THE
PHONE SNATCHERS

Also by Adrian Duncan

FICTION
Dead Men Walking
(Kindle Direct Publishing, 2020)

NON-FICTION
Shetland and the Greenland Whaling
(The Shetland Times, Lerwick, 2019)

THE PHONE SNATCHERS

Ady Duncan

Self-published by the author on Amazon's Kindle Direct Publishing, August 2021

Cover image: Lady at bus-stop, Mossbank, Shetland, April 2021
Photo by: Gary Coutts, Mossbank, Shetland

For Rose Anne

CHAPTER 1

ESKBRIDGE, MIDLOTHIAN, SCOTLAND.

MARCH 2013.

ONE THURSDAY MORNING

The elderly man's body was found lying face down on the hardwood floor of his home office. He had been strangled. He was wearing Scottish traditional highland dress, and his kilt had been deliberately hoisted over his hips to expose his smooth, bare buttocks. That wasn't what horrified the first responders. What they saw was a sight they'd replay in their minds for many weeks to come. It was a sight which shocked those who followed too – the police doctor, the pathologist, the crime examiners, and the police investigators.

It had all kicked off at just after eight o'clock that morning. When the dispatcher at Eskbridge police station answered the call to her switchboard, a noticeably pre-recorded female voice told her that she was listening to the SMS message delivery service from BT.

There was a message from telephone number such and such, the voice said, enunciating each numeral clearly. To listen to the message, she should press one; to save it, press two; to delete the message, press three; and for more information about the delivery of text messages from mobile phones to landlines, she should press four.

She pressed one.

'There's been a murder at forty-three Summerfield Terrace, Eskbridge,' said the same stilted, disembodied voice. 'Please come quickly.'

At Eskbridge Community Police station that morning, Detective Inspector Moira Quin was heading towards the rest room for her kick-start cup of coffee. As she trotted down the corridor, she had the springy, bouncy gait of a rhinoceros heading to the waterhole for that long-awaited first thirst-quenching drink of the day.

Quin was a large, pale-skinned woman with a formidable prow. She had a small, rounded, cherubic face, with the black curly hair, deep blue eyes, and pale complexion of her Connemara ancestors. She also had their marvellously-developed sense of the pessimistic – something which served her well in her present occupation.

When she entered the CID room Bob Scarth was already there, seated at the large, white, centrally-situated conference table. Scarth was a man of middle height, with short spiky greyish hair. He was in his early sixties and had the misfortune to have a distinct resemblance to Sir Alex Ferguson, the legendary football manager.

In 2012 the Midlothian Police Board, in partnership with a charity called Save Our Seniors, or SOS, agreed to fund the re-employment of retired senior police officers. These officers would return to the fray in a civilian capacity, working full-time or part-time as it suited them, to specifically tackle serious crimes involving the elderly in the force area.

Bob Scarth was one of the former detectives who for various reasons had re-joined the fight against crime by signing up as a Crime Investigator. He had served for nearly thirty years with Edinburgh City Police, the last eight of them with the Murder Squad.

Scarth and the station sergeant Gavin Balmain had been going over the 'dailies' – the incident reports from the station's officers from the previous day, which may or may not need CID input; and the 'overnights' – the reports of villainy, skulduggery, and downright stupidity which came in from Division every morning.

'Morning gents,' Quin said as she plunked herself down at the round 'pow-wow' table. 'How're they hanging Gav?' she asked solicitously.

Balmain, a large, good-natured lump of a man, acknowledged her arrival with a watery smile. It was noticeable that Quin never attempted any daft banter with Scarth. She was police and he was only a civilian, and therefore without any hierarchical standing. But his years of experience and his former rank – Detective Chief Inspector – prevented her from taking liberties.

Sergeant Balmain grunted noncommittally, and then pushed over a few A4 pages of printouts. 'Hardly anything worth noting from the dailies,' he said, 'the usual mixed bag of the idiotic and the psychotic from the overnights. Division will follow them up if they feel inclined. A couple of local phone-snatching incidents from the overnights though, which we should take heed of ... I've already got four incident reports about phone-snatching, Moira, which we haven't got round to dealing with.'

Quin groaned. 'I know. There's a Divisional conference about this effin plague this morning. Hopefully then we'll get moving on it: concerted effort and all that.'

'Phone-snatching' was a new phenomenon. Reports had started dribbling in that some passengers on public transport, who had been innocently talking on their mobile phones, had suddenly found the device snatched from them and either thrown out of a window, or destroyed before their very eyes. The phone users were all young. And the 'phone-snatchers', it seemed, were all pension-age.

The police at first pooh-poohed the reports and then tried to stifle them, but the newspapers got hold of the incidents anyway. Headlines gleefully heralded the 'Revenge of the Dinosaurs', the 'Attack of the Crones', and shite like that. Hardly a week went by without another attack being reported in Eskbridge, and it was the same in every town in the county. So much so, that Division had arranged for each police station to send at least one representative to a conference that morning at eleven o'clock. DS Scobie McIntosh and DC Heather Munro were to be the Eskbridge delegates, and they would be the ones handling any future phone-snatching incidents.

'I'm going to be forced to take Scobie and Heather off other duties, Gav. Till we start to make some headway on this. Leave the phone-snatching witness statements on Scobie's desk, will ye?'

Sonya Yuille the dispatcher stuck her head round the door.

'Knock, knock,' she said with a smile. 'Permission to approach the bench?' she asked.

'Morning Sandra,' Quin said.

'It's Sonya, Mrs Quin.'

Sonya Yuille and her twin sister Sandra were civilians employed at the station as administrators and dispatchers. Australian born, they were commonly called 'The Twinnies', after characters who had occasionally appeared in an animal TV show there. Both women had First Aid and Family Liaison qualifications. Quin excused their inability or reluctance to address police officers by their rank as an Aussie quirk, though she had no such tolerance with other civilian employees at the station, or junior officers. Other personnel suspected The Twinnies addressed her by her civilian title as an act of retaliation for Quin's total inability to differentiate between the two women.

Sonya said she'd just had the weirdest phone call. She told them about receiving the SMS message, and repeated it for her listeners. 'There's been a murder at forty-three Summerfield Terrace, Eskbridge,' she said, imitating the stilted, disembodied voice. 'Please come quickly.'

Quin was taken aback. 'I didn't know you could send a text to a landline.'

'It comes as an automated voice-message,' Sonya said. 'Like the speaking clock. I've checked out who the resident at that address is,' she said, 'and it's a Mr Colin Muir.'

Balmain said he knew who the messenger was referring to. Colin Muir was a partner in FyffeRobertson, solicitors in the town. The firm didn't practice much in the way of criminal law, and so had only rare dealings with the police, but Balmain had met Muir at a couple of Oddfellows' functions, he said. Muir had come across as an earnest, well-meaning bloke; a typical, unpretentious, small-town lawyer.

'Think she's kidding?' asked Sonya anxiously. 'Whoever sent the message, I mean.'

'Only one way to find out,' replied Balmain sourly, getting to his feet. PCs Andy Heggie and Shirley McCracken were out and about in the station's van that morning. 'I'm probably going to look like an arse,' sighed Balmain to Quin, 'but we'd better send a unit round to Summerfield Drive: just in case.'

Sonya flapped a pink post-it. 'I'll get Division to run a trace on this number too, Mrs Quin,' she said, swivelling round to leave the room.

Sonya was referring to the police ability to trace any calls which came in to their switchboards. The caller ID is always visible. Even the 'number withheld' function is defeated. This applies to both mobile and landline calls.

Quin and Scarth didn't have long to wait.

Twenty-three minutes later Sergeant Balmain was back.

'He's been murdered, right enough,' he confirmed. 'Andy Heggie and Shirley McCracken attended. Andy says it's gruesome, never seen anything like it. A heinous crime: according to him,' paraphrased Balmain liberally.

'Who's Shirley McCracken?' Quin asked.

When Heather Munro had been transferred to the CID office from his section, Balmain had applied for a replacement. Divisional had refused to supply anyone on a permanent basis, but had seconded PC McCracken to Eskbridge for three months.

'Newcomer lent by Division,' Balmain replied.

'And what's this "heinous crime" shite?' exclaimed Quin angrily. 'Who talks like that? It's newspaper-speak for God's sake.'

Balmain grinned satisfactorily. He knew all the bees the big detective had in her bonnet: all the accessible ones, anyway.

'They're cordoning off the front of the building now ...' he said, by way of a diversion.

Scarth, who was an unflappable sort and not given to flights of fancy, nevertheless had a sudden vision of Chooby Reid a second-year classmate at the school. Chooby had once told him that Peter Manuel, the Glasgow serial-killer, had been captured when the police "threw an accordion round the building" he was holed up in; and had "flooded the area with plain-faced policemen". Scarth rarely thought of old schoolmates, but when he did, he usually only remembered the laughs they had had together. Chooby had been funny, a chubby wee fair-haired rogue. What kind of life have you had, Chooby, he wondered?

Quin heaved her big body out of her chair. Everything was big about DI Quin. She had big black hair, an intimidating bosom, and big thighs that strained her black trousers to breaking point. She fixed the sergeant with a serious stare.

'You'll need to contact Division and set the ball rolling, Gav,' she said.

'I know,' he said, without much enthusiasm. Homicide was such a rare occurrence in Eskbridge that he wasn't overly familiar with the protocols.

Sergeant Balmain returned to Reception and consulted the curling blue-tacked call-out list on the wall beside his reception counter. He rang the Divisional number for Shawn Murray, the Crime Scene Manager. The CSM would call out the forensics team, the pathologist, the Procurator Fiscal's office, the whole caboodle.

Balmain then pulled a pencil from behind his right ear, and flipped open the day-book to write it all up.

The date was Thursday, 24th March, 2013.

CHAPTER 2

Like many Midlothian towns, Eskbridge evolved from a rural village into an urbanised burgh in the late 19th century. The expansion of the railways enabled a sizeable workforce to commute to Edinburgh from the expanding suburbs. Early-morning 'specials' were filled with labourers, artisans, and factory workers travelling to their places of employment. Later trains took the middle and professional classes to their offices, schools, and practices.

As Edinburgh's busy streets became more congested with private carriages, horse-drawn trams, goods vans, and delivery carts, many of Edinburgh's well-to-do chose to relocate out of town. Summerfield Terrace was the sort of place those affluent Victorians fled to, to escape the smoke and grime of 'Auld Reekie', as Edinburgh then was appropriately nicknamed. They selected suburban villas which boasted a 'vista' or a 'prospect', promised green spaces, fresh air. The houses themselves were often in the style called 'Scottish Baronial'. Crow-stepped gables, turrets, oriels, and armorial panels decorated with thistles and saltires abounded. Wide streets were laid out, cobbled with granite setts.

Summerfield Terrace led off from a busy road junction at the corner of which was a pub/restaurant, called The Covenanters' Rest.

'Looks a nice place,' remarked Scarth of the pub.

'Looks pretentious – posh,' replied Quin scathingly. 'I'll bet you an orange juice in there will set you back a fiver.'

The Terrace sat on elevated ground which rose up from the river, and faced a narrow tract of sparsely-wooded parkland, perhaps once the grazing place for the horses which pulled their carriages, or 'cars' as they were called. This green space fed gently down to the River Esk, the water pockmarked now by only the occasional pummelling raindrop, for the rain was easing.

As Quin and Scarth drove along the short, curved Terrace they could see across the river to the remnants of 'old' Eskbridge, the Kirk's high steeple and its adjoining manse. There were several slate-roofed artisans' cottages, now converted into bijoux residences. The glebe, the piece of land where the incumbent minister grew his own vegetables to augment his meagre stipend, had long since been built over. It now lay under a clutch of modern bungalows, their red-tiled roofs glistening from the downpour.

Dominated it all was the imposing, tall-windowed, old parish school. Before education became state-sponsored, parish schools turned Scottish kids out into the world armed only with the Catechism and the three R's. In most cases, it was enough to see them adequately through life. Nowadays, thought Scarth, they don't teach you even the basic survival skills.

Quin lifted a finger off the steering wheel and pointed ahead. 'No need to check the house numbers; looks like the gang's all here.'

Through the swipe of the wipers the focus of the drama was obvious. A clutch of official cars and vans, some with strobing lights, had parked on the grass verge opposite the houses. Forensics personnel moved purposely between the vehicles and a house midway along the terrace.

Muir's house built of 'blue' sandstone, quarried at Wester Hailes on the outskirts of Edinburgh. It was a building material popular with the city's architects in the late 19th century. It was used extensively in housing, and by the Edinburgh School Board. Blue and white crime scene tape stretched across the open gateway, looped around the black-enamelled gate-posts. A half-drookit PC Andy Heggie stood outside the tape, doing his best to fend off the curious. It would be worse when the ever-insistent press contingent arrived. McCracken, hunched underneath an umbrella, hovered just inside the tape. She noted the comings and goings of duty personnel on a clipboard. Heggie hoisted a dripping section and Quin and Scarth ducked under it. The young policeman followed them in.

'Shit of a day, Andy,' observed Quin as she scribbled her initials on the sheet proffered by McCracken. Heggie, who was nearly Quin's height, had a frank and open expression. When he grinned, he looked more of a boy than a man. Shirley McCracken, who was much shorter than her partner, was sexier-looking than any police officer had a right to be, Quin thought. Even in the aftermath of the deluge she somehow appeared intact, fresh, attentive. Quin offered a paw, and gave the young policewoman's leather-clad fingers an educational squeeze.

'Shirley McCracken, I presume?' she said with a grin. 'You'll have heard of me. I'm DI Quin, the dragon-lady of Eskbridge police station.'

The young PC winced good-humouredly at the introductory handshake, and gave a tolerant smile. She had indeed been briefed about the 'Mighty Quin'. Her teeth, Quin noticed with a touch of jealous satisfaction, were small, blunt, and slanted inwardly a tad. If that was the woman's only defect, she thought, she was blessed indeed.

Taking charge, Quin switched her attention to the young policeman next to her. 'What's been going on here then, Andy?' she asked.

Heggie told Quin and Scarth that he and his partner had responded to a request from the station to check out the address they were at. They found the house locked and secure, but they rustled up a next-door neighbour who had a spare key. Inside they came on a gruesome scene. An elderly gentleman, who they assumed to be Mr Colin Muir, the owner of the house, had been found on his study floor. They didn't check for a pulse. No need. It was obvious that he was dead.

'Where's this neighbour now?' asked Quin.

Heggie pointed up the street. 'Number forty-five: name of Weymss.'

Heggie said that due to the rain the Crime Scene Manager and his team had established the Rendezvous Point in the front room to the right of the vestibule. A supply of PPE, disposable gloves and overshoes would be there. The Scene Examiners were busy processing the back office, where the victim was. The pathologist had arrived ten minutes ago, said Heggie.

Quin and Scarth entered the house and stepped into an eight-by-eight ft. tiled vestibule. A small occasional table sat against the left wall. On it was a dark blue scarf, what looked to be house keys and car keys, and a new-ish mobile phone. They all belonged to the victim, no doubt. The right-hand wall was dominated by a coat rack whose pegs were full of outdoor jackets and coats. Beneath it was a shoe rack. On the wall beside the clothes was a plain mirror.

After stepping through the vestibule door, they were met by Shawn Murray, the Crime Scene Manager. He showed them into a front room, which the crime scene people were using as a temporary dressing-room. Later, suitably suited and booted in borrowed crime scene gear, they followed him down a path of aluminium squares laid out like stepping stones, to the study at the rear of the house.

The study was a high-ceilinged room, measuring roughly fifteen by fifteen feet, with ornate plaster cornices. It had been built in an age when affluence was inherited, when people knew their place in society, and the only upwardly-mobile citizens were either steeplejacks or cat-burglars. The desk was diagonally opposite the doorway, across an expanse of pleasantly-shaded hardwood. It had been specially made to fit into the corner. A captain's chair, now lying on its side, had sat in front of it. Anyone sitting at the desk would have their back to the door.

A wall on the right-hand side of the room was occupied by low shelving, display cabinets, and a collection of implements which turned out to be whaling memorabilia. A floor-to-ceiling mahogany bookcase occupied two other walls, curving round from the door to the desk. The base of the library consisted of double-doored cabinets. The top sections contained open shelves, filled sporadically with books, ornaments, framed photographs.

Directly opposite the door the fourth wall contained French windows that led out to a paved terrace. A well-kept garden could be seen outside.

Angus MacLeod, the pathologist, met the three of them a few paces inside the room. Tall, spare, with a shock of white hair above a good-natured face, MacLeod had been the county pathologist for as long as anyone in the Eskbridge police could remember. A son of the manse, he had a deep understanding of the frailties of humankind. Despite that, he had a finely-tuned sense of humour, and poker-faced banter was usually the lingua franca when police visitors were in his lab. He knew how queasy and easily-upset most of them were.

MacLeod greeted Quin and Scarth cheerily.

'Hi Moira, are ye fine? Morning, Bob,' he said.

'I'm good,' replied Quin. 'How's you?

MacLeod took his cue without preamble. He shook his head, eyes doleful, lips pursed. He patted his wheezy chest. 'Just hanging by a thread Moira,' he cantillated sombrely in his put-on beadle's voice. Angus MacLeod had been at death's door since Quin had first met him, several years before.

Quin smiled appreciatively. She peered past him to where the victim lay. Even from the doorway twenty feet away, it was obvious to Quin and Scarth that something terrible had happened there.

'Fine. Yes, fine,' replied MacLeod. He breathed in deeply, reverting to his business persona. 'Nasty business we have here, Moira,' he said. 'It's homicide, needless to say.'

The victim was an elderly-looking man who was attired in formal Scottish evening attire of a high-necked jacket over a frilled shirt, a clan kilt with the sporran out of sight below him, tartan kilt hose, knitted to match the kilt, and black day brogues. He had either recently come back from a function, or was already dressed to go to one.

The killer had displayed the body in a degenerate, pseudo-sexual tableau. He was lying awkwardly on his front. The dark green kilt had been roughly bunched up round the man's waist, to expose what a real Scotsman habitually wears below it. The victim's smooth, crinkle-free old-man's arse glistened obscenely in the overhead light.

Quin's lips curled in disgust. 'Where are his underpants?'

MacLeod smiled his understanding. 'Surely you know Moira, that a kilt is traditionally worn without underwear.'

'Yeah, I know that,' Quin said. 'Actually, I thought it was just a load of bollocks when a pal told me. Then I started to go to country dances …' Memories of half-remembered functions came drifting back to her: of hooching the night away with kilted clodhoppers. 'I found out what a Scotsman wears beneath his kilt the same night as I found out about the Squirrel Waltz.'

'The Squirrel Waltz?' asked MacLeod, the feed man.

'Twice round the dance-floor then out for your nuts,' she replied matter-of-factly. As they chuckled, she pointed downwards. 'What is that all about?'

On the man's smooth left buttock-cheek, a red-painted smiley grinned up at them.

'A tableau,' Murray said. 'For our delectation.'

The smiley face was in stark contrast to the faces of the grim-faced onlookers. The macabre representation had been deliberately designed to induce shock and revulsion in the first responders and those who inevitably followed.

Quin shivered. 'It's enough to give you goosebumples …'

MacLeod reached down and pulled back the man's shirt collar. They could clearly see the ligature mark.

'He's been strangled, probably from behind. See where the ends of the ligature have crossed at the back of his neck? Generally speaking, if the ligature is rope, electric cable, or wire, then we'd expect the mark to be sharply defined. It may even cut into the flesh. If the edges of the ligature are irregular and barely noticeable, it's usually because a soft material was used, like a scarf, a tie, or a piece of fabric. Here, as we can see, the edges are noticeably outlined, indicating that a firm material has been used.'

He bent closer.

'Yes, I can see a faint pattern, like seatbelt style webbing. And that,' he indicated an irregular mark of deeper red at the side of the neck, 'is perhaps from a buckle.'

He stood, looked around. They all looked around. On the floor beside the desk was an opened camera case. They could see high-end lenses, camera holsters, and various accessories. In the middle of the desk was a closed laptop, sitting on a black anti-static mat. At the edge of the desk furthest from them was a green retro style Trimline phone. Beside it was Nikon camera case.

Murphy pointed to the strap on the case. 'Would a strap similar to that one fit the bill, sir?'

'Something like that, yes,' conceded MacLeod. 'That type of webbing material is used for all sorts of purposes nowadays.' He pointed to the mark on the victim's neck, 'the one we have here however, may be slightly broader.' He made eye contact with Murray. 'It might be rewarding to have a look around for any possibilities, Sergeant.'

Murray nodded his head. 'It's odd that the ligature has been removed, isn't it sir? I've never come across that before.'

Macleod pushed out a purple bottom lip. 'Can't say that I have either …' he agreed.

Quin had a worried look on her face. 'What does it mean? Is it significant?'

'Everything at a crime scene is significant, Moira,' Murray stated. 'But what it tells us defeats me. As I said, it's a bit strange …'

MacLeod waited for the exchange to peter out, then knelt beside the body. The victim's head was turned to the side, with the left eye uppermost.

'And here's another strange bit,' he said to the onlookers. He lifted the man's eyelid with a pair of tweezers. 'There's no sign of petechial haemorrhaging, the tiny pinpoints of blood on the conjunctivae.'

The detectives knew that those pinpoint haemorrhages were the main indicator that a victim had been choked, suffocated, or strangled.

Quin broke the silence. 'I thought you said he'd been strangled?'

MacLeod stood up. 'Oh, he has,' he replied equably. 'We can all see the ligature marks. But I don't think he has been asphyxiated. I'll have to check to see if there wasn't some other cause of death, a natural cause, perhaps – a heart condition, for example, or some other health problem which rendered him vulnerable. But first I'll have to examine the injuries inside the neck, underneath the ligature mark.'

Something had been bothering Scarth. Something was missing. Then it came to him. Highland dress always included the sgian dubh [Gaelic: pronounced 'skee-'n doo'], the short ceremonial dagger traditionally worn tucked into the top of the hose (sock).

'Where's his sgian dubh?' he asked.

'I was coming to that,' said McLeod. He bent down a gently parted the victim's buttocks with a pair of blue-gloved fingers. Protruding from the anus was the ornamental silver pommel on the weapon's handle.

Detective Sergeant Moira Quin started visibly. She could not disguise the look of revulsion on her baby-doll face. 'Oh my God, that's disgusting!' she exclaimed impulsively. She pointed to the smiley face. 'And is that … Has that been painted in his blood?'

MacLeod shook his head. 'Felt pen,' he said. 'There were a number of pens on his desk that Shawn has bagged. No, there is remarkably little blood. I'd say the dagger was inserted post-mortem.'

Quin's mouth was down-turned. 'But it's weird. Totally disrespectful. Who would do a thing like that?' she asked.

'Someone with a lot of hate, a lot of rage,' replied McLeod.

Quin was pale. 'I can't see a woman doing that. It's just too … I'm sorry, but I just can't visualise a female as the killer here …'

MacLeod nodded his leonine head. 'I'm sure you're right,' he agreed, straightening up.

He gestured vaguely to the wood-panelled wall behind him. On it was displayed a montage of serious-looking wooden-handled iron and steel instruments, whose function was not apparent till you stepped closer and read the printed descriptions pinned below the artefact. They were designed to cut, thrust, saw, stab, chop, skin, and pierce any animal in the Arctic – whether it be from the land or from the sea.

'A woman would be more likely to use one of those implements close to hand,' resumed MacLeod. He peered at the nearest one, let his gaze drift. 'Spoilt for choice, really,' he said.

'What are they?' she asked.

Murray intervened confidently. 'Whaling implements,' he said. 'Late nineteenth century; used in the Arctic whaling trade.'

'Ah,' she said. Shawn Murray: Crime Scene Manager and pub quiz virtuoso. 'We'll take your word for it, Shawn.'

MacLeod smiled wanly. 'This isn't a woman's work, Moira. I'm sure of it. Your killer was very mission-orientated, very focused. He knew exactly what he came here for and accomplished it with a minimum of fuss. By the way,' he asked, 'as a matter of interest, how did you come to hear about this particular outrage?'

'Someone sent a text message from a mobile to our switchboard, tipping us off,' Quin said.

'Really? I didn't know you could send text messages to a landline,' said the pathologist.

'It comes as an automated voice-message. Like the speaking clock,' she answered knowledgeably.

'And what time was this?'

'Just after eight this morning …'

'Yes. Well, whoever sent the message took their time,' sniffed MacLeod. 'Talking of time, I wasn't able to estimate the time of death by the usual rectal method,' he said, pointing to the victim's rear end, 'for obvious reasons. Same goes for taking the body temperature from the liver. I have been loath to turn over the body, in case the artwork on the skin there was smudged or destroyed before we can examine it properly. However, going by the rigor present in the body, my best guess is that the time of death was not too late last night, probably between nine thirty and ten thirty. Going by the man's attire, I'd say he'd just returned from an official function of some sort, wouldn't you? Can't be all that many around this neck of the woods that require Highland dress, can there?'

Quin smiled appreciatively. 'You're full of tips and pointers this morning, Angus,' she said amicably. 'You'll be leaving no clues for us eejit detectives to find if you carry on like this.'

'Ouch,' said MacLeod, stiffening theatrically. He turned to Murray. 'I'll retrieve the elusive dagger later today, Shawn,' he said, without any hint of repugnance, 'and send it over to you for examination post-haste, along with the clothes.'

To Quin he said, 'I'll have the poor man on the table this afternoon, Moira. I take it you won't be attending.'

Quin, who had a horror of autopsy rooms smiled and said, 'You can bet on it, Angus.'

'I'll email the report as soon as I can,' MacLeod replied. He moved off towards the doorway, donning a broad-brimmed bushman's hat, and retreated down the passageway to the front door.

Murray was anxious for them to leave.

'It's going to take the SEs a few hours yet Moira, to process the place. What we can say is that there is no evidence of a forced entry. The killer was let in, or had a key. As you can see there is no sign of a struggle, a fight. No defence wounds, no trauma. He was taken by surprise. It seems probable Mr Muir was overpowered from behind. A ligature was looped round his neck and he was dragged to the floor. It suggests the killer was well known to him and was trusted by him. Generally, we don't like people we don't know standing close behind us.'

Quin and Scarth could see that the SEs were dusting all the objects in the room, as well as door handles, door frames, and such-like.

'The toilet has a push button flush,' Murray said, 'and the prints on it have been lifted. Might reveal something. The camera, laptop, and the desk surfaces have been dusted, and the felt-tip pens have been bagged to be analysed at the lab. Any special requests?'

'A report tomorrow would be better than in three weeks.'

'Ha! In yer dreams. It takes as long as it takes.'

Quin didn't take offence. 'What about the body?'

'It stays,' Murray said.

Quin shook her head respectfully. 'Honestly Shawn, I don't know how you can work with the victim lying there like that.'

'We're always aware of the victim, Moira,' shrugged Murray, 'but we have to maintain as much focus as we can. We only get one shot at this crime scene. At the end of the day, the body is just another piece of evidence: a valuable one, to be sure, but not the only one.'

Quin had heard enough. 'Give us a shout when we can poke about, will you?'

'I can have a quick look in the victim's files for the next of kin's home address if you'd like. I know he has a daughter. She has a vet's practice. Erica.'

'Whereabouts?' she asked.

'Next to Burke and Hare's, the funeral directors,' replied Murray, grinning at the well-worn chestnut.

Everybody in Eskbridge knew where that was. The funeral firm, which had been in the same premises for yonks, was actually called Burke & Eyre. But the townsfolk wouldn't be denied their wee joke, linking it sardonically with the infamous Resurrectionists.

'I don't know where she lives of course,' he said, 'but her married name's Griffin.'

'Thanks Shawn.'

Quin was renowned for her extreme reluctance to personally inform family members of a sudden death, though that onerous duty was now routinely performed by trained Family Liaison officers. She pulled out her phone, called the office, and with a shake of her lustrous hair, freed up a fleshy, bejewelled ear to press the device against.

'Hi Gav ... We've definitely got a homicide here. Listen, the next of kin's a daughter, name of Erica Griffin, owns that vet's practice in Pier Street.' She listened for a moment. 'Yes, that's the one. Find out a home address,

Gav, and be a pal and ask Division to do the death notification, will ye?'

She listened carefully to Sergeant Balmain's reply, pulled her phone down thoughtfully, resting it on her chest, before disconnecting. She turned to Scarth and the crime scene manager.

'You won't believe this one, guys. Gavin says the text message which we received this morning, telling us that Colin Muir was dead, came from the victim's own mobile phone.'

They all looked at the green retro phone on the desk, then looked around for a mobile.

'His phone's in the vestibule,' Murray said. 'On the wee table.'

Much the same thoughts were running through their heads. Had the killer remained in the house overnight, until only a few hours ago? Or had he returned to the house this morning to use the phone? Why on earth would he do either?

Murray broke their reverie. 'We'll bag it of course. Did the call originate from here?'

'We don't know yet,' Quin said. 'I'll get Heather on to it,' she said. DC Heather Munro was the station's expert when it came to tracking and cracking mobile phones.

Murray said to Scarth, his face intrigued. 'This case is certainly throwing up some weird features, Bob, isn't it?'

'You can say that again,' replied Scarth tonelessly.

'This case is certainly throwing up some …'

'Shawn,' cut in Quin amicably. 'Piss off.'

CHAPTER 3

Detective Constable Heather Munro entered the low-slung Mustang backside first. In the driver's seat the car's owner, Detective Sergeant Scobie McIntosh, glanced over appreciatively.

'Jesus Scobie,' she said, adjusting her seat-belt, 'why can't you get an SUV like everyone else?'

McIntosh grinned. 'I like this better: bought it as soon as I joined the CID. It's a statement. The guys say it's a babe magnet …'

'It's a rust bucket,' she said, but she understood. Her big brother had owned a Golf for a while which barely cleared the ground, before he got sense and bought a normal car. It was a phase they go through, she thought, automatically adjusting the air conditioning.

'At least you don't have to worry about security,' she continued. 'No self-respecting car thief would dream of stealing it …'

He patted the steering wheel affectionately. 'It's just over twenty years old now, and still purrs like a kitten. What about you?'

'What about me what?'

'You're just over twenty years old. Do you purr like a kitten, Heather? When the occasion demands?'

'Wouldn't you like to know, Scobie,' she grinned. 'Wouldn't you like to know.'

And he would too.

Munro was a pretty young woman in her early twenties. She was on the short side, with her hair piled up in a doughnut style. At one time she had been terribly self-conscious about her ears, which a dumped boyfriend had spitefully described as "nearly as big as Martha Stewart's", the American cooking guru. His name was Speug [sparrow], which she thought was cute at first, a reflection of his boyish charm. It had taken her a while to realise it was a reflection of his short attention span when it came to matters which didn't centre on him. But she had overcome her auricle phobia when she was a probationer, being obliged to wear her hair up while in uniform, and had stuck with it. She liked to think that when she let her hair down after her shift, she moved seamlessly into seductress mode.

McIntosh was a twenty-five-year-old Borderer. He was tall, fair, and thin as a stick. He was also tough, and still occasionally turned out for his home town XV. Rugby in the Scottish Borders is the very definition of 'a school of hard knocks.' He was finely calibrated, easily provoked, and his immediate boss DI Quin was convinced that his quick temper would land him in the shit sooner rather than later.

They were on their way to a Midlothian police Divisional briefing. It had been called by Superintendent Kerr, in response to the growing public concern about a rash of phone-snatchings in the county. Representatives from all eight rural police stations in the county would be attending, one per 'parish', as the local force areas were called.

He had picked Munro up at her digs, Tystie House. It was a small private hotel close to Division HQ, and the accommodation there was reserved for police personnel only – usually cadets doing probation with Division. McIntosh had also stayed there, for a year, while he waited for his divorce to come through.

'I hear your divorce has come through,' Munro said cheerily.

'That's right,' he grinned. 'No more Mr Celibacy.' He leered flirtatiously. 'So, you'd better watch out, Heather.'

She laughed. She knew he was only joking. Wasn't he?

McIntosh told her that The Bitch, as he referred to his wife after they acrimoniously split up, had applied for the divorce based on two years of separation. There were no children, or financial difficulties. He had agreed she could have the flat they had shared, providing he was absolved of any future financial implications with the property, and the divorce was granted remarkably quickly.

The only sticking point had been custody of the dog. Almost all of the 12,000 or so divorces in Scotland are heard in the Sheriff Court. Since the separation, McIntosh had lived a life of celibacy, hoping to win custody of the dog. He did nothing to give The Bitch ammunition to tell the court that he was an unfit to be a parent. However, the Sheriff, who just happened to be female, had determined that The Ex, as McIntosh now called The Bitch since the divorce, should have custody of the dog.

'The only thing I was worried about,' McIntosh confided, 'was the dog. However, the Sheriff determined that 'a pet should be with its mother.' Have you ever heard of anything as ridiculous?'

'Awwww,' Munro did her trademark tilt of the head, the sympathetic melting eyes.

'I have access rights of course,' he says, 'one day a week; and one sleepover per month.'

Munro shook her head doubtfully. 'Doesn't sound much. In fact, it sounds cruel. It would have been better if you had shared it between you: six months with its mother, then six months with its father.'

'I couldn't have handled it Heather – this job, on call all the time, never knowing when you'll be home – it wouldn't have worked, more's the pity. The Ex works from home, which apparently means not getting out of your pyjamas till lunch-time, and can look after him during the day.'

'What's the dog's name?' she asked.

'Scottie.'

'Is it a West Highland Terrier then?'

'No, he's a miniature beagle.'

'Really? I didn't know you could get miniature beagles,' she said, genuinely interested.

'You can get miniature anything nowadays. And that's not the smallest. You can get 'toy' size and even 'teacup' size.'

'Merciful Heavens,' she exclaimed. 'Who comes up with those names?' She checked his face. 'You're joking, right?'

'Hand to God,' he said.

She thought for a while. 'Seeing as he's a beagle, you should have called him 'Snoopy'.'

'He used to be a police dog, explained McIntosh. 'We adopted him when he was retired from duty. His handler had named him Scottie, her prerogative. So, we stuck with it.'

In actual fact he thought the name suited the dog. The dog's white-whiskered face and sad brown eyes and sombre-jowled look reminded him of an old uncle of his, Scottie Archibald. McIntosh had only seen him occasionally, but liked him from the first. Scottie was a gentle man who had spent most of his working life in the Borders employed by the County Council's Roads Department (motto: 'Ever Onward') as a milestone inspector.

'What sort of police work did he do?'

'Well, he was obviously too small for normal police work like crowd control, or apprehending criminals,' McIntosh said. 'But beagles have a super-developed sense of smell, and Scottie was trained to detect counterfeit perfumes. He and his handler, a sergeant called Wilhelmina, had been working strictly undercover, at street markets, car boot sales, charity free-for-alls, and kirk bric-a-brac get-togethers, that sort of thing. They were so successful that they won the 'K9 Unit of the Year' award a couple of years back,' McIntosh said proudly.

'That sounds impressive,' she prompted.

'It was for detecting a consignment of fake Armani Eau de Parfum secreted in the accordions of an Alexander Brothers tribute band who were playing at a big music festival in Duns.'

'Wow! My granny loved the Alexander Brothers. Mind you, even a teensy-weensy music event in Duns would quadruple the population. Wait a minute. How do you hide perfume in an accordion?'

'Squeeze it into the box I suppose,' McIntosh deadpanned.

She laughed, and punched him on arm.

'Anyhoo,' he continued, 'that presentation was the end of the partnership. Pictures of the award ceremony were splashed all over the newspapers. Their cover was blown. Worse than that, due to Scottie's super-sensitive nose, he and Willie became personae non grata, though in Scottie's case of course it was canis non grata, at all the local social events. You know, where ladies dressed themselves up and splashed on the whatchamacallit. It got so bad that the county's Ecumenical Council even banned them from attending church fêtes!'

'Dearie, dearie, me.'

'Anyway, when Scottie retired two years ago, he was put up for adoption, and we were fortunate enough to be given the opportunity to re-home him.'

'What sort of package does a retired K9 get?'

'Lifetime cash allowance to the adoptive parents, for food and incidentals,' he began. 'Free vet insurance. He goes to a day centre where they claim to teach old dogs new tricks; out with the old, and in with the new.'

'Is that the name of the place?

'What?'

"'Out with the Old; and In with the New'.'

'No. It's called the Eskbridge Pet Centre.'

'Well at least the name's original …'

'Isn't it just,' he replied sardonically. 'They do dog walking and pet sitting, but they specialise in de-skilling courses. Scottie likes it there apparently. The trainers there told me that being kept at home all day could have a deleterious effect on a dog's mental health. Scottie would feel he was losing out, they said, and that he might feel marginalised, excluded, maybe even depressed.'

'Well, you can see their point.'

'It's all baloney,' scoffed McIntosh. 'And of course, I'm paying for it. The costs come under 'pet maintenance' …'

'Ah,' Munro said neutrally.

'They're trying to de-sensitise that famous nose of his,' Mac rattled on, 'wean him off sniffing perfume for a living. They're also trying to teach him civilian life-skills – simple things that other dogs do naturally, such as lie on their backs to let a stranger tickle their bellies, something a police dog would never do.'

'How are they going to de-sensitize him?'

'I think they're working on the principle that the easiest way to cure an addiction is to replace it with another. They'll have to do something. As he is, unfortunately, he's a menace to society. Can you imagine what would happen if he got loose in a shopping mall? He'd go nuts. He'd be sniffing after half the women in the town.'

'A bit like his owner then?' she teased.

'You don't mean that Heather. I know you don't.' But he kind of hoped she did.

'How do I know what you're going to morph into,' she pouted, 'now that you've got your freedom?'

McIntosh didn't want to go there. 'A dog that could find golf balls would be an asset,' he body-swerved.

'Or one that could find ladies' gloves. We're always losing one of a pair. I'll give you some of the single gloves I have for him to practice with if you like.'

They were approaching Division HQ now and McIntosh turned the car into Albany Drive. It was a long, leafy, winding street bordered by the high sandstone walls of large villas. The driveway up to the headquarters complex was a smooth two-hundred-yard stretch of tarmac. At the barrier to the staff compound he scanned his ID card. The barrier lifted and he looked for a parking space.

'This is going to be a colossal waste of time, you know Heather,' he said grumpily.

'I'm looking forward to seeing her, Superintendent Kerr, I mean. I hear she's been like a new broom here.'

'Well, she's ruffled a few feathers, that's for sure …'

CHAPTER 3

The next-door neighbour to the murder victim was called Sandra Weymss. To Scarth, she looked to be in her thirties, late thirties. She was dressed for the garden: dark slacks, light-coloured shirt, black gilet, short pink gum boots. She was a thin but pretty-faced woman with short dark hair. Her face showed strain and disbelief as she welcomed the two detectives into her home.

Quin introduced herself and Scarth and she led them down a short wooden-floored passageway to a big, warm kitchen with a wide stove which might have been an Aga. Seated at a six-place polished table was a damp-eyed comely young woman. She had blonde-reddish hair, unevenly tanned skin, and a round, plump face. Hanging from her neck was a thick chain with a silver bobble at the end. She was wearing a dark print apron over a long-sleeved white t-shirt. A scrunchie scarf tied in a bow held up her hair from her forehead. She looked like a teenager, but there was a wedding ring on her left hand.

'Connie,' Sandra Weymss said in a quiet voice. 'The police are here for a quick word …'

Quin and Scarth politely refused tea or coffee, and were seated at the table, opposite the young woman. Quin's long legs touched something and when she looked down, she could see it was a green dinosaur. She looked round anxiously for its snotty-nosed owner.

The woman noticed. 'There are toys everywhere,' Mrs Weymss said, 'as lethal as landmines. I have three children, all away at the school thank goodness.'

She looked round her own kitchen as if seeing it for the first time. 'Well then, I'll leave you to it,' she said to Quin, and slipped quietly out.

Quin told the young woman their names. 'What's yours?'

The young woman told them her name was Connie Considine. She lived in one the new estates on the northern side of Eskbridge. The ones which could see Edinburgh in the distance on days when it wasn't raining. Her hands were shaking slightly, fidgeting with a packet of cigarettes and a lighter, but she hadn't light one up. A considerate young person, Scarth decided. Deferential. And obviously still in shock.

Quin reached over the table and placed a reassuring paw on the woman's wrist. Scarth noticed that the woman wore her watch on the outside of the sleeve, instead of against the skin. The woman straightened in her chair and breathed in deeply: composed herself. She was ready to begin.

'We understand you go in to clean for Mr Muir, Mizz Considine, …'

'It's Missus. I'm married. With two kids.'

'I beg your puddin',' smiled Quin, putting the woman at her ease. 'You've still got your youthful looks …'

'Well, I'm only twenty-two, efter all.'

She had traces of working-class Midlothian in her voice, Scarth noticed. Perhaps from one of those former mining villages filled with hard-faced men and rough-voiced women; where school-leaving girls had one glorious care-free summer before the babies, and the fags, and the mid-afternoon start on the booze.

The woman said she came in once a week, on Thursday mornings. 'The company I work for does the offices where Mr Muir works, on weekday nights, and I do that too. That's where Mr Muir saw me. He asked if I would do his house as well.'

'Off the books?' asked Quin.

'Well, as an obligement sort of thing ...'

The woman told them she was in the habit of letting herself in, dumping her rucksack and taking off her snorkel parka in the vestibule, and hanging them up on the coat-stand there.

'You have a front door key, obviously,' Quin asked. 'Have you ever lent it out, when you went on a holiday for instance?'

The woman smiled humourlessly. 'I don't get holidays. Can't afford them. Cleaners aren't as well paid as the polis, you know ...'

Quin let that one pass. She held out her hand. 'You'd better let me have it for now.'

When the key-ring was handed over Quin asked, 'What time did you go into Mr Muir's house this morning?'

'Same time as usual. Around half past eight.'

'Was the alarm set when you went in this morning?' Quin asked.

The woman shook her head. 'I can't remember. I'm still too confused. It usually is. He goes to work at the back of eight, and sets it before he leaves home.'

'But you're not sure?'

'No.' The woman hesitated. 'Is it important, do you think?'

Quin shrugged. She didn't know if it was. She'd check with the security service later. She put on a serious face and said 'Are ye able to talk us through the rest of it, Connie?'

The woman nodded and took a shallow breath. 'The TV was still on in the front room,' she said, 'which was unusual, for Mr Muir has normally gone to his work by the time I get here. When I saw the TV on, I thought he might still be at home.' Her eyes brimmed with tears. She wiped them with her fingertips. 'And I was right ...'

Quin stiffened involuntarily. She hated it when females turned on the waterworks. It annoyed her, for experience told her it was often a ploy.

'When you found Mr Muir,' she asked, 'did you check for vital signs? To see if he was alive?'

The woman shook her head vehemently. 'No way!' She shivered. 'I didn't go into the room. You couldn't pay me enough money to go into a room with a dead body ...'

'Why did you text us, Connie,' she said softly. 'Why didn't you just phone?'

'I was speechless. His landline phone was at the far end of his desk. I didn't want to step past his body. I picked up his mobile. I wasn't sure if I could speak. With him there. The corpse. So, I texted. The number for the Eskbridge police was in his contacts.'

'You texted our landline from a mobile?' Quin asked.

'Texting a landline is just the same as texting a mobile. Everybody knows that. I text all day long.' She twiddled her thumbs, a hint of a shy smile on her mouth. 'It's cheaper than phoning.'

Quin gave the young woman a long stare, then asked, 'Why use his phone, Connie? Why didn't you use your own?'

'Because I havenae got it, that's why,' the woman replied sharply. 'Mine got snaffled this morning by a fucken phone snatcher, when I was taking wee Theo to his nursery.'

'Really? Have you reported this incident to the police?' Quin asked.

The woman reached into her apron then brandished a crumpled piece of paper.

'Course I have. My phone's at Eskbridge police station. I handed it in at half-eight this morning for evidence: or what's left of it. A sergeant gave me this receipt for the insurance. The police number is on it. He said someone would be following it up, and I should "give it a couple of days". What good is that? I ask you. By then she'll have snatched God knows how many other people's phones …'

'We've assigned two detectives to the case, Connie. They'll soon get it sorted out.'

The woman looked dubious. She wasn't finished. 'I think it's a disgrace byraway. The way people can just grab your phone for no reason at all and then crush it to pieces and no one does anything about it.'

After an uneasy pause, Scarth broke the silence. 'Did you come straight here Mrs Considine; from the police station?'

She seemed to notice him for the first time. 'Yeah. It's only a short walk. And seeing as I was in the town anyway, I thought I'd just come round here. I usually don't get here until about eleven. Ah wish I hadnae bothered now, to be honest …'

'And then what did you do?'

'When?'

'After you'd discovered the victim, Mr Muir …'

'I just backed out. I watched him all the time, in case he moved. I backed out to the door then ran up the corridor to the front door, and waited for you lot.'

Quin's facial muscles twitched in annoyance. 'Did you not think of calling an ambulance?' Quin asked.

The woman threw her a look of astonishment. 'What for?' Her hand flew to her mouth. She went pale underneath her fake tan. 'Oh my God,' she gasped. 'He's no' still alive, is he?'

Quin shook her head. 'No, Connie. He's not alive, unfortunately.' As the woman slumped in relief Quin added, 'If it's any consolation, an ambulance wouldn't have done him any good.'

Scarth put in, 'Did you manage to notice if anything was missing, in the house? Was anything moved, would you say? Out of place?'

'I dinnae ken,' blustered the woman. 'Christ. I wisnae concentrating, how could I? All I could see was Mr Muir lying there, with his bare bum sticking up in the air. And that smiley face … Jesus …'

Her eyes grew wide, incredulous, as she stared at Quin. 'Who would do a thing like that?'

Quin smiled grimily. 'A very bad man, Connie. That's who.'

Later, when Considine had left, Quin expressed her doubts.

'I don't like that story, Bob. Do you? Why text the police? It just so … so perverse.'

'It's what young females do these days, Moira. They text each other all the time.'

'Do you think they've all of a sudden lost the use of their mouths? I don't think so.'

Scarth shrugged.

'In my experience, young females take the easy way, whatever is the most convenient for them. Composing yourself then taking the time to text instead of just phoning is not the norm, believe me …'

'Well, it wasn't a normal situation. Coming across a dead body like that …'

Quin was not persuaded. 'I still don't like it.'

Mrs Weymss was summoned then into her own kitchen. She was clearly upset when Quin confirmed that Colin Muir had probably been murdered. Upset, but not really surprised.

'I knew something bad had happened,' she said, coming into the room. 'I went round when I saw the police car arriving. The young policeman made certain I didn't come in with him. My God! Things like that just don't happen around here. It must have been done by an outsider, surely. Wouldn't you say?'

She moved to sit down at the table. 'It must have happened late on,' she said, 'for I saw him from my front window at eight o'clock, getting into a taxi. He was wearing his kilt and things. I spoke to him yesterday at tea-time when I handed in some bannocks I had made. He told me he was going out to a do last night, the annual dinner of the Midlothian Law Society. It sounded grand, but it was little more than a piss-up, he said.'

Quin asked her how long she had known Mr Muir.

'Eight years. I can't believe it's that long. Jason, my eldest, had just come on the scene. We actually bought the house from Colin, from his firm. We thought we were privileged. Houses in this street don't come on the market very often.'

'How did you come to have a key to the house?' Quin asked.

'He gave me a key because the burglar alarm went off one day when he was at work. A mouse in the garage probably. He has those motion sensors all over the place. The alarm rang for ages. Colin didn't want a repeat so he gave me a key, and the password to reset it.'

'And have you lent someone the key recently by any chance?' she asked.

'Never.' She unzipped a pocket in her gilet and pulled out a bundle of keys. 'It's always on my key-ring.'

'Who else knows the alarm password?'

'Just me; and Connie of course, the cleaner.'

'And can you tell us where you were last night?

The woman was taken aback. 'Why? Am I a suspect?'

'Everyone's a suspect Mrs Weymss,' Quin replied equably, 'except me. I know where I was last night. And you do have a key …'

'I've also got a husband and three kids to look after. Not that they will be able to substantiate it.'

'Why's that, Mrs Weymss? Quin asked suspiciously.

'Because they don't know that I'm here half the time. Until they need me. I'm the invisible skivvy. Like most mums.'

The pathologist had determined the time of death at between nine thirty and ten thirty. Quin gave herself plenty of leeway.

'I'm talking specifically between nine and midnight, say ...' she said.

'Midnight? Ha!' the woman snorted. 'I haven't seen midnight since Hogmanay. I'm in bed by nine thirty, and unless my husband feels frisky, I'm asleep by nine thirty-five.'

'When do you get to sleep when he does feel frisky?' Quin asked innocently.

'Nine thirty-six.'

They all laughed.

Scarth cleared his throat and asked, 'Mrs Weymss. What can you tell us about Mr Muir?'

'He was a good-natured, sociable man,' she answered. 'A church-goer, though I don't hold that against him. He did a lot of charity work for the Oddfellows, and the Kirk. We moved here in the winter, and a few days later, when we were having a long lie, we heard a scraping sound from outside, from the driveway. We looked out, and there was Colin busy clearing snow from our drive and pavement. That's the kind of man he was; couldn't do enough for you if you asked for something. What we used to call a "gent".'

'What age is he?'

'Sixty something: sixty-three maybe?'

'You mentioned his wife,' Quin said. 'We saw no-one in the house, apart from himself.'

'Colin and Lenore split up over a year ago. It was so sad. I think they're divorced now. He has a daughter here in Eskbridge. She's married, owns a vet's practice.'

'Yes, we know that,' Quin stated.

'She used to come round regularly, once a month at least, but not so often recently. I suspect Colin disapproved of Danny Griffin, his son-in-law.'

Quin raised her eyebrows a minute fraction. 'Oh?'

'Just a feeling; Colin and Erica got on OK,' stated the woman.

'What about contractors,' put in Scarth, 'someone to do the garden, trim the hedges?'

'We both used the services of the same landscaper. Grant Dunlop. He hasn't been here for weeks though. It's not a contract or anything. We phone him when we need him.'

Quin said, 'Has there been anyone hanging around the neighbourhood? Strangers? Suspicious-looking characters?'

The woman shook her head. 'No. It's quiet here, as you'll have gathered. It's a bit of a backwater, to be honest.'

Scarth had seen a For Sale sign outside Muir's house. 'I see the house is for sale,' he said. 'Has anyone been round viewing it – prospective buyers?'

'No, I haven't seen anyone, though that's not to say no-one's been there to view it. His own law firm is handling the sale.'

It wasn't unusual. In Scotland most homes are sold through solicitors. The buyer gains the right to occupy and use the property for as long as they own it. The concepts of leasehold and freehold found elsewhere in the UK are generally not applicable in Scotland. An estate agent advertises and promotes a property, but the actual purchase process is handled by the buyer's solicitors and the seller's solicitors. Once they have reached an agreement on price, the buyer and the seller are locked into a binding contract. The process eliminates any possibility of the buyer being 'gazumped' – that is, the seller cannot subsequently accept a higher offer from someone else. Most solicitors in Scotland who do residential conveyancing also provide some kind of estate agency service.

'It's an awfu' big house for just one person,' Scarth observed.

'Four bedrooms,' she said. 'It was far too big even when Erica was growing up. I think they expected to have more, a bigger family, but it wasn't to be. Since the divorce he's been trying to sell it, part of the settlement I suppose. The asking price is over half a million. I'm not surprised it hasn't sold to be honest.' She paused for a bit. 'As a matter of fact,' the woman continued, 'Colin told me Lenore's lawyers were getting impatient, thought he was stalling or something.'

'Maybe Lenore was getting impatient too,' hinted Quin half-heartedly.

'Ha! And what, decided to push things along? I don't think so, Missus Quin. Lenore wouldn't hurt a fly. She's moved in with her boyfriend, if you can call a fifty-year old man a "boyfriend". He's comfortably off, I believe, got his own business and things. And Lenore has her own online jewellery business. I wouldn't have thought she'd be short of a bob or two.'

Maybe it was the "boyfriend" who was getting impatient, thought Quin. 'Do you know this so-called boyfriend's name by any chance?

'Crighton, Bill Crighton. He owns a courier company. Eskbridge Express. They're at the back of Coates Crescent. He's divorced too. Children all flown the nest, I expect.' Her look went cautious. 'I suppose you all know plenty about Bill Crighton ...'

'Oh?'

'He's got a bit of a reputation ...Or so they say. I had to call your colleagues out only a couple of weeks ago because of his antics. Maybe it was three weeks ago, I forget the date. Anyway, he and Colin had a very public row out there. Don't know what it was about, but I can guess. Crighton took a hammer to Colin's car; smashed the windscreen, the bugger.'

'What do you mean you can guess?' Quin asked.

The woman smiled. 'Money; or sex. What else do men think of?'

'And you can't remember the date?' pressed Quin.

The woman shook her head. 'I was scared he might attack Colin himself, so I rang the polis. You should check.'

Out on the street the detectives met up with Sergeant Hugh Dallas. His team had been doing a door-knock of the neighbouring houses. Knocking on neighbour's doors to ask about an incident was usually a futile exercise, but one that had to be done anyway. Every now and then a snippet turned up, one which could develop into a lead. And that day's effort wasn't a total waste of time. They clambered into the rear of police minibus Dallas was using as his base, and settled on seats facing him.

'Two items of interest, folks,' said Dallas, looking down at his notes. 'The woman at number forty-one, a couple of doors down, says she witnessed an altercation between the victim and another man, who she believes was a Mr Roy McMurray. He lives at number thirty-eight, diagonally opposite the Covenanters' Rest pub. She saw him smashing the victim's windscreen. This happened about a month ago. Says she reported it to us, but I'm almost certain nothing of that nature came to our attention.'

'There seems to be a bit of confusion about that Hugh,' Quin said. 'Mrs Weymss, whom we've just interviewed, was certain that the person who attacked Mr Muir's car was his ex-wife's boyfriend. She says she reported it to the police.'

When the Eskbridge police station had been downgraded in 2012 it meant it was no longer obliged to provide 24 hr cover for the Eskbridge 'parish' – its force area. The station was operational from 7 a.m. to 7 p.m. only, with officers from Division HQ covering the remaining hours. Any incidents, which occurred during the night that required further investigation, were highlighted in the 'overnights' which Eskbridge received every morning.

'I should have asked Mrs Weymss what time it happened,' Scarth said, sharing the responsibility, 'but if it happened at night, then officers from Division would have responded.'

'I'm sure they did,' Dallas replied. 'And I'm sure it wasn't highlighted on any of the 'overnights' which I saw, but of course I'll check.'

'What was the other thing, Hugh?' Quin asked.

Dallas read from another page. 'Woman at number thirty-seven, Philippa Duguid,' he pointed down the street, 'the last house before the main road there, also reported that the victim was embroiled in a feud with McMurray.'

'We heard the victim wasn't the feuding type,' Quin said.

Dallas shrugged. 'Different witnesses, different perspectives. This woman says that both she and the victim had complained numerous times to McMurray, about the noise coming from his premises. He does joinery work apparently, at all sorts of hours ...'

He consulted his notes.

'Anyway, on one occasion the noise was so bad that she and the victim went to McMurray's house to confront him in person, and she says they were, quote …' he looked down at the page again, "… the subject of disgusting and violent verbalisation," unquote.' The victim subsequently contacted the council apparently, on their joint behalf, and the council served McMurray with an Abatement Notice.'

The detectives knew from personal experience that anything, however trivial it might seem to outsiders, could provoke and outburst of violence and result in a death.

Scarth said, 'I'm sure this guy McMurray wasn't highly delighted about being served with an Abatement Notice, but I have to say, Hugh, it doesn't sound like a motive for murder.'

Sergeant Dallas wasn't convinced that former police officers, albeit Chief Inspectors, should be able to return to duty and immediately be handed plum investigations. He adopted a studied neutral look. 'Not for me to say what a motive is, or isn't, Bob,' he said, snapping his notebook shut.

CHAPTER 3

At ten to nine that morning. DS McIntosh and DC Munro joined their colleagues in Divisional HQ's impressive new auditorium. Eight tiered rows of fabric-backed seats faced looked down onto a hardwood floor-space where a lectern stood to the side of a large white backdrop screen. The seats were of a retractable, 'telescopic', design. They could be pushed back against the rear wall, or pulled out again like a concertina. This allowed the exposed floor area to be used in different ways to suits all types of events. Lectures, conferences, and award ceremonies had all been hosted there. Training films had been shown on the big screen, and the room was a regular venue for the endless exams police officers were obliged to participate in. At nine o'clock the side door to the auditorium opened, and a small figure stalked briskly to the lectern. Someone dimmed the lights, and a respectful hush fell on the assembly.

Superintendent Kerr was born in a farm cottage in 1985. Her mother was in the habit of leaving things to the last minute and hadn't got round to making an appointment with the local midwife. Her father's experience in animal husbandry stood him in good stead. He had delivered calves, foals, kids, and the occasional llama, and out she popped with no more than a watery swoosh.

The farm cottage was near Leswalt in Wigtownshire. The village's name is Brittonic, an isolated reminder that for a long time Galloway was Welsh-speaking – part of the great British province of Strathclyde. The farm itself had a Gaelic name, as have nearly all of the farm-names and indeed place-names of the south west. Gaelic-speaking Irish settlers first arrived in the area in 6th century, following the monastic pioneers of the Irish Church. By the 12th century the south of Scotland – from Portpatrick in the west to the Dumfries in the east – was predominantly Gaelic-speaking. Nowadays however, the people of Leswalt can all speak English; when they've a mind to.

By the time Kerr was eight years old she had attended four primary schools. Her father was a farm labourer who was hired, along with many others, at 'feeing' fairs. At these fairs farm labourers would be selected by the farmers and 'feed' – offered a contract of employment for a signing-on fee. The contract was typically for six months or twelve months, and basic accommodation was included.

Only once in her early life did Superintendent Kerr stay in the same house for two years running. That year two other memorable events took place. The family shifted to Earlston in Berwickshire; and she was baptised as Betsy Kerr.

Long before she first attended secondary school, Betsy Kerr was sick and tired of explaining, to everyone who asked her, that her name was not a diminutive of Bethany or Elizabeth, or even Beatrix or Beatrice. Betsy was her given name.

The baptismal ceremony was conducted one summer's lunchtime in the Parish Church. Her father had just received his season's bonus and had decided to splash out on a decent purvey for the girl. The sprinkling of guests sprinted through clouds of demented midgies for the refuge of the Drover's Arms. Safely indoors, many partook of the establishment's award-winning pork pies, the ones enticingly flanged with crinkle-cut pastry made with fresh lard obtained from the pub's free-range pigs; though some of them settled instead for a slice of the five-meat quiche, or just the cute little shortbread stars topped with fondant icing.

Kerr's father unfortunately died when she was eight years old; having developed Q fever at a goat dairying farm they were quartered at in East Ayrshire. Her mother relinquished her nomadic life-style and took Betsy and her two younger sisters back to her native Glasgow. They set up home in a single-end in the East End of the city, where her mother obtained a job as a cigarette girl/standby caller at a nearby Granada bingo hall.

It was not one of the salubrious parts of the city, but the girls were not deprived in any way. Primary school was an uneventful journey. Secondary school was more challenging. By the time she had reached puberty, Betsy Kerr was wearing a G cup bra and had become the proud possessor of the entirely appropriate sobriquet 'Big-Boobed Betsy', or 'B-B B' for short. She had also achieved what would be her maximum height, which was 5 feet 2 inches. Her ambition, to the astonishment and disbelief of her inner-city peers, was to be a police officer.

In 2003 she wouldn't have been accepted into the police force, on account of her small stature. But the height requirement was abolished in 2004, and in she waltzed. Since then, her rise up the ranks had been little short of meteoritic. She possessed the wide range of attributes and qualities essential to become a police officer with Police Scotland, and a few more besides.

Superintendent 'B-B B' Kerr had been appointed to her position with Midlothian police in early 2013. Shortly thereafter, she'd gained an instant rapport with the troops when she had torn up a meal expenses claim submitted by a despised detective inspector.

'A Scotch Egg! Jesus Christ what a load o' shite!' she had reportedly shouted at him. 'Only a fucken cretin would think a Scotch egg constituted a proper meal! Bugger off and pay for it yourself!'

People who had never met her always speculated how a wee girl from a rough, tough, inner-city neighbourhood could rise to become a senior police officer. Once they gained an audience, and she opened her gallus [bold, cheeky] mouth, those speculations were immediately dispelled.

Superintendent 'B-B B' Kerr twisted the microphone down to suit her stature, coughed, and cleared her throat.

'Good morning ladies and gentlemen,' she said brightly. She didn't wait for a reply.

'Thank you for joining me in this briefing. I'm going to make this short and sweet, for I've got a lot of things to do today, and slavering here [prattling] isn't one of them. As ye'll all be aware we are in the middle of an epidemic, an epidemic of an anti-social activity now dubbed in the press as 'phone-snatching'.'

'This fad, for that is what it essentially is, is believed to have started in Auchtermuchty, in Fife, just one month ago. Since then, it has spread throughout Scotland at an unbelievable rate. The Fife incident started as a joke; I'm informed. A young woman, travelling on the St Andrews bus, was talking on her phone when suddenly an elderly passenger snatched it from her and threw it out of the window. The phone was subsequently run over by an 18-wheeler belonging to Eddie Stoddart – who else? – and consequently wrecked beyond repair.'

'Now admittedly the young woman was talking too long, and too loud, and her vocabulary seemed limited to words such as 'like' and 'whatever', and 'cool'. But that is no excuse for the unlawful appropriation her property, which is essentially what happened. This incident was gleefully reported in the local press, and when the national media sluts got wind of the story there was no stopping it. "Revenge of the Wrinklies" they called it; "The Attack of the Crones", and shite like that. Of course, once the idea was out there it gained traction, and before we knew it, all hell had broken loose. There were hundreds of reports of copy-catting from all points of the Alban compass, including, I'm reliably informed, some parts of Highlands where you can't get a signal anyway!'

'The press has consistently portrayed these incidents as some sort of ageist crusade. That our seniors are understandably retaliating against the admittedly irritating voices, moronic language, and boorish behaviour exhibited by the younger generation. Senior citizens, it is suggested, are coming out of retirement in their droves to join in the fun. Innocent-looking little old ladies are concealing dangerous instruments in their handbags.

Harmless-looking old codgers, as nimble-fingered as Fagin's pickpockets, are jumping on the band-wagon. 'Phone-snatching', according to one bonkers report, is the biggest craze for pensioners since they gave up the hula hoop.'

She shuffled her notes, waiting for the polite laughter to die out.

'But it's not about that. This is about criminal behaviour and the wilful destruction of property, pure and simple. The statistics are a reminder of how this epidemic has spread. In Midlothian alone, there have been one hundred and forty-three copy-cat cases. Think about it,' she urged; but before anyone could think about it, she repeated her mantra, increasing the decibels. 'In a wee county like this: one hundred and forty-three cases!' Her face an astonished look; as if she'd just been told that one hundred and forty-three was the number of orgasms a newly-wed bride could expect on her wedding night.

'And not only that, we have a new variant here in Midlothian. Instead of phones being snatched and simply tossed out of windows, we have a group of malicious saboteurs who are snatching the phones and mangling them with pliers, heavy-duty grips, and other nasty implements, before discarding them. The insurance costs, I've been told, have already topped £40,000! But members of the public here are also losing their SIM cards, with irreplaceable social contacts, photos, home-made videos – all that – on them. And, let's face it, who can survive nowadays without their mobile phone?'

Her voice dropped half an octave, took on a menacing timbre.

'We need to get across to these phone-snatchers that enough is enough, that future episodes will not be tolerated. And so today I'm announcing that here at Divisional HQ a Task Force will be set up to put a stop to this nonsense. You will all be involved. It will be a 'virtual' Task Force, so that officers do not have to waste time physically shuttling between here and their workplaces. Each station will appoint at least one representative to the Task Force. That representative will galvanise their workplace colleagues and convert them to the cause. Reports will be regularly uploaded to a dedicated folder in our Cloud, and those representatives will log in to a Cloud chat room at specific times for discussion and updates.'

'The technical framework is all in place,' she assured them. 'I already have pencilled in a name for the operation, but,' she smiled invitingly, 'I'm willing to set it aside if anyone has a better idea. Has anyone any suggestions?'

Before he knew what he was doing, McIntosh put up his arm and said breezily, 'How about Operation Wrinkly-free?'

Even as he said it, he knew it wasn't funny.

Beside him, Munro took a deep, sharp breath. She seemed to shrink in her seat. She had the sort of pained expression that you see on teenagers' faces when their Ma and Pa get up to dance to the latest hit track. McIntosh stopped breathing. You could have heard a mouse creeping along behind the auditorium's skirting boards.

Kerr's eyes turned to slits. Her face turned pale, as if she was suffering a localised infarction, but everyone knew it was from anger. Her voice, when it emerged, had icicles dripping from it.

'And you are?' she hissed in a strangled timbre.

'McIntosh, Ma'am,' replied McIntosh hoarsely, his momentary bravado dissipating rapidly. 'DS at Eskbridge…'

An uncertain pause, then illumination lit Kerr's smooth, unwrinkled face. 'Ah yes, Eskbridge. Home of the part-time coppers …'

There was a sprinkling of titters from the other participants. What Superintendent Kerr said was both true and untrue. In 2010 Eskbridge had suffered the indignity of being reduced to a community station. This was mainly due to the vindictiveness of the then Chief Superintendent Brennan, who had taken an early retirement package later that year after an excruciatingly embarrassing debacle at the station's Archive inauguration. ('Dead Men Walking' 2020) Eskbridge police station no longer had the obligation to provide 24 hr police cover, that was true, but the CID section still worked a full-time, 9 to 5 week.

'DS McIntyre there in Eskbridge is a good example of why I was selected to head this Operation,' the Superintendent continued scathingly. 'His crass, no doubt facetiously-intended, branding of the elderly as decrepit nincompoops is exactly the opposite of what we need to focus on here. This whole Division needs to embrace the idea of a policy reset. Elderly folk are a huge and essential part of the fabric of our society. We need to re-engage with them, regain their trust, not alienate them. Social cohesiveness must be our goal. These 'phone-snatchers' are not elderly people who suddenly, en masse, decide to become criminally pro-active. They are a few concerned, albeit misguided citizens, fed up with discourteous and bad-mannered behaviour on public transport, who have decided, unfortunately, to take matters into their own hands. We need to re-establish the trust the elderly used to have in the police, re-gain their confidence. It will be a delicate balancing act, make no mistake about it, but it is mission-critical that we succeed in it. We need to convince our pensioners that anti-social behaviour is a matter for the police, and draw them into our mindset …and that is why I've decided that the operation will be called 'Operation Drawstring'.'

She straightened in her chair, and glared defiantly.

'This operation will commence immediately,' she affirmed. 'To kick things off, each of youse will identify themselves to me by email today. In return, you receive the Cloud password to the Operation Drawstring folder, which has been created in the Divisional intranet.'

Kerr paused significantly, signalling the finale. 'Any questions?' she finished rhetorically, a warning gleam in her violet eyes.

Munro gripped McIntosh's forearm like a vice.

Kerr finished with a sincere-sounding, 'Thanks to all for participating,' and as the lights came up again, strode purposefully out of the auditorium.

'What were you thinking, Scobie? Eh?' demanded Munro furiously as they walked to the car. McIntosh put on a suitably sheepish expression, the boyish one that usually dampened his boss's anger. But Munro wasn't his boss. He didn't like it that she had pounced on him, and wasn't prepared to take too much.

'I can't understand you, Scobie,' Munro continued, shaking her head. 'I really can't. We've no option but to join this so-called Operation Drawstring, but from now on I think it would be prudent to keep our heads below the parapet. Okay? Let's go and see Sergeant Balmain and gather up all the witness statements about the phone-snatchers in our parish. I don't like to say this, sir, but you should keep future contacts with Superintendent Kerr to a minimum if you know what's good for you.'

'Yessir, ma'am.'

She couldn't help laughing, but showed her disapproval of his behaviour by punching him in the arm.

CHAPTER 4

It was after twelve when Quin and Scarth arrived at number 37, the last house in the Terrace. The gable end abutted the main road, and was directly opposite the Covenanters' Rest.

Philippa Duguid, the householder, had the sort of face you looked twice at, though not necessarily through interest or attraction. She had straight brown hair combed forward to a fringe which traversed across her eyebrows in a straight line. She had pale blue eyes set in a plain oval face, full lips over a silver stud, and a broad dark-inked tattoo, resembling a lace scarf, which encircled her neck and met at the front of her throat.

Duguid was visibly shocked to hear of the death of Colin Muir and immediately suggested that Roy McMurray, who lived next door to her, may have been responsible.

'Why do you say that?' Quin asked.

'Because he's a violent bugger and there was bad blood between him and Colin: bad blood between him and a lot of us.'

She told the detectives that she had first complained to the council about McMurray five months previously. A representative came out, right enough, but did nothing. She went to Colin Muir for advice, for he too had been plagued by the incessant noise, as had others in Summerfield Drive.

'What sort of noise?' asked Scarth.

'McMurray's got a big shed out the back,' Duguid explained, 'and he does carpentry work. Nothing against that. It's the noise he makes which upsets us all.'

'Week-ends or week days?' Quin asked.

'Week-ends, week days, sunny days, rainy days, holidays, etcetera, etcetera,' replied Duguid, getting into her stride. 'Sometimes he starts at five o'clock in the evening, and goes on till one o'clock, two o'clock in the morning. There's three or four of us round here, phoning each other. "It was bad last night," or "Here we go again," when he starts.'

She looked at them as if expecting a question. When none was forthcoming, she continued her rant.

'Sound does travel, you know,' she said. 'It does strange things. I didn't realise, coming from Edinburgh. In the city you know, there's always noise. You blank it out. But out here, you hear everything. Two o'clock in the morning, he's sawing away. I'm woken up. Not just me, you know, it's not just all about me …'

She led them out French windows to a wooden deck at the rear of the house. 'So, you're sitting out here, nice night, glass of wine, etcetera, etcetera,' she said, waving an arm to encompass her domain, 'and then it starts. And you think, what the hell is he doing in there?'

'What is he doing, may I ask?' Quin asked.

'Sawing, using an electric plane, who knows what tools he's got in there. Buzz, buzz, buzz. It's probably commercial work which he isn't allowed to do anyway. Not in a residential area. I've been taking anti-stress tablets for it, because I feel so wound up. It got so bad that I dreaded coming home from work. How bizarre is that?'

'Do you work locally?' Scarth asked.

'For 'INK', the tattoo shop on Elm Street? But you know what? I'd love to be able to go round to McMurray and kick him in the whatsits, but if you are a female confronting a male – especially an ape like him – well you don't feel confident enough to confront them. Do you? You put up with it. And then the neighbours phone up the next day. "Did you hear him again last night?" Etcetera, etcetera. You get bored talking about it.'

Quin hadn't noticed. 'Why did you say he was a violent bugger?' she asked.

'Because he took a hammer to Colin's windscreen. Spider cracks everywhere.'

'We heard that someone else did that.'

The woman shook her head. 'I didn't see it happening, but I heard the shouts and the bangs. I looked out the window. I saw McMurray sauntering down the road from Colin's. I called the police, and gave them a statement when they came. It was him all right.'

'Can you tell us where you were last night, Mizz Duguid, between nine and midnight? Quin asked.

'Out getting pissed. Stayed the night with a friend. If he can vouch for me, I'll be astonished. He was as rat-arsed as I was.'

Nevertheless, Quin jotted down the friend's contact number.

As the detectives took their leave, Scarth said, 'So we've got two conflicting accounts of the victim's car being damaged. We'll need to contact Division for clarification …'

'Etcetera, etcetera …' Quin mimicked. 'You know Bob, I've got the distinct feeling that we're going round and round in circles, and this is only Day One!'

Elizabeth Spence lived at 15 Summerfield Drive in a single-storey bungalow with a double garage and a husband with a triple by-pass. Summerfield Drive was a broad avenue which ran roughly parallel to Summerfield Terrace. The long back gardens behind the properties of the Terrace and the Drive were separated only by a narrow service lane. The rear of her property faced diagonally towards the rear of Colin Muir's house.

Spence was a well-turned-out woman with short hennaed red hair shed to the right, black-framed glasses, and a down-turned, thin-lipped mouth. She was wearing a black skirt and a purple cardigan, with only a thin gold chain at her neck. Quin got the feeling she was the type who was always turned out ready to meet the day. The kind of woman who would wear Rieker shoes for the gardening.

Elizabeth Spence did not know the victim well, she said, but had heard of his untimely death. 'It's a tragedy, it really is,' she'd said.

They were standing in her kitchen, looking over her rear garden to Muir's property. 'That's Mr Muir's house there,' she pointed. 'You can just see his French windows with the grey drapes.'

It was the victim's office, they knew. 'Did you see lights on last night?' Quin asked.

'I did early doors. Till about six o'clock. It gets dark then and we close the blinds.'

'Did you see or hear anyone or anything later on,' Quin said, 'say, about ten to midnight?'

'Heavens no, we were in bed then. We sleep in the front bedroom. It's on the other side of the house from here. Unless Mr McMurray is beavering away in his shed out there, we hear very little noise in this area.'

Spence had only met the victim "a couple of times", she said, when she and some of the other neighbours had met in his house to discuss a strategy for dealing with the noise nuisance emanating from Mr McMurray's property.

When Quin asked if she'd heard of the victim's car being vandalised, she said she hadn't been unaware of it, but said that she wouldn't put it past McMurray to do such a thing. He'd once physically thrown her cat over his back wall into the lane when he'd caught the wee thing prowling in his back yard.

'He didn't do that again,' she said with satisfaction, 'for my husband went round and told him he'd break his jaw if he even gave our cat a dirty look in future. It wasn't all a bluff, if you know what I mean. Matt has had burst a blood vessel already, and a by-pass operation. He has been told to avoid confrontations. But a couple of years ago he'd have done McMurray an injury he wouldn't have forgotten.'

'Do you know of any instances when Mr Muir was threatened by McMurray?'

'As a matter of fact, I do. I heard that McMurray had accosted Mr Muir in town one day, and had threatened to "get him" for instigating a Noise Abatement Notice he had been served with.'

'Oh?' Quin said. 'When was this?'

'When did I hear it?'

'Yes. And when did this incident happen?'

'Well, I suppose it happened shortly after McMurray got his notice. I think it was mentioned at one of our residents' group meetings last summer. The noise from McMurray's place is at its worst then,' she said. 'When it goes on, from morning to night, you just can't sit outside. He's got his windows and doors open, to get rid of all the dust he's creating, but even if he's got his doors closed you can still hear it. It starts to take over, becomes bigger and bigger, so that each time he fires up a machine, it annoys you that bit more. And you can't help it, because it's already made you so angry, in the first place, and it keeps going on. And you're thinking, Jesus, all I want is some peace and quiet!'

'Did your husband not consider remonstrating with him?' fished Scarth.

'He didn't dare. Matt has got a temper on him and he just couldn't trust himself to keep calm. No, we all thought the best way was for Mr Muir to organise a petition, and pursue the matter through the council and the courts.'

Scarth nodded. 'And did that work?'

'For a while, then he started up again. Last month he was served with a FPN, which is a fixed penalty notice. We all hoped that would be the end of the matter. Nobody has the right to a hundred per cent silence, we know that. But when you're listening to that racket week after week you begin to feel like screaming. It's just not acceptable. Anyway, earlier this week Mr Muir sent us round an update saying that because McMurray had continued to exceed the permitted level as far as noise is concerned, the council intended to enter his property and seize his precious equipment – his electric saws, planning machines, all that. And not before time.'

'I don't suppose Mr McMurray was overjoyed to hear that,' said Quin.

Elizabeth Spence paused. Her mouth formed a large 'oh'. 'Do you think he flipped? Went round to Colin's and attacked him? Oh my God ...'

'Well, we don't know that, Mrs Spence,' Quin soft-pedalled.

The woman's mouth became a thin line. 'I know one thing. It wouldn't surprise me one bit if he did.'

After leaving Elizabeth Spence, Quin and Scarth wandered into the pub/restaurant on the corner of Summerfield Terrace for a bite of lunch. The establishment was called the Covenanters' Rest. Legend had it that the building was once a farmhouse that gave refuge to a desperate bunch of Covenanters, fleeing from the Battle of Rullion Green near Penicuik in 1666. During the Napoleonic Wars the building became a staging post/rest stop for a stagecoach called 'The Highflyer'. This coach operated a twice-weekly Edinburgh to Carlisle express coach service following much the same route as the present-day A7.

Scarth was pleased that the interior wasn't the usual coach-house kitsch. There wasn't a bridle, stirrup, or saddle to be seen. The coaching inn had disappeared in the 1840s, along with its paraphernalia, when the steam train overtook stage coaches as the preferred method of travel. For many years the building served as an Anabaptist church, with a nearby lochan being utilised as their baptism place. And the bare, whitewashed walls of the restaurant section held small charcoal drawings, and some framed old newspaper cuttings, depicting the outdoor baptisms that had once been performed there.

The only time Scarth enjoyed eating was either when he was at home, or when he was alone. Neither was an option that day however, and he went along with the flow.

As the young waiter hovered, tablet poised, fingers drumming, Quin perused the menu. 'I was wrong,' she said to Scarth, hoisting her mouth to one side. 'The orange juice is only £4.60.'

She surprised him by finally ordering a grilled cheese and pickled cucumber bun, and a small glass of lactose-free milk. He thought she'd be a beef burger person.

The menu offered snacks as well as a la carte, and he settled for toasted muffins with scrambled eggs, and a half pint of fresh orange juice and lemonade. He'd seen the day when it would have been a couple of pints of cider and a bag of crisps, but his first heart attack in 2006 put paid to all that. Their orders taken, the young man swept up their menus and departed in a series of squeaks on the polished floor.

'Say what you like, Bob,' Quin pronounced, 'a place that can't offer up an all-day breakfast shouldn't be allowed to call itself a restaurant.'

As they waited for their food Scarth had a wander round the etchings. He read a few of the newspaper articles, some of which were from the 1850s. The Anabaptists did not believe in infant baptisms, he learned, and preferred, or at least the Midlothian ones did, outdoor ceremonies. Mass baptisms were organised, and conducted in the cold dark waters of the lochan. Naturally these spectacles drew large crowds of inquisitive onlookers. It must have been a buttock-clenching, testicle-shrinking experience, Scarth thought with a shiver, and that was only among the spectators!

At a little after two o'clock Quin and Scarth arrived at Roy McMurray's finely-panelled hardwood front door. Quin chapped on it with her elbow. A minute later the door was flung open by a big-shouldered man, probably in his early sixties, wearing a zipped pullover closed at the neck, and grey tracksuit trousers with several stripes down the side. True to his forename, McMurray was a red-haired man, now going grey, with a big red face and big red hams of hands. He had large, moist brown eyes, which gave him a slightly bovine look.

When Quin introduced them, the man immediately held out a hand. It was a hard hand, used to rough wear and tear, to physical work. The man seemed genuinely moved when Quin told him of the death of his neighbour next door.

'So that's what all the activity has been about,' he mused. 'Look,' he continued, 'it's no secret that we didn't get on. As a matter of fact,' he said unabashedly, 'I don't get on with any of my neighbours. So what?'

Quin reminded him about the noise abatement orders that had been served on him; the very real threat that his tools and equipment would be impounded.

'You must surely hold a grudge against Mr Muir, don't you?'

The man laughed. 'Oh, I do, make no mistake about it, I do. Or rather, I did.'

Quin decided to bowl in a googly. 'Did you murder Colin Muir, Mr McMurray?

McMurray looked at her as if she'd just asked him to perform an enema on her.

'No, of course I didn't. Look, I hated his guts, for what he was doing to me. OK? But murder? No way. You'll have to look somewhere else for that.'

He went to slam the door, but Quin's booted foot was in the way.

'So, you're telling me categorically that you aren't responsible?' she persisted.

'Cata-fucken-gorically. That suit you?' It was the first sign of that famous McMurray aggression.

Quin was up to it. She stepped quickly forward, her face tight, right into the man's space. Scarth held his breath. The last thing they needed, he thought, was for Quin to lose the rag and belt the man. Before she could say or do anything she might regret, Scarth said quickly, 'We've been told you vandalised Mr Muir's car, sir, and that the police who were called to the scene had interviewed you in connection with the incident.'

As Quin stepped back onto neutral ground, McMurray shook his head, a puzzled look in his eyes. 'No one's interviewed me about that. Your informant is mistaken.'

Scarth was momentarily taken aback, but not unduly concerned. He could easily check it.

'But I certainly knew the incident had occurred,' continued McMurray. 'In fact, I chased the bugger who did it out of the street.'

'Why?' Quin asked.

'Why what?'

'Why did you chase the perpetrator away? Why not just call the police?' Quin asked.

'Ha!' he guffawed. 'I like you, Inspector. You've got a sense of humour. You're obviously not from around here.'

It was the ingrained local prejudice against the police that they met now and again. Eskbridge had been a peaceful, hard-working coal mining town till the 1980s. Before the Westminster government began an ideological war against the miners' union, using the police force as its storm-troopers.

Quin's patience snapped. 'We've heard all that miners' shite before, Mr McMurray,' she said angrily. 'What you might not know is that many police officers in this country deeply resented being used as pawns by Thatcher.'

Give him his due, thought Scarth, the man did not even flinch at her aggression.

'If youse felt so strongly about it, you should have done something about it, shouldn't you?' the man replied calmly.

'We might have,' snapped Quin, 'if we had the power to go on strike, for there was certainly a groundswell of support for strike action, I can tell you.'

McMurray held up his hands, palms out in acquiescence, a broad smile traversing his thick lips as he locked eyes with her. To break the tension, Scarth asked, 'Any idea who this mysterious vandal might be then, Mr McMurray?'

McMurray shrugged, sliding his defiant gaze away from Quin's belligerent face. 'Buggered if I know. Could be any one of a dozen people Muir had swindled.'

Quin frowned impatiently. 'Swindled? Swindled who? In what way?'

'I don't know all the "who", but I know the "way" – by way of parting people with their hard-earned cash, that's how,' said McMurray, ducking inside and closing the door firmly in their faces.

In the car Quin said, 'I like him. He's kinda cute.' She chuckled. 'There was a delicious moment there when I thought he was going to take a swing at me. Pity,' she sniffed, 'I'd have liked a pop at him.'

'We'll have to check with the council, the noise people,' Scarth said, 'to see what light they can throw on this feud between McMurray and his neighbours.'

As she pulled at the wheel in a three-point turn, she said, 'I know. I'll see to that. I'll also run him through the Police National Computer, see what we have on him.'

'But apart from the fact that we have two separate candidates for the tanning of the victim's car,' Scarth said, 'and the unsupported allegation that Muir had been involved in some kind of financial dodgy dealings, we haven't really learned a lot this morning, have we?'

'Well, we know that Mr Weymss doesn't stay long in the saddle,' Quin replied.

But she had to agree. They'd gleaned precious little from all their peregrinations around Summerfield Terrace. As she negotiated the leafy streets leading back to the town centre, she remembered that when she was about ten, her parents had booked a caravan holiday in Galloway. Sections of some beaches on the Solway are cordoned off, due to the danger of quicksand. Unknown to her parents, Quin and the youngest of her four eejit brothers had gone on an adventure to test out the 'shifting sands' as they were called. To their consternation, they had found out just how quickly a person could become imprisoned in the treacherous sands, and but for a quick-thinking local lad who had hauled them out with a rope and his motorcycle, Quin and her brother might easily have perished.

She had the feeling now that she was back on the Solway. Every door they knocked on brought more uncertainty, less clarity. She glanced at the dashboard clock. Nearly three o'clock. Five hours had drifted by, and they weren't an inch further forward.

CHAPTER 5

THURSDAY AFTERNOON

Having left a suitable time to elapse for the next-of-kin to recover from the death notification, Scarth phoned the victim's daughter, Erica Griffin, to arrange a convenient time for himself and Quin to call. Her home landline was answered by her mother, Muir's ex-wife. She said Erica was 'too upset' to talk to anyone, and insisted she should not be disturbed. She said Erica's children would soon be on their way home from school – she mentioned one of the more prestigious of Edinburgh's fee-paying establishments – and that she intended to take them to her house to look after them for the day. 'It's just so distressing. For everyone,' she said.

Scarth said they had no wish to intrude. They just needed to ask some general questions, to get a better understanding of Mr Muir and the people in his life.

Erica's mother said they were all 'totally shocked' at the murder. The boys would be dropped off around four thirty, she said, but if Scarth and his colleague visited before that, and promised to 'be brief', she would do what she could to answer their questions.

As usual, they went in Quin's Volvo. The Griffins stayed in Candlemaker Wynd, in the old part of Eskbridge. It was a misnomer. It was no longer a narrow 'wynd' – but a broad tree-lined avenue. It took Quin and

Scarth less than fifteen minutes to drive there. As Quin drove along the Griffin's particular street Scarth couldn't but help noticing the pert rear-ends of Mercs and BMWs in the custom-paved driveways. Flowers grew competitively in well-tended front gardens. Nobody short of a few bob here, he thought.

The Griffins' house was a well-maintained sand-coloured mid terrace villa. It was probably in the £400k to £500k range. Quin seemed surprised. 'You'd need to neuter and spay a few pets to pay for the likes of this,' she observed, as she wobbled up the steps like a blancmange.

The ex-wife was a surprise too. She was much younger than they had somehow expected. She was a comely, carefully-made-up woman, somewhere in her forties. She had ash-blonde hair down to her shoulders, and a well-kept figure underneath a scoop-necked leopard print top. Her lower half was closely sheathed in tight black leggings. In another age she might have been described as 'Rubenesque'. She introduced herself as Lenore MacDonald, and gave them a slender hand and a tentative smile.

'My maiden name. My mother was an aficionado of Edgar Allan Poe,' she explained in response to Quin's raised eyebrow, 'and not, as I used to mischievously tell my school chums, a germaphobe.'

Quin, who had taken an instant dislike to the woman, said, 'I see,' though she hadn't a clue what she was on about. Scarth marked Lenore MacDonald down as a clever-clogs, but attractive with it.

Lenore MacDonald showed them into a large, high-ceilinged living room which was well lit by its bay windows. The room was comfortably furnished, filled with good-quality furniture scuffed by life. Or children. Erica was still indisposed, she reiterated. She was up in her room, and did not feel able to see anyone.

Quin said she understood, relieved to direct her questions to the dry-eyed mother instead.

They learned that Colin Muir was sixty-two when he died. He came originally from Oldmeldrum, in Aberdeenshire; had got his law degree from Edinburgh University; and, apart from a short stint with the Crown Prosecution Service, had been with FyffeRobertson in Eskbridge ever since.

Muir and his wife had only one child. They had met when she spent a student summer in the Procurator's office in Edinburgh. 'I was flirting with the idea of becoming a solicitor', she said. 'I decided to save myself a lot of bother and marry one instead.'

Scarth supposed that Muir would have been near middle age when he married. He could see the attraction on the solicitor's part, but what of her?

He had detected the lilt of a Western Isles accent and asked her where she came from. She said her father was a doctor, from Skye, but that she had been brought up in Perthshire, in a small village called Tibbermore.

Scarth said he knew the place. 'Tibber is usually associated with wells, or natural springs, isn't it?' he said. He wasn't sure if he was trying to impress her, or trying to win her confidence. Probably a bit of both. 'I'll hazard a guess,' he said. 'Is it the 'big well?''

She smiled indulgently. 'It could be Tiobar móire, 'big well', as you say,' she stated; 'or it might be tiobar Moire,

'Mary's well' as in Tobar Mhoire – such as Tobermory, in Mull.'

He enjoyed being put in his place. 'What do you think?' he asked.

Quin decided it was time to interrupt their flirty tête à tête. 'I think whatever kind of well it is,' she interrupted, 'it's a good one to leave behind us. We've been told that you now live with a boyfriend, is that correct?'

MacDonald smiled indulgently. 'It's ridiculous I know, calling a middle-aged man a 'boyfriend', but it's true enough. Bill, Bill Crighton, has been a rock for me during the past couple of years. When things with Colin were becoming difficult … I've moved in with him at his home at Markethill.'

'And he works for a courier company, here in Eskbridge?'

'He's the proprietor of a courier company, yes,' the woman replied tersely.

'What caused your break-up with Mr Muir, if you don't mind me asking?' asked Quin.

The woman smiled sadly. 'I think it was fatigue more than anything which brought the marriage to an end,' she said. 'Colin was one of those annoyingly cheery types who seem up for anything, no matter how dire the circumstances,' she said. 'The sort whose sheer joie de vivre takes its toll on whatever company they are in. It was very tiring.'

She paused, consulted her manicured fingernails, then said, 'Why do any marriages fail? People just drift apart. They wake up one day and find out they aren't in love anymore. Sometimes it's as simple as that.'

Or sometimes it's not as simple as that, thought Quin as they retreated to her car. Marriages sometimes fail because you find out you've been married to a rat-bastard who wasn't worth a struck match.

'Is there anyone that you know of who might wish to harm your ex-husband, Mizz MacDonald?' Scarth asked.

The woman said that as far as she knew, Colin hadn't an enemy in the world. He had a wide circle of friends, she said. He was generally well thought of. He doted on his grandchildren. Relations between her and her ex had admittedly been 'fraught' recently, because of his tardiness in getting the house on the market, but apart from that she knew of no-one who would wish him harm.

He was a solicitor, for God's sake, she said with a frown. As if the thought of a stuffy solicitor doing anything which could cause offence was patently preposterous.

Quin asked about the family. How many grandchildren are there?

She said that Erica and Danny had two children, boys aged eight and ten.

'Is Danny here at the moment?'

'No. He's on his way back from a conference in Inverness … I've informed him of Colin's death and the fact that his wife is dreadfully upset and needs his support.' She consulted her wrist. 'He'll probably be here in an hour, if you want to call back …'

'We'll have to speak to him sometime,' Quin said noncommittally. 'But there's no hurry.'

'Aren't you going to ask me to account for my movements last night, Inspector?'

Before Quin could answer the woman carried on, 'Don't worry, I was home all last night. Bill was too. He finished at eight, then came straight home for his dinner. Has it been established when, er, when the incident with Colin took place?'

'We're waiting confirmation on that,' Quin replied. 'We got an anonymous tip-off, that all was not well. Mrs Weymss, whom you'll know well, let the responding officers in. She has a key to the property.'

'Yes, I know. I gave it to her.'

'Do you still have a copy by any chance?'

'Certainly not. Why would I?'

Quin paused for a moment or two. 'Mrs Weymss happened to mention that the delay in selling the house was wearing on everyone's nerves.'

'Well Mrs Weymss can also be wearing on everybody's nerves, but she certainly got that right,' MacDonald stated. She went on to say that of course she had been greatly frustrated that the sale of the house was going so slow. She repeated that Colin's tardiness in complying with the divorce settlement had caused a 'certain amount' of tension between her ex-husband and Bill. How could it not?

'Do you know that Mrs Weymss believes Bill vandalised Colin's car about three weeks ago?' Quin asked.

She did, the woman replied stiffly, for the police have had the nerve to question Bill about it. She knew Bill had gone to see Colin about a business matter, but even if there had been a disagreement of some kind, she said, she doubted very much that matters would have got out of hand in any way. She said she would be 'astonished' if Bill had been responsible for the trashing of Colin's car. 'It just wouldn't be like him', she said. 'He's a lamb.'

'What do you make of her?' she asked Scarth later in the car. '"I was flirting with the idea of becoming a solicitor,"' she mimicked, '… pretentious cack.'

Scarth flashed an indulgent smile at her.

'Smart enough to snare a solicitor,' she continued, 'but dumb enough to leave him for a courier driver?'

He stretched his short legs comfortably in the passenger seat. 'So far, she's the only one to have a good word for this Bill Crighton …'

'I've got him on my to-do list,' Quin replied. 'We'll catch up with him tomorrow.'

Danny and Erica Griffin were home, and Lenore MacDonald was gone, when Quin and Scarth returned to the large house in 'old' Eskbridge. Two other high-end cars were already there in the gravelled drive, flanking the porticoed doorway. Danny Griffin answered the door, and directed the investigators into the same living room where they'd earlier spoken to his mother-in-law.

Erica Griffin was there, curled up on a sofa. She had long light brown hair with an understandably puffy-eyed look on her naturally pale face. What physical characteristics she had inherited from her father Scarth couldn't say, but she definitely had her mother's rather voluptuous figure and long-lashed tawny eyes.

Quin expressed her condolences to the young woman. She nodded graciously. She quizzed her gently. The woman said she was unaware of anyone who would wish harm to her dad; apart from 'Creepy Crighton perhaps.'

'You mean your mum's new boyfriend?'

'He's not new,' interrupted her husband. 'They've been lovers for years.'

'Really, Danny,' his wife admonished, 'I don't think there's any need to broadcast Mum's personal business …'

Quin said that about three weeks ago her father had been in an argument with Bill Crighton. 'Could that lead to violence?' she asked.

'Look,' the young woman said, 'Bill Crighton's a creep. But he's not a murderer.'

'Well in my experience,' pontificated Quin, 'all sorts of people commit murder. Creeps included.'

Erica Griffin shook her head. 'He hasn't got the guts for that. Lifting females' skirts is more his line.'

'Darling,' warned her husband, hoping to head her off at the pass, 'I don't think the inspector is interested in the sexual mores of a middle-aged courier proprietor …'

'On the contrary,' replied Quin keenly. 'I'm all ears.'

'Danny's right,' Erica said, rising up off the sofa. 'I should keep my prejudices to myself. After all, he may become my step-father someday.'

She moved towards the door.

'If you'll excuse me. I have to get changed to fetch our children home from school.'

Griffin was a gaunt-faced young man with dark hair and greyish eyes, dressed in a charcoal business suit. His neck, Scarth idly supposed, might be regarded by some as overly long. A slight shaving rash was visible just above the neck of his shirt. He had an easy, comfortable, professional way with him, like a dentist or a priest.

Quin studied the man briefly. 'Have we met before?' she asked suspiciously. It always unsettled them.

'No,' Griffin replied hesitantly, his confident demeanour slipping momentarily. 'I don't think so.'

'It's just that your face. It seems familiar … Never mind. We're trying to establish everyone's whereabouts last night,' Quin explained. 'Can you tell me where you were, from nine o'clock to midnight?'

'I can tell you where I was from noon to midnight,' he replied smartly, 'and beyond. I was in Inverness for a business meeting. The meeting went on longer than I anticipated, and I stayed there overnight.'

'Nice hotel?' Quin solicited with a patently-false innocence.

'The Excelsior,' the man replied smoothly. 'Pretentiously named, but comfortable enough.'

'Did you go out at all?' she persisted. 'Leave the hotel for any period – to the pub, a restaurant?'

'Where do you go in Inversnecky on a wet Wednesday night?' asked the man derisively. Rather cheekily, Quin thought. She let an uncomfortable silence built up between them.

'Look,' relented the young man, 'I appreciate you have to question, even suspect, close family members when a sudden death occurs,' he said, 'but I can assure you I stayed in my room. I had room service food sent up. I phoned Erica twice. Her phone records will substantiate that.'

Scarth noted that he did not claim that his phone records would establish his alibi.

Quin, however, seemed satisfied with the claim.

'What do you do for a living, Mr Griffin?' she asked.

Griffin, rather pompously Scarth thought, told them that he was a 'trader in digital cryptocurrency'. He had a 'portfolio' of valued clients, he said, whose funds he invested in bitcoin exchanges, mostly in the Far East.

Quin wouldn't have known a bitcoin if it had reared up and bit her. She waved an arm round the room. 'You have a very impressive home here, Mr Griffin,' she said. 'The bitumen business must be going well.'

'It's bitcoin: and yes, business is going well. For me and my clients.' He tapped the side of his head. 'Touch wood …'

They had seen the M Series BMW and the small Audi run-around in the gravel driveway. Scarth knew that the fees at the school the boys attended were in the £18,000 to £20,000 a year bracket. Griffin's business must indeed be 'going well'.

'Was your father-in-law one of your clients?' Scarth prompted.

'In a way. We were partners for a while,' Griffin replied guardedly. 'Then he got cold feet.'

'What sort of partners exactly,' Quin asked.

'Informal business partners.'

'In what way?'

Griffin hesitated. 'Some of Colin's clients were prepared to invest part of their capital in the hope of a substantial return. He introduced them to me, I made the investments on their behalf.'

Scarth said, almost reflectively. 'Well, we know that solicitors often place their clients' assets in trust funds, off-shore accounts, and whatnot. That's not unusual. What gave him cold feet?'

It seemed to be a touchy subject. Griffin's tight face seemed to tighten even further.

'Look Inspector,' he said, ignoring Scarth, 'the thing about investments is that they can go down as well as up. Understanding that is a prerequisite for any investor. Colin's clients may well have overestimated how much they stood to gain, and underestimated how much it would hurt them if those wished-for riches proved elusive.'

'How much did they lose?' Quin asked bluntly.

'I dunno. You'd have to ask his clients. Look, is this relevant Inspector?'

'How hurt is 'hurt'?'

Griffin looked at the ceiling, then returned his cold eyes to the investigators. 'If you must know, during a bad spell, around three years ago, the whole shebang went belly up. Everybody lost out. Since then, the market has recovered. It's stable now and on the up and up. It was unfortunate that some of Colin's clients lost their investments when the market nose-dived, but had they stayed the course, they would be reaping the benefits now …'

'Are any of your current investors former clients of Colin Muir?' Scarth asked.

The man regarded him for a second or two before shaking his head.

'So, your current clients understand they're in it for the long haul?'

The man looked at him. His voice was controlled, atonal. 'All of my investors are fully aware of the risks as well as the benefits. Maybe the problem for Colin,' he continued, 'was that he invested some of his clients' assets informally – without receiving their explicit blessing to do so beforehand.'

The investigators thought about that.

'Well that certainly would have been naughty of him,' Quin eventually said.

'Some people might think it is negligently naughty,' said the young man, a smug smile playing on his thin lips, 'and might be prompted to do something about it …'

It was Thursday lunchtime before McIntosh and Munro got back to the office from their Operation Drawstring briefing. As Munro took her lunch-box through to the canteen, McIntosh dropped a small pile of witness statements at the side of his desk. They were the ones pertaining solely to Eskbridge. From an inside pocket he drew out a lime-green Spork – the plastic combination knife, fork and spoon he carried with him at all times – and opened a large tub of yoghurt. He sat down, slid the top folder off the pile, and, between mouthfuls, began a keen perusal of its contents.

Fifteen minutes later, his lunch finished and his prep work done, McIntosh went about contacting those concerned.

His first phone-snatching victim worked for Ramsay's, a large department store in Eskbridge's main shopping centre, The Mall. McIntosh had a frustrating time trying to get through to her for she was in a conference when he called. When he eventually got to speak to her, Carole Dunne said she had been travelling in to work, 'yakking' to a girlfriend on her mobile phone, when she was 'attacked' by a crazy woman. This maniac, she said, snatched her phone from her hand and purposely destroyed it. This had happened, she recalled, as the bus approached the bus terminus at The Mall in Dundas Street. Her phone was a Samsung Galaxy S3 she said, as if to impress him, and cost £400.

McIntosh was indeed impressed, for it was the same model as his police issue.

Her voice sounded young. She had a masculine-sounding sudden drop of the voice at the end of sentences. It was an affectation, he knew, prevalent among females of a certain age. Penis envy, he presumed.

Dunne said that the woman who attacked her had used 'secateurs or something' and that she (Dunne) had been prevented from grabbing her assailant before she escaped, because of the pandemonium which ensued with her (Dunne) 'turning the air blue' with her outrage at the assault.

Her attacker, she said, was a trim, grey-haired elderly woman who obviously kept herself fit. When McIntosh asked why she thought that, Carole Dunne said the woman was dressed for the outdoors in the latest gear, and had 'all but sprinted' away from the bus after jumping off as the bus pulled into the terminal.

Carole Dunne wondered why McIntosh was interested, for she had already told all this to a 'pin-up girl' of a police constable. This police officer, who had been summoned to the scene, seemed more interested in the attention she was attracting than the job she was supposed to be doing.

Pin-up girl? McIntosh let his eyes drift to the bottom of the page to the officer's signature. PC Shirley McCracken. She was new and they'd never been introduced. Maybe that was something he needed to rectify.

'Just as a matter of interest, what do you do in Ramsay's, Carole?'

'I'm a security supervisor, why?'

'Were you wearing your uniform on your way to work?'

'I was, yes. Is this relevant?'

'Dunno,' replied McIntosh honestly. 'Thanks for your input …'

McIntosh's second victim was Harper Rennie, a thirty-year-old primary teacher. She had been 'too traumatised' at the time of the incident to describe the phone snatcher properly. She now did so, saying that 'the despicable woman' was of small stature, wearing a formal navy coat, with creased grey trousers. She had on expensive-looking court shoes. The woman had fair hair, probably dyed, and a narrow face with a 'sly' look.

Miss Rennie was furious that she had been forced to fork out for another mobile phone while her insurance company 'dithered around' about settling her claim for the iPhone 4S she had seen 'utterly destroyed' before her very eyes. The snatcher, she said, had used some sort of cutting device, possibly a gardening tool.

When asked to recall when the incident occurred, she said she had been on her way to the centre of Eskbridge to meet a friend. She had been talking on her phone to an elderly relative discussing her haemorrhoids, when her phone had suddenly been 'whisked' out of her hand. She acknowledged that her conversation may have sounded louder than normal, because her relative was partially deaf and habitually spoke in a whisper, and she had been obliged to put her on speakerphone to hear what she said.

But that was no excuse, surely, she stated, for such an 'unwarranted' attack – 'and on a Sunday too!'

During her rant, McIntosh found that he had to hold his phone away from his ear to avoid getting a headache. He had often noticed how loud female voices were compared to male ones, especially on phones. Or maybe it was just teachers. He'd once shared this opinion with Munro, but qualified it by saying that males probably had traits too which women found obnoxious, though he couldn't think of any. He'd enjoyed the way her jaw dropped in astonished outrage.

Her attacker, Harper Rennie avowed, had deliberately targeted her SIM card. Why she didn't know. She was lucky she'd had all her data backed up in her cloud, she said. The woman could have just as easily have just ended her call after she'd snatched her phone, if she had found the conversation objectionable, she said. There was no need to 'mangle the thing to bits', was there?

She had her phone on contract so there was no problem getting a replacement. But what if her fingers had been in the way of that maniac's pliers, eh? Could he tell her that, she demanded?

It was the first time that pliers had been mentioned.

McIntosh asked her to clarify what type of implement the phone-snatcher had used. Was it pliers, or the gardening-type tool she had mentioned earlier?

Pliers, the woman confirmed, before launching a final tirade.

What are the police doing about these phone-snatching people anyway, she demanded? Nothing; as far as she could see, she added. That's what they were doing, she declared; bugger all.

Before McIntosh had a chance to object, she hung up.

He marked her witness statement spitefully as NFA, and slipped it back into the folder.

McIntosh's third witness was Wayne Copeland, a mature student at Edinburgh University, who had audaciously given his faculty's office landline as his contact number. McIntosh held the line for longer than was comfortable before Copeland could be located. Copeland was a bore, but had one snippet of information that perked McIntosh's interest. He said that when his phone had been snatched and 'smashed to smithereens' with 'some sort of punch', he had been prevented from restraining the snatcher – a 'small besom in a dark puffer jacket' – because of other elderly passengers, who appeared to be 'running interference' as his assailant skipped down the aisle to the door.

The term came from American football, a sport that McIntosh despised, and meant the obstruction or hindrance of opposing players to make a way or a path for the ball carrier – or, in Copeland's case, the 'punch carrier'.

It was a neat tactic, McIntosh thought, and one that added a new dimension to their investigation. If it was indeed the case that some fellow-passengers had deliberately obstructed pursuit, it then suggested that some sort of concerted, combined effort, had been employed.

Connie Considine was the most recent victim, while he and Munro had been sitting through Superintendent Kerr's evangelical oratory.

Considine was a twenty-two-year-old mum who had been travelling on a number 33 bus into Eskbridge town centre. She was on her way to the Little Horrors Pre-School to drop off her eldest son Leo, aged three and a quarter. She had been on her phone, 'blethering' with a pal during the journey, when a 'crazy madwoman' had suddenly snatched the device out of her hand. Before she could react, for she had the bairn on her knees, the woman had 'spiflicated' her phone with a hand-held 'nut-crusher'.

PC Connor Reid and Special Constable Bobby Kell had responded. The attacker had fled the scene, noted Reid, leaving behind the mangled phone. They recovered it from the locus, and handed it in to Forensic at Division for examination.

In her witness statement the woman said her assailant had been a 'wee woman' wearing a dark fleecy top, dark jogging pants, and trainers. She looked old, with natural teeth that 'needed seeing to'. She was wearing a woolly hat pulled down over her ears, but a few stray auburn hairs poked out. And she was fit, said the witness, for she took off into the shopping centre 'like a demented leveret'.

McIntosh smiled. He thought he recognised a pattern. The phone-snatcher was evolving, mutating, transmogrifying – whatever. She was honing her technique; experimenting with different implements in order to find the perfect one. She was also changing her appearance each time she struck, to avoid identification. First grey hair, then hair dyed fair, then auburn: first informal outdoor clothes, then well-dressed formal attire, then ultra-informal casual wear.

A phrase came into his mind and he tried it out for size. 'The shape-shifting phone-snatcher'. It sounded good.

The first time she did it, Sallyanne had been dead scared. She had never knowingly committed a crime before, never had been in trouble with the police. So why was she preparing to break the law now? The answer was blindingly clear – because something needed to be done. Someone had to make a stand.

As a precaution Sallyanne always changed her appearance before a mission. The bus route from the south end of Eskbridge to the terminus at Dundas Mall took twenty-three minutes. From her seat at the back of the bus she could see all those who came on and got off. Sometimes she had to make several trips per day to make sure circumstances were just right. Luckily, she didn't have long to wait this time for a suitable candidate to present themselves.

After two stops a young woman, perhaps in her late twenties, boarded the bus. Shoulder hunched to trap her phone; she made her way to a seat half-way down the aisle. Once seated, she continued her voluble phone conversation. Her voice was pervasive, unembarrassed; her accent was local, undiluted. Nearby passengers glanced at each other in discomfort. Some darted reproving glances at the woman, others stoically settled in for an uncomfortable ride.

Despite her age, Sallyanne could move fast when she put her mind to it. She had an arsenal of weapons in her garden shed at home. Pliers, pincers, heavy-duty secateurs.

Her instrument of choice that day was a powerful sail-maker's punch. It was commercially used to punch holes in thick leather, and tarpaulin, and canvas. She snatched the phone out of the startled woman's hands, selected the side of the device where the SIM card was located, and pressed hard.

The screen immediately shattered. Its owner stared in disbelief at the ruins of her phone. The punch had even bulged out a bump in the back. Her SIM card, with all her contacts, photos, videos, you name it, had been shredded into mush. It was obvious that the device had been rendered inoperable, irreparable. It had gone from high-tech to scrap in less than a second.

Sallyanne had gone too. From a standing start she reached warp speed in three seconds. She had timed her attack to the moment when the bus pulled into the stop at the Dundas Mall terminus. She shouldered her way through the astonished passengers, leaving the uproar behind her, and hopped off the bus. She thought she heard a smattering of applause as she galloped into the covered mall. From there she had a hundred hiding places in shops, stores, lifts, and toilets; and a dozen ways to disappear though exits, multi-storey car parks, and fire doors.

On reaching safety, Sallyanne pulled out her iPhone and checked her Fitbit statistics.

She discovered her heart rate was 72 bpm, which was a bit elevated; her blood oxygen was 99%, which was fine; but that her wee workout had disappointingly burned only a measly 8 calories.

Still. It wasn't bad for a sixty-seven-year-old who was righting wrongs and having thirty seconds worth of exhilarating fun while she was at it.

CHAPTER 6

FRIDAY MORNING

The morning pow-wow was brief, fragmentary.

McIntosh announced that he and Munro were off to the Midlothian Buses depot that morning, to check out what CCTV footage they had of Connie Considine's incident.

When the young detectives had gone, Quin told Scarth that she had phoned the estate agent handling Muir's house sale. She had got the names of the photographers and surveyors involved, and the three prospective buyers who had viewed the property. She had emailed these details to Shawn Murray along with a contact list of people known to have been to the victim's house – the neighbours, the ex-wife, and her boyfriend, the Griffins and their kids, and the cleaner. The Scene Examiners would see that they were all fingerprinted for elimination purposes.

She told him that their friend Roy McMurray had indeed a criminal record. 'Three assault convictions. Not surprising really, given his belligerent nature. Trouble is they are from thirty years ago. Nothing since 1985 …'

'Pity,' Scarth said.

'I know,' she replied disappointedly. She reached through her notes. 'I also checked the 'overnights' from the beginning of the month. I found what I was looking for on the night of 5th March. Officers from Division responded to a phone call from a concerned resident of Summerfield Terrace, who reported that an act of vandalism had been perpetrated against a neighbour's car.'

'Who was the caller?' Scarth asked.

'Mrs Sandra Weymss, and the car in question was a black BMW 3 Series belonging to her neighbour Mr Colin Muir. It was parked in his drive. The officers who responded questioned the lady who had made the call, but were unable to get a clear description of the perpetrator. All she saw was a man in dark clothing wearing a ski cap or something similar. She did not get a clear look at his face. But from his size and shape, she 'took' the man to be Bill Crighton, boy-friend of the neighbour's ex-wife.'

'She wasn't positive it was Crighton, then?'

'Nearly positive. The officers interviewed Mr Muir, who admitted that he and Bill Crighton had argued earlier out on the street, but that he had gone inside when Crighton left in his car. He was surprised when informed of Mrs Weymss' suggestion, that his car had later been vandalised by Crighton, and assured the officers that Mrs Weymss must have been mistaken. When asked what his argument with Mr Crighton was about, Muir declined to answer.'

'Did they see what Crighton had to say?'

'Naturally. He too admitted there had been an argument between himself and Mr Muir on the night in question, but that he had not been responsible for any damage to Mr Muir's car. When invited to reveal what the argument was about, he told them it was none of their business.'

'Sounds the stroppy type,' Scarth commented.

'The officers marked their report 'NFA' – no further action required. Tell you what Bob,' Quin said. 'I think we should go round to see this guy, Bill Crighton. See what the big attraction is. You up for that?'

It wasn't a question, so it didn't require an answer.

Eskbridge Express Couriers – motto: 'Quicker Than You Think' – had their yard in a small industrial park in the north of the town. It had been built on the site of the town's old 'steamie' – the communal wash house, where women used to go to do their weekly wash of clothes, and to gossip about other women. To be the 'talk of the steamie' wasn't something any self-respecting female wanted to be.

When the investigators entered the office, a receptionist, probably in her late twenties or early thirties, looked up from her screen with inquiring eyebrows. She had platinum-blonde hair, twiffed back from her forehead, and an amused, sardonic look on her face. She was the type whose every trip to the office water cooler was like a sashay down a catwalk. A metallic sign on her desk read: The Real Boss.

'Help youse?' she asked insincerely.

Bill Crighton was in a back office. He looked to be in his early to late forties, of about middle height, with a heavy body. He had a thick covering of dark hair on his head, the kind that doesn't move in the wind.

'No calls for a while Kayleigh,' Crighton said gruffly to the receptionist as he showed the investigators into his room.

When they had settled, Quin introduced herself and Scarth and said, 'Mr Crighton, have you been informed of the homicide of Mr Colin Muir?'

'Naturally. As you well know Lenore, his ex-wife, is currently living with me.'

'Just so,' said Quin. 'We're investigating Mr Muir's homicide, and wonder if you would care to answer a few questions for us?'

Crighton opened his palms in acquiescence. 'Go ahead,' he said.

'We understand you had an altercation with Mr Muir recently. What can you tell us about that?'

'Well, I can tell you I didn't smash his stupid windscreen.'

'What was the argument about?'

'It was about money, pure and simple.'

'Would you care to elaborate?'

Wiping his nose with the back of a hairy wrist, Crighton told her the row was about the time it was taking Muir to sell the house and settle with Lenore.

He was a bit fluke-moothed, Quin noticed, with the twisted mouth of a flounder. She wondered what Lenore MacDonald saw in this man.

'I have to ask. Did you murder him, Mr Crighton?'

'Murder him?' Crighton laughed. He shook his shoulders when he laughed, like a buzzard trying out new wings. 'I'm the last bleeping person who would murder him. I needed him alive!'

He got up, went stiffly to the window. 'Can't sit for long,' he explained. 'The back's buggered with sitting in front of that computer.'

When invited to explain why he needed the victim alive, Crighton told Quin that Lenore had promised him a £50,000 cash injection for the business. The expectation was that she would get something in the region of a quarter of a million as her part of the divorce settlement. It would have given Lenore financial independence, he said, and the loan she had promised him would have given him the cash injection he desperately needed for the business.

'So,' Quin asked. 'What happens to the settlement now?'

'Who knows?' Crighton replied tartly. 'After the divorce, Erica was made the beneficiary of Muir's will. If Muir died, she would get the estate. How the financials will pan out now is uncertain,' he said, 'but there's a good chance my 'cash transfusion' will go out the window.'

'You're saying it was very much in your interests to have Mr Muir alive?'

Crighton emitted a grunt which sounded like a seal's bark. 'I'd have acted as his personal bleeping bodyguard,' he stated bitterly, 'if I'd known someone wanted to kill him!' he said.

Quin looked out of the window to the yard. There was a constant coming and going of trucks, vans, and drivers. The place was a hive of activity. She heaved a hand at the scene.

'You look busy enough to me, Mr Crighton. I hope you don't mind me asking, what was the loan for?'

Crighton explained that he needed to convert his fleet to electric, or at the least hybrid, power. Companies nowadays were stipulating that their delivery contractors must have carbon-free vehicles, he said. A huge contract with a well-known internet company was on the horizon. To have a chance of competing for that and indeed any future contracts, he needed a 'clean' fleet.

'Do you know how many metric tons of carbon dioxide the average car produces every year?' he asked.

'No,' Quin replied calmly. 'But I've got a feeling you're going to tell me.'

'Four. Four metric tons every year.'

'What's a metric ton?'

'One thousand kilos.' Crighton warmed to his subject. 'Global warming is frightening. Greenhouse gas emissions are killing us. We can see the effects now, even as we speak. Extreme weather, heat waves, glacial melting, flooding, rising sea levels … If we don't do something about it, we'll be extinct in a hundred years …'

Scarth, who more and more found his mind drifting away at a tangent, was reminded of something he'd once read about an anticipated appearance of Halley's Comet just before the First World War.

Reports began to circulate that cyanogen chloride, a deadly asphyxiant, had been discovered in the comet's tail. Rumours that this toxic gas would poison the atmosphere, and so snuff out all life on the planet, created wide-spread public panic throughout the UK.

All over the country churches held all-night prayer vigils. In the cities, wide-boy charlatans sold "comet pills" to counteract the effects of the poison. People stopped buying long-playing records for their gramophones, for it was commonly believed that the world was coming to an end.

At Dundee, naturally there were fears for the men away at the Arctic whaling. "Eh, the warld's going to end," one anxious Dundee wifie reportedly said to a friend, "and there's a' oor lads up at the whalin'. Whit on earth will they do when they come back an' fin' that there's nae warld left tae come back to?"

Quin searched for hints of mockery in Crighton's eyes. She found none. He was genuine, she thought with mild surprise, he really does believe the greenhouse gasses doomsday scenario. She let a couple of seconds go by before saying,

'Well, let's hope we don't become extinct, Mr Crighton. It would play havoc with my pension. Your future daughter-in-law, Erica, she's a vet, isn't she?'

Crighton smiled, showing ill-kept teeth. Quin wondered again what his girl-friend saw in him.

'Daughter-in-law? We haven't discussed marriage, Inspector,' he informed her. 'Me and Lenore have only been living together for a few months. But yes, Erica is a vet. Has her own business. Doing well too, from what I hear.'

'What does the husband do?' Quin asked.

'He does bugger all,' Crighton said contemptuously. 'He was a high-flying investor for a couple of years, before he got over-extended. Now he's crashed back to earth.

'We heard his business was thriving …'

'Did he tell you that?' Crighton stretched his back, wincing. 'He was making money hand over fist for a while. Bought the big house, the fancy car. Then it all went poof! Up in smoke. Maybe it was smoke all along …'

'What was he investing in?' Quin asked.

'You mean who was he investing with?'

'No,' she said stubbornly. 'I mean what was he investing in?'

'He was prospecting, is that what they call it? For bitcoins …'

Quin hadn't a clue what he was on about.

Scarth intervened before she could show her ignorance.

'Mining,' he stated. 'They call it bitcoin mining.'

'That's it,' Crighton affirmed.

'Ah,' Quin said unconvincingly. 'And who was he mining with?'

'Colin Muir,' Crighton replied. 'From what I understand Griffin has the financial expertise. Muir had been investing clients' money for forty years. When the bitcoin thing came along, it was tailor-made for a quick buck. Muir sucked them in; Griffin sucked them dry …'

'Investments can go up, but investments can also go down,' Quin pointed out knowledgably.

'Exactly,' Crighton replied. 'So, if you're looking for whoever killed Colin Muir, you're wasting your time looking at me. There must be a dozen folks round here that Colin Muir has hurt financially, through losing their money for them.'

'You know,' Quin said, 'you're the second person who has told me that today.'

'Yeah? Well, I'm sure you'll find plenty of others as well, if you ask around.'

'What an obnoxious man,' Quin said when they'd got back to her car. She stretched her seat belt to its limit, then clunk clicked. It had started to drizzle and she switched on the wipers. 'I'd like to have an excuse to come down on him like a ton of bricks …. A metric ton of bricks …'

'He was certainly only too happy to point us in Griffin's direction,' Scarth observed quietly. 'Was he being helpfully civically-minded, or trying to throw us off the scent?'

'I wouldn't trust him as far as I could throw him,' Quin replied. 'I'll run him through the Police National Computer when we get back to the office,' she said, throwing the car into gear. 'Who knows, maybe we'll find out something about him that Miss Lenore-I'm-not-a-gramophone doesn't know.'

'Germaphobe,' Scarth unadvisedly corrected.

'That's what I said, diddle I?' she snapped.

Scarth grinned. Quin with her hackles up was a beast best avoided.

She turned out of the business park, followed a secondary road in need of repair for a bit, then accelerated up the on-ramp to the dual carriageway. It would take them south into town.

'We'll need to have a closer look at Muir's business dealings, Bob,' she said, gliding into the outside lane. 'Especially this bitcoin stuff ... Would you mind going round to his office this afternoon, to see what you can find out?'

'Sure.'

'Meanwhile, I'll delve into the business world of Danny Griffin. You can't make money enough for his kind of lifestyle, without cutting at least a few corners.'

CHAPTER 7

FRIDAY MORNING

That morning DS McIntosh and DC Munro had to attend an Operation Drawstring induction at Division HQ. The way McIntosh drove, it didn't take long to get there.

Scarth came in from his East Lothian home after the young detectives had gone.

Quin began by announcing the bad news. 'Shawn has emailed me. A lab examination of the victim's camera strap hasn't yielded any epithelial tissue.'

'Hmm,' Scarth mused. 'It was worth a try.'

'I think we'll have more joy from the whiff of financial impropriety alluded to by Griffin, Crighton, and McMurray. Could you chase it up Bob, please? Shawn has left the victim's laptop there,' she said. 'Have a look through the victim's stuff today, would you? See what you can see, and bring the laptop back with you if you want it forensically examined. And the Highland dress angle. He was dressed up for some sort of occasion. Do we know where he was last night?'

Scarth admitted he was still in the dark about that.

Quin produced a glassine bag of tagged items. 'Shawn sent these over. The victim's house keys. Regarding the means of access,' continued Quin. 'The killer got in without forcing an entry. That suggests the victim knew him, trusted him.'

'Either that or the killer had a key.'

Quin nodded. 'I had a word with the estate agent. She confirmed that interest in the property had been negligible. Apparently only one has viewed the property in the last fourteen weeks; and only two prospective buyers had made inquiries in the time before that. The house is too big, too old, too expensive, she said.'

'I'll have a word with her at FyffeRobertson today when I go round,' replied Scarth, 'and see if the house-keys were ever copied, or issued to someone. Anything else from Shawn? About prints in the house, or on the sgian dubh?'

'There are prints everywhere in the house, as you'd expect. From the victim and at least three others. They're likely to be from the daughter, the granddaughters, and the cleaner. Shawn will get samples from them and send them off for comparison. Unfortunately, there are no prints on the dagger whatyamacallit or the felt pen which was used for that grotesque smiley face. The killer has left them, confident that they have no DNA on them.'

'The use of gloves. Sounds like he may have done this before,' Scarth offered.

'Could well be. Shawn has posted a discreet image of the smiley face on the PNC, so we'll know soon enough if it has been used before somewhere in a homicide. Might be a copy-cat.'

'Somehow I doubt it,' replied Scarth. 'I think that Mr Muir's murder was purely a spur-of-the-moment thing. Driven by anger, rage, frustration. I'm only surprised the killer ignored all those deadly weapons hanging on the wall, any one of which would have done the job admirably.'

'But which would have spilled a lot of blood,' said Quin. 'Messy, that. And always the chance you'd slice off one of your own fingers in the process. This is more studied, less frenzied. I think we should also flag up ligature strangling, Bob. Ligature strangling with desecration.'

'Yes, but there is tremendous animosity here,' Scarth replied quietly. 'Personal enmity. I think this is a one-off. A settling of a score.'

'You mean you hope it is a one-off,' she replied pessimistically.

It was nearly noon before Scarth got to the offices of FyffeRobertson, the law firm where Colin Muir had been a partner. Opposite the entrance door a haughty-looking woman with fluffed-up white hair and a low-slung bosom was toying with a keyboard. Her eyelashes resembled a pair of draught excluders. She was wearing a mauve-coloured long-sleeved shirt with a tiny heart-shaped pendant at her throat. Her wooden name sign said Mary Hegarty.

She condescended to notice him.

'Do you wish to see someone?' she asked expectantly.

'I'm with the police,' Scarth replied. 'I'm here to see Andrea Fyffe.'

Her formal manner relaxed. He wasn't anyone important after all.

She asked him to have a seat in the waiting area. It was opposite her desk. A high-backed chair stood casually in one corner. He sat down in it. It was an extremely busy office, with people coming and going past Scarth as he waited in a small visitor's area. He noticed that the receptionist waylaid people as they passed her desk. She intercepted them with hushed comments, eliciting frowns or startled gasps, before she freed them.

She reminded Scarth of 'Saucy Mary', the legendary Viking princess at Kyleakin in Skye, who demanded a tribute from any boat which passed through the narrow channel between her castle and the mainland. Legend has it that 'Saucy Mary' derived her nickname from her habit of baring her breasts as a thank-you to those who paid her toll. Mercifully, Mary Hegarty was content to let the office traffic pass her desk with only a whispered titbit.

He had no doubt this Mary was passing on the news of Colin Muir's death, and alerting the staff to the unwelcome presence of the police in their staid enclave.

A woman suddenly appeared before him. She was about his height, on the thin side, wearing a dark pin-stripe jacket and skirt. She had a tanned, unlined face and dark auburn hair, done in a bouffant style. It was a look that Scarth remembered fondly from his youth. The hair style made her look attractively younger. Pony-tails, he thought, had a similar effect on women. He placed her in her mid-forties, but she could pass for ten years younger. She held out a hand.

'I'm Andrea Fyffe, the practice manager here,' she said. 'You're the policeman I take it?'

'I'm not a policeman, no. I'm a civilian,' Scarth said, retrieving his hand. 'I'm what they call a Crime Investigator.'

'Crime Investigator? That's a new one on me.' She smiled, encouraging an explanation.

Scarth side-stepped the invitation. 'Well, it was new to me too, till a few months ago,' he said. 'I used to be a policeman, though.'

'I thought that. Once a polis, always a polis,' she said.

'I'm helping the Eskbridge police investigate the death of Mr Muir,' he said.

'I surmised that,' she said disarmingly. 'Come on through to the parlour,' she said, turning gracefully to lead the way to her room. She had a husky voice, a mischievous look in her eyes. She reminded Scarth of the actress Fenella Fielding. No double-entendres yet, but he lived in hope.

As they walked side by side down a long carpet-tiled corridor, he noticed she had a hint of a limp. Noticing that he had noticed she said, 'Knee surgery. Fell off my motorbike two months ago and had my knee-cap replaced. Still hurts like buggery.'

Her 'parlour' was a big room. One wall displayed photographs in dark frames; another was filled with three large portraits in gilt frames; while a third was floor-to-ceiling books. The wall with the entrance had grey filing cabinets on either side of the doorway. Her desk was a curve of pale wood propped on sturdy chrome legs. As she stepped round the side of the desk towards her chair, he noticed she had sturdy legs too.

'Please, take a seat.'

'So, you're a biker chick then?' He was surprised at how low his voice was pitched. A psychosomatic interaction?

'Ha! I was,' she guffawed at the ridiculousness of it; 'no more.' She lifted her mobile from the desk, scrolled quickly, before turning the phone so that Scarth could see the photo.

He winced. It was a bare leg, showing an expanse of skin from mid-thigh down to mid-calf. The knee-cap was bisected vertically by a raw-looking scar. It certainly looked painful. The rest of the limb, he observed approvingly, was singularly well-shaped and free from any disfigurement.

She didn't give him long enough for further appraisal. 'Took a sharp bend a bit too casually,' she explained, drawing her phone back, 'then took off over the handlebars. Black ice. Bumps and scrapes mostly, but I banged my knee quite hard. I would have waited months for the NHS to do it, but we decided to go private. The insurance paid, thankfully.'

The professional 'we' – used by nurses, doctors, and lawyers – and anyone with a tape-worm. Scarth took his seat, and fished his note-book out of his padded jacket. He had a quick look at her. She had dark-brown eyes, a thin nose, and a sprinkling of freckles. She may not have been classically beautiful, he thought, but she was certainly a good-looking woman.

'As you can imagine,' she said, 'Colin's untimely death has been a tremendous shock to all of us here.' She looked distraught, unbelieving. 'He was only sixty-two or thereabouts. What makes it all the more poignant is that I was with him last night. Well, for part of the night anyway. We were at a function in the Station Hotel.'

Scarth was awkward when he said it. 'Were you a pair? Did you do together?'

She laughed. It was a high, sharp, trill. 'Yes, we did go together, but I should explain. The function was a

Midlothian Law Society dinner, and the two of us went to represent the firm.'

'It was law professionals only then?'

'Yes. Colin and I were a pair last night, but not an item, if you follow. Andrea Fyffe is my maiden name. I'm married to Tony McGill. The MSP?'

Scarth raised a hand in defeat. He supposed he was supposed to know the name. He didn't. Like Quin and many other police officers, he despised politics and those who delved in it.

'I don't follow politics,' he lied easily; thinking: 'How could I not?'

'I can see you're not impressed,' Fyffe smiled, 'and I don't blame you. As it happens Tony is about the only politician I know. Not my scene I'm afraid.' She looked stricken. 'Do people still say something is "not my scene"?'

He smiled. 'I don't see why not. It's descriptive enough. You only use the name Fyffe here in the office, then?'

'Can't escape it.' She waved a hand at the portraits. 'That one is my father William Fyffe, the founder of firm. Robertson was a cousin, long deceased.' She pointed to an adjacent portrait, and explained it was her grandfather James Fyffe. 'He was a 'laird' you might say, local landowner.' She pointed to two portraits on another wall. The largest was a full-length study of a man elaborately dressed in furs, with a rifle in the 'rest' position at his side. He was standing on a fake patch of ice, portrayed in the style of an Eskimo hunter. The smaller one was a bust of (presumably) the same man. Inside the fur-ringed hood he was sharp-featured, dark eyed, and heavily bearded.

'That one is my great-grandfather Alexander, the source of the family wealth – or what's left of it. He was a whaling captain,' she added.

Scarth noticed a slight cast to the man's eyes. Andrea Fyffe's eyes had the merest hint of the same defect. On her it was attractive. Like one of Fenella Fielding's mischievous twinkles.

'My father wrote a book about him,' she said. 'Books about whaling don't make the best-sellers' lists. In fact, they usually disappear without a ripple. But my father is extraordinarily proud of his whaling grandfather, and his book, or booklet, was a labour of love for him more than anything else. Do you know anything about the history of Scottish whaling?'

Scarth remembered his long conversations with a Shetlander who had been to the whaling at South Georgia. 'I do, as a matter of fact. But just about the whaling in the Antarctic.'

She 'My father's one is about the other Pole, the Arctic. Would you care to give it a quick perusal?'

'Sure,' he said politely.

She got up stiffly and walked to the bookcase. She was wearing smart court shoes. She lifted clear a club chair with a well-worn pair of trainers beneath it. Like many females nowadays, she obviously walked, or drove to work in comfy trainers, then changed into court shoes at work. She retrieved a book from the shelves, closed the glass door of the bookcase, and returned to her desk.

She leaned over, offering it to him. He received it graciously.

She settled back in her seat. 'But to get back to what you asked, yes, I use the Fyffe name in the office. I've found that it's good for business.'

Scarth glanced quickly at the cover. It was a photo of the portrait of the man in Eskimo furs hanging on the wall beside him. He switched his gaze back to her, nodded his understanding. 'I know; continuity and all that jazz.' He paused with mock uncertainty. 'Do people still end their sentences with "and all that jazz"?'

'They might if they were old enough to know what it meant,' she teased.

Scarth smiled again. He liked this woman.

'Tell me a little more about last night.'

She said the function was at the Station Hotel. Formal dress. Colin as usual wore the kilt. She left the venue just after eight, due to a call from her father's live-in nurse. 'Faither has dementia, and sometimes starts crying out for me,' she explained sadly. 'He thinks I'm a child again and that I've gone missing. His keening is very distressing for all of us …'

'Let me get this clear. You don't know exactly what time Mr Muir left the function?'

'Not exactly, no. I told him to text me when got home. Before he had too many night-caps.' She smiled. Her nose wrinkled. 'Colin was fond of his night-caps …'

'When was the last time you heard from him?'

She checked her phone. 'Eight minutes to ten. We had arranged that I would be the designated driver that evening, but that was scuppered when I was called away. I asked him to get a taxi, and he replied 'No probs. See you tomorrow'.'

Her face clouded over.

'It's just occurred to me. Maybe that was the last message anyone ever had from Colin.' She lowered her eyes and stared hard at her desk for a moment or two. She dabbed at her eyes with a tissue. 'It's just so …so unjust!'

Scarth waited till she gathered herself. When she was composed, she said, 'Is the cause of death known?'

'We're not sure yet,' he hedged. 'I think the autopsy is tomorrow morning.' He found himself gazing absently at the scuffed trainers beneath the guest chair. 'What sort of mood was Mr Muir in when you saw him last,' he finally asked. 'Was he worried about anything? Anyone?'

She shook her head. 'When I left the hotel, Colin was his usual convivial self. The meal things had been cleared away and he had joined a coterie of buddies at the bar, for a round of postprandial scuttlebutt no doubt. I can give you a list of names and phone numbers. Going by past form, it wouldn't be long before they left too. We tend to eat early and leave early at these functions. Lawyers are busy people. They're of the 'early to bed; early to rise' brigade. Late nights don't agree with them. Colin was different. He liked to stay as late as possible. No one waiting at home for him, I suppose …' she paused, a sad look on her face. 'He usually mooched around till the bar closed. Hang on a sec and I'll get those contact details for you.'

She worked her keyboard, selected a short document, sent it to the printer. She retrieved the document from her small desktop inkjet and passed it over.

'Guest list,' she said, 'in order of seniority.'

He looked. Her name was at the bottom.

'As you can see, I was the most important colleague there. I'm the one propping them all up.'

He smiled, carefully folded it, and slipped it into the back of his notebook.

'What can you tell me about Mr Muir and his work here, Mizz Fyffe?'

'Andrea, please. Colin was a full partner. He specialised in conveyancing. We do have a solicitor in the practice who is involved primarily with criminal cases, but the main income stream of the firm is now from the civil side, the estate agency, and the conveyancing business. Colin was excellent with clients. He had a few old-time clients whose affairs he attended to, but the main thrust of his work was in the conveyancing. He never fancied being a criminal defence lawyer.'

'Does the firm handle much in the way of criminal cases?'

'Very little. Eskbridge is dead as a doornail, criminally speaking. Jim Baxter and his assistant handle that side of things. But since we've put in a 24-hr Helpline, one of my brainwaves, we've been run off our feet.'

Scarth was mildly surprised. 'I wouldn't have thought there are enough criminals in Eskbridge to merit a round-the-clock service.'

'There aren't. These clients need help with the Tax Credits Office, the Child Support Agency, or their Housing Benefit. It's a bureaucratic nightmare. Most of our work involves helping clients to challenge unfair or incorrect decisions made by the Welfare Benefit people. The system is extremely complicated, and it is easy for both claimants and officials to make mistakes. Some mistakes can lead to serious legal problems and dire consequences. Since we started the Helpline, we get calls from all over the county. Even from Edinburgh, and down to the Borders. Unbelievable demand. We've got four solicitors and two paralegals working flat out to cope. As I said, it was my bright idea but we've been swamped. There's a lot of inequality in this world, and I'm a committed righter of wrongs …' She paused blushingly. 'Am I blethering on too much?'

He was enjoying it. 'Not a bit.'

'As you'll have noticed from my fresh complexion,' she said in her self-deprecating way, 'I myself don't burn any of that midnight oil. But I'm not just the one waving the baton, conducting the orchestra. I chip in as much as I'm permitted. But the solicitors do the bulk of the daily drudge-work, and the paralegals do the out-of-hours call-outs. They're shattered. I'm sure their love lives are non-existent.'

'They'll find a way,' said Scarth. They laughed. 'I see Mr Muir's own house is for sale,' he said.

She tutted. 'Yes. And it has been for several months now. The house saga has been a great cause of frustration for Colin. I gathered the ex-wifie was on his back to complete the financial side of the divorce settlement. Personally, I think his asking price is too steep, and told him so, but he was stubborn. He has his eye on one of those new riverside apartments at Rosieknowe, and you don't get much change from a quarter of a million down there.'

'I'll need to have a word with whoever was handling the sale,' Scarth said, 'to check if any house keys were issued and haven't been returned. That sort of thing …'

'Jenny Sinclair is our estate agency manager. She'll give you all the gen. It will be up to the next of kin now of course, to give further instructions.'

'What will happen to the whaling collection in Mr Muir's place,' Scarth wondered aloud. 'It might be worth a lot,' he suggested.

'A lot of junk,' Fyffe replied assuredly, 'apart from the beautiful fur coats. When my father retired six years ago with the onset of dementia, his office was renovated. Colin acquired the whaling collection. It had been handed down from my great-grandfather, and had been gathering dust in my father's office for ages. Good riddance to it. Whaling is such a no-go subject nowadays, don't you think? I appreciate that our family fortune, if you can call it that, had its foundations in the whaling trade. But that was thenadays. Who needs a constant reminder?'

Scarth found himself drawn to Andrea Fyffe.

When Scarth said he'd need access to Muir's desktop computer she took him through to his office. Her limp was almost imperceptible. In a couple of weeks, it will be gone, he thought. More perceptible, was her perfume. He caught an up-close whiff as she stood back to let him pass her into Muir's room. Thankfully it was a nice, pleasant fragrance. Like most men, he had a strong aversion to being in close proximity to a heavily-scented woman.

Andrea Fyffe explained that there tended to be an overlapping workload in an office like theirs. 'We often need access to each other's computers to cross-reference files, documents, whatever, so we've created a simple password system, to avoid frustrating delays. Everyone's password is their last name, spelt backwards, an asterisk, then the firm's initials, followed by an exclamation mark.

She wrote down her password on a post-it to illustrate it for him. It read: effyF*FR! Muir's password was: riuM*FR!

'The passwords are hardly FBI standard,' she said, 'but simple as it is, it would almost certainly defeat the casual intruder.'

She accessed Muir's computer, and opened his Documents. 'These are his client files, she said. 'My, my, didn't know he had so many .... These must go back centuries!' She paused. 'That's odd, she said. 'Some of these folders are encrypted, look ...'

She clicked on one. A window appeared. Highlighted in the middle was a message. It read: VssadebtogogSirUK2w5HHlOjQn6dG_w88

They both leaned in to squint at it. 'Why would he need to encrypt his files?' asked Scarth.

'Buggered if I know,' she replied.

'I'll need to have someone take a look at the machine, Andrea. There may be stuff there that pertains to his murder.'

She looked anxious. 'Tell you what.' she said. 'Let me make a copy of all the files that aren't encrypted first. In case any of us need them. I still haven't been able to think of a replacement for Colin yet, but it's something I'm going to have to face in the very near future. Meanwhile, we'll have to share his case load amongst us. I'll need his files to distribute as and when they're needed. I must say, it very strange to have secret files on an office computer.'

'They're certainly large files. Look at that one, 42.5 MB. That's video size, movie size.'

Andrea Fyffe's lips made a moue of concern. 'Oh dear …' she said.

Scarth hoped to allay her fears. 'Probably private stuff,' he soothed. He drew breath. 'Could be all sorts of things.'

Her face turned pallid. 'I know,' she said. 'That's what I'm worried about.'

FRIDAY AFTERNOON

After leaving FyffeRobertson, Scarth returned to Colin Muir's house. His main focus was the study. While the furniture in the room was antique in style if not always in reality, the office paraphernalia was modern, though not aesthetically intrusive. The phone/answering machine, set on a charcoal non-slip mat, was on the left edge of the desk.

Scarth played back the old messages recorded on the machine. Most were from the victim's daughter, asking about his welfare, about how the sale of the house was going. A couple were from his ex-wife's solicitors, pressing for the divorce settlement agreement to be fulfilled.

Several messages were from Bill Crighton, also asking about the house sale. 'When are you going to sell it?' 'Why has the house not been sold yet?' 'How long do you propose to deprive Lenore of her share of the house?' and more of that nature. The anger didn't seem to be escalating. It was there from the start.

Scarth nosed through the drawers of Muir's desk. Correspondence, mostly to and from family, and private bank statements. He had a cursory look at the statements. More outgoing entries than incoming ones, mostly for utilities, petrol, supermarkets, booksellers, landscapers, bottled water cooler rental. There was a payment, dated three weeks previously, to Miller & McLeish of £1,100. He wondered who they were.

£6,300 per month paid was in from FyffeRobertson. Salary obviously. There was another one-off payment of £6,000 from stockbrokers in London. A share dividend? He could find out more about these payments, if need be, from the different sort codes.

Contrary to what Griffin had told him, there were no records of any business transactions between them. No doubt they were at his office at FyffeRobertson.

All in all, Muir had just under £190,000 in his current account. Not enough to settle in full with his ex-wife – she would be looking for something in the region of £230,000 – but he was not far off it. Surely, he had enough to give her an initial payment, if only to get her off his back.

Scarth replaced the documents in their drawer. As a matter of routine, Quin had contacted the victim's bank. In case robbery had been the motive for his murder, she had requested that his account be frozen immediately, and monitored for unusual activity for the immediate future.

Scarth phoned Erica Griffin to keep her abreast of developments. It was only proper. She was her father's sole heir.

Mrs Griffin told him she'd been to the bank that morning, to make sure her father's account could not be accessed.

She told Scarth that while she was at the branch, the manager had also informed her that her father had a safety security box there. She had been surprised, and had asked to examine it. The box mostly contained documents, copies of wills, and insurance stuff.

'But there were also two Premium Bond certificates,' she said, 'to the value of £10,000 each.'

'I never knew people still used Premium Bonds,' said Scarth, whose mother religiously collected them for her sons.

'Neither did I,' Griffin had replied. 'There's also a diary, or a journal of some kind, in the box. But I can't read it. It's in some strange language I've never seen before. It's probably an artefact connected to the whaling junk my father kept in his study.'

Scarth suggested that whatever it was it might be valuable – a collector's piece. He didn't state the obvious – why else would it be in a safety box? He hesitated however, before getting round to the reason for his call.

Very gently, he asked her if she felt up to doing a walk-through of her father's house, to see if anything was missing, or disturbed. The police had taken the laptop and the SLR camera, he said, and they still might have to remove documents from the filing cabinets, for forensic examination. But a good look round by someone who was familiar with the house and its contents would be helpful.

She agreed to come round the following afternoon. She said she had to collect stuff for washing anyway – bedclothes, towels, and that sort of thing.

Scarth said he would meet her, and asked her if three o'clock was a suitable time for her. She said it was.

'Would you like to see this mysterious diary, if that is what it is?' she'd asked.

'Sure. At this stage we don't know what is important and what isn't. Bring it with you, would you, Erica?'

Scarth checked the bank statements again. Many people now banked online and had dispensed with storing paper copies, but luckily Muir had kept paper statements for the previous two years. There was nothing to indicate that Muir had purchased any Premium Bonds during that time. They had obviously been bought earlier, he surmised, probably with a view to leaving them as a tax-free bonus in his estate.

Unknowingly, Scarth had saved the best for last. After tidying away the numerous paper documents, he then gently prized open the victim's laptop. When he tried to log in, he was asked for a password. On a post-it he scribbled down the formula that Andrea Fyffe had explained to him, and then tried it. It worked.

It turned out that Muir had been an avid photographer. A 'twitcher', apparently. There were lots of photos of birds. Not all of them were local, Scarth thought, from the cliffs and seascapes he could see. Many of them were photos obviously taken from ferries, going and returning from islands.

In a folder entitled Craigneuk Wildlife Park he saw some still photos of a man and a woman in what seems to be an assignation. From some preliminary shots the photographer, presumably Muir, seemed to be some distance from the beauty spot car park. Zoomed shots covered the distance effortlessly. The time was night, but the car park was well lit, if not well patronised. Only two cars were there, an SUV and a small two-door. There were about a dozen jpeg images in the folder.

Scarth opened the only MPEG-4 file in the folder. The video captured a young woman with a head of colourless hair, a white mop under the fierce floodlights, exiting her car and joining a man in the adjacent vehicle. She reminded Scarth of the receptionist at Reliance Taxis. The two cuddled then clambered into the back seat. The car began to rock on its springs. The windows steamed up. The woman exited, hurried back to her car, repaired her make-up in the rear-view mirror, then left quickly. The man got out for a leisurely stretch and a pee. His face and profile were perfectly clear in the lens.

Scarth sat back in his seat, a wide grin splitting his face. Well, well, well, he thought. Bill Crighton rides again.

He pulled out his phone and called Quin's mobile. He knew his name would come up on her screen, but he always introduced himself anyway.

'Moira, its Bob,' he said when the phone was answered. 'I'm over at Mr Muir's. Are you in the office? … Okay. Did Shawn give us back Mr Muir's camera by any chance?'

'He did. It's sitting on the pow-wow table. He kept the camera case and the strap for testing, obviously.'

'Did he say anything about the memory card in the camera?'

'No, he didn't. Should he have done?'

'I've just found some interesting photos on Mr Muir's laptop, and wondered if there was more in the camera. Could you have a quick swatch inside the camera and see if the memory stick is still in it?'

'Okay. Let's see … how do you open these wee buggers? Ah, got it I think, it's just a sliding compartment. The slot's empty, Bob. No memory card here that I can see.'

'Thanks Moira. Shawn has probably retained it. I've managed to access the laptop,' Scarth said. 'His office password worked on it.'

'Good for you. Is there anything interesting on it?' she asked.

Scarth told her of the short steamy video of the cliff-top assignation, featuring Bill Crighton and his receptionist.

'Really? I'm sure that sort of stuff is not what Mr Crighton would like posted on YouTube, or anywhere else for that matter. Listen. It's getting on. Take the machine home with you, and make sure you bring it in with you in the morning will you Bob? Okay? …'

In the world according to Quin, things were beginning to look up.

CHAPTER 8

SATURDAY MORNING

It was 7:55 a.m. on a bright Saturday morning, when McIntosh climbed out of his car in the police station compound. He changed his house towels every week, which was why he was at the office. When he had moved into his flat after his divorce came through, he had borrowed two small and two large white towels from the police station's treatment room. He returned these items every Saturday morning, popping them into the appropriate laundry basket. While there, he borrowed another four towels to last him for the following week. There was no great harm in it, he thought. The treatment room laundry was collected every Saturday afternoon and fresh replacements were left. Who would make a fuss over four measly towels?

The previous year extensive renovations had been carried out at Eskbridge police station, principally to convert the vacant second floor into Archives to hold the county's case files.

The ground floor was not neglected, however, and offices, interview rooms, meeting rooms, and tea rooms were refurbished, and fitted out with new furniture and fittings.

One new innovation was the conversion of a ground floor changing room into a sick bay/treatment room. In the bad old days of the 1980s and the Miners' Strike, it had been used by the 'snatch squads' as a place to polish their cudgels and don their battle armour.

A few months ago, the station commander, Chief Inspector William 'Oor Wullie' Robb, who suffered from gout in the ankles amongst miscellaneous other ailments, had suggested that the space might be used as a treatment room for officers who required physiotherapy.

Superintendent B-B B Kerr, whose desk the suggestion landed on, thought it was an excellent idea. She had great faith in physiotherapy, for it had once cured a nasty back injury she had incurred whilst curling. She had lost that rubber because of her affliction, and vowed it would not happen again.

A physiotherapist called Haggon was subsequently engaged on a part-time basis, and officers from the whole of the Midlothian Division soon began booking sessions for Thursday and Friday nights, and the occasional Saturday morning. Before long it became a popular venue for the sporty types, especially for the police rugby players.

Lizzie Haggon, the police physio, was well-preserved thirty-eight-year-old, with a startlingly pretty face. She was irresistible to men until they got into her personal space. Once close-up however, they found to their dismay that she suffered from the most dreadful halitosis. When the physio introduced aromatherapy massages the treatment sessions quickly became fully booked out by female officers, though many of them insisted she wore a surgical mask during her manipulations.

And so that Saturday morning, whilst rummaging in the treatment room for fresh towels, McIntosh casually scanned the notice board next to the twin-bowled sink. It was Munro's day off as well, and she'd told him she intended to have an aromatherapy session with Haggon. If she had time afterwards before joining her pals to go shopping, she'd said, she would meet up with him for a quick lunch-time drink. She'd phone him.

On the white-board was scribbled, in descending order:

Brenda: 9:15 – 9:45/ Megan: 10am – 10:30/ Eileen: 10:45 – 11.15/ TBC: 11:30: – 12:00

Heather had obviously got her 11:30 slot at the last-minute, he surmised, and Haggon had neglected to mark it up. What a lucky bugger that Haggon was, he thought, being allowed – being encouraged, to run her hands over all that delectable female flesh, and being handsomely paid for it too!

McIntosh stuffed fresh towels into his black bin bag and headed down the corridor to the main entrance. On his way out he stuck his head into the CID room. The boss and Bob Scarth were just sitting down at the conference table with Shawn Murray.

The solicitor's murder case, no doubt. Lucky them, he thought, nodding a greeting then steering past the room.

He had a suspicion that the boss knew of his towel-swapping activities and had chosen to turn a blind eye to it. But that was no excuse to take her silence on the matter for granted.

At 11 a.m. McIntosh pulled up outside The Eskbridge Pet Centre, Scottie's pretentious day centre. During his divorce, it had been agreed by the lawyers of both parties that, to avoid any possible friction and unpleasantness, the hand-over of the dog for access visits should be done on neutral ground. The Ex would take the dog there and hand it over to the custody of the centre; McIntosh would arrive at a designated, later time, to take possession. Temporary possession, for he was only a once-monthly week-end Dad.

The receptionist at the centre was wearing the staff outfit of a light blue healthcare tunic over dark blue unisex trousers. She had long reddish-brown hair, and a sulky, hungover face. She wasn't a new start, but he hadn't talked to her before. She didn't look his type.

He approached her reception counter, automatically glancing at the name-tag on her chest. 'Hi Abby,' he grinned. 'I'm Scobie McIntosh, and I'm here …'

The young woman held up a hand to interrupt him. Frowning, showing her annoyance, she pointed to a name tag on her chest. 'What does that say, Mr McIntosh?'

Definitely not his type. He leaned forward, squinting elaborately, taking his time about studying her unattractive contours. He stood back, his face a picture of puzzlement. 'Andy?'

'Short for Alexandra,' she said shortly. 'Not Abby. How can I help?'

'I'm here for Scottie,' he announced. 'Same as usual.'

The woman smiled a condescending smile. She consulted her screen. She paused, peered, her lips pursed.

'Is there a problem?' McIntosh asked anxiously.

'Well, not a problem as such,' she said raising her eyes to him. 'But we've been informed by his owner – she's your former wife, isn't she? – that the dog's name has been changed.'

McIntosh was astounded. 'How can you change a dog's name?' he challenged.

'By deed poll, I would imagine,' she said with studied neutrality. She motioned to somewhere behind him. 'If you'll just have a seat Mr McIntosh, I'll fetch Gizmo and bring him through.'

McIntosh gawped. 'Who the hell's Gizmo?' he quizzed irritably.

'Your dog,' she answered peremptorily. She allowed a hint of a smile to crease the sides of her eyes, before she lifted a flap and walking briskly to the innards of the building.

When McIntosh got back to his flat, the mail had arrived. And sure enough, there was a letter from the Deed Poll Office. He couldn't believe it. He read the letter carefully again, and still couldn't believe it. As well as a load of other guff, it informed him that, '… the canine formerly known as Scottie, shall be henceforth known as GIZMO …'

In a fury he phoned The Ex.

'What is it this time?' she demanded instantly.

'I'm not doing it,' he said in a defiant tone.

'Not doing what?'

'I'm not calling the dog Gizmo, or any other crap name you come up with. You can't change a dog's name for Chrissakes. How will he know who he is?'

'Don't be silly now Scobie,' she said, as if talking to a mentally retarded child. 'Dogs don't know their names. They respond to voice tones, to the pitch of voices, to familiar timbres …'

'He was christened as "Scottie",' McIntosh said angrily, 'and he'll die as "Scottie".'

She guffawed derisively. 'Since when was it christened?' she scoffed. 'Dogs don't get christened you stupid arse. Look, I can't talk now. Call the bloody thing what you like, but its official name is Gizmo. Look, I'm not saying another thing, Scobie. Not another word. Talking to you is like hitting my head against a brick wall,' she continued, voice raised. 'I don't need the hassle. Anyway, I have to go. Richard is taking me to Bergen for the week-end …'

'Who the hell is Richard?' he wanted to ask. Instead, he queried, 'Why Bergen?'

'Because it's somewhere I haven't been with you, that's why. And I'm warning you, Scobie, bring the thing back to its stupid day centre on time tomorrow afternoon, or I'll have you back in court for a breach of rights of access …'

Breach of rights access? Who had put that into her head? 'Says who?' he replied belligerently, stung by her unreasonable threat.

'… Says Richard. Didn't I tell you?' her voice rose triumphantly, 'he's a lawyer …'

By 11:45 a.m. McIntosh and the canine formerly known as Scottie were back at the office. He left the dog in the car and made for his desk. Once there he checked his emails. There was nothing from the bus company. He checked the office clock. Heather would be in the treatment room for another 15 minutes. Stripped down to the essentials.

He had a mischievous thought. Maybe she would like a close-up sniff of the dodgy aftershave she and Quin had bought him for his recent twenty-fifth birthday. For lying in his drawer was a small black canister ridiculously called 'Caveman'.

He'd had an investigatory smell of the stuff and it was vile. Like well-hung game wrapped up in over-ripe underpants. When he had sprayed it on his wrist one night at home, Scottie had sat in stupefied umbrage before barking the house down.

It wasn't like him. It appeared that Scottie felt justified by his behaviour. After all, he had just been exposed to an odour he'd never encountered before.

McIntosh knew the wee fella had spent many long months training to acquire his wide repertoire of smells, fine-tuning his twitching nostrils to recognise a wide but comprehensive variety of genuine, exotic, and expensive perfumes. He then had to spend untold months learning the bouquets of an equally-wide and comprehensive variety of ingeniously-manufactured fakes.

At least, McIntosh supposed, those counterfeit perfumes Scottie had become so adept at identifying had a passing resemblance to the product they purported to be. By comparison this scent, McIntosh knew, was a trashy, amateur effort. The wee fella looked to have been grossly insulted by his master even presenting it to him for adjudication.

Scottie's distinct aversion to the scent confirmed McIntosh's suspicion that his colleagues' unusual and unprecedented 'present' had been a conniving prank. It was something he fully intended to revenge one day, but decided this was not the time.

Instead, he reached into his drawer and pulled out the 'Lucky' eau de cologne his mother had bought him a Christmas. He squirted a discrete smidgeon on both sides of his neck. A couple of minutes later, chuckling quietly in anticipation, he consulted the internal phone list pinned up above his desk, and dialled the treatment room.

'Sorry to bother you Lizzie,' he said to the physio, muffling his voice behind his hand, 'but I think I see smoke coming from the front of your car.'

He hung up quickly, sat back in his seat, and ten seconds later heard Haggon thundering down the corridor towards Reception and the front doors.

He exited the CID room and crept stealthily on tiptoes down the corridor. Once at the treatment room he slipped swiftly inside and silently closed the door.

The heat hit him like a punch. It was stiflingly hot, like a sauna without the steam. The room was atmospherically lit. Only the lights from the blood pressure and heart monitor lit the room. On the treatment table Heather lay on her front. She was wearing a pink bathing cap. Her back and shoulders were bare and glistening with aromatic oil, her shapely rump was covered by a striped towel, and her legs were splayed with heels up.

McIntosh twiddled his fingers, limbering up for the task ahead. He swept aside the privacy screen, and stepped stiff-legged to the side of the couch. His legs weren't the only things about him that were stiff. He selected a vial of oil from a bed-side stand, and slowly dribbled some of it onto the patient's shoulders. He had no idea how much to use, so he used what he normally did when marinating a chicken breast.

Her skin was soft and pliable, as smooth and sleek as a seal's. He started to massage, slowly, sensually, making it up as he went along. He squeezed and teased, pinched and pressed. Outside he could hear the commotion of Haggon frantically lifting the bonnet of her car, shouting to someone who was also there, asking them to check the underside for evidence of smoke.

McIntosh knew he hadn't much time. He bent over Heather's torso, gently feeling and probing, daringly letting his fingers slip under her body to the smooth sides of her breasts. He expected her to shout out in outrage, but instead she moaned in pleasure.

'Oooooh, OOOoooooh,' she said. Or words to that effect. She mumbled something dreamily. It sounded like: 'Love the aftershave …'

I should have squirted on a blast of the crap you bought for me, he thought regretfully, his fingers kneading assiduously, and seen how you loved that …

Just then his phone rang.

McIntosh stumbled back in surprise. He grabbed a paper towel and hastily wiped his hands before, with difficulty, retrieving the bloody thing from his inside pocket. Even so it was as slippery as a bar of soap. He looked at the screen and nearly fainted. The caller display read: Heather Munro.

The room went suddenly cold and he broke out in a sweat; his throat went dry and his legs turned to water. All these things happened simultaneously.

As he stared at the phone in stupefaction, it rang again. And again.

The figure on the couch stirred uneasily, and made to turn around. Somehow McIntosh got his two-cell brain to work. He quickly declined the call, threw a diversionary towel over the head on the couch, and escaped out into the cool corridor. In a panic, he stumbled guiltily to the Gents. As he feverishly scrubbed the massage oil from his hands, he felt as if his brain was going into meltdown. If it wasn't Heather there in the treatment room, then who the hell was it?

This time his phone pinged. He looked at it warily. A text, from Heather.

"Unavoidably delayed. Doing a favour for the boss. Pie and a pint some other time?" he read.

He gathered what wits he could summon and phoned her back. 'Hi there,' he panted breezily. '… I'm in the toilet at the office. Got your text …'

'Hi Scobie. Sorry about this ... I'm on a job for the boss ... Could be here all day....'

'Ah right,' he wheezed. 'Actually, I thought you were nearer to hand, so to speak …'

'Nearer to hand? Oh, do you mean my aromatherapy appointment? No, I cancelled that first thing this morning. Wasn't sure when I'd be back. Someone else took the slot.'

He was dying to ask who, but it was bound to sound suspicious, so he said, 'No worries. No doubt we'll find out who it is later.'

He immediately regretted it. Why did he say that, he berated himself? The last thing he needed was to link himself with what had happened down the corridor.

'Why do you want to find out who it is?' She sounded mystified. 'You could find out now, if you're so interested,' she added lightly. 'Just ask Haggon. The patient's name will be up on the notice board anyway, won't it?'

'Ha! TBC? Doesn't give much away, does it?' he slavered insanely.

'How do you know Haggon's got 'to be confirmed' marked up?' she queried sharply.

Jesus. He was tying himself in knots here. 'It just slipped out. I mean I just slipped in. For an aspirin. Earlier. Listen, got to go. Catch you later …'

He emerged from the toilet, his face slick with sweat, his eyes riddled with guilt, in time to see Haggon barrelling down the corridor towards him.

'Fucken arseholes!' exclaimed the harassed physio. 'Someone's been working a load of nonsense. Claimed the bloody car was on fire! You look like shit by the way, Mac.'

'Really?' replied McIntosh, standing aside to let the woman past. He took a deep breath, for the physio wasn't wearing her mask. 'I do hope your patient hasn't been inconvenienced …'

'So do I,' puffed the physio anxiously, 'It's only Superintendent bloody Kerr!'

With his back and palms pressed against the wall for support, McIntosh felt the blood drain out of his face. As he stood there gobsmacked, Haggon explained breathlessly,

'That wee bugger Heather Munro cancelled first thing this morning. The Super agreed to come in early. For privacy's sake I always list her as TBC …' she dropped her voice conspiratorially, '… stands for 'Too Bloody Conceited' if you ask me.'

It also stands for 'To Be Castrated', thought McIntosh gloomily. And have your whatsits rammed down your throat afterwards.

CHAPTER 9

SATURDAY MORNING

When Scarth arrived in the CID room that Saturday morning, Quin waddled out of her office and said, 'Shawn's coming round to give us a briefing, Bob. But let's hear your news first.'

At the pow-wow table Scarth told her he had checked with some of Muir's colleagues who had attended the function. They confirmed the diners began to disperse after nine o'clock. 'When I remarked at the early hour,' Scarth said, 'I was told solicitors were of the early to bed; early to rise fraternity. A couple of them saw Mr Muir getting into a taxi, at around nine thirty or so – which fits with what I was told by the taxi company … I checked with Eskbridge's two taxi firms. It was a car from Alliance Taxis which took Muir home. The dispatcher told me the driver's log showed he dropped off Muir at exactly three minutes past ten.'

'Which fits with Angus MacLeod's estimated time of death,' Quin said.

Scarth nodded. 'The dispatcher said they had a contract with the Law Society,' he continued, 'and had three cars out that night ferrying a bunch of solicitors home.'

Scarth then told her of his perusal of the victim's private correspondence and bank statements. Nothing he had seen had set off any alarm bells, he said. There were no records of anything to do with Danny Griffin, or any business transactions with him or his company. It was much as he expected.

'If the victim had involved clients' money in dealings with Griffin or his company,' Scarth said, 'then we can expect the evidence to be in his office files at FyffeRobertson.'

He told Quin of the security safety box that Erica Griffin had discovered at the bank, and summarised its contents. She ignored his mention of the mysterious diary or journal, but raised a signature eyebrow at the mention of the two £10,000 Premium Bond certificates.

'I didn't know people still bought Premium Bonds.'

'Neither did I,' Scarth admitted.

Quin pursed her baby lips. 'Anything suspicious about them?'

'Wouldn't think so, Moira. Though the victim doesn't seem to have bought them in the last couple of years …'

'No mention in his statements?'

'No.'

'They're probably ancient. People used to buy them when children were born. As a future nest-egg. Either that, or they could they have been a gift from a client. Perhaps a tax-free payment for services rendered?'

'Well, it would be unconventional, but not illegal.'

'Ask the daughter for the serial numbers; just in case,' Quin decided. 'There'll be a paper trail somewhere …'

'Erica thinks that her father might have had a visitor the night he was killed,' Scarth offered.

'Really? What makes her think that?'

'It seems her father was used to getting a mug ready for his morning coffee, you know, with the powder and sweeteners in it, ready for the boiling water. Only there was no mug that we saw. Shawn says everything had been tidied away before they examined it.'

'Mmm. A woman's touch, do you think?'

'Could be. It's probably nothing.'

'I'm going to worry about this mug, Bob. Things out of the ordinary, unexplained actions, they always worry me in a murder case.'

Scarth opened up the victim's laptop. 'Then there's this …' he said.

Quin pulled her chair round so that they could both see the small screen.

'I haven't examined the files and folders in any detail,' Scarth admitted. 'Maybe Heather will have a go at it. But here's what caught my eye …'

He ran the video filmed at the Wildlife Park. The raunchy rendezvous in Bill Crighton's well-sprung SUV. Crighton's receptionist was well-sprung too, they could see, for edited into the video was a series of still shots taken from another, closer angle. Kayleigh so-and-so, her pale face a picture of paroxysmal ecstasy, was largely obscured by the love-handled Crighton. His pimple-cheeked arse was caught in the process of going like the clappers, bracketed in the cellulite-dimpled thighs of his platinum-headed understudy.

'No wonder he put his back out,' Quin observed dryly.

As the car rocked alarmingly on its suspension, its occupants heaving their way to their clandestine climax, Quin tut-tutted her disapproval.

'What would persuade any perfectly-respectable woman,' she asked incredulously, 'to enter into a relationship with a harum-scarum arsehole like Bill Crighton?'

Well, you could ask Lenore MacDonald that one, Scarth thought unkindly.

She caught his look. 'I know. I should ask Lenore whatsherface, her of the too-tight tops and the too-revealing leggings.' She sniffed. 'Maybe I'll do that one fine day …But what does his hard-pressed receptionist there get out of it?'

'Promotion?'

Quin snorted her disbelief.

Shawn Murray, his old-fashioned freshly-shaved face gleaming under the office lights, began bluntly. 'I can tell you one thing, Moira, we haven't got much. For instance, there was no indication of forced entry.

'I've retrieved the house keys from the cleaner and the neighbour, Mrs Weymss,' Quin reported. 'I presume that the victim's daughter has a key. I'll ask. So can we assume that the killer either had a key; or had been been let in?'

'Possibly. Though they wouldn't have needed a key if they came round the back. The French windows facing the rear garden were unlocked.'

'Really? That sounds awful careless in this day and age.'

'It is, if the killer knew about it,' Murray answered.

'Incidentally,' Quin said, 'the cleaner told us that the alarm is normally on when she comes in. Only when she came in on Thursday the alarm wasn't set.'

'The killer wasn't to know if the victim was in the habit of setting his alarm at night or not…' observed Murray.

'That's true,' Quin said. 'But I checked with the alarm company anyway. Just to see if anyone had attempted to set the alarm, to make it seem to the cleaner that everything was normal, but maybe got the code slightly wrong. Negative. The alarm was not set and no one had attempted to set it.'

'What about prints?' Scarth asked.

Murray shook his head. 'Nothing jumped out at us. There were hardly any fingerprints at all, other than those belonging to the victim, and of course the cleaner. The unidentified ones look to be kid's prints. Grandchildren I expect, though we'll check. There were no fingerprints or DNA at all on the ceremonial dagger, for the sgian dubh had been wiped clean. We've got a careful killer here.'

Murray added that the pathology lab had sent him some close-up photos of the victim's neck. The images supported the hypothesis that the murder weapon was a webbing strap or belt. 'The kind you see on rucksacks, gym-bags, and those sorts of things. With one significant difference ...'

He showed them a close-up of the victim's neck around the larynx.

'This bit, if you look closely, is different. There are no webbing marks. The lab says that what we see here is the bruising made by a piece of fabric being pulled tight. The ligature must be a combination of webbing and a soft material, which is confirmed here …' He slid another close-up in front of them, and pointed to a dark red mark on the side of the neck, just before the webbing marks became prominent.

'See that? At the scene, Mr MacLeod suggested it might have been made by a buckle, but there's a possibility it's an impression made by a zip.'

That was new. 'A zip?' Quin asked suspiciously. 'I thought we were talking about a belt?'

Murray nodded. 'A webbing-type belt,' he confirmed, 'with a portion made of soft material possibly fastened by a zip. Perhaps a pocket.'

'Mmm,' Quin hummed. 'Haven't a clue what that could be. And there's nothing of that order at the scene?

'No. We can assume the killer brought it with them. There's not much else to go on at this stage. If a suspect is identified, and you find such an item among their belongings, then we'll forensically examine it for epithelials, fibres, you name it. But until then, the information's not much use to you, I'm afraid.'

He returned the camera to Quin. He had examined it for prints, he said, but had found none apart from those of the victim. The surprise was that the memory stick had been removed.

'Why is that a surprise?' Scarth asked.

'You don't need to remove the stick nowadays to download the photos,' he said, 'though of course the victim may have done just that. Or of course it could have been removed by the killer. Perhaps the victim had some incriminating photos on it. And as we all know incriminating photos have been found many times to have been the motive for murder.'

'Wait till ye see this,' said a smiling Quin, motioning to Scarth to run the video again.

When it was over, Murphy looked impressed.

'What do ye think of that then?' Quin asked eagerly.

'Such energy. Such stamina,' Murray began, before a thump on his arm from Quin interrupted his train of thought. 'Talking about motives, I know CID people who would think that what you've found there is a credible motive.'

'Well, it's certainly a possibility,' Scarth opined with cautious optimism.

Quin brightened up considerably. 'I agree,' she declared. 'It's worth serious consideration. You know what? I'd love to drag that bastard Crighton in here, and beat … and squeeze him like a pluke, till he pops.'

Murray pointed a stubby finger to the screen. 'I hate to disappoint you Moira, but it looks like that's just what thon woman has accomplished.'

Scarth dutifully guffawed, but Quin had had enough of the banter. She heaved herself out of her chair like a blancmange being tipped out of its mould. 'Shawn, as always,' she smiled, sticking out a dainty hand, 'many thanks for the input ...'

As the Scene Manager gathered his things to leave, Quin moved towards her office.

'Bob,' she called over her shoulder, 'come and have a look at the victim's autopsy report that Angus MacLeod has emailed me …'

She halted suddenly, the way a kid can stop their momentum abruptly. Had Scarth been following her as she'd requested, he couldn't have avoided a squishy collision.

'On second thoughts,' she said enthusiastically, 'let's you and me go and see Angus in his lair. His report is mostly medical gobbledegook anyway. Despite the smells, I'd like to hear him spell it out for me.'

The journey to the pathology lab in Edinburgh took ages. It was only eight miles, but commuter traffic into the city on a Friday morning was slowed to crawling speed in places. Dr MacLeod had emailed the autopsy results on Colin Muir that morning, but had asked her to 'stop by' at her convenience if she required further 'elucidation'.

Once they left the Eskbridge boundary they travelled several miles though open country. The fields had been furrowed, maybe even planted with their various crops. Round Eskbridge the commonest crops were tatties and corn, with a sprinkling of sunflower.

Coming into Edinburgh's precincts they passed several small industrial estates, and a large retail park which served both Edinburgh and the surrounding country towns. Scarth smiled at a fond memory. He had gone to the retail park one summer's evening to dine al fresco with a favourite grandson. The boy had excitedly recommended a Chinese take-away situated in a converted railway carriage. His meal was ghastly, though the boy had wolfed down his own selection. For devilment Scarth had tossed a couple of wrinkled over-fried chips to the attendant sea-gulls, in whose natural habitat they were seated. The birds had huffily ignored the offerings. They knew crap when humans didn't.

They met MacLeod in his cluttered office, well away from the sounds and smells of his temperature-controlled natural habitat. He was in shirt sleeves, chinos, and crocs, having recently dumped his scrubs, apron, and mortuary willies in the locker room.

MacLeod seated Quin and Scarth haphazardly in what restricted space was available. They politely declined an offer to personally inspect the body, which produced a knowing grin from MacLeod. They also declined his offer of refreshment, though not for the same reason.

'Do you mind if I have a cuppa?' he asked. 'No?' He reached for a flask and slowly poured a cup from it. He opened a drawer, extracted a small plate of biscuits, and selected a chocolate one. 'I always get peckish after a post-mortem,' he grinned.

As Quin paled, MacLeod dug out the relevant folder from the pile on his desk, scanned it briefly, refreshing himself, and then tossed it back onto the pile.

'Right we are. The death of Colin Muir. As you'll know, I've had a word with Shawn Murray from forensics, and we agree in the hypothesis that Mr Muir was probably seated at his computer desk when his assailant surprised him. My lab technician here took numerous photographs of the ligature marks, as did Sergeant Murray. So far, we haven't reached a firm conclusion as to what the murder weapon may be, but it is likely to be an item personal to the killer …'

'Yes. Shawn told us,' Quin answered.

'Which probably also explains why it was missing from the scene,' MacLeod continued. 'We think Mr Muir was jerked off his chair and forced onto his front on the floor. Hypostasis, or lividity, shows that his arms were trapped uselessly beneath him. Bruises on his back show where the killer knelt on him, keeping him prone, if not immobile. The killer crossed the ligature at the back of his neck, and began throttling him by pulling tightly on each end.'

'Surely he resisted,' Quin opined. 'Tried to fight back?'

MacLeod shook his leonine head. 'He had been out at a formal function and returned home rather intoxicated. Inebriated rather than paralytic, but impaired nonetheless. His blood alcohol level was more than twice the legal driving limit. If Mr Muir had been sober enough to put up a fight, then we'd expect scratches or bruises along the ligature line, indicating he had attempted to pull the ligature off. But there was no evidence of that. Nor was there anything unusual in the scraping from under his fingernails – no foreign DNA there at all. At first, I believed that he was too drunk to co-ordinate a defence, and that the killer had an almost free hand to throttle him. But now I believe something different.'

'Really? How do you mean?'

'As you'll remember, Mr Muir was found dead with the unmistakable signs that he had been asphyxiated. As well as the ligature marks, the tell-tale sign of redness of the facial skin, caused by the obstruction of the veins in the neck, was easily observed. You'll have seen it before. The discolouration is caused because the veins sending blood to the brain are obstructed during asphyxiation, and the blood from the brain cannot return to the heart. That said, the main indicator of asphyxiation – whether it be the result of strangling, suffocation, or choking, or indeed some other cause – is to be found in and around the eyes. Most people who have been asphyxiated develop multiple tiny pinpoints of blood on the conjunctivae, the inner lining of the eyelids. However, as you'll remember at the time, I pointed out that Mr Muir presented with no sign of petechial haemorrhaging, as those tiny pinpoints of blood are called. Yet it was obvious, from the ligature marks on his neck, that he had been strangled. Well, that was the apparent paradox we were faced with in this case.'

'I hope you don't mind me asking, Angus. But is damage to the hyoid bone not a more reliable indicator of strangulation?' Quin asked.

MacLeod nodded. 'It can be, yes. But in fact, the internal damage caused by strangulation may not be all that dramatic, Moira. In younger people, the cartilage in the larynx and around the thyroid is relatively pliable. The hyoid bone may not show any signs of injury even though the person has been strangled. Of course, as we grow older, the cartilage becomes increasingly calcified and more brittle, so it's more likely to be fractured during strangulation.'

'That's what I was meaning, Angus. Colin Muir was sixty-six. Was his hyoid bone fractured?'

'No.'

MacLeod steepled his fingers, and gazed up at the ceiling.

'How can I put it? Lay people usually assume that a victim who has been strangled dies of asphyxiation. That constricting the neck simply cuts off the vital air supply. But those of us in the trade know that asphyxiation alone can't always be the cause, simply because some people die very quickly from pressure on the neck. Indeed, there have been several examples where a person has died almost instantly, too quickly for lack of oxygen to be the sole cause of death, presenting none of the classic signs of asphyxia.'

He took a delicate bite of his biscuit, and offered the plate to Quin and Scarth, who again politely refused.

'We know that if pressure is applied to the carotid arteries, it will cause the blood supply to the brain to be cut off. The victim will rapidly lose consciousness. If the pressure is sustained the victim will die. But we also know that strangulation also puts pressure on the nerves of the neck, which can then affect the parasympathetic nervous system … and I think now that this is what happened to Colin Muir.'

'I do hope you've typed this all up, Angus …'

MacLeod smiled indulgently. 'The parasympathetic system controls bodily functions such as stimulating digestion, conserving energy, and promoting rest. One of the main nerves in this system is the vagal nerve, and you can die almost instantly from neck pressure which in certain circumstances can instruct the vagal nerve to simply stop the heart beating. It's a reflex action. People's vagal reflex can cause them to expire suddenly for almost no apparent reason.'

Quin looked outraged. 'So could the killer claim it was accidental?' she asked. 'That they had no intention to kill?'

'They could, and no doubt some have done so in the past. In this case the tell-tale marking of the ligature, its absence from the scene, and the grotesque desecration of the body, point to a deadly purpose. It's likely the attack didn't last long. This killer was not to know that our victim would die so suddenly. But the fact that he was utterly intent on killing Mr Muir by strangulation is not in doubt.'

They thought about that for a silent moment or two.

'And finally,' Quin finally said, hoisting her bag strap a little higher, 'do you have an approximate time of death?'

'I got good readings from both the rectum and the liver. I'd say no earlier than nine thirty; no later than ten thirty: eleven p.m. at the very outside, but unlikely.'

Quin nudged Scarth. They stood, and without too obvious haste, made for the door.

'Cheers, Angus,' she said. 'Thanks for sparing us the hands-on bit ...'

CHAPTER 10

SATURDAY AFTERNOON

When Scarth phoned Broomieknowe, the live-in nurse answered on the fourth ring.

'The Fyffe residence. Gloria Rutherford speaking. How may I help you?'

'It's Bob Scarth, Mrs Rutherford. We met the other day …'

There was silence at the other end of the line.

'I came to see Andrea Fyffe if you remember …'

'You told me your name was Scarf,' she accused.

He wasn't about to argue with her. 'It's about Tony McGill, Mrs Rutherford. Just a routine enquiry. He'd been abroad, but we don't know when he arrived back home on Wednesday.'

'Why would you want to know?'

'As I said. It's just a routine enquiry.'

There was a long pause on the line, and he thought she'd gone, when she said, 'He came home in a taxi on Wednesday night, around eleven thirty. Woke me up. The driver banging doors.'

Scarth hesitated. Had Andrea Fyffe not told him she went to the airport to pick up her husband? 'Taxi drivers are like that,' he said. When they're awake, everyone's awake. It's just that I thought his wife might have picked him up at the airport …'

'Ha! Too busy gallivanting, that one …'

'She was probably in bed, at that hour.'

'She might have been in bed,' the woman said in a scathing tone, 'but if she was, it wasn't her own one. If you catch my drift.'

Scarth was intrigued. 'You think she was out somewhere?'

'I know she was out somewhere. And up to no good, likely.'

'Really? I was given to understand she spent the evening relaxing in front of the TV.'

Mrs Rutherford sniffed. 'She didn't have time. She came home at about half past eight, and left again an hour later. Didn't get back till after eleven.'

'And you're sure about that? Scarth asked.

'Couldn't be surer.'

'Would you be willing to give us a statement to that effect, Mrs Rutherford? If required at some point in the future?'

'Well, I …'

'On the understanding, of course, that your employers will not need to know, unless it needs to be produced later in court.'

'In court?' Her voice was suspicious. 'Just who are you checking up on here, Mr Scarf; Tony McGill, or his wife?'

'Well at this stage, Mrs Rutherford, it's only …'

'I know,' she laughed humourlessly. 'Routine enquiries … bla de bla de bla. Anyway, I'm not bothered what the Fyffes know or don't know. I've handed in my notice this morning.'

Andrea Fyffe was pleased to hear from him, she said, when he phoned her office later that day. When he asked if she was up for 'a bite to eat' that lunch-time, she immediately suggested the Big Kilmarnock Bunnet.

He met her at her office. She came round her desk, grabbed his hands, quickly squeezed them, then released them.

'Thank you for rescuing me,' she said, slipping into her outdoor jacket. 'This place gets manic at times.'

The pub was within easy walking distance, and Scarth and Fyffe got there after an easy stroll of five minutes. She was as tall as him and walked with her shoulder back. The Big Kilmarnock Bunnet was a well-thought-of establishment in an area of four-storey Victorian sandstone buildings. In the deprived post-war years of rationing and unemployment the neighbourhood was a place of boarded-up shops and litter-strewn streets. A place where even big Scottish polis didn't care to linger. Now it was designer outlets, health food shops, and fancy restaurants. Patrons now spent as much on an evening's sushi dishes, as a whole household earned in a single year in the 1950s.

The Big Kilmarnock Bunnet had started life in the 1950s as a working-class darts 'n' dominoes dive. It transformed in the late 1970s into a soft-rock speakeasy, before being bought by a Chinese family from Guangdong. They re-invented it as a Sino-Scottish fusion food eatery, specialising in exotic Asian dishes and traditionally-wholesome Scottish country fare.

A sallow-skinned young Asian man with dark feverish eyes took their orders. He spoke with a Scottish accent. He nodded with candid familiarity to Andrea Fyffe when he came to their table. Scarth wondered if the establishment was one of her usual haunts. Or was it perhaps because the man had been one of her firm's clients?

She daringly plumped for the vegetable and barley broth with boiled Chinese spiced-pork dumplings. A wedge of home-made crusty farmhouse loaf came on a side-plate. It was seeded, Scarth noticed, a type of bread that he disliked. He played safe, ordering a lactose-cheese toastie and a glass of bubble tea.

They made small talk till their plates arrived. During the meal, Scarth was careful not to catch her eye as she ate heartily. Each nibble of bread was closely followed by a spoonful of the soup. Chop sticks had been provided, but the dumplings were ignored.

Scarth bit a piece out of his sandwich and chewed thoughtfully, looking round the room. 'Did your father ever mention a diary being part of your great-grandfather's whaling collection?' he asked casually.

'A journal, do you mean?' she replied. 'Yes, there were several. Captain Fyffe, like all of the whaling masters those days, kept meticulous journals, and ship's logs. They were required to by the Board of Trade, who regulated the merchant marine, and regularly inspected the documentation pertaining to commercial voyages.'

'Did you ever actually see them?'

She nodded. 'Faither wrote his book when I was a little girl. I remember his study being overflowing with charts, logs, ship's journals, and stuff. I suppose all Captain Fyffe's old log books and stuff gave him the basic material for his manuscript. What happened to it all I'm sure I couldn't tell you. It's not something I've thought about.'

'Did your father ever mention the existence of a diary belonging to one of the Inuit girls?

There was a brief pause before Andrea Fyffe said. 'No. That would be interesting, though, wouldn't it? Why, has something come to light?' she asked cautiously.

'Not really. I just wondered. Diary-writing was a popular Victorian pastime. I wondered if you remembered anything of the sort among the whaling collection.'

She had finished her soup. Only now did she spear a dumpling with a chop-stick. 'Well, I couldn't really tell you everything which is in the collection,' she munched, 'after all, I was a little girl. And like most little girls it was the beautiful fur coats which interested me.'

Scarth finished his sandwich and ventured a sip of his bubble tea. It tasted incredibly sweet, which suited him. He wondered why they called it 'bubble tea'.

Fyffe caught his unfamiliarity with the beverage. 'You should use the straw,' she suggested pleasantly. 'Helps to sook up the tapioca pearls at the bottom of the glass … Bob, what is the point of all this?'

'The point?'

'Bob, you're sleuthing. And you're not telling me what you are sleuthing for. Is there something I can help you with?'

Scarth met her frank gaze. His cheeks were flushed with the syrup hit from the tea. Or maybe it was with the discomfort his next question was causing him.

'Andrea. You haven't been entirely truthful with me, have you?'

Her eyes narrowed. 'In what way?'

'Well, you told me when I first met you that you left the Law Society function early to go home and tend to your sick father. But that was not the case, was it?'

Her mouth tightened with disapproval. She pushed away her soup plate, and drew in a tiny bowl filled with palate-cleansing after dinner mints. She slid one out of its sleeve and popped it into her mouth.

'I take it Mrs Rutherford has spilled the beans on me, has she?'

Scarth tilted his head in the affirmative. 'According to her, you came home, and then went out again at about nine thirty. You weren't at home during the period in which Colin Muir was murdered.'

'And that makes you think I did it, does it?' she quizzed unbelievingly.

'Can you tell me where you were?'

He could see she was thinking it over. She unfolded the napkin by her elbow. 'OK. My dirty little secret is out. I went to meet a friend.'

It threw him. He composed himself. 'I'll need a name, Andrea.'

'No. I'm not going to divulge a name. Look, Bob, this isn't an on-going affair or anything. I'm not a slut. It's just an itch I have to scratch now and then. Okay?'

'It would help if you could substantiate your claim, Andrea,' he persisted.

Fyffe threw her napkin onto the table. 'No. Do I need substantiation? Look, Bob, I'm admitting marital infidelity to someone I've only met twice before. Does that not have the ring of truth about it?'

He opened his palms. Mr Reasonableness. 'You've admitted that you weren't at home as you previously told me you were. Now you've come up with another version as to your whereabouts. You can see how suspicious that is going to look to the police.'

She tilted her head and looked at him with narrowed eyes. 'Are you saying I'm a suspect?'

He shook his head. 'All I'm saying is that we can clear this up quickly if someone can vouch for you that night.'

'Is my word not good enough?' She shifted her eyes away from his, and looked down at her plate.

Scarth sighed. 'Andrea, you know it's not.' He pushed his plate to the side of the table. 'Where did you meet this friend?' he queried. 'Are you prepared to tell me that?'

'At a pub called the Covenanters' Rest if you must know. And yes, it's only a hundred yards away from Colin's house. And no, I didn't pop along between snifters and kill him. Satisfied?'

Scarth was surprised at the revelation, but kept his voice steady.

'The police will need a name sometime, Andrea.' He patted his napkin absently. 'What's the point in stalling? Why not tell me? I'll get your secret meeting corroborated with your friend, and that's it.'

'Definitely not.'

'I can ask at the pub, Andrea,' he warned softly. 'They'll have observant staff, CCTV, all that …'

Her smile was strained. 'Look, Bob, I'm married to an important politician. Any whiff of scandal would destroy him.' She spoke too loudly and seemed to realise it. 'He doesn't deserve that,' she said more softly. 'Can't you take my word for it?'

'I can't Andrea. You know I can't.'

Her eyes were shiny with unshed tears. She blinked them away. 'Well then bugger you, Bob Scarth,' she snapped, rising abruptly from the table.

As she marched purposefully for the entrance, their waiter drifted silently to fill her void. He proffered the bill on a porcelain saucer. 'Everything to your satisfaction, sir?' he asked with obvious insincerity.

Scarth fished out his wallet and extracted his credit card, watching absently as she neared the swinging doors.

Scarth nodded. 'Yes, fine, thanks,' he told the man.

'You handled that one well, Bob,' he said to himself self-deprecatingly. 'Congratulations.'

It was just after one o'clock when McIntosh and the canine formerly known as Scottie arrived at The Mall. First stop was Scottie's favourite fast-food drive-thru. McIntosh had got into the habit of giving the wee fella a take-away treat every time he had him for a sleep-over. This time it was a hot dog and fries for him, a beef burger for Scottie. And ketchup. They both loved tomato sauce.

The huge shopping centre was a terminus for several bus routes and was a busy place at the quietest of times. The car park for The Mall was massive, and the first space McIntosh found was a good quarter of a mile away from centre's entrance. McIntosh parked up and they ate their lunches in comfortable silence.

Afterwards, he put the dog on a lead and the two of them ambled leisurely towards the huge glass circular doors of The Mall. He was in a good mood. He enjoyed the wee dog's company, and it was obvious that it enjoyed being around him too.

The entrance was adjacent to the bus terminus, which was a large circular turnaround space, usually containing five or six buses, coming in to The Mall, or in the process of leaving it. McIntosh and the dog negotiated their way patiently through the cross-flow of crowds of people exiting from buses, or hurrying to catch one.

Just ahead of them in the press of people was a small boy being trailed along by the hand by his impatient mother.

'Mum,' implored the wee one as he skipped along. 'Can we go to Dubai Duty Free?'

She stopped suddenly. Astonished. 'What?' she snapped, before striding on. 'Of course not!'

'Oh, Mum; why not?'

'Because we don't know where it is for a start, that's why …'

'We won't need to,' argued the boy. 'The pilot knows the way. The plane will take us there …Oh, Mum, please …'

'Liam, I'm warning you …'

As McIntosh and Scottie were about to enter the centre a small woman in a pink jacket broke out of the throng, elbowing her passageway, and rushed past McIntosh. Must be a sale on, he reckoned.

Scottie thought differently. Recognising the familiar whiff of counterfeit perfume from the passing woman, he yelped ecstatically and gave chase. With an overjoyed whoop he jerked McIntosh round after her, scampering ahead among the legs of the crowd, that old familiar scent in his nostrils.

Too late McIntosh tried to apply the button brake as the extending lead quickly played out. As he tried to rein in the dog, he assumed the woman was wearing counterfeit perfume. Not an offence. Or at least, not an offence he was going to be bothered about today. Tell that to Scottie, he thought as he fought to keep up.

After a bit the woman halted, harassed so much by the happy wee dog that progress was impossible. She stood bewildered. The wee dog ran round her, barking, leaping joyously into the air on stiff legs.

McIntosh caught up. 'I'm terribly sorry madam …' he began.

She interrupted angrily. 'Are you the owner of this horrible dog?' she demanded.

Somehow the lead got entangled round the woman's ankles.

She lost her cool.

'Get it away from me!' she shrieked, trying to kick the wee beast. 'Get it the fuck away from me!'

She lost her balance. She reached out for McIntosh to stop herself falling. He stumbled over the lead himself and they fell to the ground in a tangle of limbs.

The woman, fearing she was about to be viciously attacked, went ballistic.

'Get off me, you ape!' she screamed. 'Get your hands off me!' She scratched, she struggled, fighting him off. 'You bastard …'

In actual fact McIntosh was thrashing around in a desperate attempt to get extradite himself. From her, from the lead, from the whole bonkers situation.

'Calm down, madam, please,' he pleaded in panting breaths, trying to get to his knees. 'There's no need to panic. I'm a police officer.'

'Plice!' she screeched on cue. 'Somebody please, call the plice!'

Time seemed to stop. McIntosh was dimly aware of several flashes. He realised that delighted spectators were taking snapshots of the melee, filming the embarrassing episode. He felt her teeth fastening on his left hand. He yelped in pain, and grabbed her cheeks, compelling her to release her death grip. He jerked his hand forcibly away, conscious of clipping her chin as he did so.

'Ahhhh,' she howled in pain. 'Bastard!'

The onlookers turned ugly. Three of the bolder men, urged by their wives, grabbed McIntosh and pulled him roughly away from the woman, remonstrating with him, roughing him up a bit. It took all his self-control to stop himself from going berserk and flattening them. For he could have done it, he knew. Someone shouted 'call the polis!' while McIntosh, arms pinioned, loudly protesting that he was the polis, freed himself angrily.

Two security guards arrived, panting, adrenalin pumping. They took control of the situation, asked McIntosh to accompany them to their office, where he would be given an opportunity to clear up the matter.

McIntosh indignantly refused, and an ill-tempered exchange was only dampened when PCs Dean 'Deano' Gray and Connor Reid finally rescued him. They assured the outraged citizens and the security people that the object of their attention was indeed an off-duty police officer. That the matter was now in their hands. That they would "take him into custody" for "further inquiries."

While this had been happening, another group had solicitously raised the elderly woman to her feet, comforting her, shielding her from her crazed attacker. A young man with an angry mop of ginger hair, who obviously knew the woman, gently guided her away to safety.

Gradually, the angry mood among the on-lookers subsided. They began to disperse. McIntosh looked frantically round for Scottie. The wee dog was nowhere to be seen. Or heard. As McIntosh was hustled away by Gray and Reid, they told him they had just arrived at The Mall, having been dispatched there urgently by the station sergeant in response to a report of another phone snatching. This time one aggravated by a fatal injury.

'Fatal injury?' McIntosh enquired hoarsely. 'What kind of fatal injury?'

'We don't know yet, sir,' replied PC Gray. 'We've only just got here …'

The three policemen made their way to the No. 33 bus stance. A noisy crowd had formed round two other police constables, who McIntosh recognised as Andy Heggie and Shirley McCracken. They were explaining that the bus was a crime scene, and had been withdrawn from service. People were complaining they had jobs to go to, appointments to keep. They resented being inconvenienced and weren't reticent about letting the police know about it.

McIntosh was drawn to the rear of the bus where an ambulance had pulled up onto the forecourt. The crowd fell back as a couple of paramedics pushing a wheelchair made their way from the bus to the open doors of the ambulance. Slumped in the wheelchair was an ashen faced young woman whose clothes were splattered with blood. Her eyes were shut and her face had the serenely calm look of the recently deceased.

As the paramedics lifted her out of the wheelchair and up the steps into the ambulance, McIntosh identified himself to one of them, a middle-aged woman with remarkably creased facial skin. When the patient had been loaded into the vehicle she turned and informed him that the young woman had been severely injured.

'Injured?' asked McIntosh in surprise. 'I thought she was dead.'

'Hardly,' replied the medic with professional impartiality. 'She has certainly suffered a traumatic injury though. Her right thumb has been horribly mangled by one of those maniac phone snatchers. I'd say she's going to lose the digit. It looks so damaged that amputation might be the only option.'

McIntosh needed to get things clear. 'But there's been no fatality?'

'Thankfully not,' said the medic. She raised the rear ramp noisily, banged the doors shut, and skipped round to the driver's door. The vehicle took off, tentatively at first, round the circular bus terminus; then, as the siren cleared a path, increased its speed down the dual carriageway towards the hospital.

PC Heggie disentangled himself from the crowd round the front of the bus.

'What's the score here Andy?' McIntosh asked.

'It's been a balls-up, sir. There was a phone-snatching incident on the bus, as you'll have gathered. The driver called it in to her depot. They called the Emergency Services number, who alerted Division. Division dithered then called our office. Me and Shirley were up at the football ground on crowd control duty. Sergeant Balmain diverted us here.'

McIntosh blew air out of his mouth in displeasure. 'For God's sake …'

'I know. They haven't a clue at Division. Or don't give a damn.'

'So then, when did you get here?'

'Ten minutes ago. Too late to interview any of the passengers or get statements. They'd all gone about their business. This lot,' he indicated the impatient crowd round the bus doors, 'were waiting to get onto the bus, and are obviously peeved that it has been pulled from service.'

'Were PCs Gray and Reid already here?'

Heggie shook his head. 'They came after us. From the other side of The Mall …'

'Has anyone searched the bus yet?'

'Shirley had a quick gander. Lots of blood, as you'd expect with a thumb being nearly hacked off. But no weapon or instrument found, boss. No punch, no crusher, no pliers, no nothing.'

'And no way to preserve the scene I don't suppose …'

'There have been a lot of people coming and going on the vehicle, sir, as you'd expect. There had been a serious injury; getting medical attention to the victim was the number one priority ...'

'I know, Andy,' McIntosh said regretfully.

'The Scene Manager has been alerted and is on his way.'

'Do we know anything about what happened? Any detail?'

'I've spoken to the driver, sir,' Heggie replied, pulling out his notebook, 'and taken her statement. I've noted what the medics have told us. But no other witnesses are available. The passengers had dispersed by the time we got here. That poor girl looked to be in a bad way …'

McIntosh looked over to where the driver was standing outside the doors of the bus. 'I'll need to go to the hospital and see her. But I'll have a word with the driver first.' He moved towards the throng at the bus stop. 'Thanks Andy …'

The driver was a small spherically-shaped woman, with spiky hennaed hair, and large dark-blue eyes. She had a nice, open face. She held up a tiny white warning hand as he approached.

'The bus is not in service, sir,' she said, her lips a thin line. She pointed to the blue and white tape crisscrossing the doorway. 'The police have done that. This vehicle is now an official crime scene.'

She drew herself up to her full height, which may have reached McIntosh's rib cage. 'But apart from that, no-one is permitted in the vehicle,' she said officiously. 'I've had to call it in to the Sanitation Team. Blood. Not allowed to have passengers, staff, or anyone else for that matter, on a vehicle where there is spilled blood. Union regs.'

McIntosh liked her immediately.

After he had identified himself, she told him what she knew, which wasn't much.

As she had been slowing to turn into the circular terminus, she became aware of a kerfuffle in the lower deck, she said. There was shouting, screaming, and a sudden crush of people at the doors. She had opened the doors before the bus came to a standstill, she said, because there was so many people jostling and clambering to get off. Only later did she realise that a phone-snatching incident had occurred, and that she had inadvertently let the snatcher escape.

'I could have kept the doors closed and kept everyone inside,' she admitted, 'but the pressure was tremendous. People were hammering at my Plexiglas window, demanding to get off, kicking at the doors. Like a herd of wild animals. I let them go, for safety's sake.'

The driver said that when she opened the doors the first one out was a small woman in a pink jacket. She forced her way out, and ran into the shopping centre, she said. She had the impression that several people had attempted to stop this woman, that in fact she may have been the one responsible for the attack, but that her capture had been unfortunately prevented by a large female passenger suddenly having a fainting or epileptic fit.

'Not that you could blame her,' she added, 'what with all the stramash [uproar] going on …That girl who was injured was screaming the place down. It was horrendous …'

'What did she look like?'

'What? Oh, she was young, dark haired, pretty, with blood all over her hands and front …'

'No. The woman who ran off. The one you thought was the phone snatcher?'

'Oh her. Spritely. Definitely spritely. Small and fit as a flea. Wiry, you know the type. Wearing a wool cap, and a pink padded jacket like those hill-walkers wear …small rucksack on her back, I think, though I may be wrong …'

With a horrible lurch in his stomach McIntosh knew who the driver was talking about. Knew that he had been in a position to detain her, had he known who he was wrestling with in The Mall. Hindsight, he thought bitterly. Who said it was wonderful? It was a stab in the gut. His hand was still louping where the woman had bit him. She was wiry all right.

To ease his conscience, he changed the subject. 'Did the paramedics attend to the woman who had the fit?'

'No. The funny thing was she recovered remarkably quickly after the commotion had died down. You have to hand it to her. She was a tough old bird.'

And a practiced faker, McIntosh knew. 'Where did she go: this big woman? Did you see?'

'No. She left with the others I suppose ...'

'When did you call it in to your depot?'

'As soon as someone told me there was a casualty. I couldn't get out of my cabin at first, what with the stampede, but I was told someone had been seriously injured. Once the doors had cleared, I went back to where the passenger was. I was shocked at the amount of blood, to be honest. Totally shocked. If I'd known she'd been injured by a phone snatcher I'd have called for the police right away ...'

She hadn't experienced a phone-snatching incident before, but informed him that the internal cameras would have relayed the whole thing back to the depot.

McIntosh already knew that but let her continue.

'They're not fitted with any memory,' she said, pointing to a black dome he could see just inside the doorway. 'The cameras are only capable of transmitting the video pictures back to the depot where they're stored on the servers. But that would be your best bet to find out what went on. The CCTV. The camera is the best witness. Isn't that what they say?'

McIntosh thanked her. He knew that he would have to go to the Midlothian Buses depot again, and review the camera footage.

'The screams of that poor girl will be with me for many a night now,' said the driver.

McIntosh reached down and gave her shoulder a sympathetic squeeze. 'The CCTV can wait. I'm going round to the hospital right now to try and see her. It must have been a traumatic experience for her.'

'To say the least …'

Looking for an escape, McIntosh turned and espied a policewoman coming through the crowded bus stop carrying a contented bundle. Scottie!

McIntosh felt a blush of shame rising up his cheeks. He had forgotten about the wee rogue. But there he was, tongue out, tail wagging, nestling happily against PC Shirley McCracken's delectable bosoms.

The thought crossed his wicked mind, that if he was the one nestling beside Shirley McCracken's delectable bosoms, *his* tongue would be hanging out too.

He licked his dry lips and stepped forward to meet her.

'Yours, I believe, Detective,' she said, handing the small dog over. 'What's his name?'

He liked the way her ears stuck out too. 'Scottie. How do you know he's a he?' he teased.

She smiled knowingly. 'You mean apart from the dangly bits? Us females always know a male when we see one, sir. They're the ones tripping over their tongues when we waggle our bums.'

He smiled his appreciation. PC *Saucy* McCracken, he thought.

The PC pointed to his stomach. 'Slaister,' she said with a grin.

McIntosh looked down questioningly.

'Where?'

He pulled out his top for inspection. Sure enough, he had a couple of miniscule spots of ketchup on the front of his shirt: maybe three of them if he looked closely. That was the trouble eating a hot dog in a car seat, and trying to feed an excited wee dog at the same time.

He was unembarrassed. 'How did you notice that?' he asked.

'Trained observers us policewomen, sir,' she replied. 'That's why they pay us the big bucks.'

'I'm a messy pup,' he admitted guiltily to the driver. 'My mother always said so ...'

'All men are,' she replied dismissively, but not unkindly. 'Rub some Vanish on the spots as soon as you get home …'

'What's Vanish?'

'A magic stain remover. You'll get it in any supermarket.' She looked around. Her partner PC Heggie was waiting patiently. 'I've got to go. Catch you later …'

If only, he thought.

CHAPTER 11

SATURDAY AFTERNOON

Scarth phoned Erica Griffin that morning and informed her as gently as he could of the autopsy result. Unfortunately, there was no doubt that her father had been murdered. She was remarkably stoical at the news, he thought. Many tears had been shed before now, he knew; and he also knew many more would come later. He admired her. She was holding up well. He asked her if she was willing to do a walk-through, to see if anything obvious was missing, or out of place, in the house. She agreed reluctantly.

Scarth got to Summerfield Terrace early, and waited for her in her father's study. It was a beautifully proportioned room, spoiled, he now realised, by the same off-putting expanse of Artexed ceiling he'd seen in the other downstairs rooms. No wonder the house had failed to sell, Scarth thought. The cost and inconvenience of removing the asbestos-containing ceiling coverings would be prohibitive for many prospective buyers.

The doorway was at one corner. Diagonally across the room, fitted into a corner, was the victim's bespoke work-station. It was a deep red burnished affair, with a protective glass on its immaculate surface. The victim had been attacked while sitting in the matching captain's chair, a deep-buttoned burgundy-coloured leather affair. It had now been righted and sat once more in its rightful position in front of the desk. The space of hardwood flooring where the body had lain had been thoroughly cleaned, and one of the SEs had discretely placed a woollen throw rug over it.

Scarth made his way across to the whaling memorabilia collection and examined the descriptive plaques underneath the artefacts. He saw short double-barbed harpoons (Shawn had told him they were fired from harpoon guns), toggle harpoon heads, long-handled eight-foot hand lances, a five-foot iron blubber hook, several steel flensing knives, a blubber axe, for chopping blubber into manageable pieces, and a tail knife with a two-foot blade, used to cut a hole in a dead whale's tail, through which a towing rope could be attached.

Various implements for killing seals were displayed. Wooden clubs were used to stun the seal on the nose, before an iron spike was driven into the back of its skull. There was a selection of rifles too, for every seal-clubbing party had to have a ship's officer standing by on the ice with a rifle, to provide protection from polar bears as the seals were being massacred.

There were also some Eskimo artefacts: skinners made from animal bone, tools made from narwhal tusks, a couple of 'Yakki kashes' – as the Shetland whalers called them – decorative sealskin pouches which they used to keep their tobacco dry, and a pair of tiny baby shoes made from sealskin.

Two glass cabinets occupied pride of place among the memorabilia display, and held the most precious of the artefacts. These were two beautifully-embroidered caribou fur parkas with matching boots, wonderfully preserved.

The plaque inside the cabinet stated that these impressive items had belonged to 'Agnes Napajok' and 'Betty Napajok', two Inuit girls who had come to Scotland in 1909 and 1910 respectively, to study 'religious education'.

When Erica Griffin arrived, he met her in the vestibule. She had a little boy with her. To Scarth's relief, the child immediately bounded up the stairs to the bedroom he and his younger brother used when they came for sleepovers.

She handed over a small, leather-bound journal, which from its smell and discoloured paper immediately told him was old. It was held together by a brass clasp, which was tarnished with disuse. He opened it carefully. On the fly-leaf, in an old-worldly flowing style, were the words: 'This journal is the property of Agnes Napajok.' Inside the pages were crammed with similar-styled writing, though in a language Scarth had never seen before.

'Someone called Agnes,' she pointed out, 'is given as the owner of one of those beautiful parkas in the display cabinets in Dad's office.'

'I know,' said Scarth.

'It seems remarkably well-preserved for being, what, just over a hundred years old? Do you think it is the same person?'

'I think it is very likely. It would be interesting to find out, wouldn't it? Have you given any thought about what to do with his whaling collection?'

'I have no idea. Really, I have not a clue. Do you think that maybe a museum or something would take it off our hands? It's probably valuable, but to me it's just clutter. My Mum thought so too.'

'We have an Inuit Canadian in our office,' Scarth said, 'called Lizzie Williamson. She might be able to give you advice. She's a Royal Canadian Mounted Police officer, but she is currently on secondment to the Midlothian Police. She works in our archives ...'

'A real live Mountie, wow-ee,' Erica mused. 'Does she always get her man, do you know?' she asked mischievously.

Scarth grinned amiably. 'I really don't know. Do you think I should ask her?'

Erica smiled encouragingly. 'I think you should ...'

'Ha!' Scarth laughed good-naturedly. 'But what I can ask her, if you want, is if your father's whaling collection would be of interest to a Canadian museum or cultural centre.' He tapped the journal's cover. 'And she might be able to translate your journal here, or some of it. Would you mind if I gave this to her for an appraisal? You'll get it back of course.'

'By all means. Young girls are incredibly self-centred, and girls of a hundred years ago probably suffered the same angst. It'll all be dramatically trotted out in the diary. But yes, give your Mountie a look at it. There's maybe an interesting story behind it all.'

Scarth put the journal carefully in an evidence bag, and popped it in his rucksack.

He then asked her if she would like a tea or a coffee or anything, before she began. She said she'd have a nosey round the house first, and brought out her phone to take any notes that were needed.

'Before you start,' said Scarth, 'the cleaning lady who comes in says that the burglar alarm wasn't set when she came in on Thursday morning. Was that usual, do you know?'

'Connie warned me about that. I was concerned. I got on to Dad about it and he admitted that he had set off the alarm previously by coming in with a drink in him, and fumbling with the code. I think the security company had responded a couple of times to false alarms of his. Anyway, he'd got into the habit of not setting it if he was going out to have a drink or two. To avoid bothering people. I told him he was taking a chance, leaving the house unprotected, but he insisted on doing it. You know what old folks are like.'

She looked at Scarth with startled eyes, a blush creeping up her neck into her face. 'Present company excepted of course,' she stumbled out. 'Sorry.'

Scarth smiled his forgiveness. He wasn't so old, was he? He certainly didn't feel old. Most of the time.

Griffin called her son down from upstairs, and when he had jumped the last few steps and landed beside them in the vestibule, she introduced him to Scarth. The boy's name was Jason. She introduced Scarth as 'Mr Scarth, the policeman'.

The three of them adjourned to the kitchen. 'I don't know if this will achieve anything,' she said dubiously. 'For of course my mother removed a lot of stuff. When she moved out. I'm not up to speed with what should or shouldn't be here …'

She stopped and pointed to the sink. 'That's strange …' she said. 'The drip-board …'

Scarth's eyes followed her hand. The drip-board was bare.

'What's strange about it?' he asked.

'There's nothing there. My Dad always left out his coffee mug, with the powder and sweeteners in it, ready for his morning cuppa. He did it straight after he cleared away the tea things. He was almost fanatical about it …'

Scarth looked again at the empty drip-board. 'Do you think forgot? Maybe came in a bit tiddly, and put everything away?'

She shook her head. 'No. I think he had a visitor. That's what I think.' She stared hard at him, her meaning clear in her eyes. A 'visitor' who killed him. 'A visitor who used the prepared mug,' she continued, for the boy's benefit, 'and washed it and put it away afterwards …'

While Scarth pondered on this, Griffin reminded her son to 'look after Mr Scarth', to 'be good', and then left the kitchen to begin her melancholy tour.

Scarth sat down at the small breakfast table. Jason, showing his good manners, asked him if he wanted something to drink, and fetched Diet Cokes from the fridge for both of them. No glasses were forthcoming, so Scarth followed the boy's lead and drank from the can.

The boy had his mother's wide-spaced brown eyes and caramel-coloured hair. His hair was cut short and stuck up all over his head as if charged with static electricity. He was restless.

'How old do you think I am?' he asked abruptly.

'Thirty-two,' Scarth immediately replied.

This produced a bunch of giggles. 'No. Really. How old?' He looked anxious.

Scarth held up his right hand, sideways, in front of his face. All fingers pointed to the left. He then slowly placed his left hand on top of it, with the fingers pointing to the right. The boy watched this carefully, in silence. Scarth suddenly brought his hands down.

'You're ten,' he stated flatly.

The boy was surprised, then suspicious. 'What did you do there?'

Scarth explained. 'When I held up five fingers, I could still see the top half of you. When I held up the next five fingers you disappeared; therefore … you must be ten.'

He could see the boy didn't believe him, but was too well trained to blurt it out. Children are born with a well-developed sense of suspicion, he had often thought, and were not so easily hoodwinked as adults presume.

'How old to you think I am, Jason?' he coaxed.

The boy ignored his question. 'How many press-ups can you do?' he asked, his eyes guileless.

Scarth admitted not many. He was too old for that, he said.

'I can do hundreds,' the boy bragged. He slurped noisily from his can. 'Sometimes I forget to stop …' He regarded Scarth carefully under blonde eyelashes, expecting the adult to challenge his boast. When Scarth raised no objections, the boy said,

'Who's your favourite sports star?

Scarth sat back, bemused. He'd been a sports fan for more than fifty years. How do you describe to a boy born yesterday of the stars he'd seen, in all realms of sport, during that time? Jack Nicklaus, Gary Player, Seve Ballesteros; and home-grown heroes like Kenny Dalglish, Gavin Hastings, Jim Baxter, and Ken Buchanan. What relevance would any of them have to someone as young as Jason? None, he suspected sadly.

The boy took his silence as reluctance to engage in conversation with a child, and was tempted to hurry him along. But instead of answering the boy's question, Scarth asked Jason what he really wanted to hear.

'Who's your favourite sports star, Jason?'

Jason had his reply ready. 'Andy Murray,' he declared firmly.

Scarth adopted a playful tone. 'Who does he play for?' he asked the boy.

Jason snorted with disgust. 'He doesn't play for anybody, silly. He's a tennis player. Have you not heard of Andy Murray?'

'Oh. *That* Andy Murray,' said Scarth. 'I thought you meant Andy Murray who played for Third Lanark …'

Jason small face momentarily furled up in puzzlement, but he wasn't distracted.

'Andy Murray came to our school last year, to do a coaching clinic. He spoke to me and I spoke to him …' As if conscious that this sounded a tad too boastful, the boy added: 'he spoke to a lot of us.'

Edinburgh fee-paying schools, Scarth knew, placed a lot of emphasis on the importance of sport in a child's development. And they had the resources, and the facilities to match, so he wasn't surprised Jason's school could attract the likes of Andy Murray to conduct a motivational seminar with the kids.

'Andy Murray is Scottish,' Jason informed him, in the modulated tone you would use to address a cretin, 'and he won the Olympics …' He suddenly dropped down on his knees, rolled over onto his back, and jerked his legs straight out. He did two or three laboured sit-ups, his immature stomach muscles not up to the task, before turning on his side and sitting up to face Scarth.

'I'm going to be in the Olympics when I get older,' he puffed emphatically. 'That's why I'm training. To be super-fit. I'm going to be an icon like Andy Murray.'

The boy turned quickly again to the prone position, and did five strained press-ups. The boy's jerky energy reminded Scarth of an English rock 'n' roll singer from the early sixties called Wee Willie Harris. Scarth wondered idly what sort of life Wee Willie had experienced since those halcyon days. The boy stopped his callisthenics, exhausted, and sat facing Scarth.

'I can do sit-ups all day long if I want to,' Jason panted. 'I can keep up with my dad.'

Which doesn't say much, thought Scarth, for 'Dad.'

He smiled at the boy affectionately. Little boys had such a hard time of it growing up. He didn't know what, if anything, the boy knew of his grandfather's ghastly death. But if the lad felt uncomfortable in his present surroundings, he wasn't showing it. The resilience of children, thought Scarth; even so, he was careful to keep the next question in the present tense.

'Does your grandfather keep crisps in the house?'

'You mean Papa? Sure, he has …' Jason crawled to his right and jerked open a cabinet door. Inside were all sorts of packets of high-fat goodies. 'Do you like Salt and Vinegar?'

'They're my favourites,' replied Scarth.

'Me too,' said the boy, dragging out a large packet. He opened another cupboard door, and extracted two glass bowls which he clumsily placed on the table. He filled them to overflowing with the crisps. Now that they were pals, Scarth decided to cement the friendship with a joke.

'Jason, have you heard the joke about the two man-eating lions that were walking round IKEA one Saturday afternoon?'

'No,' the boy mumbled, mouth full.

'Well as they were going round the store, one lion says to the other: "I thought you said it would be crowded with people on a Saturday? We've been wandering around here for twenty minutes, and haven't seen anyone yet" …'

Scarth gazed expectantly at the boy's sombre face. There wasn't a glimmer of amusement.

'Do you get it?' he asked anxiously.

The boy didn't get it. He remained impassively-faced. 'Was it a holiday, and the store was closed?' he asked.

'No. It was a Saturday afternoon. The busiest time …'

'Were they invisible? Yeah! The lions were invisible! Ha! That's a good joke …' His smile was wide and wet. Like a dog's grin.

There's nothing that illustrates the difference between generations more vividly, mused Scarth blankly, than each other's sense of humour. Well, that and their disparate tastes in music. Never explain a joke, his father had told him when he was young; but he had the disheartening feeling that he wouldn't get out of explaining this one.

He was saved by the appearance of the boy's mother, who just then came into the kitchen.

'Mum! Mr Scarth's been telling me jokes. He's funny!'

Her eyes were puffed. It was obvious that she had been crying. She looked at Scarth and shook her head. He took it to mean that nothing was missing, or out of place.

Catching his mother's glance at Scarth and suspecting the old man was connected to the cause of his mother's distress, the boy asked Scarth suspiciously, 'Why's my Mummy been crying?'

Scarth leaned towards him, heavy-shouldered and earnest. He patted the little boy gently on the shoulder. 'People need to cry sometimes, Jason,' he said sympathetically, 'that's all …'

'I don't cry,' the boy replied stoically.

CHAPTER 12

SATURDAY EVENING

When Erica Griffin and Jason had gone, Scarth foraged briefly through the kitchen cabinets before he found what he was looking for – the chocolate biscuit tin. He lifted his can of Diet Coke from the kitchen table, grabbed his rucksack, and wandered back down the corridor to the study.

A low armchair with a beige velvet covering and cabriole legs sat in front of the library, facing the tall, blackout-curtained French windows. Scarth opened his rucksack and fished out the book Andrea Fyffe had loaned him. It seemed fitting somehow, to read a biography of her great-great-grandfather, surrounded by his memorabilia. He settled in the deep-seated armchair, stretched his legs out comfortably onto a small matching pouffe, and opened the book.

It was a slim volume of eighty pages, more of a booklet than a book, and had been published, Scarth noticed, by the author. The biography started in an unpromising, old-fashioned manner.

"In Repulse Bay, in the upper corner of Hudson Bay," Scarth read, "there is a small group of islands called the Ship Harbour Islands. There the curious visitor will find a reminder that once these waters were the province of whaling ships from Scotland, for carved out of the rock at

Ships Harbour Islands are the names *Perseverance*, *Active*, *Albert*, and *Arctic*.

"The date chipped out below the *Perseverance* is 1892. That year, along with her Peterhead captain and crew, she had been hired by the Hudson's Bay Company as a supply vessel. It was the first time since Captain Alex Gray's grandfather had taken out the first Perseverance eighty years previously, that Peterhead had no representative at the Greenland whaling.

"The *Active*, *Albert*, and *Arctic* were all from Dundee. However, several other Scottish whaling ships, which are known to have 'over-wintered' at Ship Harbour Islands, are not recorded there. Perhaps their memorials have been eroded or erased by the remorseless Arctic winters. Among these vessels was the auxiliary steamer *Ajax*, commanded by my grandfather, Captain Alexander Jamieson Fyffe."

Scarth read that Alexander Jamieson Fyffe had been born in 1876 in Oldmeldrum, Aberdeenshire. He was the third son of a tenant farmer there. It was taken for granted that the eldest son would succeed in the tenancy of the farm. Alexander preferred to be his own man. Like many an Aberdeenshire farm boy before him, he sought employment at the 'Greenland whaling'. Whaling in the Arctic was big business. Plenty of jobs were to be had and big bonuses could be earned in a good season, and young Fyffe walked all the way to Aberdeen and secured a berth as a cabin boy.

At the time whaling companies preferred farm boys rather than town boys as deck hands. Country boys were healthier, having benefited from a wholesome diet of fresh food; they were stronger than town boys, used to the hard work on the farm; they were generally abstemious, a result of close ties between the country folk and their kirk; and were generally better educated, having had a sound grounding in the 3Rs at their local parish school.

Here the biographer drew the reader's attention to the well-known Aberdeenshire folk song, 'Fareweel Tae Tarwathie', which tells the story of a young country lad going off to the whaling, looking forward to making his fortune at 'the cold land of Greenland'.

> 'Fareweel tae Tarwathie – adieu Mormond Hill,
> And the dear land o' Crimond, I bid ye fareweel,
> I am bound out for Greenland, and ready to sail,
> In hopes to find riches, in hunting the whale.
>
> Adieu to my comrades, for a while we must part,
> Likewise tae the dear lass who first won my heart,
> The cold ice of Greenland my love will not chill,
> The longer my absence, the more loving she'll feel.

Of course, the longer his absence, the biographer reminded the reader laconically, the more chance the lad had of not coming back at all. For the whaling game was a notoriously dangerous occupation. Many lives were lost each year to ship-wreck, drowning, and to hypothermia. Limbs and digits were habitually lost to frostbite. More often than not, those riches the young men were hoping to find came at a cost.

The biographer explained that by the 1750s whaling ships from England, Scotland, and Holland were exploiting the large numbers of whales around the archipelago of Spitsbergen. In those days 'Spitsbergen' was not to be found on any map. The area was vaguely called 'Greenland'.

These ships came mainly from English ports such as London, Hull, Whitby, and Newcastle. Those from Scotland came from Dunbar, Leith, Bo'ness, and Dundee. Later Aberdeen and Peterhead would become big players. In those days a whale was always called a 'fish', and the whaling industry was called the 'Greenland whale fishery'.

The blubber was flensed from the whales at sea, and brought back to the UK in barrels. On shore, it was boiled to render it into oil. This whale oil was used domestically and commercially, for illumination and lubrication. There was a worldwide market. Baleen, the flexible horn-like substance which was obtained from the mouth of the bowhead, had many uses. It was the foundation, the biographer wrote with unconscious humour, on which the corset industry was based.

As stocks of whales at Spitsbergen diminished the British whalers expanded their activities to Davis Straits and Cumberland Sound. For many years the massive ice-fields in Baffin Bay, sometimes hundreds of miles across, limited the expansion. But in 1817, the Larkins of Leith, and the Elizabeth of Aberdeen finally broke through the ice barrier. In Melville Bay they fell in with tremendous runs of fish. Their discovery would have a major impact on the whaling industry, for it opened up a new fishing ground for a new generation of whalers. In good seasons Melville Bay produced catches whaling captains had always dreamed of. In bad seasons it was an ice-choked nightmare which claimed its sacrificial quota of whaling ships. The wooden ships, trapped between massive ice-floes, were crushed mercilessly into splinters. Within a couple of years Melville Bay would acquire such a fearsome reputation that it became known as the 'Whalers' Graveyard'.

For the next fifty years British whalers exploited the whale population in the Davis Straits region. By the 1870s, with the whale stocks diminishing, only Scottish ships persisted. With the reduced competition, those ports which persevered – such as Dundee, Aberdeen, and Peterhead, reaped a harvest like never before. But even the most optimistic ones knew that it was unsustainable. Year after year there was mounting evidence that the whale stocks were being seriously depleted.

Reports of the first contacts between the Inuit and the qallunaat – the white men – were not altogether amicable, wrote the biographer. When the people of Baffin Island first saw the whaling ships, they were terrified. They thought the sailors on the ships had come to murder them. This fear was encouraged by the shamans, who went into trances and chanted that their doom was near. The foreigners came ashore and traded biscuits and tobacco for native goods. But still the Inuit were afraid, distrustful. Then the shaman cast a spell on the qallunaat, rendering them harmless. The Inuit were no longer afraid, and went out in their kayaks to the ships, and boarded them.

Some ships probed further inland, to Hudson Bay, and established stations there. The practice of 'over-wintering' began. The whaling ships would arrive as soon as the ice would allow, usually in June and July. They would spend the summer cruising for bowhead whales. Around the end of September, the encroaching ice brought whaling activities to an end.

The ships would anchor in a safe haven, such as Ship Harbour Islands, and let themselves be frozen in. Non-essential crew would be sent home by a sister ship, leaving only a skeleton crew. Sometime near the end of April or the beginning of May the ice loosened enough for the whaleboats to be lowered again, and the spring whaling would commence. In late May/beginning of June reinforcements would arrive from Dundee, and the whaling activities were scaled up for the summer fishing. The ships would then head for home in the autumn, with the produce of two seasons in their holds.

Young Alex Fyffe gradually worked himself up the ranks. He became, in turns, a boatman, a boat-steerer, a third, second and then first harpooner, before becoming a mate. In 1900, at the relatively young age of twenty-four, he became master of a whaling vessel, the *Valiant* of Aberdeen. Eight years later he took command of the *Ajax* of Dundee, and from then on, his hunting ground was to be in the northwest corner of Hudson Bay.

'Over-wintering' would not have been possible without the help of the local Inuit. Captain Fyffe knew that his men would die of hypothermia, starvation, or scurvy if left to their own devices. Co-operation with the local Inuit was essential. The Inuit were experienced hunters who could provide fresh meat during the long cold winter – a vital weapon against the ever-present danger of scurvy. In the spring the Inuit men, who were excellent boatmen, would assist the *Ajax's* skeleton crew in the whaling. To combat the chilling cold the Inuit women kitted out Captain Fyffe's men with winter clothing.

The traditional Inuit method a catching a sea creature involved harpooning the animal and letting it swim off. The harpoon had a forty-foot line made of walrus skin attached to it, which had a drag or drogue on the other end. This was made of inflated sealskin. The harpooned animal was allowed to run. The drogue slowed the animal down and showed the hunters where he swam. Several drogues were used to retard the escape of a bowhead whale.

When the British and American whalers came, the Inuit hunters adopted their methods. The bowhead whale usually sounded after being struck by a harpoon, pulling its pursuers along for sometimes hours at a time, and towing them well out of sight of their ship, and sometimes out of earshot of the ship's bell or cannon. Most times two or three whale boats from the same ship joined the hunt, each one putting a harpoon the animal. When the whale had exhausted itself, and often its tormentors, it lay helpless on the surface. It was then dispatched with long lances.

By the time Captain Fyffe was whaling in Hudson Bay the whalers were armed with a lethal arsenal of weapons. The men of the *Ajax* used a harpoon gun, as did all the Scottish ships. The Inuit called it a 'little cannon'. It was mounted on the bow of the whaleboat, and fired a barbed harpoon. At the time, American whalers in Hudson Bay preferred a darting gun, a hand-thrown harpoon with a delayed-action explosive charge. The startled whale swam off but didn't get far before the charge detonated. It brought a new meaning to the cry of 'Thar she blows!'

Beluga whales or 'white' whales were prized for their silky-smooth white skins. White whales fed on salmon, which they followed into narrow bays or fjords. Sometimes it was possible to net the entrance behind the whales. More usually the whalers 'caa'd' them, or drove them shoreward. A cordon of small boats, with much shouting, rattling of tin cans and rifle-shooting etc., drove the whales into shallow water near the shoreline. It was a method well known in Norway, Shetland, and the Faroes for the caa'ing of pilot whales. When the tide receded, the whales were stranded. The men then took to the shallow water, and dispatched the desperate animals with lances. Great care was taken not to puncture the beluga skins more than was necessary.

Back in Scotland, these white skins were sold as 'porpoise' hide. A tanning factory in Dundee had a special department which made nothing but 'porpoise' leather boot-laces, for ladies' 'porpoise leather boots' were very popular at the time.

As payment for their services, Captain Fyffe gave the menfolk guns, ammunition, knives, and iron utensils. The women received presents of needles, thread, fabric, buttons and beads. The Inuit weren't to know it at the time, but their lives were changing forever.

In 1884 the Tannadice Whaling Company (named after the street in Dundee where their office was), established their station on the northern shore of Repulse Bay. Naturally the native Inuit, eager to continue exchanging their skills for goods and the 'miracle tools' the whalers possessed, began to settle near the stations. The traditional nomadic lifestyle was disrupted as up to two hundred Inuit congregated there. This pattern was repeated at all the Arctic whaling stations, Scottish and American. The Inuit were employed almost all year round – as hunters and suppliers in the winter, as whalers in the summer. It was convenient for all if they settled near the whaling stations.

Captain Alexander Fyffe was first employed by the Tannadice Whaling Company in the 1908/09 season, having been awarded the command of the company's 'flag ship', the 343-ton steam-powered *Ajax*. From then on Captain Fyffe 'over-wintered' at Ship Harbour Islands every second year. Before leaving Repulse Bay for Dundee at the end of a season he would commission the local Inuit to maintain the company's huts and sheds, undertake the spring whaling for him until he returned the following June. He never once suffered an instance of theft from the property while it was left unattended for those long dark months.

The Inuit loved music, recorded the biographer. They loved singing and dancing. On one of his trips Captain Fyffe brought with him a gramophone and a stack of records. It was an immediate success. The locals soon developed a fascination for Harry Lauder's songs. In no time at all, everyone could chant, after a fashion, "I love a lassie, a bonny bonny lassie", and "Roamin' in the gloamin, on the bonnie banks o' Clyde …"

Whaling ships always had musicians in their complements. Fiddlers from Shetland and accordion players from mainland Scotland were essential for crew morale, and on-board dances during the long winter months were much anticipated and greatly enjoyed by both whalers and Inuit alike.

It was inevitable that before long some of the whalers acquired 'girlfriends'. Indeed, it wasn't long before some of the Scottish whalers acquired wee half-Inuit offspring.

Captain Fyffe, the biographer claimed chastely, frowned upon such behaviour, and did not engage in any such activities. He had a business to run. Collaboration was an integral part of the way things were done. Social intercourse was unavoidable, but sexual intercourse, he knew, could be extremely detrimental to Scots/Inuit business relationships. Captain Fyffe maintained a distanced, neutral position, and strictly avoided showing favouritism of any kind.

Whaling made him a wealthy man, and in 1906 Captain Fyffe bought the small estate of Broomieknowe near Eskbridge in Midlothian. He was a supporter of the Presbyterian Church's Canada Mission, and as an ambassador for that organisation he raised funds for the Inuit settlements bordering the Hudson Bay.

In 1909 he went even further, and arranged for an Inuit girl from Repulse Bay to travel to Scotland to further her religious education. She was joined the following October by her younger sister. Both were home-tutored by Mrs Fyffe, who had been one of the first females to be accepted into Edinburgh University in 1892 (till then females were not permitted to have a university education in Scotland), and the young pupils were comfortably, and handily, accommodated at Broomieknowe.

Unfortunately for the Broomieknowe household tragedy struck in the autumn of 1911. A devastating measles epidemic swept Britain. The young Inuit girls, now practically young women, despite the assiduous attentions of Mrs Fyffe, fell gravely ill. With no natural resistance to European diseases, they succumbed quickly, and died within five days. The tragedy was tripled when Mrs Fyffe herself, who had selflessly nursed the young visitors, was also stricken with the infection, and died of complications related to it.

Alexander Fyffe had just returned from the Repulse Bay whaling station earlier in the week. He was alerted in Dundee where he was unloading his cargo of bearskins, seal skins, narwhal tusks, and ivory. He also had two live polar bears, destined for Regent Park Zoo. Captain Fyffe immediately made for home; but on his arrival there was informed by the family physician that his wife and the girls 'were no more', and had tragically perished.

Mrs Fyffe, who was only thirty-four years old at the time of her death, was the first person to be interred in the family burial plot that had been recently created at Broomieknowe.

Scarth changed his position on his chair, glancing at his watch. Startled by the passage time, he quickly scanned the following pages.

After the untimely death of his wife, Alexander Fyffe spent a listless, morose couple of years, before friends convinced him to seek solace in work. The First World War brought an end to his whaling career, and prevented him from returning to Repulse Bay. He spent the war years working with the Navy, planning, and organising trans-Atlantic convoys.

After the war, he threw himself into politics; first local, then national, then international. In 1920 he was returned as the local Conservative MP in the General Election, and perforce had to spend most of the year in London. His eldest son James, now twenty-four, took over the day-to-day running of the Broomieknowe estate.

A J Fyffe, as he was known in political circles, did not forget his Inuit friends. As soon as the war was over, he journeyed to Hudson Bay. He continued to visit the region regularly. He was a passionate believer that Canada should have the right to self-determination, and that the indigenous people of the region should have full status as Canadian citizens.

In the 1924 A J Fyffe's knowledge of the indigenous people of Arctic Canada, especially in the Hudson Bay area, earned him a seat on the Commons' influential Select Committee on Commonwealth Affairs. In 1926 he spent several months in Canada, acting as a Commissioner of the Crown. His mission was to liaise with the representatives of the Northwest Territories as they sought political and diplomatic independence from the UK parliament. In 1928 he was knighted for his services to 'His Majesty's Dominion of Canada'.

Sir A J Fyffe died in 1936. By that time his aspiration of Canada gaining the right to self-government, and being freed from the British parliament's authority to legislate for the Dominion, had come to fruition. It had been something he had been lobbying and working for since the early 1920s, and he regarded his contribution to it as his greatest achievement. His ultimate dream, to see the creation of an Inuit homeland, was not however to be achieved till 1999.

Sir A J Fyffe was buried in the family burial plot at Broomieknowe, beside his beloved wife.

Scarth felt himself nodding off so he closed the booklet. As a eulogy it had gone on a bit, he thought. But as a biography it was mercifully on the short side.

He drew himself reluctantly out of the too-comfy armchair and stepped again to the cabinet containing the caribou parkas. Poor Agnes, he thought, poor Betty.

He again examined the wonderful fur clothes and boots. The girls had obviously looked after their possessions, no doubt regarding the garments as a tangible reminder of their frozen homeland. And the superb skill and loving workmanship, which had obviously gone into the crafting of the items, had been rewarded too, by the manner in which they had been carefully looked after.

Gazing at the exhibits, so remarkably preserved long after their owners had sadly departed this earth, made him feel very humble. How ironic that they should survive the harsh climate of their native land till their early teens, only to succumb, in what must have seemed like luxurious accommodation to them, to a relatively innocuous white man's disease.

It was after five o'clock when Lizzie Williamson arrived at Muir's house from the office. She'd been intrigued by Scarth's out-of-the-ordinary summons, and curious about the artefacts he was anxious she should see.

Williamson was an extremely pretty young Canadian of mixed blood. She was a twenty-five-year-old with black expressive eyes, smooth lightly-tanned skin, and lovely teeth. She had the face tattoos of her people, which in her case consisted of a series of dotted lines which marched across her cheeks, like parallel rows of freckles.

Her grandfather was a Scot from Aberdeen who had signed up with the Hudson's Bay Company as a youth. From a lowly start in the early 1960s he had progressed up through the ranks, buying shares on the way, and was now a wealthy man, retired in Winnipeg.

Lizzie's grandmother was a native-speaking Inuit from the Baker Lake area, who, over the years, acquired many apposite sayings from her couthie, fair-skinned husband.

'Jings! Wid ye look at the time!' she'd cry; or 'Hud yer wheesht', when the 'bairns' became obstreperous. She'd say 'Ah dinnae ken' at home, or 'I'm afraid I don't really know', when she and her husband were out in the company of strangers.

The previous year the top floor of the Eskbridge police station was converted into the police archives for the county of Midlothian. When Lizzie had first arrived, as part of the staff for the archives, personnel at the station were unsure of how to describe her ethnicity in her presence. She'd settled it once and for all with an answer which endeared her to her new Scottish colleagues.

'Don't call me an Eskimo,' she'd told Quin; 'and I won't call you a Brit …'

Scarth showed her into the study. He explained that the whaling exhibits belonged to Colin Muir, a murder victim whose death he and Quin were currently investigating.

She gave the gruesome-looking iron whaling implements only a cursory glance. The smaller, Inuit-made items, such as the beaded sealskin pouches, and cute sealskin baby shoes, drew her attention. She then stood back and indicated the implements above them on the wall.

'You'd think that an eclectic collection like this probably belongs in a museum somewhere,' she said, 'but people are more reluctant nowadays to accept artefacts such as these. It's not politically correct to display items which may have been purloined from another culture. The proper place is the country of origin.' She paused. 'And you say the owner has been murdered? Where was he killed?' she asked.

Scarth was a trifle uncomfortable. 'Well in here, Lizzie, as a matter of fact.'

She shuddered, and looked suspiciously around at the floor, as if expecting to see tell-tale bloodstains.

Scarth needed a diversion. He pointed to the desk where he had laid the diary Erica Griffin had found. 'That's the journal, or diary, I was talking about Lizzie …'

But she had found her own diversion. She had caught sight of the display cabinets containing the two beautifully-preserved caribou parkas. She was enthralled.

'Oh my god,' she exclaimed, 'would you look at these …' her hand flew to her mouth. 'They're beautiful. Look. Look at the stitching … it must have taken the seamstress ages …'

Scarth pointed to the small descriptive plaques attached to the rear wall of the cabinets.

'These coats apparently belonged to two Inuit girls who came to Scotland to further their religious education. That one,' he indicated a darker-skinned parka on the left, 'belonged to Agnes Napajok, the owner of the diary. She came here in 1909.'

'Really? How wonderful. Oh yes, I'm sure several establishments at home would be absolutely delighted to have these artefacts on display. They're so beautiful, aren't they?'

She turned to him with big eyes. 'Can I feel them? Have you a key to the cabinets?'

Scarth produced a small set of keys which he had found in the top drawer of the desk. She quickly found one which fitted. She reached in and slowly drew out the coat belonging to Agnes Napajok. She pressed the fur to her cheek.

'It's like new!' she exclaimed. 'No bad smells. Thank goodness he didn't put in mothballs! Oh, these parkas are gorgeous. Lovely. I've never seen ones so old …'

She slipped the garment off its hanger, and slid a tentative arm inside it. She tried it on. It was obviously too small, and unable to be fastened, but it really suited her. Under the keen fluorescent lights of the office, her lovely dotted face peeped delightedly from inside the fur collar. She held the coat open, examining the lining, the near-invisible stitching, probing inquisitively, and marvelling at the handiwork.

She suddenly stopped, and lifted the garment up for closer inspection. Her fingers probed softly at the same spot in the lining.

'It's been repaired,' she said, shocked. She peered closer. 'Or rather, someone has made an inside pocket which the original seamstress had not intended. Look, Bob. The thread doesn't even match! It's a clumsy job compared to the rest of the garment …' her eyes were glittering as she held his. 'There's been a secret pocket here, Bob. Someone has made it. And someone has found it ...'

'Why would you need a secret pocket in a parka?' Scarth asked.

She looked at the desk. 'To hide something precious. Like a diary, perhaps?'

She picked up the diary from the desk, undid the clasp, and had a quick perusal of the pages.

"Mmm, Agnes,' she said, 'certainly a name with a lot of religious connotations … Did you make a secret pocket in your parka, Agnes Napajok, eh? What was so important in your life that you had to hide your little diary in such a dark and secret place?'

She held the diary up between them. 'Where was the diary found?

Scarth made a vague gesture, encompassing the whole collection. 'Colin Muir, the victim, had it in a bank security box. His daughter found it yesterday when she went to check his account.'

Lizzie took the parka carefully off, and replaced it on its hanger in the display cabinet.

'It's possible Mr Muir found the diary,' said Scarth, 'when he bought the collection from William Fyffe. Perhaps he suspected it was valuable, decided to keep it in a safe place, and took it to the bank. Do you think he read it?'

Lizzie shook her head. 'He probably tried to, but it wouldn't be easy.'

She showed Scarth the script on the pages. She told him that Canadian Inuit speak variations of Inuktitut, the traditional oral language of Arctic Canada. She said that Christian missionaries in the 1860s had developed two writing systems for Inuktitut. They needed a way to translate the bible and hymns for the people. One writing system was syllabic, which was easy for native speakers to learn; while the other used roman orthography – the Latin alphabet used to write English and French.

The journal, Lizzie said, had been written in Qaniujaaqpait, the written language using Inuktitut syllabics. This meant that Agnes must have had some mission school education. That would help them to find out where she lived, Lizzie told him, for missionary schools were few and far between in those days before the First War.

It was clearly written. Many pages were blank. It wasn't the continuous me-me-me screed you'd find in a young woman's diary nowadays, Lizzie said.

Having said all that, she told him she would be able to translate the text easily enough – if she was given a day or two.

'Children of Inuit descent are all taught Qaniujaaqpait in grade school,' she explained. 'Our cultural heritage is very important to us. It will bring back memories of doing my homework by candle-light in my father's iglu.'

'Really?' Scarth asked; a bit shocked.

Up close, he noticed vertical tattooed stripes on her chin. Had they been there all the time? He was too reticent to ask what they symbolized.

She flashed him a guilty smile.

'Perhaps I was exaggerating a tad,' she admitted. 'It was actually a centrally-heated suburban townhouse in Winnipeg. But anyway, I'm definitely intrigued with your Inuit exhibit. I'm off duty tomorrow, so I'll read the diary then. I can jot down the salient points, and give you an update on Monday morning. How does that suit?'

Scarth grinned. One of Scobie McIntosh's inane phrases came into his mind.

'Luvly jubbly, Lizzie,' he replied.

'You're welcome,' she chimed.

CHAPTER 13

SATURDAY EVENING

After wandering the supermarket's aisles for a good ten minutes, McIntosh finally located the Vanish. At home he laid his shirt on the small dining table, moistened the tiny reddish specks, and rubbed them with the stain remover. The spots turned a little paler, but didn't disappear. He tried again. The same thing happened, or didn't happen. So much for the magic, he thought. The garment would have to go into the wash to remove the stains, he decided. He bundled it up and stuffed it into his laundry bag, ready for the next light wash.

McIntosh's flat was in Myrtle Vale Street, in a block of sixteen apartments, usually let to students and single professional people. It had a basement laundry room with three washing machines and three tumble driers, and three ironing-boards. Use of these machines was included in the rent. Professional people are busy people, and so an arrangement was made with a personable young lady from Estonia who washed, dried, and ironed clothes for those who had signed up for her services. Her name was Anya, and she came in on Saturday and Sunday afternoons. McIntosh was one of her grateful clients.

At ten past five that afternoon, having changed into a black T-shirt and zipped fleecy top, McIntosh descended to the basement. Anya hadn't come in yet, so he dropped his laundry bag off in the corner she reserved for her clients. Twenty minutes later he pulled into the car park at the town's Strathesk Hospital. Inside the building, he sought out Dr Bashkir, one of the consultants at the hospital.

Inspector Quin was one of Dr Bashkir's favourites, her large and imposing figure a fascination to his sparse frame. His dealings with the police were normally conducted with her, but the doctor knew the young detective from his extracurricular activities. Bashkir's son was a medical student and rugby man, and he watched the lad's games as often as he could. The Medics played in the same league as the Midlothian Police First XV. Having seen the tall fair-haired young man sitting opposite him in action, he knew McIntosh was a hard nut who was best avoided on the park, if at all possible.

In his consulting room Dr Bashkir informed McIntosh that the phone-snatching patient was in no condition to be interviewed. The surgeons had not been able to save her thumb unfortunately. It was too damaged, and it had been decided amputate it. She was currently under heavy sedation.

'It really is horrendous, if I may say so Sergeant,' the doctor continued, showing his outrage, 'that folks can't speak on their mobile phones on a bus nowadays for fear of being attacked by these phone snatchers. It really is unacceptable. Are you any closer to apprehending the culprits?

McIntosh nodded. 'I'm going to nab this one, Doctor, believe you me.'

The medical man looked at him forthrightly, saw the determination on the young detective's face, and believed him.

McIntosh's left hand was throbbing with pain where the phone snatcher had bitten him. He rubbed it absently.

The medic noticed, and pointed to the detective's hand. 'Are you carrying an injury yourself, Sergeant?'

McIntosh lifted an arm. Sure enough, his left hand had swollen considerably. The bite mark had an angry-looking, reddish tinge to it. The doctor leaned over his desk to see.

'It doesn't look like a dog bite,' he said. 'From a crazed opposing forward?'

McIntosh shook his head. 'No. Something more vicious. A crazy female.' He smiled like a martyr. 'I hate to admit it, Doctor,' he said, 'but I had an embarrassing altercation earlier today in The Mall with an elderly woman ...'

'How embarrassing an altercation?'

'The kind where she got away from me,' said McIntosh with a shy grin, running a self-conscious hand through his fair hair.

'Got away from you? Tut, tut, Sergeant. That's a disgraceful admission from an experienced blindside flanker like yourself.'

'We both got tangled up in my wee dog's lead,' explained the young detective, 'and we fell to the floor. He's an ex-police sniffer dog, and was dancing around like a demented dervish. Thought he'd found a counterfeiter. During our tussle the woman bit me. She was rescued by bystanders who thought I was a maniac assaulting her.'

Bashkir shook his head in wonderment.

'And they say a detective's life is 99% drudgery enlivened with only 1% excitement …'

He stood up from his chair, fussed around in a metal chest of drawers beside his desk, and fetched out a packet of antiseptic wipes. He moved round the desk and reached for McIntosh's hand to cleanse the wound.

The tall detective stalled him. 'Could it be used as evidence, do you think?' he queried.

'DNA evidence, do you mean?'

'Yes. Saliva and all that. From the bite mark. In case she presses assault charges. Police brutality and all that …'

The doctor pursed his lips. 'Extremely doubtful, I'd say. If the skin had been pierced, then there would probably have been DNA left in the wound. But would you need it? Did you not say that a group of bystanders witnessed the affair?'

'Yes. They did. Enjoyed it too no doubt …'

'Then you don't need DNA evidence to identify her as your biter. The testimony of the witnesses, and the bite mark itself will suffice I would think. Let's have a look at it …'

McIntosh obediently held out a hairy paw for the doctor to examine.

'Do I need a jab? Tetanus?' he asked anxiously.

'No. As I've said, the skin isn't broken, so the threat of infection is minimal. The human skin is amazingly resilient, you know. But we'll clean it thoroughly anyway. Just to be on the safe side.' The doctor had an afterthought. 'And just to be on the safe side in case she presses charges of police brutality, have you got a decent camera on your phone?'

'Eight megapixels,' said McIntosh. 'More than most ...'

'Give it here a moment, would you. I'll take a couple of snaps. Where's the icon? Ah right, got it. Turn to the light a bit, Sergeant. That's it. A bit more to the right …'

When the bite mark had been photographed and meticulously wiped, the doctor returned McIntosh's phone. He proceeded to bandage the hand, talking all the while.

'Actually,' he said, 'Bite marks are more use when questioning a suspect, rather than being produced as evidence in court. Bite mark evidence relies on the assumption that the marks we make when we bite are unique to us, and that the human skin is capable of recording those marks in a way that allows analysts to distinguish them. So far, there is no scientific research to support either assumption. In fact, the research which has been done suggests both claims are false.'

McIntosh looked concerned. 'I thought bite marks could be admitted in court as evidence.'

'They can, and often are,' replied the doctor guardedly. 'But a good defence will be able to provide an analyst to contradict the prosecution's expert testimony. These so-called experts are often diametrically opposed, for no there is scientific proof that teeth can be matched definitively to a bite into human skin.'

His frown deepened. 'It beats me why courts allow it,' he continued, 'but I know one thing, that when presented as 'scientific evidence' by a so-called expert in court, bite marks can often be taken by jurors as a gospel truth.' He pointed to the jacket pocket where McIntosh had stowed his phone. 'As I said, though the science behind bite marks has been debunked, suspects don't always know that. You could, hypothetically speaking, drag a suspect into your interrogation chamber, shove the bite mark photos in front of them, and maintain that those marks are irrefutable and damming evidence. Do that and you might be rewarded with a confession.'

'Do that and I'm more likely to be rewarded with suspension …'

'Ha! I know. I'm only kidding wit ya – isn't that what your boss says, when she puts on her cod Connemara accent? By the way,' he added, switching the subject, 'the patient we're concerned with had a pal who came here in the ambulance with her. She was chumming her friend into Edinburgh on the bus when the incident occurred. She's a bit distressed, but perhaps you'd like a word with her?'

As McIntosh turned to go, Dr Bashkir flashed a brilliant white smile and added, 'Tell your ravishing boss I was asking …'

Quin … Ravishing? What was that all about, thought McIntosh.

Not long afterwards, in the Patients Waiting Room, McIntosh identified himself and sat down opposite the young woman who had arrived at the hospital with the phone-snatching victim.

The friend was a dark-haired, pale-skinned stick of a female. Her eyes were large and dark brown, almost black, and should have been beautiful. With the dark circles under them, and the clumsy eye-shadow on the upper lids, they were like two smudged bruises.

She introduced herself as Mandy Ogilvie. She said that the victim was her best friend, Leah Duffy. They were both local, and had been travelling to Edinburgh together, via The Mall.

The front of her denim jacket had been splattered with blood from her friend. She had been brushing the spots ineffectually with wipes, and had made them look infinitely worse.

He pointed to her front. 'You should try Vanish,' he said helpfully.

'You are kidding …' she scoffed, 'it'll take more than Vanish to remove this mess! No, it'll have to be dumped, probably,' she added sadly.

He switched to business mode, and asked her to tell him what had happened on the bus.

With moistening eyes, the girl told him that Leah had been 'nattering' to her boyfriend on the phone, 'flirting like', when a 'wizened wee woman' in a puffer jacket snatched the phone 'right out of her hand', and destroyed it with some sort of 'crusher'.

'A crusher? Like a nut crusher? Something like that?'

'Yeah. Look at it,' she said, pulling a mangled item from her bag. She had an astonished expression on her face. 'You wouldn't know it had been a phone.'

McIntosh looked at it the crumpled piece of black plastic in her hand. It certainly didn't look as if it had ever been a phone.

'It's only a stupid phone, and its insured,' she downplayed unconvincingly, 'but what about Leah's hand? What insurance will she get for that? It was horrendous. She screamed the place down. It must have been agony for her, the poor darling, pure agony.'

'What colour was her jacket?' asked McIntosh.

If the girl was surprised at his non sequitur, she didn't show it. 'Black leather,' she replied. 'Her favourite one. She was going for an interview …'

'No, the snatcher. The phone snatcher. What colour was her jacket?'

'I've just told you, haven't I. It was pink. A pink puffer.'

Somehow, he knew it would be. It confirmed what the bus driver had told him. A jaundiced feeling came over him. I had her, he thought bitterly, and I let her go. His good humour left him. Suddenly he had the feeling that this incident wasn't going to end well.

'There was pandemonium when Leah got her thumb mangled. I jumped up and tried to grab the wee bastard that had done it, but Leah was in the way, wailing and yelling, not that you can blame her. I couldn't get out. Then, when the wee bastard got to the front of the bus, before she jumped off and ran into the crowd here, a big heifer in a tweed coat made like she was having a heart attack or something and blocked the aisle ...'

'You think she was faking it?'

The girl scoffed. 'It was like something out of a Hollywood movie,' she said derisively. 'A Hollywood 'B' movie.'

McIntosh couldn't remember if he'd ever seen a 'B' movie. Did they still make them? But he knew what the girl was talking about. He'd seen the same pantomime several times before on CCTV footage.

He stood and patted the girl on a bony shoulder. 'Thanks for your help, Mandy. Tell Leah I'll be doing my damnest to find the woman who injured her.'

The girl dabbed at the corners of her eyes with pencil-thin fingers. 'She didn't deserve it,' she replied morosely.

By 7:30 p.m. McIntosh had parked up at the depot of Midlothian Buses. He was surprised at how busy the place was, but then supposed it would be their busiest night of the week.

In the Security Centre he requested a look at the CCTV footage for that Number 3 bus that afternoon. He was soon seated in front of one of the square viewing monitors, watching as the afternoon's drama unfolded.

The gang were all there. Leah Duffy and her buddy Mandy Ogilvie were first up. They went straight to the long back seat at the rear of the bus. The 'man in the golf cap' and 'the large lady in the tweed coat' were next to take their places. They got on at the same stop, and unusually sat down together midway up the bus. Sallyanne Seton got on at the next stop, and sat across the aisle from them. She had dyed her hair, but was easily recognisable on the video. So why had he not realised who she was when he had confronted her in The Mall, McIntosh thought?

They were all talkative, openly friendly, and clearly familiar to each other. It was perplexing. They didn't assume their usual strategic positions, and there wasn't their usual pretence of ignoring each other's presence.

Why was this?

The only thing he could come up with was that the trio weren't intent on a phone-snatching episode that journey. They were having a day off. They were relaxed and off duty, in the mood for a pleasant shopping trip to The Mall.

Then Leah Duffy spoilt it.

She had no sooner sat down than she hauled out her phone and began yammering into it. Her pal Ogilvie was enjoying the eavesdropping. The young females began nudging each other with their elbows, both of them occasionally doubling up in laughter at the repartee.

But others were not so amused. Angry glances were thrown the girls' way from several passengers. One young man, half-flirting and half-offended, asked Duffy to keep her voice down. Duffy and Ogilvie gaped at each other in mock outrage at his unwanted intervention, Duffy told him to f-off, and then the two collapsed again in fits of laughter.

Sallyanne Seton waited till the bus was slowing for the terminal. She covered the distance between her seat and the two young females in a split second. Her hand flashed out. She tore the phone from the girl's ear, taking a clump of hair with it. Duffy held on tight, was pulled from her seat, but Seton produced an implement from her pocket and, before the girls' astonished faces, clamped it round the phone and Duffy's hand.

McIntosh was grateful there was no sound on the video. Or colour either, for the blood spurted everywhere. Mandy Ogilvie shrank back in her seat, her eyes wide with fear and surprise. She was spattered with blood. Leah Duffy, her mouth agape in a silent howl, her eyes popping from her head with pain and shock, slumped sideways to the floor. Seton turned, her face streaked with blood, and fled down the aisle to the doors. McIntosh rewound the tape. When he replayed it, he could see what appeared to be blood spatter on the front of her pink puffer jacket.

Give them their due, thought McIntosh, her accomplices swung into immediate action. From the looks on their faces, he surmised that the attack on Duffy had not been planned. It was a case of Sallyanne Seton unexpectedly losing it. However, they immediately backed her up. The 'man in the golf cap' rose from his seat and impeded those from the back of the bus getting near Seton; while the 'large lady in the tweed coat' heaved her hefty figure down the aisle after the phone snatcher, then crumpled to the floor at the doors with her signature 'heart attack'. The usual pandemonium followed.

McIntosh stopped the video, and sat back in his seat to evaluate what he had just witnessed. He felt happy. Vindicated. One thing was certain. The blood on his shirt was Leah Duffy's, transferred from Sallyanne Seton's blood-spattered pink puffer jacket during their scuffle in The Mall.

Before leaving the depot, he emailed Laura Fairgrieve, the Registration Department supervisor. He needed those names and addresses of those snatchers 'URGENTLY!!!, he wrote.

CHAPTER 14

SUNDAY MORNING

McIntosh hadn't slept well, and was a bit grumpy that morning. He'd spent a lot of the night worrying about his rugby shirt, about whether the stains on it had been blood or not. Knowing it was too late now to do anything about it.

At six forty-five he and the canine formerly known as Scottie crept down the stairs from his third-floor flat and entered the building's basement. Anya had, as usual, done the Saturday night washing and ironing. His fresh-smelling and neatly folded pile of clothes was sitting on his laundry bag, on the folding table Anya reserved for finished items.

Among them nested his rugby shirt. He unfolded it, and inspected the lower front. The largest stain had been the size of the home button on his phone. Maybe slightly less. The other two stains were smaller, the size of sesame seeds. How Shirley McCracken had spotted them he was buggered if he knew.

The light wasn't all that clever in the basement, but he thought he still saw a faint mark in the area where the larger stain had been. But he couldn't be sure, even under the torchlight on his phone. Still not convinced he had any evidence to hand in to Forensics, and too lazy to climb the stairs again to the flat, McIntosh dumped his newly-done laundry in the boot of his car.

At the back of seven o'clock that morning McIntosh and Scottie were on their way for a birl to the coast. A favourite spot they had was the rocky beach near Prestonpans, situated on the shores of the Firth of Forth. Known locally as 'The Pans', the town in medieval times was a centre for salt production. The 'pans' were the salt pans. Sea-water from the Forth was evaporated over coal fires leaving the valuable residue. The salt was transported inland along recognised 'salt roads' – hence local place-names such as Salters Road, Salters Terrace, and the Salters Inn.

On the way to the shore the wee dog stood on station, his nose out of the passenger side window. Once there McIntosh and Scottie got out of the car, stretching stiff limbs. The air was cold and moist. There were seagulls aplenty to torment the wee fella.

McIntosh could see a distant oil tanker standing off the entrance to the Firth. Crude from the North Sea oil rigs is pumped to a shore processing facility at Grangemouth, the only oil refinery in Scotland. Grangemouth is situated at the head of the River Forth. The waterway is shallow, and large shipping vessels cannot navigate it. The super-tankers dock at a marine terminal nearer the mouth of the Firth, some eighteen miles from the refinery. The refined oil is pumped downstream to them from the processing facility.

At the gate from the car park down to the dunes the wee dog pushed it open, insisting on being first. He ran on a bit then stood with his tail up, impatient.

McIntosh surprised him by breaking into a jog. He zig-zagged playfully, eluding the grasps of befuddled defenders, making for a far touchline. The wee dog bounded after him, all bunched muscles and excited yap. They ran along the shoreline. Scottie didn't like the sea much. He barked at the waves as if they were attackers, intent on bushwhacking him and his master. He liked puddles, and rock pools, and fishing for crabs. He ran on ahead. After a while McIntosh shouted. The dog braked, stood defiantly where he had stopped. McIntosh turned and jogged back towards the car park. Scottie followed; big leaps, ears airborne. Soon he forged ahead, his disappointment at the brevity of the fun soon forgotten.

By eight o'clock McIntosh was parked outside the Scottie's Day Centre. When it opened, he handed him over for the day, arranging to pick him up again later that afternoon. McIntosh had too busy a day ahead to cope with work and looking after the wee fella as well.

Munro couldn't hide her delight when McIntosh picked her up outside her digs that morning. She'd got tied up with the murder case she'd been helping the boss and Bob Scarth with, she said, though she wasn't totally out of touch. 'For instance,' she added ominously, 'I know all about your antics yesterday in The Mall.'

As she shifted her truncated but perfectly-moulded legs in the leather passenger bucket seat, she beamed at him, her eyes sparkling mischievously from under her dark eyelashes.

He knew what she was talking about. A friend had already told him that some rat had posted a video of the whole performance on Facebook.

'What antics?' he asked innocuously.

She smiled, appreciating his attempt at deceit. She had planned to drag it out, to stall as long as she could, but her anticipation of his dumb astonishment when she revealed her surprise for him dissipated. She knew he knew.

She scrolled through her phone, and held the screen out to him. It was a video. From YouTube. A well-shot YouTube video featuring a tall fair-haired man rolling on the ground with an outraged elderly woman. The only merciful thing about it, as far as he was concerned, was that they were both fully clothed. Dancing around them, its delighted yelps sounding tinny on the phone's speaker, was a small dog whose excitement was evident for all to see.

McIntosh glanced at her screen quickly, then glanced away even quicker. His previous optimism for the day ahead was going down the tubes fast.

'Never thought you'd be famous, did you Scobie,' Munro goaded pleasurably. 'Yet there you are. You and your fancy-woman in The Mall. Jesus, it's disgusting. She's old enough to be your granny. Could you not have waited till you got her back to your flat before you pounced on her bones? It's gone viral … no wonder … a social media sensation …'

McIntosh's uniform, symmetrical features, looked set in stone. 'I know,' he said unhappily.

'It's on Facebook as well,' she prattled, 'under the heading: 'Deranged Policeman Attacks Defenceless Elderly Lady.' She laughed happily. 'If it's any consolation to you, it's had 3,435 likes …'

McIntosh stared ahead. In the far distance he could see the wind turbines on rolling Moorfoot Hills, overlooking one of the gateways to his native Borders country. It looked an inviting sanctuary.

An enquiring voice beside him said, 'So how did you know? About the video.'

'Deirdre told me earlier this morning.'

Munro twisted eagerly in her seat, her flamenco red lips forming an inquisitive pout. 'Deirdre? Who's Deirdre when she's at home?'

McIntosh's tone was flippant. 'Just a friend,' he told her evasively.

It had been a sort of unwritten rule between them. Teasing apart, they never seriously delved into each other's love lives; though each supposed the other to have such a thing. Of course, both of them understood that rules like that are made to be broken.

'Really?' Munro persisted encouragingly. 'Who's the dark horse then, eh?' She punched him lightly on his arm. 'Tell me all about this Deirdre, and don't tell me her bra size.'

'Thirty-four B,' he lied, 'though of course I'm only guessing,' which was true.

He had been swithering about telling her about his date with Deirdre that evening. Now with her ribbing attitude he decided to keep the information to himself.

'She's a schoolteacher. Or rather, a Headteacher …I met her in the course of some enquiries.'

Munro rapidly mulled over this snippet of news. 'Really?' she said, throwing him a darting, inscrutable look. 'And now I take it, you're conducting a follow-up to those afore-mentioned enquiries. How commendable ... You know Scobie,' she continued, crossing one rounded knee over the other, 'there are so many fascinating layers to you …'

'Piss off, Heather,' he said with a grin, his good nature returning.

When they arrived at the office McIntosh stoically ran the gauntlet of knowing looks and sly remarks from the other officers lurking expectantly in the foyer and the kitchen. It seemed that the viral world had eventually intruded into the corridors of Eskbridge community police station. He was a media star, having his fifteen minutes worth, and was hating it.

On the way to the CID office McIntosh and Munro learned from Sergeant Dallas that Scarth had left to visit Erica Griffin, the murder victim's daughter. She had phoned to ask him to call. She'd been alerted by her father's bank that there was a safety box in the vault belonging to him. As executor to his estate, she had checked it out and found something really weird. Something he ought to see. Why he was telling them this they were at a loss to know.

'By the way,' said Dallas in an aside to McIntosh, 'an envelope came for you. From Division. Your boss has it.' The look on his face said, 'you're in for it now laddie …'

In the corridor, Munro disappeared immediately to the IT room, to do a forensic examination of the laptop belonging to Colin Muir, the murder victim. McIntosh stepped gingerly into an empty CID room.

As he sauntered to his cubicle the door to Inspector Quin's office opened. She beckoned a bejewelled finger to him, her face like granite. 'Come into my parlour, detective,' she said. She had been waiting for him, nursing her wrath to keep it warm.

Quin eyed McIntosh distastefully as he squirmed in one of the visitor's chairs in her room. On her desk beside her was a photo of him wrestling on the ground in The Mall with a terrified-looking old lady. She pointed it to him wordlessly, letting the tension build.

'What on earth were you thinking, Sergeant?' she demanded frostily. Her enunciation of 'Sergeant' sounded uncomfortably like 'Arsehole'.

When McIntosh told her, that the woman he had accosted in The Mall was in fact the phone snatcher, her tone softened to one of suspicion.

'How do you know that?' she asked.

He told her of the bus-pass elimination process he and Munro had gone through, of the video footage they had viewed. Of the witness he had spoken to at The Mall.

'So why didn't you detain her then? When you had the chance?'

'I didn't recognise her. I thought she was just some shopper hurrying for a sale or something. Then Scottie chased her. We got tangled up in the dog's lead, and both of us fell to the ground. As I was trying to extricate myself, I was set upon by a group of bolshie bystanders, who misunderstood what was happening, and came to her rescue.'

Quin looked down at the photo print-out on her desk. 'Which part of the 'Deranged Policeman Attacks Defenceless Elderly Lady' did they misunderstand?' she asked, scrutinising his face. 'Because that's what it looks like, doesn't it?' She stabbed a finger at the photo. 'It's there in high-def colour on every device imaginable. How can we explain that?'

There was no answer to that, so he didn't answer.

Quin heaved her enormous bosoms in frustration. 'You know, Scobie, unless we can come up with some definitive evidence that this … this tiny woman … is involved in phone snatching, then I don't know how we can avoid repercussions…'

He nodded his appreciation of the collective 'we'.

She took a deep breath, an unnerving sight. 'However, Superintendent Kerr has got wind of it. Hardly surprising really, given the coverage.' She lifted a brown A5 envelope from her desk and scooted it over to him. 'She's sent this through for our attention.'

He opened the flap with trepidation. Inside was a still of his YouTube appearance. On the back, scrawled in black fountain pen, were the words 'SEE ME', circled with an emphatic swirl made by a red permanent marker.

McIntosh showed his boss the message.

'I've seen it,' she said gruffly.

He stuffed it back in the envelope.

'Give it a while before you head over to Division,' she suggested, 'to get your story straight. And don't try to flannel her when you see her. She's a piranha.'

McIntosh stood to go. He told Quin that he was confident that the CCTV from the buses and the footage on social media would identify the woman in The Mall as the primary phone snatcher, though he and Munro both suspected there was a gang of them, working a well-rehearsed routine.

Her left eyebrow shot up. Quin, queen of the quizzical look. 'Gang?' she queried. 'What gang?'

The woman in The Mall did the dirty deed on the bus, he explained, then her escape was subsequently facilitated by two accomplices. He sat down again, and opened the folder he had brought in with him. He slipped out the screen-shots he'd printed, captured from the video.

'The snatcher, the man in the golf cap, and the fat lady in tweed,' he explained as he dealt the images out. 'I'm just waiting for word from Midlothian buses to supply the contact details of the card holders,' he added, 'which will finally identify them.'

He paused for effect.

'Though of course there is the bite mark.'

'What bite mark?'

McIntosh showed her his wounded and painful hand, which he had kept purposely uncovered. The teeth impressions were red and puffed, but still remarkably vivid. She examined his angry-looking wound with interest.

'My, my. What big teeth you've got, Grandmother dear …' she said, impressed with the injury.

McIntosh responded in kind. 'And all the better to identify her with. Dr Bashkir took photos, but says the bite marks would have limited value in court in identifying her as the person I tussled with, after the phone-snatching incident.'

'You won't need teeth marks in court,' Quin dismissed impatiently. 'The whole effin world knows that you 'tussled' with her … But you're right. It's doubtful if the PF would even try to present bite marks as evidence nowadays. There have been too many wrongful convictions for him to be comfortable with the idea. But you haven't suffered in vain. The suspect doesn't know that. It's something we can brow-beat her with.'

'That's what the doctor said.' He paused, savouring what was to come next. 'He also sent his regards. I think you've got an admirer there, boss …'

Quin's baby-sized mouth stretched in a grin. It was the first time she had smiled that morning. 'Ha!' she laughed, disappointing him, for he hoped she would be somewhat embarrassed. 'He's a persistent devil, that one …'

McIntosh would have liked more details; knew it wasn't worth pursuing.

Quin pushed herself straight in her chair. Large and in charge. 'Listen,' she said, 'spruce yourself up and get round to Division pronto, and tell her Ladyship all this. Emphasise the CCTV evidence. And don't try and get smart with her again like you did at the Operation Drawstring briefing ...'

He was stunned. Had Munro clyped? Probably not. He had hoped that attention-seeking blunder hadn't reached his boss's fleshy ears, but remained stoical at the knowledge that it had.

Quin watched with interest as his face registered his dismay at her disclosure.

'Didn't think I knew about that one, eh Scobie?' she asked with amusement. 'Now skedaddle …'

An hour later, a scrubbed up and twiffed McIntosh sat awkwardly in Superintendent B-B B Kerr's third floor corner office.

He had passed a couple of uniforms on the way in to the building. They flashed knowing smiles at him, and he gave them a big neutral grin in return. The desk sergeant was a hard-looking veteran with thinning brown hair. This man was subjected to a fair bit of suspicion when he first joined the Division, McIntosh knew; being suspected of reporting office gossip to the high heid-yins. McIntosh had later found him to be a fair and efficient organiser of the troops. He told the man he was there to see Superintendent Kerr.

'Just to put you in the picture, Mac,' the sergeant said confidentially, 'we all know about the YouTube and Facebook posts.' He shook his head sorrowfully. 'Could have happened to any of us. So, B-B B has got to hear of it, eh? A word of advice. Just suck it up. Water off a duck's back. Don't try to argue with her. She can't stand being crossed.'

'Cheers.'

The sergeant pointed to the stairway. 'Third floor, second door on the left. Don't take the lift, reserved for high heid-yins.'

McIntosh knocked on Superintendent B-B B Kerr's office door, waited a couple of seconds for her 'It's open' response, and walked in. It was a generic, senior police officer's enclave, probably similar to ones all over the country. Only the photographs and the names on the diplomas differed.

Kerr was seated at her desk and looked up as he entered. As expected, she was in full uniform. She signalled for him to be seated on the club chair opposite her desk, then sat down herself. McIntosh realised she had already been standing when he entered the room.

He was nervous of the interview, for it could be a career-ending one if it went badly; but also strangely optimistic, because the blood smear match, he hoped, would absolve him of a multitude of sins.

Kerr eyed him with evident disfavour then shoved a photo across her desk toward him. It was the same still Quin had shown him, the screen shot from the infamous YouTube video.

'What the fuck were you thinking, Sergeant,' she demanded, her voice impartial, dangerously restrained.

McIntosh shifted his position in the inquisition chair across the desk from her. It squeaked. All inquisition chairs squeak. He didn't answer immediately. He'd rehearsed his answers in the fifteen or so minutes it took to drive from his office to Division HQ. Now his glib script had deserted him, fled irretrievably to the recesses of his brain. He didn't know if that was a good thing or a bad thing, only that it left him bereft. Out of ammunition.

Kerr searched for contrition in his eyes. Disconcertingly, she found none. He had an open-eyed guileless look she associated with retarded children, career criminals, and politicians. It wasn't going to be easy to get into this one's mind, she thought. A challenge. He's used to using his charm to disguise his deficiencies, she assessed. But he'll find he's wasting his time here.

'Well?' she pursued impatiently.

'It just happened,' he murmured lamely.

'It just happened …' she mimicked sarcastically, in her trademark Gallowgate patois. 'Do you know that, because of this – this cretinous behaviour of yours – the police force is now being laughed at by everyone in this county? And for all I know, everyone in the whole fucken country? Do you have any conception of the damage you have inflicted on the Scottish police service? Do you?'

McIntosh noticed absently that the tips of her ears were flushed with anger. He also noticed that she had a large-faced, masculine-looking watch on her right wrist. He wasn't surprised; after all, she was a Kerr. The rest of her however, was all woman. She had a physical voluptuousness that even a police uniform could not hide. The dimples at the side of her mouth suggested that, while her default setting was necessarily a serious, no-nonsense, professional one, she found time to smile a lot.

She pointed a chunky finger at the photo lying in front of him like an accusation.

'Detective Sergeant McIntosh,' she said, 'did you give anyone permission to post this video on YouTube and Facebook. It's a daft question but one I have to ask.'

'No.'

'Was that a "No, ma'am?"'

'Yes, ma'am. It was "No, ma'am,"'

She mused on what Quin had said, that the man was a jokester, an attention-seeker, but an efficient officer for all that. Maybe that assessment needed revising. She tightened her lips like a drawstring.

'Do you know who posted this … this obscenity?'

'There were a lot of people around, ma'am. During the, eh, incident, and afterwards. I was aware of several camera flashes during the, eh, duration. People had their phones out. Any one of them could have done it …' he waved an arm at the incriminating photo between them. 'The rest, as they say, is history …'

For the first time since he came into the room, B-B B Kerr smiled. The glint in her eyes was like the shimmer given off a pair of handcuffs in an interrogation room.

'Ah yes, history. A bit like your police career Detective … Was this woman drunk or behaving in a disorderly fashion?'

'No ma'am.'

'Was she carrying an offensive weapon or had given you the impression she was carrying an offensive weapon?'

'No ma'am.'

'Had you reason to believe she was on drugs or was in the possession of illicit substances?

'No ma'am.'

'Is that her dog in the photo?'

'No, he's mine. He's a former police sniffer dog. He detected something on her and gave chase. I followed.'

'What kind of a sniffer dog?'

'He specialised in counterfeit perfumes.'

'Did you smell perfume off this woman when you were wrestling in public with her?'

'No ma'am. But Scottie did. His nose can detect a portfolio of forty-odd different bouquets, all fake.'

'Really? And so you pounced on this defenceless wee woman, in a shopping mall full of home-movie enthusiasts, because she was wearing some dodgy perfume she had probably purchased in good faith at some street market?'

'No ma'am,' McIntosh declared simply. 'Our entanglement was purely accidental. However, had I known then what I now know, I would certainly have detained her.'

'And what do you know now?'

'That she's the phone snatcher.'

Kerr held up a warning hand, at a loss for words. Her gallus face was wreathed in momentary confusion. 'And just how did you arrive at that startling conclusion, Detective?' she asked him dubiously.

He told her about the CCTV footage from the previous phone-snatching incidents. He told her about the statement given by the victim's pal identifying the woman as the snatcher. He told her how he and Munro had trawled through the bus pass activations, and had identified all those concerned in the phone-snatching episodes. He was going to tell her about the possible blood spatter on his shirt when the phone in his inside pocket pinged.

He cringed a weak smile in her direction, black affronted, as he retrieved the device to switch it to mute. He glanced at the notification. It was an email from Laura Fairgrieve, the Registration Department supervisor at the bus company. It was a reply to his formal request for the contact details of his suspected phone snatchers. The delight on his face warned Kerr to be on the defensive.

'I think you need to see this as well, ma'am,' he said, 'it's from the bus company ...'

Kerr was gobsmacked at the audacity of the man, but peevishly waved a wrist in acquiescence. It was just one more nail in his career coffin.

McIntosh opened the email, and saved the images attached to it in his drive. He opened his Gallery and held the screen out to her. 'It's the ID photos, and the names and addresses, of elderly bus-pass holders who have been present at each phone-snatching incident.'

McIntosh came round to her side of the desk, careful to maintain a professional distance from her. He swiped though the images he had just received.

1. Robert Beatson, aged sixty-four.
2. Gareth Howell, aged sixty-two.
3. Sallyanne Seton, aged sixty-seven.

4. Rhoda Duffy, aged eighty-three.
5. Valerie Carmichael, aged sixty-one.
6. Mitchell Garvie, also aged sixty-one.

Kerr sniffed. 'Well, we can rule out the men, can't we?' she said lightly. 'Howell, Beatson, and Garvie …'

McIntosh stabbed a bony finger at the screen. 'That one, Sallyanne Seton, aged sixty-seven, is the snatcher. We have her on several CCTV videos from the buses. There's no doubt she's the one we're after.'

'Hang on,' said Kerr, peering closely, 'she looks like the woman you accosted in the Mall.'

'She is,' he affirmed. He decided to impress her with the descriptive phrase he had come across. 'I like to think of her as a shape-shifter …'

Kerr frowned deeply. 'A what?'

'You know, like those ghosts the Navajo believe in …'

'No, I don't know. I know very little about the Navajo. It's not something they tell you about at the Police College …'

Every instinct screamed at McIntosh to clam up, to shut his gub. He couldn't believe it when he heard himself telling her that a shape-shifter could be a wolf, running alongside your car, going at sixty miles an hour; or they could be a coyote stalking you, creeping round about you, and when you go to shoot it, they turn into a bird and fly away …

Kerr stared at him, mouth agape. Experience and intuition told her that this man was insane. Was she in physical danger? Should she summon assistance?

'When?' she ventured cautiously.

McIntosh blinked uncertainly. 'Well, the Navajo have always believed it, I suppose. Ever since they became a Nation …'

Kerr looked at him warily, the way mothers with young children would monitor a drunk approaching them in the swing park. She enunciated each word slowly and clearly. Like a teacher to a remedial class.

'When – does – she – change – shape?'

McIntosh blinked and backtracked swiftly. 'Well, I don't know that she actually changes shape, as such … It's just a phrase I had in my head, ma'am. She changes her jacket, and has dyed her hair now, that's why I didn't recognise her.'

'Most women change their jackets occasionally,' Kerr pointed out reasonably, 'and most women, at some point in their lives, change their hair colour. Many of us would also like to change our shapes, and indeed some women spend a lot of money attempting just that ... but …' she held up a warning hand, 'we are not going to go there. She's only an elderly woman, Sergeant. She can't run at sixty miles an hour. Fuck me, some of the cars I've had couldn't go at sixty miles an hour! She's not some supernatural being. She's a common criminal, and she needs to be caught.'

McIntosh relaxed, back on more familiar ground. 'We think she's not alone. Heather and I, that's my colleague DC Munro, think there are three of them, working as a team.'

Kerr looked bamboozled. 'A phone snatching conspiracy? Is that what you're saying? Gad! I've heard everything now …'

'It's more than a gut feeling,' McIntosh insisted. 'The same faces appear in each incident.' He brought up each photo in turn. 'Robert Beatson, Sallyanne Seton, and Valerie Carmichael. They're there every time. Playing an active part in the snatching incidents. They're connected somehow; we just don't know the why or the how.'

Kerr sat back abruptly in her chair.

She closed her eyes. Her features smoothed out, as if years were being erased.

After a long pause, a rapturous smile illuminated her pale-skinned face.

McIntosh gazed at her in apprehension as she slowly inflated her lungs, straining the threads of her silver buttons alarmingly.

She began to sing.

As McIntosh gawped impotently, the Superintendent trilled in a light, surprisingly-tuneful voice, "'There was Mary Seton, Mary Beaton, Mary Carmichael, and me ...'"

The tune had a Scottish feel to it. Maybe traditional. He didn't know any traditional Scottish singers. When she had finished, he guessed madly: 'K T Tunstall?'

'Not even close, Sergeant,' she beamed good-naturedly. Her face was a picture of discovery, as if she had arrived at a previously-unreachable truth.

She stabbed a finger at his phone. 'I can tell just by looking at those names,' she said eagerly, 'that there are actually four of them in it. Seton, Beaton, Carmichael, and a-n-other …'

McIntosh looked dubious. 'We don't have a Beaton, ma'am,' he pointed out nervously.

'Well, if you substitute Beatson you have,' she argued.

Her argument had an arguability about it which couldn't be denied. He played along. Suddenly all notions of rank or professional status seemed ridiculously superfluous. A daft irrelevancy.

'Okay. So we have a Seton, a Beatson, and a Carmichael …' he slavered familiarly, 'but who's the "me"?'

'It was Mary Hamilton,' she replied succinctly. 'They were all handmaids to Mary Queen of Scots. But that's not the point. The point is there are four of them. Your colleague Munro is right. Female intuition always is. They're working in conjunction.'

'You're saying we're looking for a female called Mary, or one called Hamilton?'

'Doesn't need to be a female,' Kerr hedged good-naturedly. 'Nor does it need to be a Mary or a Hamilton,' she added. 'I just know there are four of them in it, that's all.'

'So then, who is the fourth one, ma'am?' he asked teasingly.

'Buggered if I know,' said the Superintendent. She rose briskly from her chair, signalling the end of the meeting. Her height didn't change much. 'But you're going to find out for me, aren't you, Sergeant?' she smiled.

McIntosh, more relieved than he could have wished for, also stood. He held out a bony-fingered hand. He'd come expecting a grilling, a right bollocking. It had turned out better than he could ever have hoped.

After surprising herself by accepting McIntosh's offer of a handshake, Kerr escorted him to the door. The top of her head hardly reached his shoulders. He felt the soft pressure of a breast as she passed him to open the door.

She paused as she caught a faint whiff of his after-shave. She stood perfectly still. Then her ovoidal face tilted slowly upwards to scrutinize his sharp-featured phizog.

'We've met before, haven't we, Detective Sergeant McIntosh?' she said softly but distinctly. Her face was unreadable.

Here it comes, he thought. He had been wondering when she'd bring up that embarrassing faux pas at the Divisional briefing – when he'd tried to be funny in front of a roomful of colleagues.

He nodded contritely. 'Yes, ma'am. At the Operation Drawstring briefing.'

She shook her head slowly, her look inviting further speculation.

A couple of seconds went by before McIntosh twigged. His brain creaked and rattled in uncontrolled panic. The treatment-room! Jesus, he thought, she knows I'm the one who sneaked in and tweaked her boobs while she lay on the treatment table!

She was in her forties and currently unmarried, he knew. And the mess-room scuttlebutt had it she was partial to the company of younger men. It gave him no solace. His blood ran cold, his heart-rate escalated. 'Beam me up Scottie,' he prayed, before composing himself for the coup de grace.

Kerr avidly searched McIntosh's peepers for signs of guilt, of reproach, of regret. She found none. What she found was a kind of contented martyrdom, combined with a sense of irredeemable defiance.

Either that or he was shitting himself.

It pleased her. She creased her dimples, amusement crinkling the sides of her violet eyes. He'd enjoyed that wee impropriety in the treatment room as much as she had, she realised.

She lowered her voice. 'Perhaps we can work together on this one, Sergeant,' she suggested seductively. 'Closely together …'

McIntosh licked dry lips. The sound of his voice, when it came out, wasn't one that he recognised. 'Certainly, Ma'am,' he croaked in response. 'It'd be pleasure.'

Yes, she thought. I'll make sure it is.

CHAPTER 15

SUNDAY AFTERNOON

When Scarth retired from the Edinburgh City police, he and his wife sold the Craigentinny bungalow where they'd brought up two daughters, and decamped to the small village of Kilspindie on the East Lothian coast. The renowned 'Golf Coast'.

It suited both of them. His wife was a keen watercolourist. The often-wild seascapes on her doorstep gave her endless vistas to try and capture. Scarth had played 'parkland' golf at a club in Edinburgh for more than twenty-five years, and wanted a taste of 'links' golf before he hung up his clubs for good. The golf club at Kilspindie had a course he enjoyed. It was on the short side: perfect for beginners, retirees, and golfers past their prime. It suited Scarth fine. He was out at first light that morning. The first three holes meandered along the coastline. A hundred yards offshore, new-born seals lay on a sandbank. Brilliant white, they lay against their mothers' glossy dark skins in the weak spring sunshine. Scarth spent a pleasurable couple of hours before his nagging thoughts got the better of him, and he found he couldn't concentrate on his game. At least, that was what he blamed for a couple of missed birdie chances.

He'd had an espresso in the clubhouse before phoning Andrea Fyffe's mobile on the pretext of returning her father's book. She said she was at home, at Broomieknowe. It took him slightly by surprise.

'Is that the Broomieknowe your whaling ancestor bought?'

'Of course. It's been in the family now for over a hundred years … Why don't you come over, and meet the author?'

Broomieknowe sat on the southern outskirts of Eskbridge. When it was built, it was a good three miles from the town, but Eskbridge had expanded, creeping stealthily, gobbling up the surrounding countryside. Now a suburban carriageway passed busily not a hundred yards from the rear of the house.

Scarth turned off the carriageway, and passed through an open pillared entranceway. He slowed as he met a reddish-coloured gravel drive. It was flanged on both sides by cherry blossom trees. He had noticed in his own village how the blossoms had suddenly burst forth, as if from nowhere. For the previous five or six weeks, they had showered the neighbourhood with tiny coloured petals, like multi-coloured snowflakes.

Broomieknowe seemed to be two houses joined as one. As he approached along the short, curved drive, a rectangular two-story grey-slated sandstone building loomed ahead of him. Was this the main house? It had four south-facing windows on the upper floor, suggesting at least three bedrooms.

Adjoining it was a narrower, tower-shaped building. Four small upper-story windows were visible from the drive, suggesting the building had three storeys. An extension of some sort?

A pillared portico, an adjunct between the two buildings, faced the drive like an afterthought. The impression was of two separate buildings placed randomly together, but somehow the juxtaposition worked.

He parked his Jazz beside a pearl-coloured Audi two-seater and a white Mini, and was crunching self-consciously across the gravel towards the doorway when the door opened. A tight-curled middle-aged woman dressed in a blue hospital uniform raised a pair of enquiring eyebrows. She didn't wear a name tag. He told her who he was, and that he had been asked to call by the daughter of the house. The woman pointed to the tower-shaped building fifty yards away.

'If you mean Mrs McGill, her and her husband live in the Old Tower there …'

Scarth was about to question her further when a voice rang out from the far end of the building. 'I'm here,' Andrea Fyffe called. With a resentful glance, the woman in the uniform retreated, and the door closed silently.

Andrea Fyffe waved, and came across the gravel to meet him. She was dressed for the country. Checked shirt, olive sleeveless jacket. A long dark-coloured skirt and black high-laced commando-style boots. She held a thin-wristed hand up to shield her eyes from the low southerly sun.

Scarth waved a hand towards the house. 'Well, as family piles go, Andrea, it's certainly an impressive one …' He pointed downward. 'How's the knee?

She lifted her right leg and flexed it. He was disappointed she didn't show him the scar. Then she put her foot down and slowly, tantalisingly, drew up her skirt over her knee. Innocent as it was, the gesture struck Scarth as mildly erotic. The scar on the knee looked better than he remembered it. The general shape of her leg looked better too.

Was she flirting with him? He was buggered if he knew. Should he respond? Scarth hadn't flirted for thirty years. He'd forgotten the signals. The protocol. She broke the spell, dropping her skirt and stepping slightly to the side.

'It's getting there ...' she said with that deep husky voice. 'I'm even doing light jogging now …'

Something blasphemous in him wished he was getting there too.

'How's the investigation going?' she asked lightly.

He hesitated. Many years of withholding police information from the public was a habit that was hard to break.

She caught his look. 'Don't tell me you're not able to divulge anything. Isn't that what the police say?'

'Well, I'm not the police, Andrea …'

'No suspects yet?' she enquired.

'No, not really.'

'No clues, promising leads?'

'A few,' he relented uncomfortably. 'Here and there …'

'But still mainly hypotheses and circumstantials?' she teased.

'Yes, and no …' he hedged.

'Ha!' she laughed derisively, enjoying his discomfort. He cracked a smile, and laughed with her. One nil to the lady with the gammy leg, he thought.

She slowly composed her face. 'You don't need to tell me. I don't really want to know. It would be too painful to hear. By the way, I phoned Erica last night. That poor woman. I just had to. She's holding it together for the most part. At least, for now.'

Scarth nodded. 'Do you know her well?'

'No, I can't say that I do,' she replied. 'We've met a few times, of course. Colin used to inveigle her into accompanying him to dos when I was unavailable. She's a lovely girl. I feel incredible sorry for her. It's just the ghastliest thing to have happened …'

Scarth had no wish to encourage her line of conversation. He looked back towards the house. The portico had a flowery flange he now noticed. Wisteria?

Small talk seemed a safer avenue. He pointed to the low-slung two-seater.

'Nice jeep …' he said, though it certainly wouldn't have been his choice of transport.

She laughed. 'It's only a standard TT, nothing fancy. It's my husband's. Hence the AM MSP registration plates. Mine's the wee Mini run-around; handy for parking in the nooks and crannies other cars can't access.'

Scarth smiled at the ridiculousness of it. Anthony McGill, the well-known Member of the Scottish Parliament, who needed daily reminding, via his personalised plates, of his ephemeral status. He remembered the time his father, on being shown a photo of a Porsche Carrera that one of his pals had bought for twenty-eight thousand pounds, commenting: 'Jings! You'd think they'd give you four doors for that kind of money …'

Andrea Fyffe interrupted his thoughts. 'Tony's away a lot,' she said. 'So I sometimes use his car, and his petrol. He can claim the expenses, of course. That's why I was free to accompany Colin the other night. Tony is at some daft conference in Texel. I'd never heard of it. Had to Google it.'

Scarth had. He knew it was pronounced Tessel. 'It used to be the haunt of picaroons and privateers,' he said. 'John Paul Jones skulked there a while too …'

'Oh?' she sounded profoundly uninterested. 'Who's John Paul Jones?'

'A Scot who founded the United States Navy. What's the conference about?'

'It's about, and I quote 'The Sustainability of North Sea Fisheries.'

Scarth snorted. 'I'd have thought that by now politicians might have realised that the North Sea fisheries and 'sustainability' don't belong in the same sentence.'

'A sceptic, eh. Yes, I'm sure there are many who'd agree with you, Bob. We have a house rule here – no politics to be discussed in the house. It was my idea, of course.'

'How long have you lived here?' he asked.

'Since I've been a bairn.'

She turned, and they walked away from the front of the houses. 'As you'll know from Faither's booklet, Sir Alexander Fyffe bought this place in 1906. It was a large estate then, built for the wealthy. But time and expediency has whittled that away to just the house and the grounds, I'm afraid ...'

The book! He'd forgotten all about the book. It was the reason he was there, after all, wasn't it? He excused himself and retrieved the book from the passenger seat of his car. Thirty seconds later he stood pleasurably again at her side. As he handed the booklet over, he realised he'd forgotten how tall she was. And better looking in the natural light than in her fluorescent-lit office. She was wearing jewellery which was unashamedly costume. It was colourful, frivolous. It gave her a carefree, girlish look. He wondered if she was always this airy when her husband was away.

'I enjoyed reading it,' he said. 'It reads like one of those Boy's Own books I loved as a kid.'

'Yes,' she agreed. 'It was self-published. Vanity publishing, they used to call it ...'

And still do, thought Scarth unkindly.

'... but it was very well received for all that. He regarded it as his life-time's achievement. And rightly so. I've read it many times, of course. Compulsory reading, you might say, being the daughter of the author. Speaking of which ...I'm sorry, but I may have brought you here on false pretences. I'm afraid that Faither hasn't managed to get up and about today. He has dementia, poor dear, and some days are just too overwhelming for him ...'

Scarth didn't know what to say, so said nothing.

'We have a full-time help here. Gloria,' she continued, leading him towards the tower. 'You met her at the door. She's a qualified nurse, and has her own apartment in the main house. My mother is still alive, hale and hearty, but she's off on a botanical cruise to the Flannan Isles at the moment. Gloria is a treasure but she can be stroppy at times I'm afraid ...'

'It's difficult to get the right kind of help nowadays, I suppose ...'

Andrea Fyfe's eyes darkened with anger. She frowned, annoyed. 'Bob, that is unworthy of you …'

Scarth immediately held his hands up. 'Apologies, Andrea. It was indeed uncalled-for.'

She paused, letting him stew, before accepting his contrition. He felt the heat of her umbrage thankfully dissipate. He was glad, for he genuinely didn't want to cause her offence.

'Yes well,' she began again, 'Gloria generally copes well, but as I mentioned to you the other day, she had to call me out on Wednesday night when my father had a bad turn and became uncontrollable … a state which is becoming more frequent, unfortunately.'

He bit back the urge to ask more about that evening. And the inclination to quiz her a bit more about the live-in nurse. They strolled for a while in silence. They arrived below the tower. She lifted a slender arm and indicated the edifice.

'Tony and I live here. The inside's been totally modernised, of course. Three bedrooms and what-have-you …Would you like the tour?'

Scarth looked at his watch and declined politely. He shrugged helplessly.

'No time, I'm afraid. Maybe some other time?'

He looked more closely at the solidly-built structure. In the bright spring sunlight, it had looked newer than the house. Now he took in the wide wooden double-doorway on the ground floor and the tell-tale small windows keeking out from above.

'Was it a fortified house at some point?' he asked.

She nodded. Her jewellery remained static. 'Yes. We think it was a bastle house, from the French "bastille".'

She pointed to one of the small windows. 'That's where our bedroom is. I keep a bow and a quiver full of arrows below that window, ready to fend off all those border reivers who might come and plague us.'

She laughed at the daftness of it all. Scarth laughed too.

'I dare say someone did just that … in days of yore,' he said.

'Nae doot. That part …' she continued, pointing to the wooden doors set in the middle of the building, 'used to be the stable, for the horses and a milch cow or two. Originally there was no internal access to the apartments above. Access was by an outside wooden ladder or staircase, which could easily be withdrawn inside if the house was attacked. My grandfather used it as a garage for his Austin 7, a car which he was inordinately proud of. Family tradition has it that in the winter-time, when heavy frosts were about, Grandpa used to cover the car's engine with a horse blanket. In the mornings he'd forget of course, and after a couple of turns with the starting handle, when the engine kicked into life, the fan shredded the blanket to pieces …Ha! It happened regularly; I'm told.'

Scarth smiled with her. So, the rectangular building, which he had thought was the original dwelling, had come later. As if reading his thoughts, she said, 'The main house is probably only early nineteenth century.'

She indicated a large gap in a high hedge which ran away from the tower house.

'Let's go through here.' The gap was framed by a tarnished, ten foot high, whale's jawbone. 'One of the main sources of income from the Arctic whalers was the sale of jawbones to the public,' she told him as they approached the arch. 'They served as gates, porches, and decorative garden entrances. Local authorities were fond of erecting them as entrances to public walkways. Did you know that the jawbones of Edinburgh's famous Jawbone Walk came originally from Shetland?'

He didn't. Though he had been told, by an old ex-South Georgia whaler, that jawbones from large whales had been utilised in the past in Lerwick as 'A' frames to unload cargoes from flit-boats.

She motioned him to follow her through the entranceway. She still a bit of a hirple, he noticed, and wondered how long her limp would be with her.

They came out on a paved path which bordered a long narrow lawn. It was probably the original rig which was an integral part of medieval houses, Scarth thought. The housekeeper's personal market garden, for growing soft fruit and vegetables. She pointed to the bottom of the lawn, to an area fenced in with black enamel railings.

'Come and have a look down there,' she said.

Trees bordered the manicured grass all the way down the right-hand side of the lawn. As they approached the fenced-off area he could see a small temple-like structure off in the woods. A grotto of some kind. Or was it a gazebo? The Victorians liked their gazebos. They walked for a short distance over grass till they arrived at the end of the lawn.

'That is what I wanted you to see,' she said.

It was a family cemetery.

Scarth was intrigued. She saw the look on his face and again second-guessed him.

'There's no specific restraint under Scots law on a family setting aside a portion of their ground as a family burial plot,' she informed him. 'And as you can see, there's plenty of room for the rest of us …'

She pointed out the headstones of her great-grandfather, great-grandmother, grandfather, and grandmother. There was another, smaller headstone. It was the grave of her grandfather's twin sisters, she explained, who had died in childbirth. They were called Mary and Margaret. All the gravestones had fresh flowers sitting in stone vases in front of them. There were also several small crosses, family pets, judging by the names, and a smaller memorial stone, set aside from the others. Scarth went over and bent to read the names and the dedication:

'In memory of Agnes Napajok, (aged about 16)
and Betty Napajok, (aged about 14)
from Hudson Bay, British Canada.
Innocent victims of the measles epidemic of 1911.
Now with their Maker.'

'Ah,' he said. He knew who they were.

'Sir Alex had the stone erected as a remembrance for the two Inuit girls he had brought over from Canada. Agnes and Betty weren't their birth names of course. Poor Agnes and Betty, they had no natural defences against Western diseases.'

'Yes, I read about it in your father's book. A tragic episode …' he pointed to her great-grandmother's headstone, 'It seems fitting somehow, that they were buried near their mentor.'

She looked puzzled. 'No, no: they're not actually buried here,' she contradicted gently. 'Family tradition has it that Sir Alex repatriated their remains to their home settlement … just before the First World War broke out. It was his last whaling voyage.'

'Ah right,' replied Scarth, retreating swiftly. 'It's just that your father's book didn't specifically say what happened to them.'

'Didn't' it?' She turned away from the cemetery, to lead him back across the lawn. 'Well, Faither would certainly have been able to clarify the point for us at one time, bless him, but any knowledge he once had is now totally unrecoverable … He doesn't even recognise my mother or me sometimes …'

It was the third time she'd used 'Faither'. It sounded so stand-offish. Impersonal almost. She walked silently for a moment or two. From somewhere nearby he could hear the electronic chimes of an ice cream van. A modern-day Pied Piper, touring the housing estates. It was a testament to how much Eskbridge had expanded into the country.

'I've heard it said,' she intoned sadly, 'that having a friend with dementia is like waving to someone who is sailing away on a boat. They get more and more distant as the boat sails away, but you keep on waving, just in case they're waving too ...'

They reached the paved path, and she stopped.

'Your question about where the girls are buried was perfectly valid,' she said. 'When I was a young tomboy, running wild around here, I was fascinated that two Eskimos, as I thought of them, had come from the frozen wastes of Canada to be taught here at Broomieknowe. After my great-grandmother died, the school was closed, of course. My great-grandfather's whaling collection was housed in what used to be the schoolroom.'

She pointed to a pair of French windows on the rear of the house as they looked at it. 'That's where the schoolroom was. It was the largest room in the house. When my grandfather died, the whaling stuff was moved to my father's office at FyffeRobertson. Clients were enthralled by it, apparently, though I can't think why. My parents transformed the schoolroom into a beautiful lounge with a study off it. They were healthy then to enjoy it ....'

They skirted well-tended daffodil beds, some of the flowers seemed to be struggling. Spring hadn't fully sprung in Midlothian yet.

'Yes, when I thought of those Inuit girls,' she continued, 'I was sad that they had died here. I didn't know anything about them, of course, but I used to spend ages staring at their beautiful caribou parkas in their air-tight cabinets, just longing to try them on.' She laughed unexpectedly at the frivolousness of it all.

'My great-grandfather was devastated at the death of his young wife,' she said, her face turning sombre. 'He never re-married you know. I think that he lost all his energy at that time. Family tradition has it that he suffered greatly from depression for a couple of years. The 'blue fog' he termed it. By the time he had fully recovered a reason to go on living, the First World War had broken out, and the North Atlantic was a no-go area for British shipping. It was the end of his career as a whaling captain. Whether he missed winters in Arctic Canada I don't know, but I'm sure he missed the people, for he returned to Canada many times after the War.'

After a respectful few paces, Scarth said, 'We don't tend to think of measles as a serious threat nowadays. Do we?'

'No. We don't,' she replied, as they passed under the jawbone arch. 'But measles was a killer in those days. It still is in some parts of the world. It must have been a dreadful time for everyone here. Admittedly, the epidemic wasn't as deadly as the Spanish Flu pandemic of 1918/1919. I doubt very much if we'll see a pandemic anything like as deadly as that in this country again.'

They stepped out onto the gravelled area in front of the house.

'However, it's true to say that the measles certainly killed thousands of victims that year in the UK: and not just in the cities, it's traditional breeding ground. The 1911 outbreak in Edinburgh spread quickly out to Midlothian, apparently. There was no NHS then, of course. Local doctors, nurses, and of course funeral directors, were overwhelmed.'

'Did the council not try to intervene, to help?' Scarth asked.

'The local authorities did apparently urge people to act sensibly, to avoid socialising and gathering in crowds. They found that if people are given a choice of accepting social restrictions, for the greater good, or of carrying on normally with their lives and recreations, they almost always act selfishly. The outbreak could have been easily contained if folk had acted responsibly. It was not to be, however. I hope that if we ever have a raging epidemic like that in this country again, we'll have learned from the past, and people will take sensible personal precautions to limit the spread of disease. But I doubt if they will ...'

'There's nowt as strange as folk …'

'My great-grandmother nursed the girls, as best she could, and sadly, paid the ultimate price for it. She too became infected and died. She was just thirty-four. Her name was Andrea, and I'm named after her …' she finished proudly.

Scarth, his mood somewhat deflated, declined the invitation to stay for afternoon tea. He said his goodbyes at his car, and trundled it slowly down the driveway to the asphalt carriageway. He was glad he had visited Andrea Fyffe. She was an exhilarating person to be with. But the grave markers had somehow put a dampener on his feelings, and in the end, he was glad to leave Broomieknowe and its rather solemn atmosphere.

Lizzie caught him just as he was leaving Eskbridge for home.

'Are you free to talk?' she asked. The usual police precautionary greeting. Meaning: 'Are there civilians within earshot?' Sometimes his colleagues forgot he was a civilian.

'Sure, Lizzie. I'm on the hands-free. Just heading home from Eskbridge.'

'Have you got time to turn around and come into the station? I need to show you what I've found out in this diary.'

'Something juicy?' he joshed lightly.

'Something ghastly, Bob. I'm not kidding. It's horrendous,' she stated with restrained indignation. 'I've been up half the night transcribing Agnes Napajok's diary, and I have to tell you Bob, it was grim reading.'

He hadn't thought the diary would be of much interest. What startling revelations could a teenage girl come up with? A Victorian teenage girl.

'Really?' he queried. 'How so?'

'That man, Captain Alexander Fyffe, was a monster. A sexual predator of the worst type, and, I certainly believe, a cold-hearted murderer ...'

She had his attention. Scarth was dumbstruck. What was she on about? It took all his concentration to stay on the road.

'Are you still there?' she asked anxiously.

'Looking for a place to turn,' he said without enthusiasm. 'I'll see you in fifteen, Lizzie ...'

The police archives were of course open every day, and Lizzie and Scarth found a sheltered reading desk well away from the doorway traffic. With the diary and her transcript lying on the table between them, she began by giving him an introductory run-down.

'Agnes, then aged fifteen, arrived at Broomieknowe in October 1909. The following year her sister Betty, aged a year younger, joined her. The girls had separate attic bedrooms. A pantry-maid was also accommodated up there under the eaves. The rest of the domestic staff came in every day.'

She flipped open her transcript in front of her. 'Broomieknowe at that time was run as a private school. It had a number of children, mostly females, who attended day classes. The school was what you call here a 'crammer', its function was to prepare students for their public-school entrance exams. The Fyffe's would probably charge handsome fees for their services. Mrs Fyffe was in charge of the schooling. When she was not teaching the day pupils, she gave religious instruction to her two boarders, Agnes and Betty. In the diary Agnes refers to Mrs Fyffe as 'My Lady', and to Alexander Fyffe as 'The Master' ...'

She paused, a tortured look on her face. He thought she misunderstood the term.

'Well, he was a 'master' of a ship, after all,' he said. 'It was a common address back then. Still is in the merchant navy …Or did she mean 'schoolmaster' do you think?'

'Look, Bob,' she said, 'in the light of what I've been reading in the diary, the term has connotations I'm uncomfortable with. Can I just refer to him from now on as simply Fyffe?'

'Sure. Fine by me.'

'Okay. Well, Agnes says that while Mrs Fyffe was in charge of the academic side of things, Fyffe seemed to involve himself in any physical activities the students engaged in. He would find hours to spend with the young pupils. They went hiking in the woods, for instance, had picnics. He taught the girls how to swim, and they all swam in the River Esk when it was warm ...'

Lizzie found the part she wanted in her text, and showed it to Scarth. 'This is what Agnes says.' She began to read aloud:

'We feel special, even loved. He is kind and gentle. I feel God had something to do with this, that God was happy with me. And when The Master chooses me, it is in fact God who has chosen me.'

Lizzie's eyes were clouded. 'In the diary, Agnes tells of systematic abuse; but in the beginning she was unsuspecting. She says she wanted to do her best, and to be picked out by Fyffe to do a task was an honour.'

'What sort of tasks?' asked Scarth.

'Agnes sometimes helped Mrs Fyffe to set up the desks, for the classes. As she was a boarder, she was always there early, and would do little jobs before the day-pupils arrived. As a reward, Fyffe would give her chocolate, and sweets. He had a special way of dispensing the sweets.'

She found the page:

'He would present me with the chocolate and give me a kiss on the cheek. I was quite comfortable at the time, because sometimes my uncles would kiss me on the cheek. Sometimes he would rub noses with me. Then as time went on, he would kiss me on the lips. This created a huge turmoil within me. But I did not want to appear like a little child and I did not object.'

'Sounds like grooming to me,' stated Scarth suspiciously.

'Yes,' Lizzie replied tersely. 'That is exactly what it was. She goes on …'

'The first time The Master touched me we were playing hide-and-go-seek at the grotto in the grounds. All the other children were there too. His rule was that if he found you, he would grab you roughly. Sometimes he puts his hand underneath my clothes. He always says it was an accident, but he tells me not to tell anybody. Afterwards I have this guilt. I don't know what he was doing to me. All I know is that I didn't like it. It feels like I am caught in a whirlpool. And that I have no control.'

'The progression was so slow,' Lizzie explained, 'that her natural reaction was that if she felt uncomfortable, it was as if she had done something wrong. Because she felt bad, she thought she must have done something bad for him to do that to her.'

Scarth found it difficult to look at her, felt a shame for his gender. It was a story he knew was all too familiar.

'Fyffe suffered from insomnia,' Lizzie continued. 'He regularly slept on a reclining armchair in his study. One night, she heard the pantry-maid crying in the night. She got out of bed and saw Fyffe creeping back down the stairs. Not long afterwards, the girl was dismissed. Agnes was terrified he would come to her bedroom.'

She pressed her lips together, and engaged his eyes. 'Fyffe worked hard to make the girls feel guilty for his sins. Young victims of sexual abuse can't always tell when a line has been crossed. When it happens, they often feel it has been part of a long-standing behaviour, so they might not even recognise it as something that is the abuser's fault. They believe it is something they allowed to happen, and in fact somehow encouraged.'

Scarth nodded. 'Yes. Plus the fact that Fyffe's social standing commanded respect,' he said. 'So much so, that other adults around might ignore the evidence before their very eyes …'

Lizzie nodded her agreement vigorously. 'She says that.' She flicked over a few pages, flicked some back. 'Here …'

'Today The Master grabbed me in public and felt me over my clothes. Everywhere. It didn't matter who was watching. They laughed at his playfulness.'

'But Fyffe's escalating behaviour became worse when he got the girl alone,' Lizzie stated. 'Agnes says he met her one day in a hallway, and told her to go into a nearby room. She suspected he wanted to feel her up again, but he went beyond touching. He exposed himself to her. He then forced her to do things no child should ever have to do. He told her that if she told anyone, she would go to Hell, her parents would go to Hell, her sister would go to Hell. She was terrified as she confessed the incident to her diary. He said he might be able to stop her going to Hell, if she did as he asked, he said. Shortly after that, he came to her room at night and raped her.'

'I am ashamed. I am no longer whole. He has stolen my most precious asset, my illitkosetsiak, my virtue. How will I find a husband, now that I am incomplete?'

Scarth had no words to say.

'The following year, when her younger sister Betty arrived, Agnes feared that she too would be abused. If that happened, she told her diary, she was determined to tell 'My Lady', Mrs Fyffe, to put a stop to it. Sure enough, just before Christmas, Betty told her Fyffe had overpowered her in his study. He told her she would be his special little pullak, Christmas bauble, and digitally raped her.

'Agnes was shocked and reported it to 'My Lady'. She told Mrs Fyffe of the on-going abuse she and her sister were suffering. She also told Mrs Fyffe of the suspected abuse of the pantry-maid Paula Reid. Mrs Fyffe is outraged, and ashamed. That night, Agnes records hearing a huge row in the schoolroom between 'My Lady' and

'The Master'. The fight is followed by screams. Agnes is petrified. Later that night, the family doctor is summoned. He has a hushed conference with Fyffe. Next morning, to everyone's astonishment, Mrs Fyffe is pronounced dead of the measles. She was buried in the garden plot two days later.'

'For God's sakes,' Scarth muttered.

Lizzie sat back. 'It's unbelievable. How could that happen?'

'It was a rough time,' replied Scarth. 'Thousands of people in Britain had already perished. The family doctor, whether incompetent or suborned, pronounced the cause of death as the deadly flu, and no-one questioned his competence or integrity. And there was no autopsy to contradict him ...'

'Do you think Fyffe killed his wife?' she asked bluntly.

'Well, we only have the word of a schoolgirl,' he cautioned. 'But yes, if things transpired as Agnes tells it, it seems a distinct possibility that that's exactly what he did. Mrs Fyffe's death is too sudden for a disease to strike her down. But what happened after the wife's burial?'

'Well naturally,' continued Lizzie, 'Agnes feared for her life, and that of Betty. Typically, she tells her diary it has all been her doing, her fault. She realises her diary and its confidences could bring harm to her if Fyffe finds it. She says she will hide the diary in the lovely parka her mother made for her, and pray that God will deliver her from the evil around her.'

Lizzie paused, tears springing up in her eyes. She found the last page, pointed to it. Scarth leaned over and read the pitiful words:

'I know I cannot stop The Master. I can only confide in you, my secret friend. But for now, I will hide you safely in the amauti my Anaana made for me. I hope someone will find you some day, and will pray for me, poor sinful Agnes Napajok. Adieu!!!'

'I wonder what happened to them?' said Lizzie tearfully. 'To Agnes and Betty … were they sent home, now that their mentor had died?'

Scarth shook his head. He looked at his young colleague with sad eyes. 'Fyffe's biographer says not. He says the girls also died in the pandemic. No natural resistance. I've just read Fyffe's biography, written by his grandson, who is still alive. In the booklet he says the girls caught the measles. Mrs Fyffe nursed them, but could not save them. After the girls died, she too succumbed. He surmises that she must have caught the disease from her young patients.'

Lizzie gaped in surprise. 'But that can't be true,' she protested. 'Agnes says nothing in her diary about the measles epidemic, nothing about being ill. And she actually records Mrs Fyffe's death and burial in the diary, which she obviously couldn't have done if she'd died before 'My Lady'.'

He thought of the modest stone marker in the Fyffe family plot. He had wondered why a commemorative stone would be erected in a family cemetery, for two girls who weren't even part of the family, and who purportedly weren't buried there. Surely a plaque in the old schoolroom, or a framed photograph, would have sufficed? Was it in fact a grave marker? He told Lizzie about the commemorative stone.

'So, there's a possibility those girls are still at Broomieknowe …' Lizzie said. She stood up, a determined look on her speckled face. 'It would be good to find out …and nail that bastard Fyffe for what he has done.' She sighed. 'It's too late now I know to do anything about him, the so-called 'Master'. To all intents and purposes, he has escaped justice. But his memory shouldn't remain untarnished, should it? That would be criminal.'

Scarth was silent. Eventually he said, 'I can't devote official time to this, Lizzie. I'm an employee of the police, and I can't just shoot off on tangents, much as I'd like to. I'm being asked to investigate the murder of Colin Muir, and that's what I'll have to stick with. Sorry.'

Lizzie smiled for the first time since he'd met her that afternoon.

'No worries, Bob. I understand. But there are no restrictions on me looking into it, in my free time, are there?'

'Look into what, Lizzie? The possibility that Sir Alexander Fyffe killed his wife?'

'No,' she said soberly. 'The probability that Sir Alexander Fyffe killed his two Inuit boarders.'

CHAPTER 16

SUNDAY AFTERNOON

McIntosh downloaded and printed out the information he had received from Midlothian Buses. He was stuffing it into a beige folder when Quin strode into the CID room.

'Well, well, well,' she said languidly. 'Home is the hunter, home from wherever ...' She shook her head in wonder. 'You should have been a snake charmer, Scobie. Superintendent Kerr has just been on the phone, telling me what a wonderful detective I have on my team ...'

McIntosh was surprised, but acted as nonchalantly as he could. 'Maybe she liked my aftershave,' he said innocently, deciding to get his retaliation in first.

Quin stood back suddenly, consternation on her face. 'What aftershave?'

'That stuff I had in my desk drawer… the birthday present you and Heather gave me … I gave myself a blast of it before I went to see the Super.'

Quin was aghast. It was true that she and Munro had clubbed together to get him something for his twenty-fifth. And she knew he'd put the awful stuff they'd got from the joke shop in his desk drawer. In the novelty place, it had been a toss-up between the fake aftershave and a fart cushion, but they'd plumped for the pong. Ever since they bought the stuff, they'd been waiting anxiously for him to try it, ready to hoot their delight when he fell for the prank.

'Oh my God, Scobie,' she blustered apologetically. 'You are kidding. That was just a joke. It's not a real aftershave!' Her hands flapped wildly. 'We got it from a novelty shop ...' Her face crumpled into a disbelieving, fearful grin. 'Don't tell me you went and sprayed yourself with it before seeing the Super. You didn't, did you? It's totally disgusting! It's meant to be totally disgusting …'

McIntosh's face masked his pleasure at her obvious consternation. He spread his big palms. 'I think it's okay, boss. Unusual. Quirky. Superintendent Kerr must have approved of it too. She never said otherwise …'

Was he having her on? Surely no female in the world, she thought with a shiver, could stomach such a stench willingly.

Her expression, McIntosh noted with satisfaction, was a sublime mixture of suspicion and revulsion.

As they seated themselves at the pow-wow table, he handed her the beige folder: the print-outs from the bus company, complete with the photos, names, and addresses.

'We know from the CCTV footage on the buses that this Sallyanne Seton is the phone snatcher,' he said as she opened the folder. 'And we have the names and addresses of the other two that Heather and I suspect of assisting her.' He paused dramatically. 'The Super thinks there may actually be four of them, working in cahoots, so to speak …'

'What makes her think that?' Quin asked, obviously curious.

'The Four Marys,' McIntosh announced enigmatically. 'Mary Seton, Mary Beaton, Mary Carmichael, and me.' He straightened his back; he always found the conference table chairs uncomfortable. 'Hand-maidens of Mary Queen of Scots,' he finished knowledgably.

'Really? Well, that's good to know,' Quin replied flatly, her interest faltering. 'Who's the 'me'?'

'Mary Hamilton.'

Quin scanned the surnames, forehead furrowed. 'There's no Hamilton here …'

'No, but we haven't identified the fourth one yet, boss.'

'What fourth one? And there's no Beaton here either,' Quin pointed out stubbornly.

'As the Super indicated to me, substitute Beatson, and you have it.'

Quin scanned his sharp features for duplicity. Was he winding her up? Her baby lips pursed. 'And the Super said all this, did she?' she pursued sceptically. 'Was she serious?'

'Couldn't have been more serious,' he affirmed offhandedly.

'Mmm. Sounds like a heap of pish to me …' Quin stated with a sigh. 'Makes you wonder where they get senior officers from nowadays, doesn't it?'

McIntosh knew better than to comment on that one.

Quin straightened in her chair. 'Listen,' she said, closing the folder and tapping the cover, 'if it's a conspiracy, as the Super supposes, then we need to prove they know each other, associate with one another. We need to put them together. We need to review any tapes in The Mall, see if they meet up. Shops, cafes, supermarkets, and so on. It would be good if the Mall security people have any footage of your famous YouTube incident.'

'I'll go round to The Mall security centre this afternoon, boss …'

'And why have we never found a weapon? Can you tell me that? The snatcher uses different instruments, we know that. But does she take them away with her or does she discard them? For instance, it doesn't look like she had one on her person when you were wrestling with her, does it. Did she pan it off to an accomplice, dump it in a bin before you encountered her? Maybe the CCTV cameras can tell us.'

As McIntosh stood to go, Quin planned aloud. 'We need to get a search warrant for this Seton's home,' she stated, 'to search for the implements she's been using to disable the phones. While you're at The Mall,' Quin continued, 'I'll get a report off to the PF to put the search warrant application in motion.' She flipped her wrist around. 'It's getting on. He likely won't be able to submit it to the Sheriff now till the morning. Right then Scobie, get yourself round to The Mall, and let me get on with that report for the Fiscal.'

McIntosh dithered. He was thinking about Scottie. He daren't take the wee fella with him into The Mall again. Should he return him early to the day centre and risk the Ex finding out about it? If she did, she might use it as an excuse to curtail Scottie's future week-end sleepovers.

Quin took his hesitation as the need for further clarification.

'Once we have a search warrant for Seton,' she assured him, 'we'll haul the three of them in simultaneously for questioning. I'll see Sergeant Balmain later today about organising the troops so that we have enough uniforms and transport to carry out the arrests.'

The Dundas Street Mall in Eskbridge was a two-tiered shopping centre built on the site of what used to be a huge carpet factory. On the ground floor it had a total of eighty-six shops and supermarkets. The second floor was home to four restaurants, and two pubs – Gilligan's Irish Pub; and a bar which opened as The Classic Contradiction, then inexplicably changed its name to The Unavoidable Affliction. Lyle Lovett fans waited for the day it would change its name again, to The Inevitable Conclusion.

The centre also had three coffee shops – The Buttered Bannock, The Chatterbox, and Jessie's; and an eclectic mix of take-away joints. It housed a gym, a soft play centre, and a multi-screen cinema. Surrounding the centre were car parks for 1,800 vehicles.

What was of interest to McIntosh that afternoon was that it had lots of CCTV cameras. They were mounted to monitor the car parks, entrances and exits, and the main concourse. In-shop and in-store cameras were also in abundance, targeting entrance doors, fire doors, aisles, and check-outs.

The security centre was an impressive operation, with shifts of personnel monitoring the banks of cameras for the sixteen hours daily that The Mall was open. McIntosh was met by a young man wearing a white uniform shirt rolled up to his elbows. His epaulette insignia resembled those of a Warrant Officer in the Gendarmerie. He introduced McIntosh to the head man. The boss was a serious-looking thick-set man somewhere in his fifties. He was above average height, and the only one in the room wearing a suit. His name tag said: Donnie MacKay, Security Supervisor.

Donnie took charge of McIntosh personally, and led him to a corner of the room where a large, square monitor sat. The CCTV system was state-of-the-art digital, he related, with video storage for up to three months.

McIntosh began by explaining that he was investigating a series of phone-snatchings on public transport. The perpetrator, he said, was female. She always alighted at the bus terminal outside, and darted into the shopping centre. There had been a pattern to the phone snatchings, he said. They always occurred in the mornings between 8:30 and 9:30 a.m. – peak commuter period. What he needed to do was have a look at what the CCTV video could tell him on those times and dates. He hoped they could track the phone snatcher through The Mall, as she made her escape after a snatching incident on a bus. Did she meet anyone? Where did she go? All that sort of stuff. He showed the man a screen-shot he had of her on his phone.

'Shouldn't be a problem,' Donnie said, seating himself before a viewing monitor. He quickly found the first day McIntosh was interested in, and cued the tape. 'Take a pew,' he said to McIntosh, indicating a free desk chair nearby.

The first incident of phone-snatching brought to the attention of the Eskbridge police had occurred two weeks earlier, on the 10th. Carole Dunne, the victim on that occasion, had described her attacker as an elderly woman wearing newish-looking 'outdoor' clothes. This person had destroyed her phone with 'secateurs or something', she said, before 'sprinting away' from the bus and disappearing among the mass of people entering the Mall.

Donnie hit the 'Play' button. The snatcher, wearing a dark green insulated snow jacket, was identified hopping off the bus as it pulled into the terminal. She easily dodged through the crowds of commuters, and entered the covered shopping mall.

McIntosh and Donnie laboriously tracked her with multiple cameras as Seton ambled through the shopping centre. Several times McIntosh asked Donnie to stop the video and take a close-up screen shot of her in The Mall surroundings – all date and time-stamped.

Seton reached the escalator to the second-floor food court, and rode up it. She dithered at the top of the escalator for thirty seconds, apparently to see if anyone was following her, before leaving the shopping centre by descending the east stairwell. She emerged not far from a taxi rank. She went to the head of the line of taxis, all private cars, for no black cabs operated in Eskbridge, and disappeared inside the first one. The vehicle left the area.

From the time that she emerged from the bus till the time she entered the taxi, she had not spoken or interacted with anyone.

Much the same performance ensued on the other days McIntosh selected.

On the 14th, when Harper Rennie had her phone snatched and 'utterly destroyed' by the snatcher, Seton was wearing an olive outdoor fleece, she said, with skinny jeans and walking shoes. Rennie had also stated that her attacker that day had on a tasselled woollen cap. This proved not to be the case, for McIntosh and Donnie were able to get a clear screen-shot as she approached the escalators. She had no cap, or had removed it. Her hair was short and dark-coloured. She appeared to be her usual genial-looking self.

On the 17th, Seton had used some sort of punch to destroy the phone of Wayne Copeland. He had not been able to give an accurate description of his attacker, only that she was small, had dark brown hair which he assumed had been dyed because it didn't go with the lines on her face, and was wearing a dark puffer jacket.

On the 19th, when Connie Considine was attacked with her wee bairn on her lap, Seton again rode the escalator up to the second-floor Food Court, checked for anyone shadowing her, before descending the rear stairs and leaving as before by taxi.

Then came the day McIntosh was dreading seeing. He saw himself and Scottie innocently approaching the entrance to The Mall. He saw a small woman in a pink puffer jacket burst through the crowd towards him. As she bustled her way through the milling bus passengers, Scottie, the wee eejit, caught her scent, whirled after her, and began his delighted pursuit. Eventually, in his daft enthusiasm, the wee dog brought both the snatcher and his master down in a tangle of embarrassed limbs. McIntosh witnessed again his 'citizen's arrest', as several bystanders physically intervened and subsequently 'handed him over' to PCs Gray and Reid.

Donnie, to his credit, never laughed outright. He let the video run on, showing the aftermath of the incident, something the YouTube footage hadn't captured.

As a dishevelled McIntosh was 'taken into custody' by the two young policemen, the snatcher was briefly comforted by a small group of bystanders. Among them was a red-haired youth in a dark blue hoodie. He led her towards the ladies rest-rooms, before veering off alone towards the nearest exit.

But something had caught Donnie's eye.

He ran the footage again. As the phone snatcher dodged through the crowds she bumped rather heavily into the same young red-haired man in the hoodie, almost knocking him off his feet. Donnie ran the sequence again. As the snatcher careered off the youth he clutched his stomach, doubling up as if in pain.

'Did you see that?' Donnie asked.

'Yeah,' McIntosh replied amiably. 'Looks like Seton cracked one of his ribs.'

'No. She slipped something to him,' said Donnie simply, fiddling with his controls. He selected another camera angle, wasn't satisfied, and selected another. He cued the footage to the point when the snatcher ran into the youth, watched the action carefully in slow motion. He froze the screen.

'They're good,' said Donnie in admiration. 'Did you see what happened? She doesn't just pass something to him, she actually stuffs the item quickly into his top. Even bystanders would miss it. He turns away, as if his chest has been injured, but he's actually making sure the item is safely lodged in his hoodie.' Donnie sat back, a wide grin on his mug. 'Oh yes, they've done this before I think …'

McIntosh was alive to the possibilities. 'It could be the phone-crushing implement she used,' he stated. 'Do you know,' he added in a bemused tone, 'we've never found any weapon, or implement that she uses. Up till now we didn't know if she took them away with her, discarded them in The Mall or somewhere else, or panned them off to an associate, or what. Now we've seen one instance where she apparently slips it to an accomplice. Maybe there are others.'

Donnie took the hint. 'No probs,' he replied. 'I'm as interested as you are.' His fingers flashed over his keyboard as if on automatic pilot. 'I'm usually tracking shoplifters, monitoring drunken or boisterous behaviour, that sort of thing. Occasionally we have a missing child to search for. This is more interesting …'

Donnie was a wizard, displaying an enviable familiarity with the workings of his system. As he reviewed the footage for a second time, McIntosh was amazed at how much he had missed. In the aftermath of each incident the snatcher 'accidentally' bumped into, among others, the red-haired youth.

Donnie was impressed. 'He's always there, or thereabouts,' he observed.

'Yes. To take possession of the phone-crushing implement, in case she gets apprehended.' replied McIntosh. 'How did I not see what was happening the first time around?'

'Because we weren't looking for it. Once we saw one instance, the others became obvious.'

Donnie was able to get a close-up of the youth. 'There,' said Donnie, pointing to the screen, 'look at his front.'

McIntosh peered. 'Is that what it looks like, Donnie?'

'It certainly looks like a blood stain to me. From when she slipped him the weapon ...'

'Pity it's not in colour,' McIntosh said, but he was obviously highly pleased nevertheless.

Donnie stabbed a button on his keyboard. The image transformed itself into full RGB colour. 'We run the cameras on black and white to save storage space,' he explained. 'They all have a colour facility when we need it …'

The stain on the front of the youth's hoodie was a dull red.

'Yep,' Donnie said. 'It's blood all right. Tell you what, though, if she transferred blood from her hands or clothing to that young guy when she bumped into him, then she most likely did the same thing to you, when you were wrestling with her later.'

McIntosh's brain went into a spin. Were the pin-prick marks on his shirt blood? Is that why they didn't come out with the stain remover? He felt a sweat coming on, and a flush creeping up his cheeks. Anya would have done the washing by now. Destroying any evidence there was to be had. And it was his fault, there was no denying that.

'Can we have a look again at that transfer?' he asked.

They watched again as the snatcher progressed through the crowd and collided with the youth, and then continued on her way towards the unwitting McIntosh and Scottie. Donnie slowed the action. They scrutinised the images on the small screen. The results were inconclusive. If she had blood smears anywhere on the front of her jacket, they were too small to be seen.

McIntosh couldn't hide his disappointment. He looked absently round the room, taking in the slow-moving images on the myriad of screens mounted around the walls, and the white-shirted operators gazing intently upwards at them. He moved his head closer to Donnie and lowered his voice conspiratorially.

'There's something else, Donnie, and it needs to stay between us. Okay?'

Donnie nodded attentively; his eyes bright. He raised his right hand in the air like Maradona. Hand to God.

'Let's say, for argument's sake, that I found tiny stains on my top. After that incident with the snatcher. And then, because I assumed the stains were ketchup from my lunch – because I was trying to feed myself and my wee boisterous dog at the same time – I tried to get rid of them with fabric stain remover … what would happen?'

Donnie's voice was a conspiratorially low half-whisper. 'What would happen to the garment, you mean? Well, if they're blood stains, if that's what you're getting at, stain remover won't work anyway. The stains'll still be there.'

McIntosh pursed his lips. 'And what if, let's say, to compound the error, the shirt was then run through a hot washing machine cycle … would the blood evidence, if there was indeed any blood evidence there in the first place, be destroyed, do you think?'

Donnie shrugged. 'I don't know for sure. I would hazard a guess that your forensics people will still be able to retrieve some kind of workable sample from the stains. You'd have to hand it in to them to see.'

McIntosh looked reluctant. His laundry was still in the car, and it would take only twenty minutes to get to the lab at HQ. But it would mean he'd have to admit to his carelessness and stupidity in the first place. He decided to wait it out.

'But why do you need your shirt for evidence?' Donnie quizzed. 'If the blood we can see on the boy's hoodie there is a match for the victim's DNA, then you've got her. It could only have got on his clothing by being transferred from the snatcher. And she could only have got it from being spattered by the victim during the phone-snatching attack ...'

McIntosh's pale face lit up with a grin. 'By God you're right.'

'So, forget your top,' Donnie advised. 'Focus on the snatcher and the boy. What you need to do now is find her and seize her puffer jacket, for she won't be able to remove any stains either, and find the boy and seize his hoodie …'

McIntosh set his jaw. 'We know who she is, and my boss is preparing an application for a search warrant, but we don't know who the youth is yet …'

'I can't help you there, I'm afraid,' replied Donnie, 'all I know is that he isn't on our radar.'

McIntosh looked at his watch. It was after four o'clock already.

'Listen Donnie,' he said with a sigh, 'you've been a tremendous help. Thanks a bunch.' He nudged the man amicably. 'You should have been a cop, you know.'

Donnie hesitated. 'I used to be a cop, Sergeant,' he admitted. 'Before Brennan swung his axe.'

McIntosh was astounded. He automatically glanced at the man's name tag again: Donnie MacKay. The name meant nothing. 'Chief Superintendent Brennan?' he asked.

'The very bastard. I was a DI at Penicuik.'

A Detective Inspector! McIntosh was impressed.

In 2010, CS Brennan had been the architect of the deeply-unpopular force-reduction measures which had seen Eskbridge police station, among others, being reduced to part-time operations. Penicuik was a couple of parishes to the east Eskbridge, but might as well have been in Papua New Guinea for all the intercourse there was between them.

'Is the gorgeous Mighty Quin your boss?' Donnie enquired.

Jesus, thought a gobsmacked McIntosh. Small world. You never know who you are talking to nowadays.

He grinned. 'She is, yes,' he admitted. Gorgeous? Where did that come from?

Donnie grinned back. He beckoned McIntosh closer. 'This needs to stay between us, Sergeant …'

McIntosh raised his right hand solemnly in the air, before bending forward, all ears.

'We were close friends for a time, Moira and I,' Donnie whispered. 'Really close.' He smiled ruefully, 'Till my wife found out, anyway …' He straightened up in his seat. 'If you remember, tell your boss I was asking.'

'Certainly,' McIntosh replied, also straightening up. He nearly said 'sir'.

Well, well, well. The Mysterious Moira Quin. Who'd-a thunk it?

They lapsed into a comfortable silence.

McIntosh broke the spell by producing his phone and saying, 'I hesitate to take up more of your time Donnie, but I still have a couple of loose ends …'

He scrolled to his photos and showed Donnie the bus company screen-shots he had of Valerie Carmichael and Robert Beatson.

'We think these two are acting as accomplices in the phone-snatching instances,' McIntosh said. 'Acting as decoys, running interference sort of thing. Have you ever seen them here in The Mall?'

'Well, I can tell you right now that they all know each other.' Donnie replied instantly. He tapped a temple significantly. 'Pornographic memory,' he said with a sincere smile, 'never forget a face. Those two, and your phone snatcher, are in our Rogues Gallery … Hold on a sec …' he said, his fingertips a blur on his keyboard, '… here we are,' he announced after an impossibly short time. He leaned back in his chair, having brought up their faces on his widescreen monitor.

McIntosh peered eagerly. Beatson was without his golf cap. The man was flanked by two other women. It took McIntosh a second or two to recognise Sallyanne Seton, for in the line-up, as she had appeared on her bus pass, showed her with grey hair. All three stared sullenly at the camera. The captions below their names read: Valerie Carmichael, Robert Beatson, and Sallyanne Seton.

'This is them in our Interview Room, prior to being handed over to the police. Caught shoplifting in Ramsay's department store.' said Donnie. He swivelled to face McIntosh. 'I don't know if they were ever prosecuted. Probably not, for it usually means store staff have to take a half day off to testify in court, and employers are reluctant to give them time off. All I know is that they're barred from The Mall now. Maybe that's why your phone snatching woman has dyed her hair. Yeah, it was a strange one. Gina Fraser, one of our floorwalkers, or Loss Prevention Officer to give her full title, brought them in …'

'Is this Gina on duty today?' asked McIntosh.

Donnie swivelled his chair and spoke loudly to someone behind them. 'Is Gina on today?' Hearing an affirmative, he said, 'Give her a shout, will you?'

Gina Fraser, the plain-clothes security officer, was dressed for the outdoors. Or dressed as if she had just popped into The Mall for a few things before going on somewhere else. She blended in perfectly with the hundreds of other women in the shopping centre who were intent on doing just that.

She was a tall, well-shaped woman, with thick, fair hair, cut short. Around forty, McIntosh thought. Under her expensively-branded cagoule she was wearing a colourful knitted cardigan buttoned down the front. Under the cardigan was a white shirt or blouse. She was wearing skinny jeans which showed off her shapely limbs favourably, and soft-soled black shoes. The shoes were the only give-away to her profession.

McIntosh explained the reason for his visit, and showed her his screen shots of his persons of interest. 'I believe you caught this motley crew in Ramsay's store, Gina,' he said. 'What can you tell me about them?'

'I know all three of them by sight. They stay not far from me. I live in the Marionville area. They had a well-rehearsed act. God knows how often they got away with it. And God knows why they did it, for they are all comfortably off.'

'Boredom?' suggested McIntosh. 'For the buzz of it?' He thought of the phone-snatching incidents. Was that the motive? Sheer bloody boredom?

'Anyway,' Gina continued, 'they first came to our attention in Binns. The three of them pretended not to know each other, though they moved through the store more or less at the same pace, going from one department to another. One of Binns' floorwalkers suspected the large woman of shoplifting expensive lingerie in the ground-floor Ladies department. When she was challenged by the floorwalker, this woman had a heart attack or a seizure of some kind. The old man came to her aid, went into a panic, and began shouting for a doctor. He created such a fuss that the security guard on the door was summoned to give assistance. The woman recovered of course, but by that time the small one had slipped away with the big one's shopping bag, and with the purloined goods inside it. It was as easy as that.'

McIntosh smiled grimly. 'The heart attack scenario is the same as the ploy they've used on the buses. When the small one did the phone-snatching.'

'But that wasn't the only instance,' Fraser continued. 'When practically the same thing happened a second time in the Miss Selfishness store, I scrutinised the in-store video with their security staff. It was clearly a set-up. We decided to keep a special look-out for them, and the third time they tried it, in Ramsay's department store, we were ready for them.' She pointed to McIntosh's phone. 'That image was taken just before we handed them over to the police.

'Were they charged?'

Gina nodded. 'Case came up in the Sheriff Court just last month. I went there with Carole to testify. Each of them was fined the total value of the goods – £120 – and given a written warning. In addition, The Mall management issued a ban on them entering the premises. We haven't been bothered by them since. I presume that's why she has dyed her hair, so that the security staff here wouldn't recognise her.'

'Presumably. Who's Carole?'

'Carole Dunne. Ramsay's security supervisor. The lady who detained the three of them.'

Carole Dunne? Where had he heard that name recently. Then it came to him. The first phone-snatching victim!

Gina Fraser had plain face, but when she smiled, as she did now, McIntosh thought her smile made her look almost pretty. 'You look as if you've won the lottery,' she said. 'Was it something I said?'

McIntosh nodded happily. 'Carole Dunne was the first victim of the phone snatcher,' he replied, a wide grin splitting his fizzog. 'The snatcher must have known her.'

'Really? So, the phone-snatching is what, revenge? Pay-back time?'

'Could well be.' McIntosh pulled up his notes on his phone, scrolled through them. 'Do you know a Harper Rennie, a Wayne Copeland, or a Connie Considine?'

She pulled a face. 'Don't think so. Should I?'

'Not especially. No worries. Thanks Gina. Oh, before you go, have a gander at this one.' He showed her the screen shot of the red-haired youth. 'Have you seen this guy knocking about?'

The floorwalker peered, pursed her lips negatively. 'He's not one of our clients, the ones we look out for. But I know he works here. Not here in the security centre, but in The Mall. Up in the Food Court somewhere I think …'

'Any idea where?'

'Not really. But it should be easy enough to find out if you show that screen-shot around up there …'

McIntosh turned to go. 'Right you are. Thanks again.'

'You're welcome,' she said smiling broadly. Why had he thought her face was plain? When she smiled, she was good-looking by anyone's standard.

'One more thing, Gina,' he said, 'we've been informed by Midlothian Buses that both the women live at the same address. Do you know anything about that?'

She smiled that special smile again, inviting him to continue.

'It's just that my boss thought they might be in a relationship, or something,' he lied, for Quin had no idea that the women shared an address.

'Oh, they're in a relationship all right,' affirmed the floorwalker, 'but maybe not the kind your boss envisaged.' She breathed in though her nose, looking round the room cautiously. 'They're related through the ballop, as we used to say...'

McIntosh raised his eyebrows expectantly. It just got curiouser and curiouser.

'They have a sexual connection,' she explained to him. 'I forget the details, but I know that the fat-faced one, Valerie Carmichael, and your phone snatcher, Sallyanne Seton, are sisters. They have an unusual domestic arrangement. They take turns to spend their days with Bob Beatson at his house. Week about, apparently. One stays at home while the other spends her week with the boyfriend. But whichever one is with him during the day always returns home at night, to sleep in her own bed. I've been told the sisters still sleep in the same bedroom they had when they were children.'

'You get told a lot.'

'They were the talk o' the steamie for a while …'

'It all sounds a bit weird.'

'And wait till you hear this. What I also heard,' Fraser continued, 'is that the old guy, Beatson, is servicing both of them. Though not simultaneously, of course …'

McIntosh was gobsmacked. 'Really? Sounds exhausting. But they're pensioners …' he protested in disbelief.

Gina gave him a worldly smile. 'Amici e vini sono meglio vecchi' – Friends and wine improve with age,' she translated. 'It's Italian. Maybe the same thing goes for sex as well, eh? … Here's hoping anyway,' she finished cheerfully.

A long-forgotten phrase from his schooldays leapt into McIntosh's brain. 'The only Italian I know,' he replied bashfully, stuffing his phone in an inside pocket, 'is that old Julius Caesar quotation: "veni, vidi, vici" – "I came, I saw, I conquered."'

'Yeah, well, it's much the same thing, isn't it?' Gina retorted wittily. She had freckles too, McIntosh noticed, which danced when she grinned.

The second-floor Food Court was only sparsely populated. It was too late for the lunch crowd, and too early for the pubs and the cinema patrons. It was almost too late for the café and bistro set.

The first unit he came to, The Buttered Bannock, was open, though the staff seemed to be clearing up. The two women busy cleaning the tables eyed him with jaundiced expressions.

McIntosh held up an appeasing hand. 'Police,' he said. 'I'm not looking for refreshment.' He focused on the nearest one, who was studiously ignoring him.

'Do you have a minute?' he politely asked.

She was a sour-faced girl with an unfortunate hairstyle, and the square shoulders of an asthmatic.

'Are ye talking to me or chewing a brick?' she demanded belligerently.

McIntosh smiled dutifully. He showed her the screen shot of the red-haired youth and asked if she knew him, or where he worked. She pointed vaguely down the long corridor to the rest of the food outlets.

'He works as a delivery boy for one of the pizza places down there,' she said.

McIntosh's eyes followed her arm. They were all there: Pepe's Pizza, Pizza Paradise, Dominos, Papa John's, and Pizza Express. He also noticed The Happy Haddock, Chico's Fried Chicken, and MacStovie's. How many Happy Haddocks had he seen, he wondered?

'I can save you the bother of looking,' she said laconically. 'They're all closed. Open evenings only …'

'But you're sure he works for one of them?'

'I just said so, didn't I?' she replied testily, anxious to get on with her work and get out of there. Carnaptiousness suited her, McIntosh thought.

He decided to turn on the boyish charm. 'His name's not Hamilton, is it?' he asked amiably.

She shook her head impatiently. Looped bronzed earrings jangled. 'How would I ken? Is that the name your grass has given you, then? Hamilton?'

'Who says I've got a grass?'

She snorted her contempt. Her hands flew to her hips, her head tilted challengingly. She'd had enough. 'What so-called detective hasn't? Well, you'll no' hear more frae me, mister polisman, because I'm no' a grass …'

Jesus, McIntosh muttered to himself as he left. What would she have been like if I'd asked for a bannock and jam, and a nice cup of chamomile tea?

He needed a rest, he realised. He'd get a couple of uniforms from Division to ask around for the youth that evening.

CHAPTER 17

SUNDAY AFTERNOON

McIntosh reached Shawn Murray, the forensics manager, later that afternoon. He apologised for disturbing him at home. He then explained that several tiny stains had been 'discovered' on the front of his shirt. He had suspected they were ketchup slaister stains sustained when he had lunch in his car with a wee dog jumping all over him, he said. But he now suspected that they may have been blood stains, transferred from the phone snatcher, sustained whilst making contact with her during the unfortunate fracas in The Mall.

'By 'whilst making contact',' Murray drolled, 'I take it you don't mean contact in an other-worldly, spiritual way, but rather in a very down-to-earth conjunction, somewhat in the style of all-in wrestling?'

'Gloat if you like, Shawn, but think about it: if I hadn't grappled with her, I wouldn't have got the evidence, would I?'

'Well, it still remains to be seen if it is in fact evidence, of course.'

'The thing is, as I thought the spots were tomato sauce, I used a stain remover on them …'

'And what happened?'

'They didn't disappear.'

'Well, that's encouraging …'

'And then I put them in the wash. Or rather, the cleaning lady put them through the wash.'

'Ah. That's not so encouraging …'

'The thing is, the stains are still visible. Just. Is there any way they can be tested? To see if its blood or not?'

'You realise that any sample which may be retrieved will be hopelessly contaminated, don't you?'

'I'd still like to know.'

'And you fully understand that we may have to cut samples from your garment to perform presumptive tests?'

McIntosh had anticipated this. 'It's my favourite top, Shawn. My Scotland away kit one. But I'm willing to sacrifice it,' he replied, his voice a parody of loss, 'in the interests of justice.'

Murray let an uncomfortable silence build up. Eventually he said, 'Bring it in to the lab then, Mac,' he said with mock-weariness. 'Mrs Slocum's on duty, busy with a case for Galashiels, but I'll phone her and tell her you've to get priority'.

'No probs. Thanks, Shawn.'

'But it's going to cost you mind …'

Mrs Slocum, McIntosh knew, was in fact a forensic scientist called Mrs Riddell. Her nickname stemmed from her officious and bossy manner, à la the television sit-com character well-known to a previous generation. She did in fact have a passing resemblance to the aforesaid character, being border-line middle-aged, and having carefully-twiffed platinum-coloured hair.

Mrs Riddell had come to them the previous year from another Division. She was almost immediately disliked because of her stern, unforgiving, and demanding manner. She had no discernible sense of humour. Nobody knew anything about her. No one had met Mr Riddell, though they all supposed he had existed, at some point. But whether he still existed, they were too scared to ask. After nearly a year in the same team as nearly a dozen other forensic scientists and officers, Mrs Riddell remained a mystery to them; an enigma wrapped up in her own obfuscation.

McIntosh received a baleful look as he handed over his washed and ironed rugby shirt.

'What exactly do you expect me to do with this, Sergeant?' she asked. 'I've been given to understand that you've already polluted the sample with stain remover, and put it through a high-speed wash. What do you expect me to find?'

'Well, I don't know that the wash was in fact high-speed, Mrs Slo …, er, Mrs Riddell, but …'

'I don't care a hoot what kind of wash it was,' she interrupted fiercely. 'The fact is that any evidence that may have existed, has now been contaminated. Probably terminally.'

She spread the garment out on an observation table, took up a magnifying glass, and began a careful examination of the area which McIntosh indicated.

'I thought the marks were ketchup,' he explained lamely. 'That's why it ended up in the wash.'

'What's left of them you mean …'

'But now I'm thinking there is a possibility that they may be blood.'

'What makes you think that?'

He told her briefly about the victim of the latest phone-snatching incident having her thumb crushed, and about him 'coming into contact' with the suspected perpetrator in The Mall.

She looked at him keenly, a miniature smile on her vermillion lips. 'You're the one they're all talking about, aren't you? You're quite a media star, you know Sergeant.'

McIntosh came over all bashful. 'Yeah. So, Superintendent Kerr told me.'

'Yes. I heard you'd got a bollocking,' she said dismissively. 'And now what? You've been in contact with suspected perpetrator, this phone snatcher, and you suspect she might have transferred some of the victim's blood onto your clothing? Is that your hypothesis?'

'It's a leap, I know …'

'No, no,' Mrs Riddell said, surprising him. 'It's perfectly feasible.'

McIntosh pointed to his shirt. 'Then again, I know I'm a messy pup.'

'All men are. Well, there's an easy way to find out if it's blood or the ubiquitous tomato sauce. Take a seat.'

Mrs Riddell selected an array of small bottles from a shelf, and lined them up on a small wheeled table beside the long examining table.

'I love doing this,' she admitted. 'When I was a schoolgirl in Shawlands my ambition was to be a forensic scientist, or maybe a coroner like Quincy. Remember him?'

McIntosh was puzzled. Was that Shawlands in Glasgow? Is that where she comes from?

She saw his uncertainty. 'Of course you don't remember. Quincy's too ancient even for the golden oldie re-runs now …'

She fished in a chest of drawers and dug out a tub of cotton buds. She moistened the tip of one with a drop of distilled water, and gently rubbed it on McIntosh's shirt.

The tip of the swab was then cleaned with a tiny drop from the first bottle.

'Alcohol,' said Mrs Riddell. 'Cleans the sample and exposes more haemoglobin. If haemoglobin is there.'

Mrs Riddell then added a minute drop from the next bottle in the line. McIntosh noticed that she was one of those people who stick the tips of their tongues out of their mouth, when concentrating on a tricky task.

'It's a reagent called phenolphthalein,' she explained. 'Don't ask me to spell it. You'll notice the sample turns colourless.' She reached for the last remaining bottle on his desk, and gently allowed a drop from it to drip onto the sample. 'However, when I add a spot of hydrogen peroxide, which will react with any blood present …it will change colour … there, see? … The tip is turning pink ...'

'That's amazing … Is it blood after all?'

'Not necessarily,' she stated. 'This doesn't prove that what you have on your shirt is blood. There are several other possibilities – some paints for instance. It is only what we called a presumptive test, meaning that the presumption may now be made that the sample could be blood. However, I can state categorically that those stains on your shirt are not ketchup.'

'Well, that's encouraging ...'

'Isn't it just,' she smiled. She had very good teeth, McIntosh noticed, and a sturdy wee frame which went in and out at all the right places. She caught him looking and said, 'What else were you wearing when this incident occurred?'

'These jeans, and these trainers …'

'You'd better whip them off then,' she said. She took in the dismayed look on McIntosh's face.

'Go over there,' she pointed to the door, 'and turn off the overhead lights. Get your togs off, and bring them to me.'

Seeing the mortification in McIntosh's eyes she said, 'Don't be shy Sergeant, I've seen a pair of bollocks before now. Here,' she reached into a drawer, pulled out a disposable scene jump-suit, and tossed it to him. 'Climb into that to preserve your chastity, and in case I get any funny ideas ...'

McIntosh did as he was told. Just before he plunged the room into darkness, Mrs Riddell clicked on a small table lamp. When he dutifully brought over his jeans, she laid them out on the examination table, picked up a spray bottle from her small dispensary table, and gave them a couple of exploratory squirts.

Pst. Pst.

An area the size of a tennis ball, just to the left of his crotch, lit up like it had been stippled with stardust. McIntosh knew that Luminol could detect the most minute specks of blood, invisible to the naked eye. But it was still mightily impressive.

'Wow,' he said. 'Looks like the Hogmanay fireworks at Edinburgh Castle.'

'Really?' she dismissed. 'We never stay up. Looks more like a knee print to me …'

McIntosh had a brief mental recap of his struggle with Seton. 'You know, you might be right. I'm sure she tried to knee me at one point, in the whatsits.'

Her face was spooky in the reflected green light from the table. 'Hmm,' she said. 'You're a lucky man then …'

McIntosh grinned proudly. 'I know. Could have done me a serious injury that.'

Mrs Riddell switched on her desk lamp. 'I mean lucky in the sense that you were fortunate she didn't miss. It can only be transfer from the suspect, and if a sample of the DNA matches the victim's blood, it's what we call in the trade a slam dunk.'

She pulled the jeans closer to her, then gazed absently at her selection of scalpels.

'Oh, yes,' she continued, 'you've been extremely lucky, otherwise we wouldn't have the potential evidence, would we?'

He should have been pleased, but he wasn't. 'When you say sample,' he queried tentatively, 'do you mean you'll have to carve out that piece from my jeans? It's just that they're Tommy jeans. Cost me over £80 ...'

'Ha! Vanity, Thy Name is Man. Well, I'll need to do a comparison test with a swab from your jeans there, and the victim's DNA.' She pointed to a wooden stand holding several vials of dark coloured liquid. 'Shawn has already brought in samples of her blood from the bus. We'll soon know whose blood it is.'

Mrs Riddell escorted him as he squeaked his crinkled way to the doorway. He said, 'So there's a possibility I'll get the jeans back in one piece?'

She smiled enigmatically. 'Probably. I'll just tickle your crotch area with one of my little cotton buds and see what happens ...' She grinned, knowing full well what would happen if she did it while he was still wearing them, '… And with any luck I'll have a result for you by this evening some time. That do you?'

'Luvly jubbly, Mrs Slo … eh … Mrs Riddell,' he replied falteringly.

'Grizel,' she said sharply.

McIntosh stood very still. At first, he assumed she was reproving him for his slip of the tongue; using perhaps some sort of matronly swearie-word outwith his ken. Then he wondered if it was some sort of technical term. Was it a forensic or police anagram that he probably should have recognised, been aware of?

She then surprised him by sticking out a bony hand.

'Grizel,' she repeated with a bashful smile. 'It's short for Grizelda …'

Ah. So that's it. But why was she telling him her name? He was at a loss to know but he grinned and extended a hairy paw.

'Scobie,' he said. 'It's not short for anything that I know of. Mac, on the other hand, is …'

'Yeah, I know,' she said, withdrawing her hand, 'it's short for a couple of sandwiches shy of a picnic. Only kidding. I'll email you, Sergeant.'

She held open her door for him to exit.

'Love the suit byraway,' she whispered as he rustled self-consciously past.

And they said she had no sense of humour?

CHAPTER 18

MONDAY MORNING

Despite the constant onslaught of salted sea air, Scarth's coastal village was respectably wooded. In the mornings, the air reverberated with bird-song. Prominent among the participants was of course the blackbird, with more songs in its repertoire than an Irish showband. In the early-morning half-light, as Scarth lay in bed listening to the pigeons cooing in the sycamore tree at the foot of his garden, a startling thought came to him: what would Andrea Fyffe do if she knew of the existence of Agnes Napajok's diary?

She would be mortified, that went without saying. Her fierce pride in her illustrious ancestor's achievements would take a severe, perhaps fatal, blow. She would have no need to hide the diary's shameful contents from her father, for he was probably past comprehension, but would she try to distance herself from it, and from her beloved ancestor?

No, he thought. Given her social standing, her first reaction would surely be to attempt to acquire the diary, and then suppress its contents from becoming public knowledge.

That would certainly be the course of action her husband would take, he decided, for any whiff of scandal would be certain to derail his cushy ride on the public gravy train.

Did he get to know of its existence, wondered Scarth? Did he decide to confront Colin Muir and end up murdering him while attempting to retrieve the diary?

Andrea was at the Midlothian Law Society dinner at the time of the homicide. But was Tony McGill where she said he was?

At the conference table later that morning, Munro and Scarth sat awaiting their boss. Munro had on a royal blue cotton jacket, with the cuffs rolled back. It was over a white t-shirt. She told Scarth that once McIntosh arrived, they'd both be briefed before going to interview the suspected phone snatcher, Sallyanne Seaton.

Quin, wearing a red striped top under a navy suit jacket, soon joined them. She was in a vexsome mood. She dislodged a rucksack strap which had been draped over her left shoulder as she pulled up a chair.

'Me first,' she announced peremptorily.

Scarth turned to give Munro a sympathetic sigh.

Quin drew air in noisily through her nose. 'With regard to the actual murder investigation,' she continued, 'we're really not much further forward. We've got a time of death at the scene, a possible point of entry to the scene in the French windows, and several candidates who might conceivably want Mr Muir dead.'

She paused.

'When we came across the video Muir had of Bill Crighton having it away with his receptionist, I thought we had cracked it. Unearthed a prime suspect. I was thinking Muir maybe tried to blackmail him, and got silenced for his trouble. You can see his motive. If word of that video reached Lenore MacDonald's bejewelled ears, she'd have ditched him in a hurry. And bang would go the £50 grand she had promised to invest in his zero-emissions courier company.'

'Why would Mr Muir need to blackmail him?' Munro said. 'Surely lawyers are wealthy enough …'

'Bob's been looking into Mr Muir's financial affairs,' Quin replied. 'He was in deep doo-doo. Andrea Fyffe, the office manager at Muir's law firm, has confirmed Colin Muir was about to be sued by needy creditors. So much so, that he was a potential walking bankrupt. He needed every penny he could get to fight that action. We also have the fact that Erica Griffin, his daughter and heir, has discovered Premium Bonds worth £10,000 in a safety deposit box in Muir's name at his bank. There's been no withdrawals or payments from Muir's bank account. So where did the money for these certificates come from?'

'Yes. They could indeed be from the proceeds of blackmail, boss,' Munro said. She flicked a glance at Scarth, who winked sagely.

Quin nodded her agreement. Fingers of very dark hair fell to the corner of her mouth. 'Exactly. But who from? Crighton doesn't have the money. He's hanging on by a thread waiting for his girlfriend's cash injection. I've been checking out his finances. He hasn't got that kind of money lying around.'

'Premium Bonds have serial numbers,' Munro observed. 'They can be checked. With a bit of digging, the buyer will be revealed. Do you want me to look?'

'Do that Heather,' Quin said. 'When you have a moment …'

'It's doubtful that Crighton would kill Mr Muir,' Scarth said, 'after all, as he told us himself, with Muir dead, the estate money, what will be left of it after the sharks have done with the estate, will go to Erica. Crighton desperately needed Lenore, the ex-wife, to get her divorce settlement from Muir, so that she could give him his much-needed loan. He needed Muir alive …'

'Good point,' Quin agreed. 'But I'm not totally convinced.' She sniffed. 'Then there's McMurray. A brute of a neighbour who is no stranger to violence, and who had good reason to hate the victim's guts. Was the murder just a vicious act of revenge, with no hint of blackmail around?'

Scarth's face showed his doubts. 'McMurray seemed to me to be the blustering, bull-shitting type. He will try to push you around unless you stand up to him. I don't seriously think he's a killer.'

'You're probably right,' Quin said. 'I'm clutching at straws.'

'Then there's Danny Griffin,' Munro said.

'Yes,' Quin said. 'Tell Bob what you've found out Heather …'

'Well for one thing, I've found that on the night Mr Muir was murdered, Griffin was in Edinburgh, not Inverness as he claimed.'

Scarth was all ears. 'Was he now? Whereabouts in Edinburgh?'

'He stayed all night at the Rasmussen, one of the airport hotels.'

Scarth pursed his lips. 'Meeting a secret girlfriend? A secret business meeting? It could be innocent enough. What motive would Griffin have to murder Colin Muir?'

'To save his business reputation, maybe,' Munro replied. 'I've had a look at the encrypted video files on his office computer. They weren't naughty videos, as Andrea Fyffe feared, they were endless recordings of the Shanghai bitcoin exchange.'

'Showing what?' Scarth asked.

'They're not recent. They are a few years old. The videos followed the day-to-day fluctuations of the bitcoin market. Mr Muir seemed particularly interested in the doings of a company called Candlemaker Holdings.'

Scarth sat up straighter. 'Where have I heard that name before?' he asked Quin with a smile.

'The Griffins stay in Candlemaker Wynd,' she confirmed.

'Candlemaker Holdings traded up till three years ago,' Munro explained. 'It was a partnership. The two partners were Danny Griffin and Colin Muir. I think Mr Muir was taping the transactions on the floor of the Shanghai bitcoin exchange in order to monitor the activity of Candlemaker Holdings. To keep an eye on his investment.'

'Or to gather evidence of any dodgy dealings on Griffin's part. As ammunition for the forthcoming lawsuits over the loss of clients' money …' Quin put in.

They all thought about that for a moment.

'Yet according to Andrea Fyffe,' Scarth said, 'the news that Colin Muir's creditors were about to move on him wasn't common knowledge yet. We know it. But Griffin doesn't.'

Quin harrumphed. 'If Griffin's so squeaky clean, why did he lie to us? Don't answer that. We all know that when someone lies to us, there's dirt beneath the carpet.'

'I never said he was squeaky clean, Moira,' Scarth reminded her. 'He may be the opposite. For instance, I've discovered that his claim that Colin Muir surreptitiously used clients' money for investment purposes was a lie. Andrea Fyffe told me it just could not be done. He had no more access to clients' money than he has to mine. A personal signature witnessed by one of the other solicitors was required. She did admit there was a possibility that Griffin would be sued at some point; whether the impending action against Colin Muir was successful or not.'

'But if Muir was out of the way,' Quin speculated, 'his wife could get her inheritance. She could bail him out when the inevitable law suits started.'

'Possibly,' Scarth conceded. 'But there is nothing currently on the legal horizon that would cause Griffin any concern …' Scarth objected.

'So maybe his antennae were picking up danger signals from another source,' Quin said. She changed tack. 'Here's something that's been gnawing at me. Is there a possibility that one of Mr Muir's creditors did it? I mean, even if there is a pending court action, what's to stop one of them going ahead and killing Mr Muir anyway? They'd get revenge for the heart-burn and trouble he's caused them. And there's a strong possibility that they'll also be getting their money back as a result of suing his estate. Like a win-win double-whammy.'

Scarth smiled. 'You've got a very tortuous mind, Moira. And you've just opened a huge can of worms ...'

'How many creditors are there, Bob?'

'I don't know,' Scarth admitted frankly.

'Think you could find out?'

'Sure. But I'm due in court later,' he reminded her. It was a follow on from his old days with the Edinburgh City force. 'I might be there all day. The creditors' lawyers are Sharpe & Shuter. Maybe they'll tell us, if you ask politely,' he said hopefully, not looking very hopeful.

'Mmm. Then again …'

'Griffin would know who the creditors are,' Scarth interjected. 'After all, he was the one who actually lost their money for them.'

Quin brightened up considerably. 'You're right. And I know he'll be dying to tell us. Especially after I ask him if his little wife knows of his all-night tryst at the Rasmussen.'

'You're a devious woman, Moira.'

Quin simpered happily. 'Why thank you, Bob. Anything else that's new?'

Scarth paused. 'Well … there's just the puzzle of the Inuit girl's secret diary.'

Quin gave him a questioning look. 'What diary?'

Scarth told Quin and Munro the story of the Inuit girl's diary he and Lizzie had discovered, and gave her the gist of Lizzie's subsequent translation. Quin was visibly moved, but was adamant that it did not concern them.

'Bob,' Quin said firmly. 'We are not going to get involved with a hundred-year-old mystery. We have a murder case right here in front of us. That's what we need to concentrate on.'

'Maybe the cases are connected.'

'How so?' Quin asked testily.

Scarth was not to be discouraged. 'What if Colin Muir's murder was all about the diary? If word of the revelations in the diary got out, the Fyffe family name would be irrevocably tarnished.'

'Are you including Andrea Fyffe in this daft hypothesis?'

Scarth shook his head. 'She's not on my radar at all …though Tony McGill's whereabouts on the night in question have not been firmly established,' Scarth pointed out.

'Who?'

'Andrea Fyffe's husband. He's an MSP. We haven't questioned him, but she says he was out of town that night. If the Fyffe family is scandalised, then by implication, he would be too. Whether he would be prepared to take action over it I couldn't speculate. Politicians are notoriously thick-skinned.'

'Find out about him Bob, will ye?' Quin said. 'Find out something juicy about him. I hate politicians. I despise the very ground they walk on.' It was the voice of old anger which had found a new outlet.

As Scarth gathered up his papers and dumped them on his cubicle desk on his way out, Quin turned to Munro.

'Heather,' Quin said. 'I think I hear Scobie's heap of scrap coming into the car park. Go and fetch him in to me, will ye? I want a word with that bugger …'

When Scarth phoned Broomieknowe, the live-in nurse answered on the fourth ring.

'The Fyffe residence. Gloria Rutherford speaking. How may I help you?'

'It's Bob Scarth, Mrs Rutherford. We met the other day …'

There was silence at the other end of the line.

'I came to see Andrea Fyffe if you remember …'

'You told me your name was Scarf,' she accused.

He wasn't about to argue with her. 'It's about Tony McGill, Mrs Rutherford. Just a routine enquiry. He'd been abroad, but we don't know when he arrived back home on Wednesday.'

'Why would you want to know?'

'As I said. It's just a routine enquiry.'

There was a long pause on the line, and he thought she'd gone, when she said, 'He came home in a taxi on Wednesday night, around eleven thirty. Woke me up. The driver banging doors.'

Scarth hesitated. Had Andrea Fyffe not told him she went to the airport to pick up her husband? 'Taxi drivers are like that,' he said. When they're awake, everyone's awake. It's just that I thought his wife might have picked him up at the airport …'

'Ha! Too busy gallivanting, that one …'

'She was probably in bed, at that hour.'

'She might have been in bed,' the woman said in a scathing tone, 'but if she was, it wasn't her own one. If you catch my drift.'

Scarth was intrigued. 'So, you think she was out somewhere?'

'I know she was out somewhere. And up to no good, likely.'

'Really? I was given to understand she spent the evening relaxing in front of the TV.'

Mrs Rutherford sniffed. 'She didn't have time. She came home at about half past eight, and left again an hour later. Didn't get back till after eleven.'

'And you're sure about that? Scarth asked.

'Couldn't be surer.'

'Would you be willing to give us a statement to that effect, Mrs Rutherford? If required at some point in the future?'

'Well, I …'

'On the understanding, of course, that your employers will not need to know, unless it needs to be produced later in court.'

'In court?' Her voice was suspicious. 'Just who are you checking up on here, Mr Scarf; Tony McGill, or his wife?'

'Well at this stage, Mrs Rutherford, it's only …'

'I know,' she laughed humourlessly. 'Routine enquiries … bla de bla de bla. Anyway, I'm not bothered what the Fyffes know or don't know. I've handed in my notice this morning.'

Andrea Fyffe was pleased to hear from him, she said, when he phoned her office later that day. When he asked if she was up for 'a bite to eat' that lunch-time, she immediately suggested the Big Kilmarnock Bunnet.

He met her at her office. She came round her desk, grabbed his hands, quickly squeezed them, and then released them.

'Thank you for rescuing me,' she said, slipping into her outdoor jacket. 'This place gets manic at times.'

The pub was within easy walking distance, and Scarth and Fyffe got there after an easy stroll of five minutes. She was as tall as him and walked with her shoulders back. The Big Kilmarnock Bunnet was a well-thought-of establishment in an area of four-storey Victorian sandstone buildings. In the deprived post-war years of rationing and unemployment the neighbourhood was a place of boarded-up shops and litter-strewn streets. A place where even big Scottish polis didn't care to linger. Now it was designer outlets, health food shops, and fancy restaurants. Patrons now spent as much on an evening's sushi dishes, as a whole household earned in a single year in the 1950s.

The Big Kilmarnock Bunnet had started life in the 1950s as a working-class darts 'n' dominoes dive. It transformed in the late 1970s into a soft-rock speakeasy, before being bought by a Chinese family from Guangdong. They re-invented it as a Sino-Scottish fusion food eatery, specialising in exotic Asian dishes and traditionally-wholesome Scottish country fare.

A sallow-skinned young Asian man with dark feverish eyes took their orders. He spoke with a Scottish accent. He nodded with candid familiarity to Andrea Fyffe when he came to their table. Scarth wondered if the establishment was one of her usual haunts. Or was it perhaps because the man had been one of her firm's clients?

She daringly plumped for the vegetable and barley broth with boiled Chinese spiced-pork dumplings. A wedge of home-made crusty farmhouse loaf came on a side-plate. It was seeded, Scarth noticed, a type of bread that he disliked. He played safe, ordering a lactose-cheese toastie and a glass of bubble tea.

They made small talk till their plates arrived. During the meal, Scarth was careful not to catch her eye as she ate heartily. Each nibble of bread was closely followed by a spoonful of the soup. Chop sticks had been provided, but the dumplings were ignored.

Scarth bit a piece out of his sandwich and chewed thoughtfully, looking round the room. 'Did your father ever mention a diary being part of your great-grandfather's whaling collection?' he asked casually.

'A journal, do you mean?' she replied. 'Yes, there were several. Captain Fyffe, like all of the whaling masters those days, kept meticulous journals, and ship's logs. They were required to by the Board of Trade, who regulated the merchant marine, and regularly inspected the documentation pertaining to commercial voyages.'

'Did you ever actually see them?'

'Naturally I did. Faither wrote his book when I was a little girl. I remember his study being overflowing with charts, logs, ship's journals, and stuff. I suppose all Captain Fyffe's old log books and stuff gave him the basic material for his manuscript. What happened to it all I'm sure I couldn't tell you. It's not something I've thought about.'

'Did your father ever mention the existence of a diary belonging to one of the Inuit girls?

There was a brief pause before Andrea Fyffe said. 'No. That would be interesting, though, wouldn't it? Why, has something come to light?' she asked cautiously.

'Not really. I just wondered. Diary-writing was a popular Victorian pastime. I wondered if you remembered anything of the sort among the whaling collection.'

She had finished her soup. Only now did she spear a dumpling with a chop-stick. 'Well, I couldn't really tell you everything which is in the collection,' she munched, 'after all, I was a little girl. And like most little girls it was the beautiful fur coats which interested me.'

Scarth finished his sandwich and ventured a sip of his bubble tea. It tasted incredibly sweet, which suited him. He wondered why they called it 'bubble tea'.

Fyffe caught his unfamiliarity with the beverage. 'You should use the straw,' she suggested pleasantly. 'Helps to sook up the tapioca pearls at the bottom of the glass … Bob, what is the point of all this?'

'The point?'

'Bob, you're sleuthing. And you're not telling me what you are sleuthing for. Is there something I can help you with?'

Scarth met her frank gaze. His cheeks were flushed with the syrup hit from the tea. Or maybe it was with the discomfort his next question was causing him.

'Andrea. You haven't been entirely truthful with me, have you?'

Her eyes narrowed. 'In what way?'

'Well, you told me when I first met you that you left the Law Society function early to go home and tend to your sick father. But that was not the case, was it?'

Her mouth tightened with disapproval. She pushed away her soup plate, and drew in a tiny bowl filled with palate-cleansing after dinner mints. She slid one out of its sleeve and popped it into her mouth.

'So, Mrs Rutherford has spilled the beans on me, has she?'

'She says you came home, and then went out again at about nine thirty. You weren't at home during the period in which Colin Muir was murdered.'

'And you think I did it?' she scoffed unbelievingly.

'Can you tell me where you were?'

He could see she was thinking it over. She unfolded the napkin by her elbow. 'OK. My dirty little secret is out. I went to meet a friend.'

It threw him. He composed himself. 'I'll need a name, Andrea.'

'No. I'm not going to divulge a name. Look, Bob, this isn't an on-going affair or anything. I'm not a slut. It's just an itch I have to scratch now and then. Okay?'

'It would help if you could substantiate your claim, Andrea,' he persisted.

Fyffe threw her napkin onto the table. 'No. Do I need substantiation? Look, Bob, I'm admitting marital infidelity to someone I've only met twice before. Does that not have the ring of truth about it?'

He opened his palms. Mr Reasonableness. 'You've admitted that you weren't at home as you previously told me you were. Now you've come up with another version as to your whereabouts. You can see how suspicious that is going to look to the police.'

She tilted her head and looked at him with narrowed eyes. 'Are you saying I'm a suspect?'

He shook his head. 'All I'm saying is that we can clear this up quickly if someone can vouch for you that night.'

'Is my word not good enough?' She shifted her eyes away from his, and looked down at her plate.

Scarth sighed. 'Andrea, you know it's not.' He pushed his plate to the side of the table. 'Where did you meet this friend?' he queried. 'Are you prepared to tell me that?'

'At a pub called the Covenanters' Rest if you must know. And yes, it's only a hundred yards away from Colin's house. And no, I didn't pop along between snifters and kill him. Satisfied?'

Scarth was surprised at the revelation, but kept his voice steady.

'The police will need a name sometime, Andrea.' He patted his napkin absently. 'What's the point in stalling? Why not tell me? I'll get your secret meeting corroborated with your friend, and that's it.'

'Definitely not.'

'I can ask at the pub, Andrea,' he warned softly. 'They'll have observant staff, CCTV, all that …'

Her smile was strained. 'Look, Bob, I'm married to an important politician. Any whiff of scandal would destroy him.' She spoke too loudly and seemed to realise it. 'He doesn't deserve that,' she said more softly. 'Can't you take my word for it?'

'I can't Andrea. You know I can't.'

Her eyes were shiny with unshed tears. She blinked them away. 'Well then bugger you, Bob Scarth,' she snapped, rising abruptly from the table.

As she marched purposefully for the entrance, their waiter drifted silently to fill her void. He proffered the bill on a porcelain saucer. 'Everything to your satisfaction, sir?' he asked with obvious insincerity.

Scarth fished out his wallet and extracted his credit card, watching absently as she neared the swinging doors.

Scarth nodded. 'Yes, fine, thanks,' he told the man.

To himself he said, self-deprecatingly, 'You handled that one well, Bob. Congratulations.'

CHAPTER 19

MONDAY MORNING

Confirmation that the blood on McIntosh's jeans matched Leah Duffy, the most recent phone-snatching victim, had dropped into McIntosh's Inbox first thing that morning.

Shawn Murray had pulled out all the stops to get the result to him ASAP, and 'Mrs Slocum' had duly obliged. McIntosh had immediately phoned Murray with his appreciation at the Forensic team's efforts, and had emailed Mrs Riddell, for he knew she would be home asleep now. It was such a huge fillip for the investigation, that he took the unusual step of phoning Quin at home. She too had been delighted. She said she was having a catch-up with Bob and Heather first thing, and asked McIntosh to pick up some treats and coffees on his way in to the office.

Scarth said a brief hello and goodbye to McIntosh as he left for his court duty. And when Munro and McIntosh took their seats at the CID room conference table, Quin scanned her notes briefly, cleared her throat, and then began.

'Here's where we're at. We now have the ID photos, names, and addresses of our phone snatchers. We have footage from the bus company showing them collaborating in the assaults. We have witnesses who can place them there. We have footage from The Mall showing the suspect wiping blood off her hands after her assault on her last victim. And we have confirmation from Shawn Murray that the blood on your shirt Scobie is a match for that victim, and video proof that the blood was transferred from the suspect to you as she made her escape after the incident.'

She scooted her chair round so that both of them could see the folder's contents.

'We need to concentrate on this Sallyanne Seton,' she stated. 'Are we sure about where she stays?' They both peered at the folder. 'It says here that Seton and Carmichael stay at the same address,' said Quin, 'in Bridge Street Lane. Is that correct?'

'It is,' McIntosh confirmed. 'They're sisters apparently. Carmichael has been married, and widowed. That's her married name. The other one was married, I think, but divorced. She uses her maiden name.'

'It says here that they stay at Galadale Villa. Sounds very grand.'

'Several villas were built in that street for the gunpowder mill management,' McIntosh said. 'They're mostly all gentrified now, of course.'

'What gunpowder factory?' Quin queried.

'There was a gunpowder mill in that area,' replied McIntosh, 'where the big Galadale council housing scheme is now. Big employer in its day. Hundreds of workers at any given time. The operation closed in the 1950s I think.'

'Never heard of it,' said Quin. 'Hardly surprising really …'

'The Second World War was over, so no more need for its products I suppose …' Munro speculated.

'Before my time ...' replied Quin, showing her disinterest.

McIntosh, the fount of all knowledge, continued: 'The factory started during the Napoleonic Wars apparently, and …'

Quin, like most women, despised history lessons. 'That was before my time too, though you probably won't believe it … I was about to say it is hardly surprising that I've never heard of it. When you become a cop, people stop telling you things.'

'Except other cops. And who would believe them?' McIntosh grinned at his own wit.

Quin ignored him. 'This Sallyanne Seton,' she said, 'she's probably a nice wee wumman, clean in her habits, but we can't allow her to attack members of the public just because they are blethering on their mobile phones. Go and interview her. Intimidate her. If she isn't forthcoming, bring her in and I'll squeeze her.'

McIntosh rose from his chair.

'Oh, and Scobie,' she said as he turned to go, 'apologies about the after-shave.'

She gave him a placatory dunt on the upper arm. 'It was a joke in bad taste. I admit it. I'll make it up to you, you know that.'

He nodded. When it came to ribbing, it was as important to take it as to dish it out, he knew.

'I've applied for a search warrant for Seton's home,' she said before he left the table. She looked at her Fitbit. 'With any luck the PF will get a warrant from the Sheriff in a couple of hours and you can go and pick her up. Take

Heather with you,' she smiled solicitously, 'in case the wee wumman takes it into her head to beat you up again …'

Something in McIntosh rebelled a little.

'Does the name Donnie MacKay mean anything?' he asked innocently. He knew immediately he had hit the bulls-eye.

Quin's mouth became a thin line. 'No, I don't believe so. Why? Should it?'

'It's just that he was asking for you.'

'Where did you see this Donnie MacKay?' She acted nonchalant, but he knew he had perked her interest.

'He's the boss at The Mall security centre,' McIntosh replied helpfully.

So that's where he is, she thought. She filed the information away for future use. Possible future use.

'Never heard of him.'

McIntosh turned to go. He knew she was lying; and she knew he knew she was lying; and he knew that she knew he knew she was lying; and … and anyway, he thought, what's the point of pursuing the matter? If she wanted it forgotten about, then so be it.

A few minutes casual gossiping in the rest-room with PC Gray, gave McIntosh some more details of the Carmichael and Seton sisters. Dean 'Deano' Gray, played semi-pro football with a local Junior Club. The sisters had been brought up in Galadale Villa, he said, which their father had bought in the late 1950s.

'Their father, Bobby Seton, was a hero to my granddad's generation,' Gray announced. He soon warmed to his subject. 'Bobby was a professional footballer, a 'goalkeeper to trade' as he used to say. We all know nowadays about Billy Bremner, Archie Gemmill, Souness and Dalglish, legends and giants of the game. But twenty years before them Billy Seton was a household name in England. In the 1950s, the English football leagues, the professional clubs, were stuffed with Scottish players. Footballers were one of Scotland's most valuable exports. There was lots of unemployment here after the war, and football was a way out for hundreds of lads.'

'He obviously made good, being able to buy Galadale Villa.'

'He was a top-flight player; won League Cup medals. He was only awarded about a dozen Scottish caps, but of course they played a lot fewer internationals then ... That house was reserved for the manager of the gunpowder mill. It closed in the early 1950s, and the house was sold off. The factory was demolished in the early 1960s, and the council built the Galadale scheme on the site.'

McIntosh nodded. 'I know that bit. Do you know anything of the two daughters that live there?'

'Only what Sergeant Balmain has told us. That they are a pair of pests. One of them, I think it was Seton, has called the switchboard a couple of times complaining about the bad manners of young people yapping on their mobile phones on the buses.'

'Has she now? Well, thanks Deano. You've been a big help. Are you playing today?'

Gray flexed his knee, tightening his mouth, shaking his head. 'Sidelined. Cruciate ligament injury. Could be out for weeks.'

McIntosh grimaced his sympathy. He held up his bandaged paw. 'Me too, Deano. It's a bugger. But your knee will heal, don't worry. Just don't go chasing criminals for the time being.'

Gray, a talented but fatally lazy player on the park, one who preferred the ball to come to him rather than having to hustle for it, gave the tall detective a lopsided smile. 'Do I ever?' he cheeked amiably.

They laughed. Warriors missing the fray.

The warrant came through a couple of hours later. Just after ten thirty McIntosh and Munro were ready to leave the station. They stopped at the reception on their way out. The station's SUV was away to Edinburgh, being used to pick up stationery supplies from a wholesaler. Sergeant Balmain cast McIntosh a jaundiced look when he announced he intended to bring at least one suspect in for questioning, and asked what uniforms were available to transport prisoners back to the station.

'My Mustang's not suitable,' he explained. 'The suspect is known to be violent. We'll need the Black Maria.'

Balmain guffawed his derision. 'Ha! The last time I saw a Black Maria was when I was a school-bairn in short trousers. So, who's this violent suspect then?'

'The phone snatcher. Her name is Sallyanne Seton.'

Balmain's craggy features creased into a genuine smile. 'That nutter …'

'Do you know her?' asked Munro.

'Oh, we know her all right. She's been warned about making nuisance calls to the station here, and to Division.'

Munro was intrigued. 'What kind of nuisance calls?'

'The waste-of-police-time kind of calls …Tell you what, PCs Gray and Reid will be out and about with the van this afternoon, up at the football, I'll send them round if you give me a shout when you need them.'

It said a lot for the law-abiding nature of the Eskbridge community, thought Munro, when only two policemen were required for crowd control at local matches. Of course, it also said a lot about the size of the crowd the local Junior League games attracted.

It was nearly eleven o'clock when McIntosh and Munro pulled up outside the terraced villa in Bridge Street Lane. The house was an unremarkable two-storey Victorian building, made of light-coloured sandstone, set in a short terrace of similar structures. Between the two second-floor bedroom windows, a square stone insert said 'AS. 1884'. McIntosh didn't know if it was a builder's mark, or the initials of the architect. It might even be the initials of the building society which provided the finance, he thought with distracted interest. More likely the architect, he guessed.

When Sallyanne Seton opened her door to McIntosh and Munro, she seemed delighted to see them. As the detectives held out their wallets for identification, the woman's hand flew to her chest, her face a parody of relief.

'Come in, come in,' she urged pleasantly. 'I've been expecting you.'

McIntosh and Munro exchange perplexed glances as they stepped over the threshold, McIntosh ducking under a low lintel, blacked from decades of passing exhaust fumes.

Seton was a short, slim woman with a tight expression on her face. She had disconcertingly pale, piercing eyes set above high cheekbones. There were wrinkles round her mouth which didn't look like laughter lines. She wore a burgundy lambswool sweater, light blue jeans, and fluffy pink slippers.

'Thank goodness you've arrived,' she announced breathlessly, leading them into a stifling livingroom. 'Actually, I'm just off the phone to the police station,' Seton said. 'I didn't expect you so soon ...'

From the adjoining kitchen there was a strong odour of something McIntosh could not identify, but did not particularly care for. Like most police officers, he dreaded going into old folk's homes. Sometimes the smells which assaulted them were awful. And distressing too, for it was often not the occupants' fault. Nowadays double-glazed windows were hermetically sealed, and small transom windows, which could admit at least modicum of fresh air, were often ill-situated at the top of the window. For old people, they were difficult to reach, and difficult to open. They were often forced to breathe in and out yesterday's dead air.

However, the livingroom McIntosh and Munro entered was airy and well-ventilated. Fresh flowers sat on the marble mantle-piece and on a sideboard. The furniture was from another era, but looked clean and comfortable. A corner display cabinet held medals, tasselled caps, and wooden-studded football boots Dubbined to a high sheen. Below the football memorabilia lay several glistening objects which appeared to be from a more recent era.

'My Daddy's trophies,' the woman said proudly.

Munro piped up. 'In our display cabinet we had stones. We used to collect stones. From the beach,' she said.

McIntosh and Seton looked at her questioningly. Munro felt the pressure to elaborate.

'Every time our parents took up for a picnic to the beach my brother and me would collect a stone each. As a memento. We must have been to hundreds of beaches ...'

'I never had a brother,' Seton replied dismissively. She indicated the lower shelf. 'Though I do have my own commemorative trophies ...'

McIntosh bent closer to the cabinet. It suddenly dawned on him what he was looking at. Pliers, an industrial punch, a pair of secateurs. Souvenirs of the phone-snatching attacks, polished and arrayed proudly for everyone to see! He couldn't believe the audacity of it.

He straightened and turned accusingly to the woman. She was vigorously wiping her hands on a kitchen towel. The stains on the towel were bright red. With a start he identified the smell that had been bothering him. It was blood! Had she committed another bloody phone-snatching assault, or had she been cleaning the implement used to hack off Leah Duffy's thumb? Her brazenness was astounding.

'Excuse me, Mrs Seton,' McIntosh said calmly but menacingly, 'but is that blood on your hands?'

She lifted her high thin shoulders in objection. 'It's Mizz,' she said sharply to him. She held up her red-stained hands. 'And of course, it's blood. It's pig's blood. We make our own black pudding. I'm doing a basinful now ...The secret is in the suet, you know ...'

McIntosh felt his stomach flip. He had no further questions on the subject.

'Are you going to arrest these people or not?' the woman demanded of him.

He was momentarily taken aback. 'What people?' he questioned.

Munro, who always took the lead when they were interviewing females, lost her patience with McIntosh's dithering. 'We're actually here to serve a search warrant, Mizz Seton …' she interrupted mildly, but firmly.

The woman continued to focus on McIntosh. She had an astonished look on her face as she answered his question. 'What people? What people he asks? I'm referring to the people who are living in my attic of course, officer.' She jerked a thumb towards the ceiling. 'The aliens. Why else would you be here?' She glared at McIntosh, then Munro, then McIntosh again.

Munro was insistent. 'Mizz Seton,' she interrupted again impatiently, trying to gain the woman's attention, 'could we perhaps return to the matter at hand …'

Seton interrupted. 'Oh, never mind that now, woman,' she said fiercely. She gritted her teeth. 'I've been terrorised for months now by these people. You need to catch them, and lock them up. You,' she jabbed a stick-like finger at McIntosh, 'make yourself useful and follow me ...'

She swivelled on her heel and returned the way they had come in. At the livingroom door she turned and put a cautionary finger to her lips, urging stealth.

As Munro, astounded, stood rooted to the spot, McIntosh, without quite knowing why he did it, followed the woman out of the room to the hallway. Stretching upwards was a broad, gently sloping staircase, built in the days when females wore bustles and needed extra passageway. At the top of the stairs McIntosh could see a triangular occasional table, set in the corner of the landing. It held a colourful vase, but no flowers. The vase was blue-tinged. It looked expensive, porcelain, possibly Oriental.

The woman began creeping slowly, carefully, up the stairs. McIntosh reluctantly followed suit, moving with elaborate secrecy. After a few steps she turned, her face lit by excitement, and whispered to him. 'They've come down. They're in the back bedroom …'

McIntosh turned to Munro, who was standing at the bottom of the stairs, looking bemused. He shrugged his shoulders helplessly. She used the back of her hand to wave him on, her grin the width of her face. She put a hushing finger to her lips. In her softest voice, she cautioned him delightedly, 'No hanky-panky mind ...' She got a scowl in return.

McIntosh slowly climbed the steps. The old dear was afflicted with wind, and every second step resulted in a soft puff being emitted from between her buttocks. Pfft. Pfft. The smell was instantaneous and ghastly. McIntosh held his hand over his nose and mouth as he gagged and gasped his way upwards. The chortles from Munro down below set his teeth on edge.

At the landing he carefully manoeuvred around the small table with its exotic vase. To his left a short corridor ran the length of the house. It had four doors. Two bedrooms, a bathroom, and a cupboard? The woman stepped forward silently and stealthily opened the first door. She beckoned to him conspiratorially, and entered.

It was a large, high-ceilinged room, with a large double bed. It had an unused, fusty, smell about it. As if all the air had been sucked out of it and the windows nailed shut years ago. The curtains were heavy and partially drawn. In the dim half-light McIntosh could make out the woman as she approached the far side of the bed. She motioned him to move round the near side, a pincer movement. She pointed sharply downwards several times, her face full of meaning, then cupped her hand to the side of her mouth. 'Underneath the bed …' she whispered.

McIntosh hadn't a clue what she meant. 'What?' he mouthed.

'There's one underneath the bed,' she hissed.

One what? McIntosh hoped it wasn't a full chanty. He dropped awkwardly to his knees, and gently lifted the musty counterpane. He lowered his head to the rough carpet, and peered underneath the bed.

With a start, he encountered a pair of mad, red-rimmed eyes staring right at him. Through the dust motes and fluff he could see they were a pale ice blue, brimming with mischief. They resembled the cold, weird eyes of a rabid Husky dog.

Then he realised they were from the other side of the bed. It was Sallyanne Seton, on her knees and squinting anxiously from under the bedspread.

McIntosh and the woman lifted their heads simultaneously, and looked at each other, still on their knees, across the dusty bedspread. Her eyes had a brightness McIntosh didn't like.

'No one here,' she stated, rising to her feet. She sounded disappointed. Deflated.

'Listen, Mrs Seton …' he began.

'It's Mizz,' she reminded him frostily.

' …. I'm not here to chase away your demons …'

'Who says they're demons?' she replied angrily.

'We're here to serve you with a search warrant, in connection with …'

'Well search then!' she snapped impatiently. 'Isn't that what I'm asking you to do? Search. Search for the aliens who are plaguing our lives …Oh look! Behind you! Look! There's one there!'

McIntosh spun round instantly, semi-crouched to ward off an attack. Behind him was a tall double wardrobe. One door was mirrored. His dishevelled figure stared stupidly back at him. His suit was dust-stained and crumpled, as if he had been sleeping in a skip. In the mirror, he could see Sallyanne Seton staring in horror at his reflection.

After what seemed to be an eternity, he stepped smartly to the side. His reflection disappeared from the glass. She could no longer see him in the mirror. Her face dissolved into relief. He was fascinated. It was like Pavlov's dog, he thought, or whatever.

He stepped again in front of the mirror.

'AHHHH,' the woman wailed. 'THERE IT IS! IT'S BACK AGAIN!!'

He stepped to the side again. Her face immediately flattened into peacefulness. The mirror was like an on-off switch. He'd never seen anything like it.

'Is everything all right up there?' Munro called anxiously.

'Fine,' McIntosh shouted in reply. He'd had enough of this ridiculous farce, he told himself, and marched out of the bedroom. On the landing he waited for the woman to emerge. Munro was still at the bottom of the stair, her neck craned upward.

'That was quick, sir,' she called. 'Might be a new record for the 'wham bam thank you ma'am' award ….'

Sallyanne Seton hurriedly joined McIntosh at the top of the stairs.

'I know you don't believe me,' she panted. 'No-one does. But there have been aliens living in the attic for two years now. They used to come down into the bedrooms, and interfere with us while we were asleep. When we were in our flimsies. We weren't safe from their evil intentions. Me and Val have been sleeping in the livingroom ever since …'

McIntosh took pity at the obvious distress on the old woman's face. 'I sympathise, Mizz Seton, but there's not much the police can do. Perhaps a spiritualist, a medium or somebody, could help …'

'Or an exorcist,' piped up Munro from the foot of the stairs.

'Yes, an exorcism,' McIntosh retorted enthusiastically. 'That would do it.' He nodded officiously at Munro. 'Excellent idea Constable. Remind me to mention you in despatches …'

'Maybe there's another way,' said the woman, still looking fearful. She engaged McIntosh's eyes feverishly. 'What if you threatened them? You know, officially, in a loud voice. Told them to clear off out of here, and that if they came back, you would arrest them and throw them in an underground dungeon …'

McIntosh saw his way out. 'Well, it might work,' he conceded. He looked to Munro for confirmation. She nodded enthusiastically. She was enjoying this.

McIntosh filled his lungs dramatically.

'FOR THE ATTENTION OF YOUSE ALIENS,' he bellowed stentoriously, 'WHO ARE CURRENTLY OCCUPYING THE ATTIC IN GALADALE VILLA, ESKBRIDGE, I AM THE POLICE, AND I ORDER

YOU TO CEASE AND DESIST YOUR DEPREDATIONS FORTHWITH …'

Seton nodded vigorously, urging him on. At the bottom of the stairs, Munro looked up at her superior officer's commanding figure in admiration. 'Threaten them with jail time if they don't leave, sir,' she encouraged, unable to hide the smirk which played on her cute little face.

McIntosh gave her a warning glare, then cleared his throat again.

'I ORDER YOU TO VACATE THESE PREMISES IMMEDIATELY,' he dutifully roared, 'YOU ARE NOT WELCOME. IF YOU DO NOT WITHDRAW AT ONCE, YOU WILL BE INCARCERATED INDEFINITELY!'

He coughed discretely then turned to the woman standing behind him. 'That do you?' he asked, taking a tentative step downward on the well-worn stair carpet.

'That was very well put, officer, thank you,' she said from her elevated position, then hit him an almighty clatter on the back of the head with the porcelain vase.

The last thing McIntosh saw, as he tumbled head over heels down the stairs towards her, was Munro's stupefied face as she stood paralysed in shock, fearfully awaiting the inevitable collision.

CHAPTER 20

MONDAY AFTERNOON

'Oh My God,' laughed Quin, searching for her phone, 'I have got to get a photo of this …'

She was in the Patient's Waiting Room at the hospital. On the sofa opposite her, sitting morosely, were Detective Sergeant McIntosh and Detective Constable Munro.

Not that they were immediately recognisable.

They each wore hospital gowns and flip-flops. Both had their foreheads trussed in turbans of gauze and bandages. McIntosh had a tape across his broken nose. Munro had come off worst. Propped against the sofa beside Munro was a ferrule-tipped, adjustable-length NHS walking stick; for she had a foot encased in an off-white stookie. Her left arm was in a sling.

'Dearie, dearie, me,' clucked Quin as she zoomed in for her snap-shots. 'What on earth have you two been up to?'

When McIntosh had come tumbling down Sallyanne Seton's stairs towards her, Munro had neither the room nor the time to take evasive action. His momentum slammed her against the solid front door. The impact had fractured her right ankle. Her left collar-bone had been fractured. Her head had been lacerated as it bounced off the solid front door. She now sat, one wing in a sling, one foot in plaster, giving her hard-hearted boss a resentful one-eyed look from under her bandage dressings.

McIntosh had got off lightly. He was used to tumbling, breaking his falls, being trampled on the rugby field by opponents who were intent on doing him significant harm. He had sustained a few bruises on his arms and back during his rapid and unplanned descent, but his soft landing on his startled colleague's pneumatic body had prevented serious injury, and he had emerged relatively unscathed.

Apart, that is, from the head wound. And his dented nose.

Sallyanne Seton's vase had gouged a furrow on the back of his head which had required fourteen stitches. He sat now, his bandaged noodle making him look taller than he already was, clearly not in the mood for his boss's banter.

Quin eyed McIntosh and Munro without sympathy. 'Two experienced police officers,' she droned on, while shoving her phone in her bag, 'and you can't even bring an old age pensioner in for questioning? Jasus. If Deano and Connor Reid hadn't shown up at Seton's house to help with the search warrant, you'd still be lying there, bleeding all over that woman's hall rug.'

Quin let the silence build up. Savouring the downcast looks from the sofa.

'What the hell happened?' she asked.

Despite her wooziness from the pain-killers, Munro gave her the gist of it: – how they'd been decoyed by the woman's whimsicality into thinking she was a harmless old eccentric; how McIntosh had been blindsided at the top of the stairs; and how she had been an unwilling buffer to break his fall. It was a wonder they both had not been more seriously injured, she added.

Quin harrumphed. She addressed McIntosh. 'And what about you, Detective? What dismal tale do you have to tell?'

'She bushwhacked me, boss. Simple as that. I underestimated her. More deadly than the male and all that …'

'Don't talk pish, Sergeant. I'm not in the mood for it. She's an old woman, not an effin commando. Do you know that, only a couple of hours ago, I advised Superintendent Kerr that the phone snatcher who had been plaguing Eskbridge for the past month was on the verge of being arrested? Do you? How am I going to wriggle out of that one, eh?'

She might as well have been talking to the wall.

Her eyes narrowed as she focused on McIntosh. 'You know, Scobie, I'm beginning to think that you are too accident-prone for this investigation: you are insolent to the Superintendent in front of dozens of other officers; then you appear on social media rolling on the ground in a public place with an elderly female civilian; then you inflict such serious injuries to yourself and a colleague that you both end up in the A & E department …'

McIntosh sighed in relief. She doesn't know about the treatment room. Thank Christ.

'I'm beginning to think you need your head looked at …'

'I already have, boss. They did a CT scan of my skull. They didn't find anything …'

'Ha!' Quin guffawed humourlessly. 'My point exactly! Only someone as totally effin brainless as you could get themselves into the kind of scrapes you do.'

McIntosh grinned in spite of himself. 'I meant pieces of pottery from the vase the old bastard hit me with.'

'Not hard enough as far as I'm concerned. And how do you know it was a vase?'

'Heather told me.'

'What, when youse were getting your stories right? I'm going to need you both to write this up. Before you go on sick leave …'

'I vaguely remember Dean and Connor helping us before the ambulance arrived,' said Munro. 'But what about Seton. Did the boys arrest her, boss?' asked Munro.

Quin shook her head. 'No sign of her. She'd skedaddled. After Gray and Reid found you and Scobie curled up cosily together in the hallway, they called in for an ambulance. Then they called me. We went round to Robert Beatson's place, and there she was. We pulled the three of them in. They're quaking in the office now, awaiting the interrogation chamber.'

Quin smiled enigmatically as she recalled the shocked look of umbrage on the conspirators' faces as they were brusquely taken into custody. For his good work in comforting the injured detectives, and promptly calling for the medics, she had thrown PC Dean Gray a bone.

'Book 'em, Deano,' she'd growled with a straight face, even though she knew it was not applicable in the Scottish police service.

His grin had been wide and appreciative. 'Yessir!'

Quin had smiled appreciatively. She hated the bleating "Ma'am" which came with her new rank.

'Ever since I joined the police,' Gray had rabbited excitedly to her, 'I've been waiting for someone to say that to me ...'

She'd known that of course: which was why she'd never said it. He was such an egocentric little shit, that she'd purposely withheld the gratification from him.

She'd told Heather the story before McIntosh shuffled in from his ward, and they'd had a quiet giggle about it.

McIntosh interrupted her ruminations and startled them both with a sudden burst of laughter. They both looked at him questioningly.

'What a laugh it would have been, boss,' he wheezed, leaning forward, 'if you had said to PC Gray, "book 'em Deano" …' He sat back, grinning widely.

Quin had a face as emotionless as a Sphinx. Then her features morphed into a frown of puzzlement. She looked at Munro questioningly. Munro looked at McIntosh questioningly.

'You know,' he prompted, his confidence faltering now, 'like Steve McGarrett in Hawaii Five-O …'

There was a moment's silence as they stared at him in dumb incomprehension.

'Who?' they chimed in ragged unison.

McIntosh scrutinised their impassive faces. He couldn't believe they were missing his point. He didn't believe they were missing his point. Oh yes, he told himself, what he had here were two wind-up merchants from the Eskbridge School of Pathetic Acting.

A slow grin played on his cracked lips. It developed into a wide smile, then he burst into a raucous laugh.

The two females had struggled to keep it in. They couldn't wait to join him, and vented their hilarity accordingly, their wild laughter echoing round the plain-walled room.

'Jesus,' McIntosh admitted after a while, gathering his breath, 'youse had me going there for a split second …'

'Didn't we just,' laughed a contented Quin, a hand raised to quell her heaving chest.

Munro was the first to curtail her amusement. She looked at Quin and piped up in a worried voice. 'They might be keeping us in here overnight, boss, because of the head injuries, but do I need to go on sick leave afterwards?' she asked anxiously. 'It's just that there's so many loose ends we need to tie off …'

'Officially yes, Quin replied. 'Time off after being admitted to hospital is mandatory, and justifiable so. Unofficially, I'm not ordering you to stay away from the office. Have a good night's rest, and see how you feel the morning.'

She lumbered stiffly to her feet. 'Listen kids,' she said, 'I've got to go. Before Dr Bashkir gets wind that I'm here …'

Just then the door creaked slightly open, and the consultant's smiling nut-brown face peeped round the opening.

'They told me you were here, Moira …'

'Yogi!' Quin cried in apparent delight. 'How're they hanging?'

MONDAY EVENING

When McIntosh answered his door-bell that evening, Deirdre Clarke recoiled in surprise.

'What the hell happened to you?' she gasped in horror; her eyes glued to his turbaned head.

He stood grinning. 'It's a bit of a story,' he said bashfully. 'The nub of it is, I fell down a flight of stairs.'

He'd only been detained at the A & E Department for the statutory four hours before being discharged. No concussion, so he was allowed to leave. But his head stitches still needed careful looking after. He'd gone straight round to the pet centre to pick up Scottie. The wee fella was on the last night of his monthly sleep-over and he didn't want to deprive him of his morning jaunt to the beach.

'Dear, oh dear, oh dear,' she said, as he stood aside to let her into the flat.

Deirdre stepped cautiously into McIntosh's flat. It was the first time she'd been there. She was a self-reliant-looking woman with a trim, lissom frame and red hennaed hair piled up in a doughnut. She was several years older than McIntosh, but looked younger. They'd had two dates in the previous six weeks, but apart from a bit of light-hearted petting the occasions had passed unremarkably. She was curious to see how he lived.

She passed through a short hallway into the livingroom. Actually, it was his livingroom and galley kitchen combined in a long, orderly room. At least it looked and smelt presentable. A four-chair dining table had been set out in a corner, complete with sputtering red candles, fresh flowers, white napkins. She smiled. She liked a man who was prepared to spend some time wooing a girl before jumping her bones.

That morning McIntosh had sprayed and wiped the galley kitchen worktops and the loo, and after a quick whizz round with the Gtech had declared everything ship-shape. He religiously changed his bed-sheets and duvet covers twice a month, whether they needed changing or not. And that morning he had risen early and stripped his bed. He'd crammed the bedding into the washing machine, set the cycle, and hit 'go'. New sheets from Marks and Sparks – Egyptian cotton like his mother recommended – were ripped from their wrapping and smoothed out on the bed. Hopefully, Deirdre would stay the night.

As she moved into the room Scottie rose to his feet and immediately went over to check the new arrival.

She had heard all about the famous Scottie, his extraordinary sense of smell, his exploits with the police. McIntosh had even told her about the outrageous name change The Ex had instigated behind his back. She was scandalized.

'You can't just change a dog's name,' she had exclaimed. 'How will it know who it is?'

'My point exactly,' McIntosh had replied sanctimoniously.

Nevertheless, she was nervous. She hadn't met Scottie in the flesh, so to speak, and she didn't really like dogs. She knew the dog stayed with McIntosh occasionally; she just hadn't expected him to be there that night somehow.

As she plunked herself down on the sofa, Scottie took up a position on the floor in front of her. He barked twice, then waited, his eyes watching her suspiciously. When McIntosh didn't respond, for he had wandered into the galley to fetch Deirdre a glass of her usual Prosecco, the wee dog barked twice more, loud, insistently, its tail standing straight up like a dorsal fin. He was on station.

'I don't think he likes me,' Deirdre called over her shoulder.

'Nonsense,' grinned her host affably, returning to the sofa with two fistfuls of drinks. He handed her a glass of wine, remained standing, chugging at a beer. 'What's not to like?'

As he sat down beside her, the dog started a low, rumbling, warning growl, the sound deep in its throat. He barked again. Sharply, angrily. Not an official bark this time. More like a jealous one.

McIntosh was surprised. He'd never seen Scottie act this way before with a stranger. Usually, he was all sniffs and wagging tail, his mouth slavering excitedly.

As he slithered an exploratory arm along the back of the sofa towards Deirdre's bare neck, Scottie emitted the loudest protest yet. Deirdre jumped in surprise and fear; McIntosh reacted sternly.

'Quiet!' he ordered the pet crossly. 'That's enough!'

Even as he chastised the wee fella, McIntosh realised two things at once: 1) The dog thinks he is still at work; and 2) If he didn't shut it up quickly, I'll lose the chance of seducing the delectable Deirdre.

He rose quickly, scooped up the little dog, and hurriedly carried him into the bedroom. He dumped him unceremoniously inside the door, and closed it tight before the wee fella could react.

As McIntosh returned to the sofa, he suddenly realised that the worst place he could have stashed the wee fella was in the bedroom. Wasn't that where the best chance of success lay?

'Maybe he thinks I'm wearing fake perfume,' Deirdre suggested when McIntosh was seated beside her.

'More than likely,' McIntosh replied. 'He has a smell repertoire of the usual brands – Kilian, Penhaligon's Halfeti, Hana Hiraku, Rose d'Arabie – that sort of thing.'

'I've never heard of them.'

'The usual luxury brands I should have said ...'

Deirdre was puzzled. 'But if the perfumes were fake, Scottie wouldn't need to differentiate between them, would he? He wouldn't need a super-sophisticated nose. They'd all smell much the same, probably. They'd all smell like crap …'

McIntosh chose to miss the point. He shook his head in wonderment. 'Beats me how he does it, really. He's amazing.'

She relented. 'Maybe the counterfeits have just a hint of the perfume they're supposedly representing. Enough of a whiff to fox the uninitiated. Like me. What's Hana Hiraku?'

'Japanese. It's everywhere apparently,' replied McIntosh knowledgeably, though he'd had to ask the handler. 'That's why he's barking,' he continued confidently, 'he knows you're wearing counterfeit perfume.'

'Well, I bought it off the internet, so I wouldn't be surprised really …'

But McIntosh was keen to get on with the seduction. Keen to change the subject.

'Have you thought about food?' he asked.

Deirdre smiled, happy to get away from Scottie and his wonderful attributes. 'What have you got?' she enquired.

'Come through to the kitchen and we'll explore the larder,' he said. 'Bring your drink ...'

In his narrow galley kitchen, he made a show of showing her the contents of his stuffed freezer.

'I've got mince 'n' macaroni in there: if you'd like that.'

'That sounds interesting,' she fibbed.

'It's available with a red sauce, or a cheese sauce …' he offered. 'Ladies' Choice.'

'Mmm,' she said thoughtfully, noncommittally.

'It doesn't have to be mince 'n' macaroni,' he said, offering her a way out.

She could see that was what he wanted, but wasn't ready to give in. She nibbled her lower lip. 'What else have you got?' she asked nicely.

'Spaghetti mince; which is similar to mince 'n' macaroni obviously, both being of Italian extraction. Except for the mince of course, which is home-grown Aberdeen Angus. Or stovies – made with chipolatas. Cordon bleu quality. Delicious.'

'You certainly seem to be well stocked …' she said diplomatically.

'I cook stuff for the freezer every once in a while,' he said with bachelor pride, 'then defrost it in the microwave when I need it. Saves time ...'

She looked impressed with his forward-thinking. But still hesitated.

'Or we could order in a pizza ...' he suggested. He'd already ordered a pizza from every one of the pizza joints in The Mall. Just to see who delivered it.

She relented, nodding her head. 'Pizza,' she said, finally convinced.

'Thank goodness for that,' he smirked. 'I've already ordered it …' he admitted sneakily.

'Bastard,' she laughed, punching him on the arm. 'We'd better set the table.'

The narrow galley space made it difficult for them to pass as they howked out plates, cutlery, condiments. McIntosh couldn't avoid getting bumped now and then with a rounded hip. Deirdre hummed to a tune in her head. She looked amused, tricky, and smug, darting challenging glances his way. The infrequent small talk bore no relation to what was going on; to the tension in him that she was building.

The chores done, they rested at the work-top. She took a modest mouthful from her glass then set it down. She was wearing an unseasonal vest-type top; low cut, figure-hugging and purposely sensual. She leaned on the counter, half-turned to him, her arms folded under her breasts, presenting them almost.

Their eyes locked. He couldn't look away. He didn't want to look away. He fidgeted. There wasn't enough air in the room. He wanted to ease his erection to a more comfortable position, but was scared to draw attention to it. She looked down at it, then up at his face.

'At least you've got something interesting for afters,' she smiled.

He put his glass down and put a fingertip to her check. She kissed his wrist. As their mouths came together, he could taste the nicorette chewing gum. He put his hands on her buttocks and pulled her close. She pressed herself hard against him, her arms snaking round his neck. He could feel the elastic of her panties under his thumbs.

When he came up for air he put on a wobbly act, pretending his legs were going from him. 'I feel faint,' he said feebly. 'I think I need a lie down.'

'Don't we both,' she breathed suggestively.

The doorbell rang.

'Damn and blast!' exploded Deirdre.

'That'll be the pizza delivery,' he said happily. 'I've been looking forward to it for ages.'

'Yeah,' she replied bitterly. 'So was I.'

At the door, McIntosh automatically took the pizza from the delivery guy, then did a double take. He was a tall slim youth, with red curly hair. McIntosh recognised him instantly as the one who had 'rescued' the old lady in The Mall.

The youth looked at McIntosh, said, 'Oh shit', and turned and ran for the stairs.

McIntosh thrust the pizza box into Deidre's arms, pecked her on the cheek, said, 'Must dash', and dashed after the youth.

'Where are you going?' she wailed helplessly after him.

McIntosh chased the pizza lad down the stairs, and up the street. After a hundred breath-sapping yards the youth turned left into a courtyard. McIntosh pulled up, a daft grin on his face. It was a cul-de-sac, he knew, and all he had to do was block the entranceway. He'd done something similar a million times before, when an opposing forward charged his line.

Realising he had painted himself into a corner; the youth decided attack was the best form of defence. The youth surprised McIntosh by putting up a struggle. In spite of his slim build, he was strong, a handful. Eventually McIntosh backed him up against a wall.

'I'm a policeman,' McIntosh panted. 'I need to talk to you. Is your name Hamilton?'

Thinking that McIntosh was confusing him with someone else, the youth grinned. 'Naw,' he said, 'It's Archie McLurg …'

McIntosh tried to hide his disappointment.

It would have been fitting, for Superintendent Kerr's sake, if the lad had been a Hamilton. It would have rounded it off nicely, validated her theory of the link with the Four Marys. But this McLurg had scuppered that. Probably on purpose. McIntosh was filled with a sudden irrational rage against the youth for spoiling the symmetry of it all. The young man's face was momentarily creased in bafflement before McIntosh's big fist buried itself in his solar plexus.

'That's for screwing it all up,' McIntosh puffed with satisfaction.

The youth doubled up and slid slowly to the ground. McIntosh waited patiently till, after a bout of violent retching and having, the youth slowly revived. McIntosh handcuffed him. He knew that the Eskbridge station had closed at seven. What he needed was a lock-up for his prisoner the night. He managed to hold on to the guy, pull out his phone, and call Division.

'It's Scobie McIntosh in Eskbridge,' he announced breathlessly to the dispatcher.

There was a pause.

McIntosh wondered insanely if he had entered the wrong number for HQ into his Contacts.

'I'll need some proper identification,' said the dispatcher stiffly.

With a heavy heart McIntosh recognised the cultured Kirkcudbright twang of Vicky Guthrie.

Many moons ago, when he'd been an unmarried uniformed probationer, he'd once gone round to Vicky's place for an afternoon quickie. It had ended badly. When they'd got all bare-naked and needy, he'd handcuffed her to her bed, to add a bit of spice to the proceedings. Afterwards he'd discovered that he'd left the keys for the cuffs in his locker at the station. It was a sticky situation. In more ways than one.

He hoped she didn't still hold it against him.

'Vicky, I'm in a rush here,' he pleaded desperately.

'Be that as it may,' she said frostily, 'I still need your ID number, DS McIntosh. Standing Operating Procedure, protocol, whatever. I'll give you a clue,' she said, her voice dripping sarcasm, 'it's on your warrant card.'

And so it was. McIntosh, with his mobile trapped between shoulder and chin, and one hand gripping the handcuffs to subdue the youth, fumbled for his wallet. He fished it out, pried it open, and read out the number. It seemed familiar somehow.

'That's your date of birth, you stupid git,' she said icily.

'For fuck's sake Vicky,' he protested, 'can't we let bygones as bygones? I'm sorry. OK? Will that do?'

She pounced. 'No, it will not do! Do you know how *black affronted* I was when that incident got out? Do you? Do you know how much humiliation I suffered when the *whole fucken* Division got to know about it?'

McIntosh had made the mistake of using his airwave radio to ask a mate to take the keys out his locker, and bring them to him pronto. Might as well have broadcast it with a loud-hailer.

'Bring them where, mate?' the so-called mate had asked solicitously.

'Vicky Guthrie's place', McIntosh divulged insanely, letting the cat out of the bag.

The mate, knowing they were on an open channel, and hoping to elicit more titillating information for the delectation of the listeners, asked innocently, 'Is she a prisoner?'

God knows how many people were monitoring the conversation, McIntosh recalled bitterly. You could practically hear the ears of every cop in the county pricking up.

Yet he couldn't resist stepping into the trap, eejit that he was.

'You could say that,' he'd replied enigmatically. 'I've gone and cuffed to her headboard …'

Jesus. The laughs the lads had enjoyed when that got out.

But all that was in the past: a different country. Wasn't it?

'What the fuck do you want anyway?' Guthrie quizzed brusquely.

'I need help,' McIntosh panted, thankful that she was at last seeing sense. 'I've just slapped the cuffs on someone, and I'm ...'

'Oh my God!' she gasped in disbelief. 'I can't believe it! You're at it again aren't you, you dirty filthy bastard!'

'No, Vicky, I …'

'That poor woman, whoever she is,' interrupted the distraught dispatcher. 'Oh, you need help all right, McIntosh, you need psychological fucken help!'

'I've got a problem here with a prisoner, if you must know.'

'Ha! Oh, I know all right. I know what it feels like to be one of your prisoners! I can't believe you've got the brazenness to tell me this. I really can-not believe you're telling me this …'

'Vicky, would you listen just a minute…?'

'Get off the line McIntosh!' she shouted. 'This is for emergencies only!'

'That's what I'm trying to say, dammit. This *is* an emergency!'

'Well, just deal with it!' she yelled. 'PERVERT!' she screamed finally, severing the connection.

Eventually he had managed to drag and frogmarch the youth to his car, and bring him to Division HQ himself. He handed him over to the custody sergeant.

'Keep him snug for a few hours Bert,' he said. 'I'll be back for him first thing in the morning.'

He rushed home to Deirdre. He had only been away an hour and thirty-five minutes, yet she wasn't in the flat.

The pizza box had been folded and stuffed into his letterbox.

Why had she done that? What harm had the pizza done?

In the lonely bedroom, Scottie was barking the place down.

McIntosh trudged across the carpet to release the poor wee soul. Scottie greeted him with feverish licks and a tail wagging like a windmill.

Thank goodness dogs don't hold grudges, he thought as he tickled the wee fella affectionately behind the ears.

CHAPTER 21

TUESDAY MORNING

Unusually for him, Scobie McIntosh was the first one in to the CID room that morning. Big day ahead. He had been informed by email from Superintendent B-B B Kerr's office that she would be conducting the initial interviews with the phone-snatching suspects in person, and that he would be required to assist her. Fame at last.

Pinned to the office whiteboard were the crime scene photos from the Muir murder case, and snapshots of the main players. A portion of the board had been reserved for the phone snatching investigation. He had pinned up the bus-pass photos of the three primary suspects. To them he added a print-out from The Mall security footage featuring young James McLurg. The Fourth Man.

He noticed the boss had mischievously added the photo of him rolling about on The Mall floor with Sallyanne Seton. He flipped it over, showing Superintendent Kerr's blunt summons: 'SEE ME' on the reverse side. He stood back and admired it. It was a privileged communication, representing a select invitation. An evocative reminder of his unique, lubricated encounter with the formidable but delectable lady in question.

Quin had just joined him from the tea point, carrying her morning coffee, when Scarth breezed into the CID room.

'Morning Moira; morning Scobie,' he said cheerily. 'I hear congratulations are in order. Regarding the phone snatchers ...'

Quin harrumphed. 'Congratulations are a bit premature, Bob; though of course we're chuffed we've got them in custody. Scobie brought in the fourth one last night. Suspected fourth one. They're all being held at Division. Scobie and the Super will be interviewing them today.'

She nudged Scarth and lowered her voice conspiratorially. 'Between you and me, Bob, I think the Super has a bit of a thing for our Scobie here …'

Once again McIntosh wondered feverishly how much his boss knew, or indeed if she knew anything, of the massage room tryst. He had a mutilated right ear, the result of a bite from an over-zealous rugby opponent. He felt it tingling. The last time he'd blushed was when he was fifteen and had farted in a scrum, but nowadays self-consciousness presented itself in a vivid redness of the said ear. It was embarrassing.

Quin enjoyed the young detective's discomfort, before changing the subject. She pointed to the whiteboard on the wall in front of them.

'Listen guys,' she said after a slurp, 'is it just me, or is there something funny about this whiteboard?'

McIntosh owned up immediately. He pointed to the photo he had turned not long before.

'It's my doing,' he admitted. 'I flipped over the embarrassing photo of me and the phone snatcher in The Mall. It wasn't one of my best moments.'

Quin and Scarth looked casually at B-B B Kerr's 'SEE ME' directive, the bold letters circled with the red permanently-markered swirl.

Quin shook her ear-rings. 'That's not it,' she said. 'It's the swish or swoosh she has made round the 'SEE ME' bit. It's like the Asics logo, isn't it, only different?'

Neither of them could guess what she was getting at, so said nothing.

She pointed to a photo of the murder victim, a close-up of the smiley face on Colin Muir's left buttock. 'She could have done that. The Super.'

It was a leap too far for McIntosh. 'The murder, boss?'

She punched him on the arm. 'The swoosh, ya eejit. Any fool can see the similarity.' She turned to Scarth. 'Bob, can you see any resemblance?'

'Well, perhaps a tad …'

'It's obvious! I tried to replicate it last night. Did it dozens of times, but couldn't get it right …'

'You'd have to do it left-handed, boss,' McIntosh said. 'Right-handed people draw a circle in a clock-wise fashion. This swirl goes anti-clockwise. That's because the Super is left-handed.'

'How do you know that?'

'All the Kerrs are,' replied McIntosh knowledgably. 'Or were.'

He told them quickly but animatedly of the days of the Border reivers. In medieval times, he said, castles were almost always built with a clock-wise spiral (when looking up from the bottom). Right-handed attackers, as most people were, had their swings blocked by the inside wall. But the defending swordsmen, who would either be advancing down the stairs, or backing up in reverse, could swing their swords freely, without being blocked by the wall.

The Kerrs were trained to use their swords left-handedly. This meant that when they were attacking up a conventional clock-wise spiralled staircase, they could chop at the feet and legs of the defenders, without their swings being hampered by the wall.

The Kerrs also built their castles with anti-clockwise spiral staircases, which made them easy to defend if you were left-handed, while simultaneously disadvantaging right-handed attackers.

'Fascinating,' drolled Quin, clearly uninterested.

'That's why left-handed people are called 'ker-handit', or 'car-handit',' McIntosh continued. 'Named for the Kerr family.'

'I thought it was 'corrie-handit',' Scarth said.

'Same derivation,' McIntosh stated confidently in parting.

As he gathered his things, and made his way out of the room, Quin raised her eyes momentarily to the ceiling, shook her dark locks, then turned and moved back to the conference table.

'Bob,' Quin called over her shoulder, 'come in to the body of the kirk. You too Heather. Time for a pow-wow.'

To kick things off, Quin addressed Munro.

'Shawn's sent me a helpful email. Or rather, he's sent me an email he thinks will be helpful.' She then looked specifically at Scarth. 'Remember he said the ligature may have been a belt with something made of soft material with a zip on it. Forensics have come up with a suggestion. A fanny pack, bum bag, or a waist pack; take your pick of the various terms.' A dubious expression clouded her deep blue eyes. 'Was it Muir's? Do middle-aged men have so-called bum bags, Bob?'

'Certainly,' he asserted. 'I know of several of my golfing buddies who wear something similar, especially on holiday; to carry phones, money, sun lotion, that sort of thing.'

'Really? As we all know,' Quin continued, 'when a murder weapon is removed from the scene, it is usually because it can be readily identified as belonging to the killer. But bum bags, fanny packs, call them what you will, are generic, ubiquitous. They're on sale everywhere, especially on the internet. They're worn everywhere. Finding this one will be infinitely more difficult than looking for the proverbial needle in a field of haystacks.'

They sat in silence, contemplating that enormity.

Scarth was thinking that he couldn't remember ever seeing a haystack. Even fifty years previously, when he was a young boy, most farms used baling machines. Sheaves and stooks were a thing of the past. He'd once stayed for a week with a pal who was a farmer's son. Scarth and his buddy had earned pocket-money by lifting the newly-formed bales of hay onto the prongs of his dad's fork-lift, which transferred the bales onto a waiting low-loader. It took the two of them all of their strength to lift a single bale of hay together. The field stretched forever. He thought he would have to spend his whole holiday there. He found out later that it was only seven acres.

His ankles and shins, he remembered, were covered in cuts from walking through the sharp-edged stubble. His mother had gone ballistic when he'd returned home, and had forbidden his return to the farm.

Doddie, his pal was called. Doddie Weir. Not the famous one. The wee bandy-legged one. Doddie knew a number of amazing things for a boy: he knew where to get girlie magazines even though he wasn't an adult; he knew how to shoplift without getting caught; and he knew where there was a field white with button mushrooms if you went at a certain time in the morning. In the tortured life of an adolescent, when adults were absolutely the last people you'd trust with a confidence, Doddie was the kind of boy you went to if there was trouble on your mind. Did he ever take over the farm as his father intended, Scarth wondered?

Munro interrupted his reverie. 'But they'd be local haystacks, in local fields, wouldn't they, boss?' she asked hopefully. 'That would narrow it down considerably, wouldn't it?'

Quin had her doots. 'Marginally, Heather,' she said. Feeling she had been a bit sharp on the girl, she gave the young detective an encouraging look, and said, 'So Heather, have you managed to check those phone numbers I gave you?"

Munro nodded. She looked down at her notes.

'I've got some results here, boss. To begin with, Bill Crighton was where his wife said he was on the night of Mr Muir's murder. He was home with her from ten past eight onwards.'

'Snuggled up close beside the fresh-smelling Mizz Lenore MacWhatshername,' Quin scoffed. 'What about the bitcoin entrepreneur of the year, Danny Griffin?'

'As we suspected, he never left the Rasmussen Hotel last Wednesday night.'

'So he says,' Quin answered. 'I had a word with him last night. He admitted being at the hotel all night, and not at Inverness which he had previously stated. Lying bastard. I warned him that wasting my effin time any further would result in charges being brought against him. He says he was meeting a financial adviser, in an attempt to negotiate a capital loan. I didn't mention anything about impending law suits or anything. I asked the adviser's name, and he told me it was someone called Aimee McPherson.

'I know her,' said Munro. 'She's a charismatic go-getter, apparently ...'

Quin pursed her small lips. 'Really? I asked Griffin if the negotiations went on all night, and he said, 'Pretty much', the lying prick.'

'The other numbers you gave me was for Tony McGill and his wife,' Munro continued. 'His wife had told Bob he was away at some conference in the Frisian Islands, and that's exactly where he was. So that's another loose end tied off.'

'I know. It's a bugger,' Quin said unhappily. 'We're running out of loose ends ...'

They sat in silence for a moment, then Scarth stood up from the table. 'I've got to love you and leave you kids,' he apologised. 'I'm due back in court his morning, Moira. This bloody thing is dragging on and on. Hopefully, my tuppence worth will be heard today, and I'll get back into the saddle.'

Quin said, 'Which is where Danny Griffin probably spent the guts of Wednesday night if I'm not mistaken.'

Scarth looked mock-shocked. 'Moira Quin, go and wash your mouth out this instant.'

'Oh, and another thing, Bob, before you go,' Munro interjected. 'Andrea Fyffe wasn't where she told you she was.' She let the tension build up 'Her GPS signal puts her at the Covenanters' Rest on Wednesday night from 9:30 p.m. till 11:03 p.m.'

Quin beamed happily. 'Thank you, Heather, for a lovely loose end …'

Scarth sat down again. 'Actually,' he intoned, 'I knew that … That she'd been to the Covenanters' that night. She told me.'

Quin was aghast. 'She told you? When?'

Scarth shrugged. 'Yesterday. We had lunch in the Big Kilmarnock Bunnet …'

'For Chrissakes, Bob! Would ye listen to yourself! A suspect tells you she was a hundred yards from the scene of a horrific murder, at the time of the murder, and what, you don't think it's suspicious? You don't think it important enough to report it? What am I running here – a dating society?'

As Munro drifted discretely away from the table, Scarth faced Quin.

'I should have reported it, Moira. I'm sorry I didn't. She told me a plausible story of meeting an old friend there, and I swallowed it. Sincere apologies ...'

As Quin seethed inwardly, struggling to manage her temper, a couple of sharp knocks came from the room door. They all turned their heads sharply at the unexpected intrusion.

'Knock, knock,' Sergeant Balmain said insincerely, marching briskly into the room. Trailing somewhat nervously behind him was a thin-looking, thin-haired man, and an even thinner-looking youth.

'Someone to see you, Inspector Quin,' he said formally, ushering in the pair towards Quin. 'A Mr Liam Shinnie and his son Bobby …' he announced.

'Robbie,' corrected the sulky youth.

'That's the one,' replied Balmain cheerily, retreating backwards to the door. 'They've got a video tape of someone entering the rear of Mr Muir's house on the night of the homicide,' he explained.

Quin was all ears. Scarth, who was again hoisting his rucksack onto a shoulder prior to leaving, hesitated. Quin laid a hand on his arm.

'Bob,' she said, 'can you stay for a bit? This might be interesting.'

Scarth consulted his wrist somewhat anxiously. The drive into Edinburgh was something he'd gladly cancel altogether, but there was no way out of it.

'Twenty minutes, Inspector,' he said, mindful of the civilians present. 'Then I've definitely got to make tracks.'

Quin seated the boy and his father beside Munro at the conference table. Scarth joined them. Sergeant Balmain said, to no-one in particular, 'right then. I'll leave youse all to it …'

Mr Shinnie told them that he lived in Summerfield Drive, the street which ran parallel to Colin Muir's street. The rear of their house faced the rear of Mr Muir's, he said, and that was what this visit was all about.

The boy, he told the investigators, was part of Spring Lookout. It was an ornithological survey, sponsored by a national TV company, monitoring the behaviour of birds in typical Scottish gardens during spring time. As part of the scheme, the boy had acquired a camcorder, with night vision, which he had set up in his bedroom. The room overlooked the Shinnie's back garden. Partly in shot was the rear of Mr Muir's house, and the service lane which divided the two properties.

Quin arranged for the small portable TV in the rest room to be brought in and set up on a table near them. The investigators and the Shinnies arranged their chairs to suitable viewing angles. The camcorder was connected, Mr Shinnie produced a remote control and said: 'That's us; ready to roll.'

Shinnie ran the tape forward looking for the place he wanted. Several times the tape was stopped to check its position. The views all looked the same: darkness, mainly. The trees and bushes at the bottom of the Shinnie's garden partially obscured the right-hand side view. There was a street-light further down the lane, which threw out a meagre light to help them.

For what seemed to Scarth like an eternity they watched intently as nothing happened. Quin shifted impatiently in her seat, like a jelly settling in a desert dish. She was about to remonstrate about the time it was taking when suddenly a figure appeared on screen. It moved purposefully up the lane to Muir's garden gate, let itself in, and scooted up the concrete path to the house rear. The figure moved to the left, onto an area that was decked, and stopped at the French windows. These were swiftly opened, and the figure slipped inside.

No alarms sounded.

Scarth glanced at the time-stamp on the camcorder film. It read: 21:50.

'That's what I wanted you to see,' said Shinnie. 'It's Roy McMurray …'

Quin and Scarth were gobsmacked.

'How did he get a key?' Quin asked the company, not expecting an answer. No one bothered to answer anyway.

The study light came on, but went off again after half a minute. McMurray, for they were in no doubt it was he, suddenly appeared again at the French windows, and, as swiftly as he had entered, slipped out again. He nipped down the garden path, through the gate, and out into the lane. They watched as he ambled to their left, slowly moving out of shot.

The group at the conference table watched and were surprised as the study light went on again. No silhouette was visible through the thick black-out drapes.

After a long while, Quin broke the silence. 'Is that Colin Muir getting home?' she asked.

Scarth looked at the time on the camcorder. 21:52. 'No,' he said. 'Mr Muir doesn't get home for another eleven minutes yet.'

'Then who is it? Quin demanded.

The boy spoke. 'It's a buglur. Mr Muir always checks the glass doors and the kitchen door before turning off the lights. This night he didn't do it. It's unusual. The lights stayed on for ages. I was hoping they would go off, because I wanted to see if there was bats flying about, but they might have been scared off by the glow.'

Quin regarded the youth as if a foul taste was in her mouth. She despised young males, especially little boys, and this plooky specimen did little to alleviate her odium.

'So, when did the lights go off, Bobby?' Quin probed as blandly as she could.

'It's Robbie,' the boy replied.

'Beg your pudding, Robbie,' Quin said through her teeth. 'When do the study lights go off then?'

'I said. After half an hour.'

That was another thing Quin detested about youths – their uncouth surliness. She stared belligerently at young Shinnie. Was he being deliberately obtuse? She racked her brain for an ordinance under which she could detain the little shit. Finding none, she nodded to the father, who ran the tape forward.

When the study lights duly went off, Scarth noted the time on the machine. It said 22:27. The taxi company had told him Colin Muir had been dropped off at 22:03.

'Colin Muir's home by now,' he said. 'The taxi dropped him off twenty minutes earlier.'

'So why hasn't he checked that the French windows are secure?' Quin asked.

'Shawn said they'd been left unlocked,' Scarth reminded her.

The investigators stared morosely at the screen.

The boy pointed. 'He comes back into the room about now, though he only stays ten minutes.

They swivelled their eyes back to the screen. The lights in the study duly came on again at 22:45. They went off again at 22:53.

The boy stood up. 'That's about it. The tape finishes at eleven. They only gave me a four-hour tape. I'm supposed to review it, and note down the various species I see in the garden, then fill in a questionnaire. I'd have liked an all-night tape, to film the bats and things, if they were about, but it was too expensive.'

Quin looked questioningly at Scarth, who gave an imperceptible shake of his head. He had no questions for the Shinnies.

Quin commandeered the tape, but not the camera, and guided the Shinnies back to reception, all the while regaling them with her most sincere thanks.

Afterwards, Scarth said, 'I think we have to accept that it was McMurray entering the house, given the size and everything, the way he moved, and Mr Shinnie's identification.'

'Yes, Quin sighed, 'but why was he there at all? The fact that he gains entry to someone else's house, around the time they were murdered, is definitely suspicious.'

Scarth consulted his notebook then spoke. 'The taxi driver told me Colin Muir was dropped off at three minutes past ten. Going by the tape, McMurray had already left the house by that time.'

'So who's the mysterious 'buglur' then, as the spotty nincompoop called him?'

'I'm pretty sure it is the killer,' Scarth stated. 'McMurray heard him coming in, probably suspected it was Muir, and scarpered. Whoever it was stayed there till Colin Muir came home, before switching off the lights and leaving at 22:27.'

'After having strangled him.'

'Yes. Angus was sure that short time frame was when it occurred …'

Quin clenched her teeth in a grimace. 'So, we haven't dotted all the t's and crossed all the i's yet,' she snapped, lumbering to her feet, her chest heaving unnervingly. She threw her bag strap over her shoulder. 'Let's go and get

McMurray,' she said enthusiastically, 'and drag him in here by the nostrils.'

Scarth looked alarmed. 'I'm afraid I can't help, Moira. This court thing …'

Quin looked momentarily discomfited, but recovered swiftly. 'Don't worry, Bob,' she soothed, her tiny mouth curled in determination. 'Mummy here will get it sorted …'

CHAPTER 22

TUESDAY AFTERNOON

Scarth had felt bad about not being able to accompany Quin to arrest Roy McMurray, but at the time he couldn't get out of his court commitment. Then, to his utter frustration, after hanging around the court's corridors for a couple of hours, he wasn't called to give evidence. It was just like the old days when he was a police officer. Hurry up and wait.

On the way back to Eskbridge he was glad to hit open countryside again. He gazed out of the window at the magpies as they swooped from hedgerow to hedgerow in their incessant search for food. Ominous birds, his grandfather had told him, (he'd called them pyats) for in the old days, folk believed a pyat landing on your window sill meant there would be a death in the house. Scarth had been an impressionable child, possessed of a formidable memory, and drank it all in. Now, as he sailed past middle age, he struggled to remember the previous month's events. Soon the magpies would have insects aplenty, he thought. When spring had finally sprung. Until then it was a case of each day at a time. He knew the feeling.

It was after lunch time when he reached the office. Quin was out, no doubt bringing in Roy McMurray. Heather Munro was busying herself in her corner cubicle with her gadgets. McIntosh's chair was empty, his desk top was littered with photographs, folders, and documents. He wandered upstairs. Lizzie Williamson had a surprise waiting for him in the archives.

Lizzie had set up a video conference with Repulse Bay Interpretive Centre. A college pal she had known in Winnipeg had recently been appointed to the position of Curator at the Centre. It was an incredibly out-of-the-way spot, but her friend was studying for her Master's degree in Natural Resources Management, and the experience she would gain in the wilds would be invaluable.

Scarth and Lizzie adjourned to a 'Quiet Room' and sat at a burnished table. On it was a large monitor and a small PC. Lizzie made the connection via Skype, and they were off and running. After a few moments, two women who were obviously Inuit appeared on the screen in front of them.

Sheila Ann McKay, the Curator of the Centre, was a pretty young woman with wide-spaced intelligent eyes. Beside her was a much older, heavily-tattooed woman. Both were smiling. They were sitting at a small table in a room decorated with children's drawings. At Sheila Ann's elbow was a small projector. Mounted on a stand beside them was a white screen backdrop.

'*Ulaakut*,' said Sheila Ann. 'Good morning. It is eight o'clock in the morning here, but I do not know what time you have there. Today I am honoured to have with me Rosa Temela, who is our most respected elder here in the Repulse Bay settlement. Lizzie, I hope you are settling in there in Scotland; and that the weather is not too cold for you. Ha! I'll get to the point quickly, for the Centre is due to open in half an hour. As you know, the Centre has old photos,' explained Sheila Ann, 'some dating back to the early 1900s. They were taken by whaling captains who had cameras, rare items in those days. We have spent many weeks digitising this collection, but we think it is worth it. This slide,' she said, flicking a switch on the projector, 'may be of interest to you.'

It was a group photo. Inuit men, with identical soup-bowl haircuts, stared fixedly at the camera. The women, their hair parted in the middle and drawn tightly back, were shy and withdrawn. A smiling white man, hands on knees, sat in the middle. Scarth recognised Alexander Fyffe from his portrait in Andrea Fyffe's office. But he had also seen the photo, for it had been one of several in a photograph section in the middle of William Fyffe's booklet.

'I have gazed at this photograph many times,' said Rosa Temela. 'My grandmother, and then my mother explained all the old photos to me.' She looked at the slide with a fond smile and then pointed to the screen.

'There is your Captain Fyffe,' she said. 'The others are some of the people who worked for him; the hunters and their wives and children. I know them all by name.' She pointed to a young woman at the left-hand side of the group who had her arms round the shoulders of two young girls. 'That one is Nutaraq.'

She sat back suddenly, content with what she had said. There was an awkward pause before Sheila Ann said, 'Tell us about Nutaraq, Rosa, for we do not know of her.'

'Nutaraq was one of the chief's three wives,' stated the old woman. She took a breath. 'In those days a hunter had two or three wives. He needed his wives to work on the skins of the animals he killed. Usually, the chief's second or third wives were given to a captain of a whaling ship as his 'girlfriend'. It glued the bond between the Inuit and the whalers, and raised the chief's status. Nutaraq became the girlfriend of *Illungak*, which was our nickname for Captain Fyffe.'

Lizzie sniggered. She gave Scarth a sheepish look. '*Illungak* means he was bandy-legged,' she whispered.

Scarth was surprised, perhaps mildly shocked. The booklet Andrea Fyffe's father had written had firmly stressed that Captain Fyffe had taken great pains to avoid any such fraternisation.

Sheila Ann took over. 'As you can imagine, wrapping their tongues round local Inuit names was a problem for the whalers,' she explained, 'so they gave out Scottish names, like Betty, Maggie, Tommy, and Billy and so on, to make life easier. Sometimes the names identified helpers with specific jobs, like Harpoon Willie, Starboard Tam, or Kayak Jock. One man was called Handy Andy, for he could do many jobs. Inuit nicknames for the whalers tended to focus on physical characteristics. There was a well-known captain who was called *Nakungajuq* – Cross Eyes. That was why Captain Fyffe was nicknamed *Illungak* – the bow-legged one.'

Just then Rosa leaned forward and tapped the white screen. 'See how fancy-dressed Nutaraq is ...'

Lizzie and Scarth peered. The young woman in the photo was wearing a much-embroidered fur jacket embroidered, with bangles at her wrists.

'Before she became the captain's girlfriend, she was really poor; afterwards – covered in beads and bangles.'

Scarth needed clarification. 'Bob Scarth here, Rosa,' he said. 'I'm a bit confused. I was told that he did not have a girlfriend. Did not approve of the men having girlfriends …'

'Ha!' Rosa guffawed toothlessly. 'All the captains had girlfriends. Who else would keep them warm through the winter – the bosun?'

They all laughed.

'And I can tell you that some captains had more than one girlfriend,' Rosa continued salaciously. 'Sometimes they had girlfriends in every station where they visited! Those two girls in the photograph with Nutaraq were from her first husband. They were called Agnes and Betty. She also had two children with *Illungak*, your Captain Fyffe, who were also girls. They were twins. There is a story about this. Just after they were born the shaman went to Nutaraq and told her she must destroy them. She already had two girls, he said. That was enough. Infanticide really did get practiced in those old days. If the twins had been boys, they would grow up to become producers and providers, said the shaman, but two girls would only be a burden on her and the community. When Captain Fyffe heard of this, he threatened the shaman, and said he would tie an anchor to the man's ankles and drop him in the Bay if he ever came near Nutaraq again. The twins grew up healthy. In fact, there is a photo here that they are in ...'

Sheila Ann clicked through a few slides till Rosa said, 'Stop!'

It was a modern-era group photo, with too many people in it to differentiate the faces.

'This photograph was taken in 1966 when an Inuk from our settlement was elected to the territorial council,' the old woman explained. 'It was a very proud day for us in Repulse Bay. The twins were grandmothers then. Oh! I've just remembered something,' she chortled, 'the Scottish whalers used to chant, "Ye cannae shove your granny off a bus!" – which meant that you had to look after your granny, be kind to her ...'

Scarth saw a chance to establish a rapport with the old woman.

'Hi Rosa. It's Bob Scarth here again. I'm a friend of Lizzie's. I heard that Captain Fyffe brought a gramophone to the settlement,' he said, slowly and clearly. 'He had a stack of records. Apparently, a great favourite song among the Inuit people there was: "Roamin' in the gloamin, on the bonnie banks o' Clyde …" by Harry Lauder …'

'Who?' Rosa asked the young woman sitting beside her.

'Harry Lauder,' replied Sheila Ann. 'He was a famous Scottish singer.'

The old lady looked blank.

Sheila looked uncertainly at the camera. 'Wasn't he, Bob?'

'Well,' Rosa intervened, 'I certainly don't remember seeing him here …Are you a relation of his Mr Bob?'

'Not that I know of …' he replied carefully.

'I remember one Scottish song my mother taught me when I was little. She coughed, then sang in a wee high tuneful voice: "Will ye stop yer tick-e-ling, tick-el-lickel-ickel-ing. Stop yer tickling Jock!"

They all hooted with delight.

'That's Harry Lauder, Rosa,' chuckled Scarth. 'He wrote that song.'

'Did he?' Rosa giggled. 'He must have been a very clever man, for that song is still known here, after all these years …'

There was a transatlantic pause. When everyone stopped talking so that someone else could be heard. After a second or two Lizzie piped up to attract the old woman's attention.

'Rosa, Lizzie here. Can you see the twins in the photo?'

'There!' Rosa pointed. 'The ones without the head scarves. See how their hair is tousled. This photo was taken one time when a big bowhead was caught by the hunters. We had a great feed of *maktaaq*. My, what a day that was ...'

'What maktak?' Scarth whispered to Lizzie.

'Whale's skin,' Lizzie whispered back. 'It's eaten raw or boiled. The bowhead *maktaaq* is an Inuit delicacy surpassing all other. To be honest, it turns my stomach, but don't for heaven's sake tell anyone! Such a sacrilege …'

Rosa was rattling on. 'By the time this photo was taken the twins would only be in their late fifties. Just youngsters! I'm eighty-two,' she said, a wide grin spreading her wrinkled face, 'though of course you wouldn't know it. The twins are called Mary and Margaret. They live in Fort McMurray now, a long way to the south of here.'

The names registered with Scarth. Mary and Margaret were the names of Alexander Fyffe's twin daughters who unfortunately died in childbirth at Broomieknowe. Had his Inuit twins been born after his Scottish ones perished? Were they a poignant reminder?

Rosa was thoughtful for a moment; then spoke up again.

'Yes, I was told that when Nutaraq lost Agnes and Betty, her two darling girls, the shaman claimed it was God's way of balancing things out. For a woman to have four girls alive was excessive, greedy. That was the way shamans thought back then.'

Lizzie and Scarth exchanged glances.

'You say they were lost, Rosa,' said Lizzie. 'What do you mean?'

'I can only say what my mother told me. Captain Fyffe took Agnes and Betty over the oceans to Scotland, for their education. It was hoped they would learn to be teachers, and come back to us and teach the children here. But they passed over in Scotland, because of the measles. It was very tragic. Captain Fyffe broke the sad news to Nutaraq when he came to Repulse Bay here for the final whaling season.'

'Excuse me Rosa, its Bob Scarth here again,' Scarth said. 'You say that Captain Fyffe reported that Agnes and Betty had died when he came for his last whaling season. When was that? Do you know?'

'It was just before the big war broke out. He came early that year with two ships from the whaling company in Dundee. We were told a big war was coming. Captain Fyffe loaded what had been stored from the winter hunting, the fur and seal skins, ivory and narwhal tusks, and stuff, onto his own ship, the *Ajax*. The other ship was smaller, and took what was left.'

'And that was when he reported that Agnes and Betty had died of the measles?

'Yes.'

'Did he bring them with him?' Scarth asked. 'Are they buried at the settlement?'

'No,' the old woman replied patiently. 'Captain Fyffe said he had arranged for them to be buried in a special mausoleum in Scotland.'

'And this was just before the war started?'

'Yes. In 1914. Captain Fyffe and his men packed up what they wanted from the storage sheds, for I think they knew they wouldn't be back. They gave their Inuit friends and helpers all the tinned food, the guns, ammunition, whaleboats, and things. It was a bonanza for the settlement, that was for sure, but it was a sad time too, for I think everyone knew it was the end of an era. The war stopped the whaling, and it never started again. Captain Fyffe never came back till after the war was finished. He couldn't, because of the German submarines prowling around in the Atlantic Ocean.'

'And Captain Fyffe was definitely not Agnes and Betty's father?' asked Lizzie.

'Yes. That is true. Everyone knows that. His granddaughters will tell you that. The girls all had Inuit names, of course, but all the girls were also given Scottish names, by Captain Fyffe. He was very good to Nutaraq and the twins after the war. Every time he visited, he brought loads of gifts and presents for them, and for Nutaraq's father, when he was alive.'

She paused.

'Do you think that Agnes and Betty could be returned here? I think that would be good; so that their souls will feel at home, and be at peace. I think the twins would want that too. Can you find out if it is possible, Lizzie?'

'Wow,' said Lizzie, sitting back in her chair. 'That was a bit intense. If Rosa's information is correct, and there's no real reason to doubt it, then the revered Sir Alexander Fyffe, the bastard, was abusing his own step-children. What kind of man does that?'

'A very sick one.'

'Would it be the normal practice in those days for remains to be repatriated?'

'I doubt it,' replied Scarth. 'Unless there was some fame or historical importance connected with them. Or the family privately arranged it. Communications between Scotland and the settlement at Repulse Bay were spasmodic at best. The war severed them completely. Poor Betty was in the invidious position of being unable to alert her mother about what was happening, but she was astute enough to leave a record for others to find.'

'Meaning your victim Mr Muir. He finds the diary, and sews the secret pocket shut again. Then what does he do? Does he go onto the internet for a crash course in the syllabics which would enable him to translate it, or at least get the jist of what was in it?'

'Well, you're never too old to learn new skills …'

'And then, perhaps, decides to utilise that information for his own devious purposes.' She stared directly at him. 'Blackmail,' she enunciated. 'Targeted at someone in the Fyffe family; or someone closely connected to them. That would be my guess.'

Scarth nodded. 'Blackmail, which resulted in his premature death.' He capped his fountain pen and slid it back into his front zipped jacket pocket. 'Well, it's entirely possible. Though I have to say Lizzie, that we already have a strong suspect for his death. A neighbour. New evidence just came to light this morning, though I must admit I'm a bit confused about the motive behind it. It could be blackmail, as you suggest. If it is, Moira will squeeze it out of him today.'

'I'll leave that side of things to you, Bob, if you don't mind,' Lizzie said. 'But I agree with Rosa. It would be fitting if the girls' remains were repatriated. Could that still be arranged? Even after all this time?'

'I don't see why not,' Scarth stated. 'There would be a cost of course, but I don't think there would be a legal impediment.'

'Maybe Andrea Fyffe could tell us,' Lizzie suggested, not altogether playfully, 'if there is a legal impediment.'

'Maybe Andrea Fyffe would have her reasons for not telling us. As I said, she is adamant that the girls' remains were returned. Indeed, I wouldn't be surprised if she saw it fit to go out of her way to prevent a repatriation request. It would be like an exhumation.'

'But it wouldn't be an exhumation though, would it? If, according to her, there are no remains there ...' She frowned. 'I think those poor girls were murdered, Bob.'

Scarth was tight lipped. 'Yes,' he said, 'so do I.'

'There's another reason why there needs to be an exhumation order. I think that Sir Alexander Fyffe also murdered his wife. Agnes practically says it in her diary. It's Mrs Fyffe's remains which need to be examined.'

'I've no idea what an exhumation of Mrs Fyffe could tell us, Lizzie. She died a long time ago. But I do know that getting an exhumation order would require jumping through many bureaucratic hoops. A sheriff would need to be convinced by strong reasonable cause before he would allow such a drastic action to take place.'

'It might be easier, if you could convince him that Colin Muir was murdered in an effort to conceal the truth of what lies at the bottom of that garden.'

'It all comes back to the diary, doesn't it?'

'Find out who wanted the diary the most,' she answered firmly, 'and you'll find out who killed him.'

CHAPTER 23

TUESDAY LATE AFTERNOON

Later that afternoon, when Scarth slipped into the station's only interview room, Quin and McMurray were staring at each other across the single table with mutual loathing. McMurray had the pissed-off look of a Belted Galloway bull with the toothache. No lawyer was present. A good sign, thought Scarth.

He took his seat beside Quin, nodding cordially to McMurray. He didn't intend to take a very active part in the interrogation. Long ago, as a young detective, he had learned that the best way to make people talk more than they care to, is to listen. Listen as intensely as you can. Make nods of agreement, sounds of approval. Don't try to fake it. When people find a genuine listener, they want to extend the experience. They will prattle on, sometimes more than is good for them.

Listening, however, wasn't Quin's way; at least, not that day. She cleared her throat.

'For the record,' she said into the recorder, 'the time is now, er, three seventeen; joining the interview is Crime Investigator Robert Scarth. Is that okay with you, Mr McMurray?'

McMurray shrugged. 'I'm not bovvered,' he said.

Quin turned to Scarth. 'I have informed Mr McMurray that he has been captured on video illegally entering the property belonging to Mr Colin Muir on Wednesday night. The night Mr Muir was murdered. Mr McMurray claims it is all a misunderstanding. That we have put two and two together and got five.'

She turned to the suspect. 'For the benefit of Mr Scarth, tell us your story again Mr McMurray. And try and make it believable this time.'

McMurray let out a huge, exaggerated sigh.

'As I've told Mrs Quin here, I made and fitted the garden entrance gate, the kitchen door, and the French windows. This was years ago, when relations between me and him were cordial. The work was all done in my workshop, and most of the work was done with mahogany. No expense spared. I refuse to work with cheap wood anyway, and told him that upfront.'

'Sounds like a lot of work,' Scarth said, in an empathetic tone.

McMurray was bored, disinterested. 'It was joinery work,' he dismissed. 'Any idiot could have done it. I'm a carpenter. I make bespoke furniture, not IKEA look-alikes.'

'How did you come by the keys to the garden gate, and his house?' Quin asked.

'I always keep copies of doors that I make. In case the customer loses theirs. Cheaper and less trouble than replacing the locks.'

'What else did you do during this entente cordial with Colin Muir?' Quin queried.

'I designed and fitted the bespoke cabinets and bookcases in his study. Took me weeks, working all hours.' His face grew animated. 'Then he goes and reports me for making a noise at night, when I'm doing stuff for other folk? Has my tools seized? What kind of a bastard does that?'

Quin replied. 'As far we know Mr Muir was only one of several of your neighbours whom you had pissed off sufficiently for them to ask the council for protection.'

'Muir was the instigator,' McMurray replied. 'I wanted him to suffer for it. I wasn't lying about trashing his windscreen. Bill Crighton did that. I saw him. But it gave me an idea. I went into Muir's house that night to get his car keys. I knew he was out. I'd seen him in his Heilan' Laddie outfit. I wanted to steal his car, drive it somewhere, maybe Bill Crighton's yard, and torch it.'

'Instead, you decided to kill him,' Quin said flatly.

McMurray's nostrils flared. He flexed his bull-like shoulders and fixed her with his formidable stare. 'You can't be serious,' he finally said.

His left ear, Scarth noticed, was markedly more prominent than his right one. It gave him the appearance of signalling to make a sharp left turn.

Quin's face hardened. 'We're investigating a murder here. You can't get anything more serious …'

'If you're hoping to intimidate me, Mrs Quin,' McMurray replied menacingly, 'you can forget it.'

Quin stiffened. 'That'll be *Inspector* Quin to you, McMurray …'

The man ignored her, looking directly at Scarth. 'Just so that Mr Scarth here, and that wee recording machine of yours get it right,' McMurray said, 'I did not kill Colin Muir. End of story.'

'I'll decide when the story ends, McMurray,' Quin barked, her bosoms quivering in temper. 'Not the likes of you.'

McMurray sat back and peeled back thick purple lips to reveal blunt-edged grey teeth. It might even have been a smile. His goading had won.

Scarth stepped into the breach. 'Why didn't you take the car? It was still outside the house when I went round the following morning.'

'Couldn't find the keys. Simple as that.' Muir's car keys were in his sporran, Scarth knew. 'Plus, I didn't have time. The bastard arrived home early. I had to scarper.'

'What time was this at?'

'I dunno. Ten o'clock? Five to? Look, I could have stayed and brazened it out with him. But I knew it would lead to violence. I removed myself from the scene to avoid a confrontation.'

Scarth remembered what Erica Griffin had said about her father leaving out a prepared instant coffee for his morning livener.

'Did you tidy up in the kitchen?' Scarth asked.

'What?

'Cups, plates and things. At the sink. Did you tidy anything away?'

'Listen, I don't clear away my dishes in my own house, never mind anyone else's …'

'Did you speak to Mr Muir that night?' Scarth continued. 'When he came home?'

'What? No. I've told you. He came home earlier than usual.'

Quin perked up. 'How do you know it was Colin Muir?'

'I walked down the lane, turned the corner into Summerfield Drive, and as I was walking up my drive, a taxi pulled away from outside Muir's.'

'What time was this at?

'As I said. Ten o'clock or thereabouts. The news had just started when I switched on the telly.'

It fitted; the investigators knew. The taxi company had confirmed Muir had been dropped off at five to ten.

'Did you see anyone else in the street,' probed Quin, 'as you left Mr Muir's house, and before you went inside your own house?'

'Not then. It's a quiet area,' he said with a grin. 'Nothing out of the ordinary ever happens there, does it?'

'So: you've no-one to provide you with an alibi …'

'Well, I waved to the taxi driver. When he did a U-turn. He's a mate of mine.'

Quin was staggered. 'Did he wave back?'

McMurray's grey-toothed grin was a thing of wonder. 'Gave me the finger, cheeky bugger,' he said.

'What do you mean by 'not then'?' Quin asked.

'Pardon?'

'You said 'not then',' she repeated. 'When I asked you if you saw anyone in the street. What did you mean by that?'

'Oh that. Yeah. A jogger went past my house. I always sit in an armchair at the window. The window's north-facing, doesn't get a lot of light; but perfect for the TV picture. Anyway, she went past me about half ten. I was surprised. I've never seen a jogger out our way before. We're mostly all past that in my neighbourhood.'

'What did she look like?'

'Not old, but older than her figure suggested. Shapely …nice bum. Sexy.' The man ran his hot brown critical eyes over Quin's impressive upper torso. She felt scorched, as if from a blow-torch. 'Though not as sexy as you are, Mrs Quin ...'

Scarth inhaled a sharp, shallow, nervous breath. He'd seen the day when he would have reacted decisively to the man's impertinence; instead, he sat and gritted his teeth. That was one of the irritating things about growing older: the number of compromises you had to make. But the last thing they needed now was for Quin to off the deep end and bop the guy one.

Quin flushed. She was flattered. She didn't know why she should be, but she knew she shouldn't be. Then her discomfort turned to irritation. It made her angry that the man had found a weakness in her. Her chest swelled as she took a steadying gulp of the room's charged air. Instead of going ballistic, she smiled her trademark crocodile smile – showing small pointy teeth; her eyes like flints. She centred her attention on his smug-looking mug.

'What other anatomical observations did you make about her?' she enquired through her teeth.

'She was on the tall side, dark-haired, wearing the same gear all those joggers wear. It's like a uniform. Hard to tell them apart, apart from the bums. They're like clones.'

'Describe this particular clone,' Quin encouraged.

'Multicoloured tights, sweat-band on forehead, stop-watch on her wrist, water bottle in her hand …'

'But you didn't think she was local?' Quin probed.

McMurray shrugged. 'I didn't think so at first, I suppose. But then I saw her again.'

'That same evening?'

'Yes.'

'When was this, Mr McMurray?' Scarth asked.

The man wasn't going to be hurried. 'Around closing time. Eleven o'clock-ish,' he said. 'I often go across the road to the Covenanters' pub for a pint just before last orders. That's when they sell off that day's pies at half price. Anyway, I went out my front door, and as I was walking down my driveway, I saw her start her jog from Muir's house …'

'Colin Muir's house?' Quin spluttered.

'Well, I don't know of any other Muirs in the street,' McMurray replied sarcastically.

Quin's eyes darkened with anger. 'And then where did she go?'

'I waited till she had passed my drive. She kept her head down. Didn't acknowledge me.'

'Did you recognise her?' Scarth asked.

McMurray shook his head.

'For the record, Mr McMurray just shook his head,' Quin said. 'So, who did you think she was?'

'I didn't know who she was, and I wasn't interested in knowing who she was,' McMurray replied wearily. 'A girlfriend staying over at Muir's for a bit of the old rumpy-pumpy? His social worker? The Avon Lady? I presume youse two know. Am I getting hotter?'

'No. You're getting obnoxious,' Quin replied, before lapsing into a sudden silence.

Scarth stirred. 'Where did she go? After she passed you?' he queried.

'She nipped round the corner of the Covenanters' towards the car park. It's at the back of the pub. You can't see it directly from my street.'

'And you've no idea who she was? No? Okay then.' She stacked her notes, slipped them into the folder in front of her, and flipped the folder closed. She regarded Mr Murray seriously. 'But you do know she came out of Colin Muir's house at what … just before eleven p.m.? Is that correct?'

Quin leant a little to her left. 'Mr McMurray just nodded his confirmation that the suspect came out of Mr Muir's house at the time stated.'

She sat back, looked at Scarth. 'Anything else, Bob? While we still have Mr McMurray with us?'

Before Scarth could answer, McMurray intervened.

'One more thing. The jogger. She ran funny. As if she had a limp ...'

For a moment the investigators were speechless in surprise. Quin recovered first. She glanced at Scarth. It was a sad, commiserating look. Then her face hardened as she regarded the man opposite her.

'And you're sure about this, are you Mr McMurray?'

'As sure as I'm sitting here with you in my face …'

Quin clenched her fists and stood up abruptly. Uh-oh, though Scarth; here we go. McMurray, unworried, grinning like an eejit, stood up and faced her. PC Gray, who had been in attendance on door duty, told them later in the rest room that it was 'like Godzilla versus King Kong'.

After Gray had escorted McMurray out, Quin, her eyes still dark with anger, turned and faced Scarth.

'Since I turned forty-never-you-mind a few weeks ago, I've foresworn the drink. But you know what? That man sorely tempts me to jump back off the wagon again …Jesus. What have we got then Bob; we've got a tall brunette, one who walks with a limp? Ring any bells?'

Oh yes, Scarth thought bitterly as he made his way to the door. The bells are ringing loud and clear all right. The tell-tale signs had been there, he thought. I just chose not to see them. Didn't want to see them.

Quin read his face. 'Don't worry,' she commiserated. 'I never saw it coming either.'

It was nearly six p.m. when Quin and Scarth returned to the CID room. Quin summoned Munro to the pow-wow table, and the three of them took their seats.

'Heather,' Quin smiled encouragingly. 'What have you gleaned from that electronic gadgetry you have cluttering up your corner?'

'A hundred things, boss. Not all of them relevant, or even remotely interesting. First things first. Bob asked me to check the numbers of the Premium Bonds which were found in Colin Muir's safety deposit box. It turns out they were bought online, earlier this year, by a credit card belonging to a Mr Anthony McGill. He's the husband of Andrea Fyffe.'

'Now why would Anthony McGill buy Premium bonds for Colin Muir?' Quin asked.

'Because once Colin Muir had found the diary,' Scarth said, 'he knew he could use it to his advantage. He needed money, because of the impending court cases, and decided to blackmail McGill. Any whiff of scandal would be extremely detrimental to McGill's political career, so he paid two tranches of blackmail money, by Premium Bond.'

'And then what? He decided enough was enough and killed him?' Quin queried half-heartedly.

'The problem with that, boss,' Munro put in, 'is that McGill wasn't even in Midlothian that night. I've had it confirmed that he was indeed in Holland.'

'But his jogging wee wifie most certainly was ...' Quin said pointedly.

'Yes, she was,' Munro said. 'I've had a go at tracking Andrea Fyffe's phone. And I'm sorry to say, Bob, that Fyffe wasn't where she says she was …'

It wasn't a great surprise. As the investigation had progressed, and especially since the interview with McMurray, he had felt himself becoming more and more uneasy over the dark suspicions of Andrea Fyffe which had been festering in his mind.

'By pure coincidence,' Munro continued, 'like something out of a daft detective novel, I came across her whereabouts while I was looking for something else.'

She held up a small glassine bag. In it nestled a SIM card.

'Remember Connie Considine, the cleaning lady whose mobile phone was crushed by the phone snatcher? Her device was retained here as evidence. On a hunch, I extracted the SIM card, just for curiosity, and had a glance through her photos. On the night of Mr Muir's death, Connie Considine and a bunch of girlfriends were having a baby shower at the Covenanters' Rest.'

'A what?' Scarth asked.

'One of Connie's friends is expecting and it was decided to 'shower' her with gifts during a night out at the pub. Connie took a number of group photos on her phone, outside in the car park, and that's the point I'm coming to. Here,' she said, pushing some print-out copies towards Quin and Scarth, 'see for yourselves.'

A group of under-dressed, hyper-looking females tottered tipsily on high heels as the camera caught the jinks of them. In the background of three of the images, a well-shaped female, obviously not part of the brightly-dressed 'shower' party, was captured moving behind them on the way to a car parked off to the side. She had on multi-coloured running leggings, almost luminescent in the car park lights. The heading on the last image, as the mystery woman was opening the car door, said 'Eskbridge, 24 March, 22:32.'

Scarth pursed his lips. The car was a low-slung silver-coloured Audi sports car. 'Nothing fancy' Andrea Fyffe had described it to him.

Munro seemed to read his thoughts. She waited a moment to let him gather his thoughts.

'That's Andrea Fyffe, isn't it Bob?' asked Munro.

'Yes,' he confirmed wistfully. 'And I've seen the car before. She has a Mini. Handy for parking in the nooks and crannies other cars can't access she told me …'

'But useless for a monthly shopping,' replied Munro, attempting to lighten the mood. 'I know. I've got one.'

'Hang on,' Quin interrupted impatiently. 'Is it or isn't it Andrea Fyffe's car?'

'I can check the plates to make sure,' suggested Munro. She looked at Scarth hopefully.

Scarth pushed his glasses further up his nose. 'No need, Heather,' he said heavily. 'It's her husband's car. She uses it while he's away.'

Quin made a noise like a snorting buffalo. 'Will youse stop talking in riddles? Okay. We've pinpointed Andrea Fyffe a hundred yards from Colin Muir's house, on the night he was murdered, and at roughly the time he was murdered. So what? Does that make her a murderer?'

'She's wearing the murder weapon,' Munro said flatly.

They scrutinised the image carefully. They had to agree. Andrea Fyffe was definitely wearing a bum bag.

'Well, well, well,' Quin remarked with evident satisfaction. 'Would you effin Adam and Eve it …'

CHAPTER 24

WEDNESDAY MORNING

As Scarth joined Quin and Munro at the pow-wow table the following morning, McIntosh was noisily busy at his desk. To cover the shaved patch at the back of his head where the stitches had been inserted, he was wearing a black police-issue baseball cap. His twin black eyes looked watery, giving him the appearance of a panda about to sneeze. His broken nose still had a sliver of plaster across it. His right hand was still partially strapped up. He shouldn't even have been at work. He was loading all his documentation concerning the phone snatchers into archive boxes, ready to be transported to Division.

He glanced self-consciously towards the others.

'We haven't made much progress during our interviews with the phone-snatching suspects,' he said to no one in particular. His liquid eyes passed over them earnestly. 'They've lawyered up. Their briefs have told us their clients will be invoking their right to silence.'

He jerked his hands out from his sides, a posture of helplessness.

'Nothing we can do,' he said. 'The Super says it'll be a case of sitting down and preparing a report for the Fiscal, then crossing our fingers as we wait.'

He indicated the archive boxes he was loading. 'Superintendent Kerr has asked me to go over to her office so that we can compile the investigation report together,' he explained.

'What charges are being considered?' Scarth asked.

'Sallyanne Seaton will be facing multiple charges,' McIntosh replied. 'With relation to poor Leah Duffy, Seton is going to be charged with 'Assault to Severe Injury and Permanent Disfigurement'. Could get five years for that. And rightly so. She will also be charged with 'Assaulting a Police Officer', and 'Criminal Damage' for the destruction of the victim's mobile phones.

Munro, sitting with her now much-autographed stookie sticking out, said: 'What about my injury?' she asked with a hard-done-by look. 'Does that not count?'

'The 'Assaulting a Police Officer' charge refers to the incident at her house when we attempted to execute a search warrant. Your injury will be included as well Heather, don't worry,' McIntosh soothed. He looked again at Scarth. 'As far as Valeria Carmichael, Robert Beatson, and young McLurg are concerned', he continued, 'they will be facing charges such as 'Accessories or Accomplices to Criminal Damage', and possibly 'Perverting the Course of Justice'.

'Well done, Scobie,' Quin said, genuinely impressed. 'You've done well. A difficult case, God knows ...'

The young detective acknowledged the compliment modestly. 'Well, it isn't over till the shouting stops, of course. After the report's been compiled and sent in, it's a question of waiting to see what action the Fiscal decides to take, regarding prosecution.' He hefted the boxes under his arm, and made for the door.

'I do hope the good Superintendent's not trying to steal you away from us,' Quin called after him, a tiny smile on her cherubic lips.

'There's no question of that, boss,' McIntosh answered over his shoulder. He stopped and faced the room, switching his load to another arm. He smiled, a gruesome sight. 'Actually,' he said, 'I've found her easy to work with. Very accommodating.'

Quin adopted her most corrosive tone. 'Yes. I've heard she can be …'

After McIntosh had cheerfully left, Quin explained to Scarth that she had asked Heather Munro to prepare a timeline for Colin Muir's murder. Quin said she would then use it as a basis for her report to the Procurator Fiscal.

'It'll be good practice for her,' she said, smiling at the young detective. 'During Heather's presentation,' Quin said to Scarth, 'feel free to chip in if there's anything you want brought to our attention. We'll both act as Devil's Advocates. If you think of any impediments or objections a defence lawyer would come up with, let's hear it, so that we can find a credible work-around.'

Quin nodded to Munro to begin. The young detective used her stick to limp to the office flipchart. She turned it to a fresh page, and half-turned to face her audience, a disarming smile in place.

She really was an attractive young female, Scarth thought, all the more so because she seemed oblivious to her charisma. He wondered why no mention of a boyfriend had surfaced by now. She was a country girl.

Was she privately spoken-for back home in the hinterland?

The object of his reverie called him to attention with a brief clearing of her throat.

'The obvious place to start is when we were first alerted to Mr Muir's death,' Munro said, her voice professionally serious. 'As you'll recall, a pre-recorded telephone message informed us that Mr Muir had been found dead. What Sonya heard, was an SMS message delivery service which had been texted to our switchboard number. The original text had come from Mr Muir's mobile phone.'

Addressing Quin, Munro said, 'I've since had a look through Mr Muir's phone, boss, and made a copy of his phone calls and texts in chronological order. It's interesting. And it gets more interesting as the story progresses.' She picked up a marker pen from the flip-chart easel. With a disarming smile she said, 'Please feel free to talk among yourselves while I scribble on the flipchart for a while …'

They watched intently as she wrote, in large letters, the heading:

COLIN MUIR'S PHONE TIMELINE.

She turned and faced her audience.

'Mr Muir did not use his mobile phone during the day of his murder,' she told them. 'Hardly surprising, since he was at his office for most of his day, and the majority of his business communications were conducted by his office phone and by email. However, there is some traffic on his mobile during the evening we can look at.'

After a quick glance at her notes, she began writing again in bold strokes. As she did, she started a commentary about the items as she listed them.

'Right then. The background we all know. Andrea Fyffe and Mr Muir were scheduled to go to a Law Society dinner that evening at the Station Hotel. She was the designated driver, and came round to his house and picked him up. They got to the hotel at around seven in the evening. In her interview with Bob, Andrea Fyffe said she was called away from the function at just after eight o'clock. This was corroborated by several attendees. Her father has dementia, and sometimes the live-in nurse found it difficult to cope with him if he got boisterous. There are several texts between Andrea Fyffe and Mr Muir subsequent to her leaving the hotel, and I'll use them to get the ball rolling …'

She busied herself for a while at the chart, then stood back so that they could see the result. 'So, here's what I've got,' she said, 'though it doesn't look much just yet. The recipient of the first text, at ten past seven, I'll reveal later if you don't mind.'

Wed:
19:10 – Muir texts a-n-other:

20:45 – Fyffe texts Muir: 'Faither in a tizzy. Apologies for upping and leaving you.'

20:46 – Muir texts back: 'No apologies reqd. Sorry to hear about your father.'

21:20 – Muir phones the taxi firm, and arranges for a 21:40 pick-up.

21:48 – Fyffe texts Muir: 'Have to stay here. Can you get a taxi home?'

21:52 – Muir texts back: 'No probs. Plenty of taxis.'

Thurs:
08:34 – Muir's phone texts our switchboard: 'There's been a murder at forty-three Summerfield Terrace, Eskbridge. Please come quickly.'

'It's mostly all innocuous stuff. Bare bones at this stage. But let's see what the chart looks like when I highlight a few details which we know about, and pencil in some of the things we don't.'

She busied herself with her marker pen. Behind her, Quin squirmed uncomfortably. She fished for a bra strap, and adjusted it. Scarth fingered his notebook, the way a believer sought the reassurance of a string of rosary beads.

After a half minute Munro dropped her hands to her sides, and stood back from the flip-chart. She indicated it. 'Right then. There we go. The entries in the brackets are suppositions at this stage. The ticks are entries which can be corroborated.'

Wed:
19:10 – Muir texts a-n-other

[20:15 – Fyffe gets phone call while at function.]

20:30 – Fyffe leaves function.□

20:45 – Fyffe texts Muir: 'Faither in a tizzy. Apologies for upping and leaving you.'

20:46 – Muir texts back: 'No apologies reqd. Sorry to hear about your father.'

21:20 – Muir phones the taxi firm, and arranges for a 21:30 pick-up.

21:48 – Fyffe texts Muir: 'Have to stay here. Can you get a taxi home?'

21:52– Muir texts back: 'No probs. Plenty of taxis.'

21:55 – the time the taxi driver confirms Muir dropped off at house.□

[22:03 – 22:30 – Muir probably killed.]

Thurs:
08:34 – Muir's phone texts our switchboard: 'There's been a murder at forty-three Summerfield Terrace, Eskbridge. Please come quickly.'

Quin squirmed uneasily. 'Heather dear, I hope this isn't one of those prolonged and embarrassing dénouement thingies like those awful Agatha Christie films. What is the first entry? Who the effin hell is the 'a-n-other' Muir texted at ten past seven?

Munro looked mock-surprised. 'Oh, didn't I mark it up?'

They all laughed.

'Okay. I'll do it now then.' On the flip-chart she wrote:

1910 – Muir texts Tony McGill: 'Regarding your query, the final settlement price is £250k. Look forward to hearing from you.'

They gaped in astonishment.

Quin recovered first. 'So *that's* what this is all about?'

Munro cleared her throat. 'I think so. Muir was demanding a final blackmail payment of a quarter of a million. Andrea Fyffe decided to search Colin Muir's house that night, to find the Inuit girl's diary and put an end to his blackmail. As we know, she or her husband, or both, had already spent £20,000 on Premium Bonds. No doubt they wanted the extortion to cease.

'She invented a ruse to leave the function early. She told colleagues at the dinner that her father had taken ill again, and that she had been summoned there by the live-in nurse. But she didn't go to her father's house till later, did she Bob?'

Scarth shuffled in his seat and shook his head. 'I found out by accident from the live-in help that Andrea never appeared at her father's house till the doctor summoned her,' he said. 'That was at about eleven fifteen.'

'I think Andrea Fyffe left the function and went to her own home,' said Munro. 'She texted Mr Muir, pretending to be at her father's house, and apologised for leaving the function early. She changed into the jogging gear we saw in the photos. She then drove her husband's car to the Covenanters' Rest, parked the car, and went round to Mr Muir's house and let herself in. She banked on Mr Muir staying at the Law Society dinner till last orders, as he usually did. We know that the photos outside the pub were taken between 22:31, and 22:32, by which time Mr Muir had been murdered.'

Quin stared at her for several seconds. 'Okay,' she said slowly. 'I'm the Devil's Advocate here. How did Andrea Fyffe get into the victim's house?'

'She was spoiled for choice,' Munro replied confidently. 'Sergeant Murray has already confirmed that the French windows at the rear of the house were unlocked. She could have gone that way, but I think she used one of the keys Mr Muir had left with the estate agency section at her office, who were handling the sale of the property. We've all been there in that office, boss. The keys for the properties for sale are all sitting openly on a peg-board, each one conveniently tagged. Andrea Fyffe could have taken or copied Mr Muir's house keys anytime without any problem. The neighbours probably knew she was a colleague. I think she just went boldly up to the front door and let herself in.'

Quin nodded her agreement. 'And McMurray, who was in the process of creeping round the place, heard her, panicked, and beat a hasty retreat back out the unlocked French windows. He thought it was the victim returning home early. But it was Fyffe. Okay, so she let herself into the victim's house, intent on searching it for the diary, the source of all her worries. Then what?'

Munro capped her marker pen back and placed it back on the flipchart's easel.

'Then she got caught. Unbeknownst to her, Mr Muir had decided to leave the function early and had called a taxi. He unexpectedly arrived home early and found her in the house. She got a fright. I'll bet he was surprised too, and probably pretty upset at finding her there in his house. They had a fight. We don't know the ins and outs of it. What we do know is that Mr Muir ended up dead on his study floor.'

Munro paused, letting them ponder on that one. It was a scenario which worked for both of them. But there was something which had been bugging Scarth.

'I phoned Angus MacLeod this morning, Moira,' he put in. 'There's something which has been bothering me. I don't know if I told you but Andrea Fyffe is a so-called biker chick. Or was. She came off her motorbike not so long ago, and needed knee surgery. She actually lifted her skirt and showed me the scar.'

'Oooo. Did she now?' Quin teased.

Scarth smiled and nodded. 'Twice, in fact. I was struck how the stitches made quite a distinctive mark, a raised scar across her knee-cap. Anyway, Angus told us that Colin Muir was lying on his front when he was strangled. There were bruises on his back where the killer had forced him to lie prone. I told Angus about my unease and suspicions about Andrea Fyffe, and mentioned her scarred knee. I wondered if there was physical trace evidence on the victim's body to suggest that she was the one who kneeled on him …'

Quin got it. Her doll's face split into a wide grin. It made her look six years old. 'Bob, you crafty old devil … Don't tell me there was a scar mark running though the bruises on the victim's back. Was there? That would be fantastic …'

Scarth shook his head. 'No such luck, Moira, I'm afraid …'

'Fuck!' Quin exclaimed in exasperation. 'Bob, don't wind me up like that. My heart can't take it.'

Scarth was taken aback. 'Sorry, Moira. Angus told me the bruises could have been made by anyone. Or at least any adult, regardless of gender. He also told me I was likely on the wrong track. He was at pains to inform me that female stranglers are extremely rare, almost non-existent. He said he had done thousands of post-mortems and had never come across a case of a female strangler yet.'

'Yes, well he has now,' Quin said sourly.

Munro had been scribbling furiously. She turned again to face her bemused audience.

'Here's my final chart version,' she said. 'I've added bits of information which we've gathered from other sources, to give us a fuller picture. My own comments are in the brackets.'

She looked puzzled.

'I had been puzzled why Andrea Fyffe would return to the scene of the crime. It seemed incredibly risky. Had she left something? Forgotten something? Then I realised how incriminating that first text would look to the police when they were investigating the murder. The police will want to know what the 'final settlement price' thing is all about. It is a direct link, connecting her and her husband to the blackmail, and a prime motive for a homicide. Fyffe realises she must go back to Mr Muir's house, find his phone, and delete that text …'

She stepped back.

'Anyway, that's what I think happened. See what you think. I'll give you time to peruse it …'

Wed:

1910 – Muir texts Tony McGill: 'Regarding your query, the final settlement price is £250k. Look forward to hearing from you.'

[20:15 – Fyffe gets phone call while at function.] (Probably from her husband. She decides to leave the function early, and go and search Muir's home for diary.)

20:30 – Fyffe leaves function.□

20:45 – Fyffe texts Muir: 'Faither in a tizzy. Apologies for upping and leaving you.'
(She's pretending to be at her father's house.)

20:46 – Muir texts back: 'No apologies reqd. Sorry to hear about your father.'

21:20 – Muir phones the taxi firm, and arranges for a 21:30 pick-up.□

21:45 – Fyffe arrives at Covenanters' Rest?
(Still pretending to be at her father's house, she texts Muir):

21:48 – Fyffe to Muir: 'Have to stay here. Can you get a taxi home?'

21:50 – McMurray enters rear of Muir's house. (Seen on camcorder).□

21:51 – Fyffe enters front of Muir's house. McMurray hastily leaves by French windows. (Seen on camcorder)□

Lights go on in study. (Seen on camcorder)

(Muir, who is on his way home in a taxi, replies to Fyffe's last text.)

21:52– Muir to Fyffe: 'No probs. Plenty of taxis.'

21:55 – The time the taxi driver confirms Muir dropped off at house.
(While Fyffe was searching his house, Muir arrives home unexpectedly. A row ensues, which gets physical. Whether intentional or not, Muir is killed. She then leaves.)

[22:03 – 22:30 – Muir probably killed.]

22:27 – Lights go off in Muir's study. (Seen on camcorder)

22:30 – McMurray sees 'jogger' go past his house. Assumes she's local. He describes her in interview with DI Quin & CI Scarth. The description fits Andrea Fyffe.

22:32 – Fyffe seen at Covenanters returning to car.

22:45 – The lights go on again in Muir's study. (Seen on camcorder)
(Is this Andrea Fyffe searching frantically for Muir's phone, and realising it is not there? The lights go off again after ten minutes.)

22:55 – McMurray decides to go for a pint before last orders. As he is exiting his house, he sees the same 'jogger' he had seen before. She is leaving Muir's house.

Was she a colleague of Muir's? A girlfriend? He isn't sure. He nods to her as she goes past. She goes into Covenanters' car park, gets into silver-coloured Audi sports car, and drives away.□

Thurs:

08:34 – Muir's phone texts our switchboard: 'There's been a murder at forty-three Summerfield Terrace, Eskbridge. Please come quickly.□

'Wow,' Quin said, her face full of admiration. 'Well done, Heather. What a brilliant presentation. You're a genius. Isn't she a genius, Bob?'

Munro glowed with pleasure as she hobbled over to the pow-wow table and plunked herself down. She stretched her stookied leg out in front of her.

'Andrea Fyffe was unbelievably unlucky that night,' she resumed. 'She couldn't have anticipated that Muir would leave the function early. He was usually the last to leave the bar. Nor could she have anticipated being caught on camera by the baby shower girls when she was returning to her car after the murder, thus placing her at the scene.'

Scarth spoke. 'Her excuse for leaving the function must have seemed perfectly feasible at the time. Her father often took turns which necessitated her having to drop everything and rush round to him. What she couldn't have predicted was that her father would in actual fact have a horrendous evening. Such an eventful one that the nurse felt obliged to call in the doctor. It destroyed her alibi.'

Quin got her oar in. 'So there she was, having just set up a perfectly acceptable alibi for a quick in-and-out house-breaking, when she suddenly found herself with a murder on her hands. Then what?'

Munro nodded. 'She had of course no idea that she had been captured by that phone camera outside the Covenanters'. But I'm sure she realised round about then that she had to get hold of Muir's phone, and delete the incriminating text to her husband. Or better still, remove and destroy the phone. In either case, it was important enough to risk a return to the murder scene ...'

'And that was when she ran into our old friend McMurray,' Quin supplied. 'The monkey-faced night owl ...'

'Yes,' Munro smiled. 'Again, Lady Luck was against her. Her error in returning to the scene was compounded when she sneaked out again, and the ever-vigilant Mr McMurray was around to spot her exiting the victim's house.'

'Wait a minute,' Quin objected. 'The victim's phone was lying on the vestibule table, along with his house keys,' she said. 'I saw it. Why didn't she?'

'I wondered about that,' Munro admitted. 'When we come home, we leave our keys somewhere near the door, don't we? At least I do. So that I don't forget to pick them up on the way out. But I never leave my phone there. I keep it with me. We all do. So why would Mr Muir leave his mobile on the vestibule table? And more importantly, if he had left it there, why didn't Andrea Fyffe find it?'

'My point exactly,' Quin said.

Scarth had a guess. 'She didn't find it because it wasn't there when she was in the house.' He grinned. 'Am I right, or am I right, Heather?'

'Why wouldn't it be there?' Quin asked impatiently.

Munro told them the answer. 'Because Mr Muir had inadvertently left it in the taxi. On a hunch I phoned Alliance Taxis. The driver who dropped off Mr Muir told me he found Mr Muir's phone on the back seat of his car, at the end of his shift. He was annoyed at having to go all the way back to Mr Muir's house to return it.'

The room fell silent.

'How could he return it?' Quin quibbled; still peeved at having assumed the cleaner had just used the phone and then replaced in on the vestibule table, where they had found it. 'Muir was already dead.'

'The taxi man dropped it through the letterbox at 02:25 a.m.,' Munro replied. 'That's what Connie Considine meant in her statement when she had 'picked up' the phone. I asked her. It was lying on the inside doormat when she came in that morning.'

Quin looked at Scarth. He looked back. They had both missed it. Scarth held up his hands to Quin.

'Sorry Moira. I missed it. Should have followed it up properly.'

'I missed it too,' Quin admitted.

Munro broke the embarrassed silence. 'I think Andrea Fyffe's rage and frustration then boiled over when she couldn't find Mr Muir's phone, and prompted the defacement of his body. She must have been livid. That damn phone. It has been the bane of this whole investigation ...'

She pointed to her flow-chart. 'The text which sparked off our whole investigation had been sent on the morning after the murder, as we know, by Connie Considine. In her statement she explained that her own phone was out of order, having been crushed the previous day by

Sallyanne Seton. It's a weird link to the two cases, the phone-snatchers, and Mr Muir's murder. Anyway, we know she didn't use Mr Muir's land-line, because the message came from his mobile. So I asked myself, why did Connie Considine state she had 'picked up' Muir's mobile? Surely the man would have had it on him, in his pocket, or in his sporran. Mr Muir was lying dead in the study. She was adamant that she did not enter the room. So where was his phone? That's when I thought of phoning the taxi company.'

Quin sat back in her seat; her cherubic face wreathed in dimpled smiles. 'Heather, you're an effin genius.'

Munro shook her head modestly. 'There's still loose ends. For instance: why was the memory card removed from Mr Muir's camera?'

'To point us in Bill Crighton's direction,' Quin said firmly. 'The photos of him and his receptionist doing the fandango at the cliff-top could have screwed up his life big time. It would be only natural for him to try and retrieve them.'

Munro pointed to the office whiteboard, where McIntosh's 'SEE ME' memento from B-B B Kerr was still prominently displayed. 'And we've yet to come up with a credible motive, to explain the grotesque smiley face she drew on Mr Muir's bare bum.'

Quin spoke. 'I've been thinking about that. Were you not here when Scobie told us all that left-handed shite about the Kerrs, Heather? No? Well, I've always thought there was something weird about the similarity of that swirl and that gruesome smiley face. I tried to replicate it and couldn't. Scobie said Kerr could do it because she was left-handed. I checked with David Simes; the handwriting expert Division consults sometimes. He says when right-handed people draw a circle, they are apt to do it anticlockwise. Try it yourself without thinking, and you'll see. Anyway, Simes says most lefties draw a circle clockwise. Most, he admitted, but not all. Since it is so arbitrary, he said that in his opinion it probably wouldn't be considered reliable evidence. Pity.'

Scarth was remembering his lunch with Andrea Fyffe: the way she used her left hand to spoon her soup; the way she laid the spoon on her napkin, and used her left hand to convey her crusty bread to her mouth. There was little doubt she was left-handed.

'Just hypotheses and circumstantials?' she had jokingly asked at Bellevue. He knew now she had been fishing, not joking. He was more disappointed in himself for getting drawn in, than resentful at her for manipulating him.

'Andrea Fyffe is left-handed,' he announced flatly.

Quin's jaw dropped, then she clapped her hands delightedly. 'Brilliant! Are ye sure?'

Scarth nodded, though without much enthusiasm. He'd liked Andrea Fyffe. Felt duped by her. He felt older than his age.

'Then the swirl is in,' Quin stated. 'Bugger what Simes says. If he won't testify, we'll get another expert witness who will.'

'And now we know why the ligature was removed,' Munro put in. 'Because she brought it with her, and took it away with her. It was the jogger's companion, the so-called bum bag …'

Quin was equally animated. 'That's right! Is it visible in the photos, Heather?' She scrutinised the prints eagerly.

'Jesus. You're right!' Her dimpled fist pumped the air. 'We've got her, kids. We've effin well got her!'

Then a sudden thought clouded her expression.

'Do we need it, Bob. The bum bag?' she asked. 'For the DNA evidence on it – epithelials, fibres, and such-like whatnots? What I'm saying is: if she has disposed of this bum bag, do we have enough evidence without it?'

'Enough evidence to arrest and charge her? Yes. I think we do,' he replied. 'We certainly have enough circumstantial evidence here to bring her in and question her about Colin Muir's death. The pathologist will testify that the murder weapon was something identical to her bum bag. We can prove Andrea Fyffe was in Colin Muir's house at the time of his death. We can prove she was wearing a bum bag at the time. I think we have enough to build a strong case against her.'

'I'll get a warrant,' Quin stated, 'to search her house, and the apartment at Broomieknowe, for that bum bag. But her phone is going to be her ultimate undoing. Heather, can you run a GPS location check on her mobile number straight after this meeting? I'll apply to get her phone records. Witnesses can lie, but their mobile phones can't. Thank Christ.'

She turned and beamed at Scarth. 'Does the blackmail theory work as a motive for you Bob?'

He had his doots. 'I don't think this is about Andrea Fyffe protecting Tony McGill's political ambitions. From what I hear he's the kind that would throw it off; laugh it off. Politicians are like that. He'd use it to command attention at dinner parties. "Did I ever tell you about my wife's most infamous ancestor? The one who got away with murder?" No, I think Colin Muir's murder was all about the Fyffe family's reputation. And given her father's failing health, Andrea Fyffe was the guardian of that.'

'What about that text message to McGill?' Quin asked. 'The price for the final payment? Doesn't that point us towards blackmail as the motive?'

'I think McGill certainly told Andrea Fyffe about the message,' Scarth said. 'They both knew that blackmailers don't stop. There would be another final settlement to follow. And another one after that. I think that when McGill got Colin Muir's text that night, he phoned his wife to warn her of the predicament they were in. Her phone records will tell us.'

'Was that what the call at the function was about, do you think? Not her father's sudden illness, as she claimed?' Quin asked.

'Perhaps,' said Scarth. 'That's another mistake I've made, Moira. I didn't check with the live-in nurse, to find out exactly when she called Andrea Fyffe that evening. I think Andrea Fyffe left the dinner and went home to gather her thoughts, and it was probably then that she decided to take the violent action she did. I suppose Colin Muir had previously given her a sight of the diary, maybe even a précis of the contents. She knew it would be damming if it got into the public domain. Her great-grandfather would be exposed as a sexual predator, and more than likely, a murderer ...'

'A trait which runs in the family, apparently,' Quin muttered.

'He is long dead, however,' Scarth continued. 'He cannot answer for his crimes. But her father, who had written such a glowing biography of Sir Alexander Fyffe, is very much alive. He would be totally discredited in the eyes of all those he cared about.'

'Do you think he deliberately covered up his grandfather's misdeeds?' Quin asked.

'It's hard to say, Moira. There are a lot of things we don't know. Was he a naive dupe: blinded with pride by his ancestor's distinguished career? Or did he suspect that something was amiss? For instance, his grandfather's ship's logs and private correspondence, which would almost certainly have contained unpalatable details, have never surfaced. Did Andrea Fyffe's father destroy any incriminating material and set out to create a new myth for Sir Alexander Fyffe, to hide the sordid truth?'

'That's a lot of ifs, Bob,' Quin said equably.

'I know. And almost all unanswerable.'

He took a steadying breath.

'Look Moira,' he said, 'when we've finished preparing the case against Andrea Fyffe, I'm going to need some leave time.'

Quin wasn't surprised. She knew the woman had captured his affection.

'You're a civilian contractor, Bob,' she said, as if he needed reminding. 'You can take leave any time you want. She's a murdering bastard when all's said and done. She's not worth your sympathy. You're a golfer. You're used to disappointment and heartache. You'll get over it.'

Scarth gave her a sad smile. 'It's not that, Moira. Or at least not all that. Lizzie Williamson is determined to have the remains of those two Inuit girls repatriated to their homeland, and I've promised to help her in that quest. An exhumation of Mrs Fyffe's grave will also be requested. We're convinced that Sir Alexander Fyffe was responsible for his wife's death, and may possibly have murdered his two young house-guests to cover his tracks. I feel I owe it to the other victims in this case to try and get a satisfactory resolution for them.'

Quin laid a gentle hand on his arm: 'Take all the time you need, Bob. Do what you have to do.'

She withdrew her hand and sat back.

'Listen, it doesn't matter how noble Andrea Fyffe's motives were. The fact remains that she murdered another human being, and she needs to pay for that ...'

She fixed him with her dark, depthless eyes.

'End of story ...'

CHAPTER 25

EPILOGUE

The prosecution of the phone snatchers was heard in the Sherriff Court only a couple of months after they had been charged. Though the phone-snatching 'epidemic' had now spread to all regions in Scotland – especially large towns and cities – the case was the first in the country to come to trial.

As Superintendent B-B B Kerr and DS McIntosh had hoped, the Prosecutor Fiscal had taken a tough line against Sallyanne Seton. In relation to the injury and loss of a thumb suffered by Leah Duffy, Seton was charged with 'Assault to Severe Injury and Permanent Disfigurement'. In relation to the removal from the possession of, and the subsequent destruction of the various mobile phones belonging to her victims, she was charged with 'Theft' and 'Criminal Damage'. In relation to the assault on DS McIntosh and the injury suffered by DC Munro, she was charged with two counts of 'Assaulting a Police Officer'.

Valerie Carmichael and Robert Beatson were charged with being Seton's accomplices in the various phone-snatching incidents. Archibald McLurg was not charged. This was in return for him withdrawing a complaint of assault by DS McIntosh, prior to his arrest.

The case against Seton in particular was strong. She was seen on CCTV footage from the buses where she selected and attacked her victims; was identified by victims and witnesses; was observed by CCTV footage in The Mall passing her bloodied phone crusher to an alleged accomplice; and was identified by Detective Sergeant McIntosh as the person who had transferred blood from the victim onto his clothing.

Seton pleaded 'Guilty'. She admitted injuring Leah Duffy, and apologised to her publicly, saying it was accidental. She admitted to the other incidences of phone-snatching, though she declined to produce an explanation. She claimed she had acted alone in this felonious behaviour, and denied the involvement of any accomplices or associates.

The jury believed her. The prosecution against her alleged accomplices was shelved. Seton was found guilty. With regard to the severe injury suffered by Leah Duffy, the Sheriff said that though she had shown the court 'genuine remorse', he had 'no option' but to impose a custodial sentence. She was given two years. On the other charges the Sheriff said that 'justice would be best served' by a 'robust' Community Payback Order.

The murder trial of Andrea Fyffe, before Lord Hay, took fourteen months to come to the High Court. The prosecution was led by Hugh McSporran, QC. Defence Counsel for the accused was Liz Turnbull QC. The trial heard evidence for eighteen days.

On the nineteenth day Mr McSporran summed up the case for the prosecution. He began by thanking the members of police investigative team, the forensic technicians, the pathology department at the Infirmary, and the expert witnesses who had contributed to the prosecution's case.

McSporran reminded the jury that the accused was the office manager of a respected law firm in Eskbridge, Midlothian. She was a trusted colleague and friend of long standing, of the murder victim, Mr Colin Muir. He asked them to recollect that the nub of the matter lay far in the past. It was the existence of a girl's diary, written more than a hundred years previously, had been discovered in a secret pocket in a fur coat belonging to her. The girl, who was a Canadian Inuit, had come to Scotland at the invitation of Sir Alexander Fyffe, the great-grandfather of the accused. The contents of the diary were explosive. They revealed that Sir Alexander was a determined sexual predator, and possibly a triple murderer.

The victim, who had been experiencing financial difficulties due to an arduous divorce and a plethora of potentially crippling civil court cases, had seen a way out of his difficulties He knew that if the contents of the diary ever came into the public domain, both the accused and her husband would be acutely embarrassed. Their reputations and careers would suffer serious, perhaps even terminal, blows. In the knowledge of this, the victim had foolishly embarked on a blackmail scheme.

The accused and her husband subsequently paid Mr Muir two tranches of funds in response to his initial blackmail demands. These were in the form of Premium Bonds. These items were later found in a bank security safety box belonging to the victim. As we have learned, he said, the police were able to establish that these bonds were bought online from an account held by the accused and her husband, so there was no doubt as to their provenance.

However, as is the nature of blackmailers and their nefarious schemes, the accused and her husband were soon faced with further demands. The price for a full and final settlement, they were assured, was the sum of two hundred and fifty thousand pounds. They decided enough was enough. The accused then devised a ruse whereby she could enter the victim's home, while he was out, in order to search his premises for the incriminating diary.

We have been able to supply evidence gleaned from mobile phone tracking systems, he told the court, which showed, contrary to her statements, that the accused was in or near the victim's house on the night of the murder. We have shown the court photographic evidence, taken in the car park of a pub not a hundred yards from the victim's house, which shows the accused near the scene at a time when the pathologist has stated the murder took place. We have an eye-witness account of her actually leaving the victim's house on the night of the murder.

Then, he said, we have the evidence of the murder victim himself. You have seen and heard the evidence presented by Mr MacLeod, the eminent pathologist for the county of Midlothian. Mr McLeod has demonstrated to you how the victim was suddenly attacked from behind, by someone he trusted, and strangled by a ligature. You have seen the photographic evidence from the post mortem of the bruises and ligature marks on the victim's body. You have heard expert testimony from the pathology lab that the ligature used to strangle the victim, the murder weapon, was a ubiquitous item commonly referred to as a 'bum bag'. You have seen, from the photographic evidence of that night, that the accused was in fact wearing such an item.

Unfortunately, McSporran stated, the prosecution could not avoid giving you sight of the photos depicting the despicable way the victim's body was desecrated after death. It must have been deeply distressing for you, he told the jury, and you have my sympathies. The grotesque 'smiley face' portrayed in the photos, drawn in provocatively-red marker pen, was a display deliberately designed to shock whoever was unfortunate enough to find him. You have heard the opinion of Dr David Simes, the notable and experienced hand-writing expert, who stated that the defacement of the victim was 'more than likely' done by a left-handed person. You have heard the evidence from the civilian Crime Investigator employed by the police, a person who was at the heart of the investigation into the accused, who confirmed that the accused is indeed left-handed.

Finally, you have heard the evidence of the accused herself. She has brazenly admitted to being in the victim's house that fateful night. Indeed, faced with the weight of evidence which proved it, how could she not? She has stated that she and the accused 'got into a bit of an argument'. However, she denies intentionally murdering the victim. She said he 'flew into a rage' when she refused to pay any more blackmail money. She stated that she 'may have tried to restrain him', in order to 'protect herself' from potential violence on his part.

This, of course, is ludicrous poppy-cock, McSporran assured the jury. 'Blethers', his granny used to call it. We do not lasso someone from behind with a ligature; pull it tight enough to strangle them to death, as a means of self-defence, he said. No, ladies and gentlemen, Andrea Fyffe did not act in self-defence. Our contention is that Andrea Fyffe went to Colin Muir's house that night with the intention of bringing the blackmail to an end, he said, and if that entailed murdering him, then so be it.

Liz Turnbull, QC, Counsel for the Defence, didn't deny that her client had caused the death of Colin Muir. But she argued that the death was unintentional, accidental, and unpremeditated. An expert witness – a retired forensic pathologist – was called.

Though Turnbull explained to the jury that she did not intent to question the validity of Angus MacLeod's testimony, it was obvious to the prosecution and investigative teams that she intended doing just that. They'd seen it before. Introducing just enough doubt in the eyes of the jury to re-evaluate previous expert testimony is a courtroom ploy frequently used by defence lawyers.

Turnbull asked her expert witness if it was possible that Mr Muir died not from strangulation, but had expired almost instantly as a result of vagal reflux.

Not unsurprisingly – for there is no point in calling in an expert witness who will refute your theory – the expert agreed. The vagal nerve, he reminded the jury, was one of the main nerves in the parasympathetic system. In certain circumstances, pressure to the neck can instruct the vagal nerve to simply stop the heart beating.

Turnbull then asked the expert if, in his opinion, this is what happened to Colin Muir. The expert said yes, it was. Just as the investigative team feared, for MacLeod himself had warned them of the possibility, some members of the jury bought it.

The jury were out for ten hours before returning with their verdict.

Juries in Scotland are composed of fifteen people. A simple majority of eight is enough to secure a conviction. In Scots law juries have a choice of three verdicts: Guilty, Not Guilty, or Not Proven. Not Proven is a verdict which allows a jury to express the belief that the accused is guilty, whilst acknowledging that insufficient evidence has been produced to merit a conviction. In practice, it is the same as an acquittal. In the case of The Crown v Andrea Fyffe or McGill, the jury returned a verdict of Not Proven.

Quin was disgusted. Scarth was disappointed. Munro was stunned. Quin knew the forensics team would be gutted. The prosecution team were philosophical; hopes of a conviction had been high, but in a murder trial where the accused is a female, the possibility of defeat is always there.

Andrea Fyffe and her defence team were of course highly delighted. She left the High Court that afternoon a free woman. As her entourage triumphantly paraded through the marbled halls, they passed a grim-faced Quin, Scarth, and Munro.

In the courtroom, Fyffe had texted Scarth a parting shot before the jury returned. 'Whatever way it turns out, goodbye, Bob Scarth. I thought we had a promising rapport going there for a while ... But once a polis, always a polis, eh?'

It was a cheap jibe which blindsided him.

In the corridor he showed the message to Quin. As Fyffe and her supporters swept by towards the converging media scrum, Quin hissed, 'Don't say a word, Bob. Don't give that insufferable woman the satisfaction of upsetting you.'

'I'm not upset, Moira,' he replied mildly. They watched as the excited crowd of reporters tracked Fyffe and her supporters down the hallway and out towards the building entrance. 'I know that Andrea Fyffe has many unhappy days and fretful nights in front of her; and she richly deserves each and every one of them.'

He tapped the pocket where his phone nestled.

'Lizzie Williamson has texted me in the last hour,' he said. 'She says the exhumation at Broomieknowe has been given the go-ahead. Andrea Fyffe is going to face some unpalatable truths in the very near future.'

'Glad to hear it, Bob,' Quin puffed, the exasperation in her face softening to a look of anticipation. She linked arms with him and Munro. 'Come on kids, let's go. Jesus, I need an effin drink …'

On a misty June morning an exhumation team assembled at Broomieknowe. Andrea Fyffe, as was her right as a representative of the family, was present. Lizzie Williamson attended, but Scarth stayed away.

The first surprise, to Lizzie Williamson anyway, was that the ground below the remembrance stone to Agnes and Betty Napajok was undisturbed. There was not, and never had been, a grave or graves there.

The second surprise, which affected everyone, was that the grave of Mrs Fyffe contained not one, but three skeletons. The deepest one was found in a disintegrating though still-intact coffin. This was presumed to be the remains of Mrs Fyffe. The other two skeletal remains, which were wrapped in shreds of shrouds, had been placed on top of the coffin, probably after Mrs Fyffe's interment.

The two shrouded skeletons, found lying adjacent to one another on top of the coffin, had been covered in quicklime, probably shortly after burial. The use of quicklime was once thought to hasten the destruction of a body, but in fact it can have the effect of delaying decomposition. What it did do, however, was to help prevent the odour of putrefaction from escaping into the air.

The remains were transported to the Dalkeith lab of Dr Lori Hay, a forensic anthropologist retained by Midlothian Police. When Dr Hay's examination was complete, Lizzie Williamson was invited to Dalkeith to receive the anthropological determination first hand.

Lizzie Williamson, wearing gloves, mask, lab coat, and a protective cap over her hair, nervously took up a position just inside the door of the mortuary. She was surprised at what little smell there was. The three skeletons were laid out anatomically on separate examination tables.

'First of all, Lizzie,' Dr Hay said to her after a brief introduction, 'we can tell by the pelvic girdles that all the skeletons are female.' She stood by the table on which the remains of Mrs Fyffe lay. 'The female pelvis, as you probably know, is noticeably larger than the male. I haven't got a male one here to show you, but like the male pelvis, the female one is designed to keep our guts from spilling out, and to enable us to walk on two legs. The female pelvis also has to accommodate the biggest thing ever to pass through it – a baby's head.'

She glanced across the table at Lizzie. 'Are you a mother, by any chance Lizzie?'

When Lizzie shook her head, neither regretfully nor hopefully, Dr Hay gleefully continued. 'The amazing thing is that the female pelvic canal is about an inch narrower than a normal baby's head. It's a squeeze getting that precious head safely through the birth canal. Nature sees to it that a compromise is made; but once the baby's head descends through the pelvic outlet here … you sure as hell want to get it out as quickly as possible, believe me.'

Dr Hay moved nearer to the two tables furthest from the door.

'These two specimens are of immature females,' she announced. 'At birth, the pelvic girdle is comprised of twenty-one separate bones. By the time a female reaches the age of twenty to twenty-three, as we can see on that first specimen, these bones have fused to form the innominate bones, also known as the hip bones. If we look carefully here,' she pointed to one of the other two skeletons, 'we can see that final fusion hasn't taken place. If it had, we would see a crest of bone which runs along the top of the bone. Without that crest, we can conclude that the skeleton is therefore that of an immature female.'

Again, Dr Hay shifted position, returning to the table holding the remains from the coffin.

'The examination of the skeleton from the coffin, identified as Andrea Fyffe from the tarnished brass plate on the lid, showed that in life she had reddish hair, was slight of build, had a full set of teeth, and stood five foot two inches in height. The two other specimens both had jet-black hair, strong teeth, and were less than five feet in height.

'The causes of death,' the woman continued, 'were initially less easy to determine. But there was a clue. In the case of Mrs Fyffe, that favourite bone of crime writers, the hyoid bone, had been fractured, suggesting that she had been strangled. The problem with that is,' she explained, 'though pressure placed at the side of the neck by an assailant can break the rather flimsy horns of the hyoid bone, a dead body found to have a fractured hyoid hasn't necessarily been strangled. The fracture could have occurred earlier during their life. It isn't fatal.

'The hyoid bones of both the young girls were intact. Conversely, that does not mean they had not been strangled,' stressed Dr Hay. 'For in fact, it is estimated that around two-thirds of all deaths by strangulation, especially in young people, do not result in a fractured hyoid.'

To Lizzie, it was confusing: had the three females been murdered, or not? She didn't dare ask.

'Hyoid bones are like twigs,' Dr Hay told Lizzie. 'When you snap a green twig, the broken ends will usually be irregular, with strands of stubborn wood hanging from them. This is the way a hyoid looks if it has been broken perimortem – around the time of death. When you break a twig that is dry and dead, the ends tend to be clean, uniform. This is the way a hyoid fracture looks when the break is done post-mortem – after death, when the bone has had time to dry out. However, under the microscope, Mrs Fyffe's fractured hyoid was examined in greater detail, and clearly showed the tell-tale signs of perimortem trauma. I'd say she suffered a violent death,' Dr Hay concluded. 'I can't say for sure that asphyxiation was the direct cause, it may have only been a contributory cause, but I can tell you that she has definitely been strangled.'

Lizzie found courage from somewhere. 'What about the girls?' she asked.

Dr Hay pursed her lips. 'The cause of death?' Can't say for sure. There's not enough to go on, unfortunately.'

'What about ethnicity. Could they be Inuit?'

Dr Hay studied Lizzie's tattoo-freckled face as if seeing it for the first time. 'Of course! Why didn't I think of that? I was about to suggest that due to the high cheekbones, they were Asian, or Native American.' She paused. A horrified look came over her. 'Oh no,' she cried, 'they're not related to you are they, Heaven forfend!'

'No,' Lizzie said, 'we are not closely related; as far as I'm aware. My family's origins are from further west. They occupied the tundra landscape around Aberdeen Lake, following the rhythms of the season and the migrations of the caribou. Those two Inuit girls whose commemorative plaque was set next to Mrs Fyffe's grave, were from Repulse Bay, on the western side of Hudson Bay.'

A crafty look creased the make-up on Dr Hay's elfin face. 'Ah. But you've a theory as to why Mrs Fyffe had them for company in her final resting place. Am I right? I'm intrigued. Do tell ...'

'I have a diary,' Lizzie told her. 'It was written at Broomieknowe by a girl called Agnes. She was a young Inuit brought over here by Sir Alexander Fyffe who was a whaling captain when he was young. The reason for her visit was to further her Christian education. She was later joined by her sister, called Betty. Agnes was aged sixteen, and Betty was aged fourteen. Their place of burial has not been established. I was hoping these are their remains …'

'Well, the ages certainly fit,' Hay said. She pointed to the legs of the girls. 'If the pelvic bones had been missing, I could tell by the extent of fusion of the epiphysis, the caps on the long bones there that fuse completely after the age of twenty, that these two people were young when they died.'

'They are believed to have died at Broomieknowe in the measles epidemic of 1911,' Lizzie informed her. 'I had a researcher look for some documentation in the National Records of Scotland to substantiate that claim. She found the death certificates I was after. At the time a Dr Chalmers, who was the family doctor, entered 'Measles Encephalitis' as the cause of death for Mrs Fyffe and both the girls.'

Dr Hay shrugged and raised her hands. 'Well measles certainly was a killer in those benighted times. And encephalitis, inflammation of the brain, can be fatal in a surprisingly short time. I can't substantiate or decry the doctor's opinion just by looking at the bones. But it sounds plausible.'

'Could Agnes and Betty have been strangled as well?'

'It's possible. As you can see, the hyoid in both girls is still intact, though as I've explained, in young people that can be misleading. Asphyxiation can be caused by smothering, choking, suffocation, and several other methods.'

'In her diary,' Lizzie said, 'Agnes makes no mention of measles being in the household at all. There were other pupils there at the time as well, yet she does not mention any of them being sick. You'd think she would if it was the case. However, she does state that she was being sexually abused by Sir Alexander Fyffe, the husband of that woman there, the woman from the coffin. Agnes says that she had the temerity to report this abuse to Sir Alex's wife, and that later she heard a furious argument between them. The next day Mrs Fyffe was found dead. The family doctor claimed it was measles.'

'A trifle sudden, isn't it? And convenient.'

'There was a measles epidemic here at the time. But I think Sir Alex murdered his wife, and then went about silencing his two Inuit witnesses. He murdered them, and had them secretly buried in his own wife's grave. Then, with the complicity of the doctor, he had them declared as victims of that measles epidemic.'

Dr Hay nodded her head in agreement. 'I have to say, that the fact they were buried without coffins, and covered in quicklime to disguise that they were in the ground at all, certainly indicates foul play. But did no one miss them? Friends, relatives?'

Lizzie shook her locks. 'Canada was a long long way away in those days. Sometimes more than a month of hard sailing. Andrea Fyffe, the living one, claims that Sir Alex repatriated the girls' remains. But I have been in contact with their settlement village in Canada, and the elders refute that. They can remember no such thing, for it would have been a memorable event. Now we know why they can't remember.'

Dr Hay escorted Lizzie to the locker room where they took off their gloves, masks, scrubs, and wellies. They rinsed their hands and wrists in the wet room. Dr Hay heaved a huge sigh. 'What a heart-rending saga, Lizzie. It seems we all have a responsibility to do the right thing by these girls now, even though it is nearly a hundred years after their deaths …However, my job now is only to write a report to the Procurator Fiscal. In it, I will certainly express the view that Mrs Fyffe was murdered. I will also state that it is my opinion that the two Inuit girls were murdered too. If you intend to take this further, and I sincerely hope you do, the PF will need sight of that diary you mentioned. Whether he will instruct the police to initiate an investigation I cannot say. I should warn you though, that he might not think the public interest would be best served by a police enquiry all these years after the fact.'

'Could I do it privately?'

'Of course. But what would be the purpose? I'm sorry to say, Lizzie, but Sir Alexander Fyffe, monster that he no doubt was, is beyond the reach of justice. To all intents and purposes, he's gotten away with it …'

Later that afternoon Lizzie phoned down from the archives and invited Scarth up for an update. When they were both seated at a quiet desk, she related her meeting with Dr Hay, and the anthropologist's conclusions.

'Bob,' she continued, 'my time here is nearly up. The RCMP hierarchy need me back to help them fight crime, and my people need me to help fight injustice. I need to return to Canada to earn a living. I've loved being in Scotland, enjoyed the Scottish culture, which is of course – with my grandfather being an Aberdonian – partly my culture. I've learned so much, collected so many Scottish phrases that I can't wait to teach my Inuit grandmother. For example: 'Yer bum's oot the windae', and 'Are ye aff yer heid?'.'

They laughed, then her face turned serious.

'I've got official permission to arrange for Agnes and Betty Napajok to go home. I'll be phoning Canada later today with the news. It will not happen for a few weeks yet, but the people there at the Repulse Bay settlement will want as much warning as possible in order to organise a proper home-coming. It will be quite an occasion; I can assure you.'

'Thanks for seeing to it, Lizzie,' Scarth said. 'It can't have been easy for you. I haven't been much help I'm afraid ...'

She smiled and laid a tattooed hand over his.

'Dinnae talk daft, Bob,' she said, sounding just like a Musselburgh fish-wife. 'Listen, you've been a tremendous help. It couldn't have been pieced together without your instincts and input.'

She withdrew her hand. Her lovely face turned serious.

'They dig the graves in the summer at Repulse Bay. It's the only time the ground can be penetrated. It used to be that when people died in winter, all the relatives could do was make a cairn over them. Babies were left out to mummify. Now I'm told the grave-diggers prepare a dozen graves in advance, in case the winter is a really bad one. Pneumonia might take a grandparent or a grandchild; a surprise winter storm might catch out a hunter; depression or alcoholism might persuade someone to take their own life. A child might be stillborn, or a worn-out old person might just die simply of old age.'

Scarth remained silent as she continued:

'The graveyard there is small, and overlooks a beach of black, soft sand. I've asked the elders to set aside a couple of graves for Agnes and Betty. Their commemorative plaque will stay here, as a reminder of their short stay in Scotland. The beach I'm talking about faces Ships Harbour Island, for that is where they embarked on the whaling ship *Ajax* which brought them here to Scotland, all those years ago.'

He had made up his mind about it long before. Now was the proper time to tell her.

'I'm going to go there, someday,' Scarth avowed, 'to Repulse Bay.'

Lizzie smiled. 'Keep me posted,' she said, 'and I'll meet you there.'

'Who knows,' he joshed, 'we might even have a bite of maktaaq together …'

Lizzie balked, laughed, then smiled disarmingly.

'Piss off, Bob,' she said inoffensively. She followed it with a proud grin.

'That's one Moira Quin taught me.'

THE END

Printed in Great Britain
by Amazon

77605459R00231